CASSANDRA'S CASTLE

D.L. Gardner

DEDICATED

to

To my granddaughters and great
granddaughters
may they find what they are looking for!

CASSIE

D aydreaming again, Cassie?" Her mother's voice sounded no kinder than an alarm clock.

Cassie slowly closed the curtains, sealing out the lights that glistened against the twilight, and danced on the surface of the water. She turned from the picture window and peered at her mother, Abbi Wilson, who leaned over the kitchen table leisurely flipping pages to a magazine.

A faint beep sounded from the pocket of Cassie's hoodie. She glanced at her mom, who ignored her, and her father hadn't moved from the couch. She peeked at the screen. Odd, she thought as she studied the unfamiliar bearded face. He looked like a child in a Halloween costume.

"Who's that?" her father mumbled. With his back to her, his agile hands moved rapidly as he labored at his sketch pad, inventing creatures of a fantasy world for the next video game he was commissioned to design.

"No one."

She tucked the phone back in her pocket and soon forgot about the image as she watched her father. How she wished she had been born with more of his creative genes. Every character he ever drew seemed to come to life.

"Are you done with your homework?" her mother asked. "It's near nine o'clock. If you're spending the weekend at Monica's, you need to get your homework done before Friday."

Cassie took one last look outside and finished pulling the curtains closed.

"Cassie, your mom asked you a question," her dad murmured from the couch.

"Yeah, I'll get it done soon."

She moved closer to him and leaned over his shoulder. "Hey! Is that Xylon?"

"Not quite." He didn't look up, but kept sketching, his hand quick and sure of every line, every detail. Cassie watched mesmerized as the features of a little man took shape; first his eyes with his lids half open,

9

his round nose and mustache, and then his mouth bent in a crooked smile.

"True. He's different from that Xylon guy you made," she said.

Her father chuckled. "You remember what Xylon looked like?"

"You kept a print of your original drawing of him in one of our photo albums."

Xylon was the star of her father's personal fairy tale. Before she was born, he claimed he had traveled with Grandpa Alex, whom she never met, through a portal into a magical realm. The two experienced a most remarkable journey, which lasted off and on for almost six years. A world where little computer characters like Xylon came to life. A world made up of everything a young girl dreamed of—horses, green meadows, mountains, and mysterious caves. Her dad met pirates, sailed on tall ships, and fought dangerous battles. But the most exciting encounter of all was Stenhjaert, the dragon. Throughout her childhood, Cassie begged to hear every detail of her father's adventures, and she soaked up the saga as though it were her very own. Even Mom said the stories were true.

Dad was usually eager to tell his account of all that had happened. Whenever the family took a vacation, they would gather around a campfire under the stars, or on lazy summer days around the barbecue, or on the couch in front of the fireplace just before bedtime. He told her everything.

Everything except the ending. Whenever the story concluded, his voice trailed off, and melancholy crossed his face. Whenever she asked why he never went back, or why grandpa stayed, her father always fell silent, or he would change the subject, or send her to bed.

Cassie swore that someday she would enter through the portal and discover the answer to those questions herself. Maybe she would even find grandpa.

"Take me there sometime."

Cassie's mother laid her magazine on her lap and looked her daughter in the eye.

"No. Your destiny is to finish school. Now answer me. Do you have homework?"

A ring tone came from her pocket and Cassie pulled her phone out. Daemon. She smiled sweetly at her mom and held the phone to her ear.

Daemon's voice exploded. "Cassie have you even thought about our thesis yet? It's getting down to the wire and nothing's been done. When are we going to start? It's due next week, you know?"

Cassie turned the speaker down and walked to the hallway, keeping her voice as low as she could.

"Tomorrow after school. I have a really cool idea," she whispered.

"I hope so because Monica and I can't agree on anything."

"Trust me, she'll love this. Talk in the morning." Cassie hung up and turned around to a piercing look from both her parents.

Her father spoke first, his calm concealing the disappointment Cassie knew was there.

"You have a project due?"

"It's just a term project. Nothing to get bent out of shape over."

"Bent Out of Shape?" He waved his hands as if trying to avoid saying more, but her mother interrupted in the tone she'd been expecting.

"A term project? At the end of the semester, you finally decide to do your term project?" Mom asked. "Term projects are projects you're supposed to be working on for the entire semester. You can't expect a decent grade if you haven't even started yet."

"It's not like that, Mom. Don't worry. It's covered. I've done all the prep work already. We just need to write it up. I'll take pictures. We'll have photos, flags, and costumes. It will be the best project anyone has ever done. I promise."

"Costumes? Where are you getting costumes from?" her father asked.

"I don't know, somewhere. Don't worry! I have it all under control."

Their stares followed her as she walked calmly to her room and shut the door. When she switched the light on, her phone beeped again.

"What now?" she mumbled to herself. She was surprised to see nothing but a blank screen. She tapped the phone with her hand. "What?"

Was her phone dying? A white light flashed on and off, and then a strange, bearded face appeared, scowling at her. The more she studied the image, the more real it looked.

"Who are you?" If she didn't know better, she'd swear it was Rumpelstiltskin. He was dressed in a robe and had long, straight hair that glowed like a silver moon. His crooked fingers held what looked like the top of a walking stick.

Cassie tapped the screen again and the face disappeared.

"I must be really exhausted," she sighed, plugging her phone into its charger.

THE TERM PROJECT

Daemon held up a red cardboard cone and smirked at Cassie. "Are you serious? You want me to wear this? I mean the Khaki's I can understand but this... this thing on my head? Who made this thing?"

"I did, and it'll look like a uniform in the photo." Cassie positioned him next to a stump and placed the make-believe fez securely on his head. She pushed his wavy, overgrown hair behind his ears and took off his dark-rimmed glasses. He blinked and then squinted.

"I don't know Cassie," Monica complained, tossing her hair over her shoulders and stepping next to Daemon. Her sneakers caught the hem of her long skirt and she stumbled.

"This outfit is disgusting. Suffrage? Seriously? I'm suffering in this dress all right! I don't see why we couldn't have done our term project on something cool instead of dressing up like dorks. Everyone's going to laugh at us. Besides, cool things happened in 1908, you know. Like Ford and the Model T, or Orville Wright and the airplane! Why did you have to choose a war?"

Cassie sighed. "Our project isn't just on war. It's about revolution, which is entirely different."

"Why the fez?" Daemon snickered.

"The Turkish revolution is the easiest to make accessories for." Cassie returned the sour look as she rummaged through her backpack.

"This is not a Turkish accessory. It's a paper plate?"

"Does it matter? Who else will dramatize their projects like this? No one, that's who. Just wait and see. We're going to ace this."

She pulled a toy rifle from her pack and placed it in Daemon's hand.

"Hold still now. Look serious." Cassie stepped back and held up her camera. "Move in closer, Mon."

"Are we supposed to smile or what?" Monica asked, scowling.

"No. Look like revolutionaries who believe in what you're fighting for."

"I don't," Daemon dropped the gun and crossed his arms over his chest.

Cassie lowered her camera.

"You don't? You don't believe in freedom? You don't think these are causes that people were passionate about? C'mon Daemon this is real. These people changed the world. Think Les Mes!" She picked up the toy and handed it to him again. He reluctantly accepted.

"Les Mes was overrated. No one was singing during the French Revolution. They were dying. People killed each other in these wars, Cassie. I'm not into that. The world can be changed without killing."

"Maybe so, but it wasn't. Besides, what could be better to report on?"

"You want my opinion? I think we should do our report on Ed Ruelbach's shutout against the Dodgers."

"That'd be even more hilarious! We could all wear baseball jerseys and beat each other over the head with bats!" Monica sneered.

"Which would be a lot more interesting than standing in the woods letting Cassie take pictures of us in our pajamas with red paper cones on our heads!" Daemon returned.

"Ah! Perfect!" Cassie exclaimed. That's the look I wanted. There!" She held her cell phone up again and snapped several more shots.

"Sacrifices had to be made for freedom." She clicked to the gallery on her phone, curious to see how the shots came out.

"Easy for you to say. You wouldn't have had to fight in the trenches. Are we done yet?"

When she enlarged the photos on her screen, her mouth fell open.

"What's going on?" Daemon asked.

Cassie looked up at them and then at her camera again. Behind the still of Daemon and Monica were three soldiers. The men were along a coast shooting out toward the sea.

"What's the matter?" Daemon dropped his gun, pulled his glasses out of her pocket, and pushed the spectacles onto his nose. He inspected her phone.

"Holy Toledo!" Daemon whistled. "Something's wrong with your camera."

Cassie didn't answer, though her heart throbbed against her chest. "The Realm. My dad's Realm."

Daemon tried taking the phone, but Cassie pulled away.

"Monica, take a photo of me," Cassie said.

"No." Daemon snapped.

"It's here, Daemon. The portal is right there by that tree! Dad's world!"

"Cassie what are you talking about?" Monica asked.

"She thinks this is a portal now because there's a glitch in that crazy camera of hers. Probably some website sent you those images," Daemon said.

"No, Daemon, it's not a glitch. Look. Those are real people. Another click of the camera, and I bet I go in. In fact, I'm sure of it."

"Go in where?" Monica asked.

"The Realm. The portal."

"Don't do it, Cassie," Daemon warned.

"What? You believe her?"

"I believe her dad. I've talked to Mr. Wilson about his adventures. There's a world that runs parallel to ours and Mr. Wilson says portals exist that can take you there." Daemon faced Cassie. "He also says it's dangerous. He wouldn't approve of you going. I'm sure of it."

"The dragon's gone, Daemon. Dad knows that. He's the one who got it out."

"Dragon?" Monica turned white. "Are you guys joking?" Her eyes bulged.

"No!" Daemon and Cassie both answered in unison.

"You aren't going to disappear. Not an option. No," Daemon reached for her phone, again.

Cassie stumbled away from him and tripped into the ferns. "You can't stop me, Daemon. I'm going in with or without you two."

"That's insane, Cassie," Monica said.

"I'll have my cell phone. You can text me." Cassie scrambled to the spot where Daemon and Monica had posed and held the phone in front of her.

"No!" Daemon lunged for her.

Cassie clicked the shutter. Monica screamed. A great blue flash lit up the woods and when Cassie blinked, her friends were gone... or rather she was.

No sooner had she taken the first breath of fresh air in the new world than her ring tone sounded.

"Come back here," Daemon's voice cracked amid a layer of static.

"Later," she laughed, "Good grief let me look around first." She turned the ringer off and put the phone in her pocket, mesmerized by the alternative universe she had entered.

What a pleasant fragrance of damp earth and clean air! The sky was bluer than she'd ever seen! The field she stood in overlooked a marshy meadow blanketed with bull rushes, cattails, and field grass. Cassie squinted from the brilliance of green under the bright noonday sun. To the right of her stretched a dark wooded forest that bordered the meadow.

In the distance, the landscape touched a turquoise sea. Overlooking the water on a golden cliff was a colossal white castle and courtyard that glistened like jewels. To the left of the castle wound a road into the hills, ending at a cluster of adobe-colored houses with red rooftops that dotted the hillside.

"Wow!" Cassie said, and pulled out her phone. "Hey guys, there's a castle by the water not too far away. A real castle."

"Come back," Daemon shouted. She could hear Monica's protests in the background.

"Gosh you guys, where is your sense of adventure? You should see if your phones will get you here."

"Not a chance," Daemon said.

"Well, I'm not leaving until I do some exploring!"

Cassie shoved the phone back in her pocket and started walking toward the sea, but the ground was softer than what she expected. Her boots sank into damp soil and after taking only a few steps she dropped so low that the grass towered above her head, blotting out her view. "Oh. Oh!"

As Cassie tried to climb back up onto solid ground, each step took her deeper into a muddy tunnel instead, until roots and tubers formed an arch over her head, and the bright of the sun became a speckle of dancing light peeking through blades of grass over her head. Soon, her feet were stuck, and the only direction she could move was deeper into the belly of the earth. She had no control over where she was going. Some odd force of gravity sucked her downward.

THE NOMAD'S CAMP

Jimmy shifted in his saddle as he rode up to his uncle. Every night they sat still as stone on their horses guarding the camp. From what? Jimmy had no idea.

"You see that, Jimmy?" Whitefox asked after acknowledging Jimmy's presence.

"What?"

"Those men crossing Point de Tratado Bridge."

"So?"

"It's a sign that they may have been raiding the king's militia again."

"Why do you think that? They could have been in the city trading their wares,"

Whitefox shook his head, but Jimmy released a sigh of frustration and fidgeted in his saddle. "I don't know why you watch them so closely. Sure, they slipped up once, but it doesn't mean they're going to keep on stealing."

"More than once. Did you forget what I had to go through to save their necks last time?" Whitefox asked.

Jimmy and his uncle had come to the Isle of Refuge as strangers from the ice country with others of their clan, but when the ship sailed back, Whitefox stayed and made a new life for himself and his nephew. They had been accepted by the Gitanos, but never assimilated into the outlaws' light-fingered traditions. Because of his moral standards, Whitefox became a watchdog over them instead, gently persuading them in their crafts to make an honest living.

"They can take care of themselves," Jimmy concluded.

"Jimmy, we keep our word." Whitefox spoke softly, referring to the latest smooth-talking with the current ruler of Alisubbo, King Chavez. He even drew up a treaty between the residents of the Isle of Refuge and Alisubbo.

"They've been behaving themselves," Jimmy argued.

"Have they?"

"Well, yes!"

"They've put on a good front. But ever since we agreed to the king's terms, they've been resentful."

"Can you blame them?" Jimmy snickered. "Basket weaving and trading in textiles isn't all that adventurous."

Whitefox turned to face him. "You just made my point. Now that you agree, it's your turn to keep watch tonight."

"What are you going to do?"

"I'm going to sleep."

***

Jimmy did not watch the Gitanos with the same critical eye as his uncle. He enjoyed their company and found minor fault in their gallivanting. In fact, occasionally he would join their celebrations.

This night found Jimmy caring little that the nomad's whiskey burned his throat, only that the raw tasting liquid eased his mind and calmed his nerves. The girl he'd had his eye on, Elena, was paying closer attention to him than ever before.

He watched her put another log on the fire before she sat next to him. She smelled like the woods, the campfire, and the fragrant herbal oil she rubbed on her hands. Her hair was dark, long and curly, and tickled his cheek as she leaned her head on his shoulder. He wrapped his free arm around her and chugged another drink.

Men congregated around another campfire, their voices loud in song and laughter. Geno, a short, stocky fellow whom Whitefox had instructed Jimmy to keep an especially careful eye on, held up his flask and waved to him.

Elena stood and took Jimmy's hand. "Come on, Jimmy, they want us to join in the fortunetelling." She pulled him up and led him to Geno.

A bare patch of dirt in front of the group was scratched with a circle divided into uneven sections. Images were drawn in each of the sections: symbols of owls, eagles, a pyramid, an eye, a wolf, and a heart. All curious shapes to Jimmy, and though familiar with the ritual though, did not know what the symbols meant.

"Tonight, you will get your fortune told, Jimmy Boy!" Geno said as Jimmy settled closer to Elena on the blanket. Geno's female friend Ibbie gave Jimmy a flirtatious smile. When Geno tossed a stone into the circle, everyone cheered.

"Good work Geno! I see light in your future!" a tall, dark-skinned man named Cruz said as he patted Geno on the back and sat down. He lifted a pitcher as an offer to Geno.

"Light? "Geno asked.

"You know. Sunshine."

"Light from the barrel of a gun, maybe?" Geno took the pitcher from Cruz and poured himself another drink. When his cup was full, he offered to fill Jimmy's mug.

Jimmy hesitated. Elena took his flask and held it out for Geno to fill.

"Or maybe the light of a woman." Ibbie plucked at Geno's whiskers, and everyone laughed.

It mattered little to Jimmy what the Gitanos did when they were away from camp. They were alive, happy, colorful. Even in the light of the flaming campfire, the woven patterns on their clothes, their beads, and anklets on their bare feet told the story of adventure, risk taking, and bounty. The fire lit their faces like devilish spirits against the backdrop of a starry sky.

"You try, Jimmy Boy!" Geno handed Jimmy a handful of stones.

"Me? I don't know how," Jimmy said, already woozy from the alcohol.

"I will help you," Elena assured him and took his hand. Her gentle touch sent a thrill through every part of his body.

"Go on. Toss. We'll see what tomorrow brings." Geno said.

Maybe if Elena wasn't leaning on him, he'd have tossed better, but his pebble rolled out of the circle. Laughter came from everyone, and Jimmy, being a good sport, laughed with them.

"You missed! You aren't even in the ring!" Elena scolded teasingly.

"Next time," he said.

"Next time may be too late. This is your fortune. Your life. Don't make fun of it. This is serious. Let me show you how." She picked up the stone. "Concentrate, or Geno and his friends will laugh you out of camp."

Elena blew into her hand, shook the stone, and then tossed it into the circle. The stone bounced into the owl section and rolled into a heart. Elena clapped her hands and gave him a kiss on the cheek.

"There! You see? That is my fortune."

"What does that mean? Love?" Jimmy asked.

"Maybe. We'll see. Now you go ahead. You toss love too and we'll know we are meant for each other."

Jimmy followed her example and shook the stone, blowing into his hands for added luck. He tossed. The stone landed on a wolf. Everyone moaned.

"What? What does that mean?" Jimmy asked.

Elena stood and brushed off her skirt. "It's all right. It's just a stone in the sand. Means nothing."

Jimmy, stunned and disappointed, watched her walk away. When Geno slapped him on the back, he turned to him. "What does it mean?" Jimmy asked again.

"That wolf, you see his face. It's a mask. Maybe it means you're pretending to be something you're not." Geno poked a stick at the fire and stirred the coals.

"What do you mean? Pretending to be what?"

"Your uncle's servant. Maybe you aren't supposed to take orders from him. He bosses you like a soldier."

"That's crazy."

"No. It isn't crazy. He wants you to police us like we're criminals. We were on the island before your people came. You should be our prisoners. "

"He's just looking out for you folks, Geno."

"What? Do we look like children? We don't need to be watched over." When Geno nudged Cruz, the man nodded and looked deep into Jimmy's eyes. His were dark, and the whites glimmered with fire light. He winked at Geno, stood, and sashayed into the woods.

Jimmy shook his head and tossed the rest of the whiskey in his cup at the fire. A minor explosion hissed into the air. "Look at all the trouble you got into last time you went to Alisubbo. You're lucky you all didn't get killed. Who knows what would happen if it weren't for my uncle keeping peace with the king? "

"That was a chase, is all. Did we get caught? No! We're too cunning to get caught. Your uncle doesn't save us. All he does is talk a lot."

"Don't talk bad about my uncle, Geno! He keeps the cavalry from riding out here and taking you all to jail."

Geno stared at a lone figure disappearing into the trees.

"You should listen to my uncle because he knows what's best for you. He knows what's best for all of us!" Jimmy said.

Elena appeared again with another jug and a sweeter smile than before. Thinking he'd impress her this time, Jimmy threw the stone more carefully. She pursed her lips when he looked up at her, though he did not know where the rock landed. She walked to the circle, knelt, and brushed the sand.

"There! Look! It's true! Your stone is in the heart! You will find love tonight!"

Tickled, Jimmy let out a cry of excitement. "I can handle that. Come sit by me Elena!"

"Ah, Jimmy, maybe you and Elena can't get together tonight! Maybe tonight you must report to your uncle?" Geno interrupted.

Sure enough, Whitefox appeared out of the brush. His expression was not a pleasant one.

"Crap!" Jimmy said with a hiss. Before he could think of an excuse, Whitefox had him by the collar and pulled him to his feet.

"What in the king's name are you doing? Not what I asked you to, that's for certain."

"Hey! Slack on the reins, there Whitey. He was just having fun with us." Geno complained.

"Get back to the yurt, Jimmy." Whitefox slapped the dust from Jimmy's shirt, causing him to lose his balance. Jimmy reached for his flask, but Elena grabbed it first. She gave his uncle a deathly glare and walked away.

"See what you just did? You got her upset," Jimmy slurred.

"She's not the only one upset," Whitefox grimaced.

"Why? We were just having a drink. They were reading my fortune."

"You were supposed to be checking on the horses, not stirring up trouble." Whitefox glanced into the woods and then at Geno. "Geno, I've told you before not to get my nephew drunk."

Geno laughed and wiped his mouth. "He got himself drunk. He's a man, not a boy. He knows what he's doing."

"Come on, let's get you back to where you belong."

When Whitefox let go of him, Jimmy staggered, His head spun and suddenly his stomach rolled. He grabbed his uncle's arm and hung on to him.

"Look at you." Whitefox turned to Geno. "No more of this, do you hear? Where is Elias?"

"In the woods. He'll be back," Geno replied curtly.

"You'd better be right," Whitefox said.

At that moment, Jimmy doubled over. His stomach turned inside out. If it hadn't been for Whitefox's brawny arms, he would have landed face down in the dirt, perhaps in the fire. He didn't remember much after that, just that his uncle guided him away from the camp.

***

"Get up Jimmy, we need to ride!"

Jimmy rolled over on his sheepskin. The hide over the window had been tied open and moonlight shone in his eyes.

"Jimmy!"

His uncle banged on the door, and then he heard horses. He sat up a bit too exuberantly, for as soon as he did, his head pounded. White fox let himself in.

"Get up. We're riding to Alisubbo. Elias has been taken prisoner."

Jimmy groaned. The headache raced through his body and settled in his stomach.

"Jimmy! Did you hear me?"

"Yes."

"I already saddled your horse. Don't give me any excuses about your head hurting, either. You ought to know better than to drink Gitanos' brew. Who knows what's in it?" Whitefox pulled him to his feet.

Jimmy stumbled to the door and snatched his hat and his coat from the peg. He had slept in his clothes, with his boots on.

"He's a prisoner?"

"And from what Geno said, they're giving him a trial at daybreak. Let's go."

They rode hard to Ponte de Tratado, and crossed the bridge at sunrise, reaching Square de Regem at shortly after dawn. Jimmy followed Whitefox directly to the plaza, where he reined in his horse next to his uncle's mare. His heart skipped a beat at what he saw.

Scents of newly cut pine still hovered in the air as a scaffold baked in the morning sun. Cavalry units inundated the plaza. There, among the decorated soldiers stood a dirty, ragged Elias, one of the shiftiest of the renegades. His hands were tied behind his back, and a blindfold was knotted behind his head. Bound as a prisoner in the presence of a heavily armed guard, the dark-skinned man stood relaxed, a broad smile stretched across his face.

Soldiers strolled leisurely about, their sabers and helmets so polished that when the sunlight flashed on them it left spots in Jimmy's eyes. Despite the blinding heat, Jimmy's vision was as clear as ever. The sight had sobered him. There was no mistaking that grin.

"What are they going to do? Hang him?"

"It appears so!" Whitefox said.

"And he's smiling?" Jimmy whispered to Whitefox. "There's nothing that bothers that guy!"

Whitefox shot him a grimace. "Well, it bothers me!"

Jumping from his horse, the rugged northerner handed Jimmy his reins. "If you'd done what I asked you to last night, this wouldn't have happened." he said.

"It's my fault?" Jimmy asked. Whitefox spun on his boot heels and jogged past the castle guards into the canopy of the colonnade. He disappeared into the castle.

Jimmy took a deep breath, assessing the scene in front of him. The guards stood stiff at the base of the plaza's central attraction; a monumental statue dedicated to a king of yore; a bronze rider mounted proudly on his brazen steed.

Sweat dripped down the troop's temples as they waited in the sun, all too patiently. Several ranking officers gathered in the shade and spoke casually with one another. Other than the soldiers, there was no audience to speak of.

Hangings usually drew a civilian crowd. Where was everyone?

Journalists in top hats, three older women wearing long black dresses and huge bonnets, and an elderly gentleman in village attire loitered in the square. However, the crowd of spectators that often congregated for public hangings was absent.

Maybe Elias wasn't worth their time of day, Jimmy surmised. Or maybe it's the growing distaste for the military that's keeping the commoners away. It made sense. Valerio, the young cavalry commander in all his pompous ceremonies, his brigade of infantry patrolling the streets as though every citizen were the enemy, was intimidating to the humble residents of Alisubbo. Why the man was lauded a hero in the newspapers was a puzzle to Jimmy. Still, the few times he and his uncle rode into town, the headlines displayed the cavalry captain's portrait. Perhaps hanging Elias was a potential entry into his portfolio.

Jimmy's uncle had few words of praise for Valerio.

Whitefox appeared at the gated entry. He walked vigorously alongside King Chavez, a white-haired gentleman with a short beard, handlebar mustache, and solemn countenance. The king wore his dress uniform, high shiny boots, and pristine gloves. One hand rested on the guard of his rapier.

In the king's shadow walked his two sons, Marques, the Prince Royal, heir to the throne, his head held high, alert to his father's commands. Farther behind strolled his seventeen-year-old son, Martim, a boy only a year older than Jimmy.

They never met. Whitefox had mentioned once that maybe they should, that maybe Martim could teach Jimmy some manners, and respect for the arts. To Jimmy's relief, the opportunity never arose. He could think of better things to do than paint pictures or listen to violin music. Manly things, like hunting wild boar in Bandene Forest, or flushing grouse in the grasslands on the isle.

Valerio marched several steps ahead of the king. Magnificent in his presence, Valerio was proud, and carried himself straight-backed. With his plumed helmet tucked under his arm, his other hand rested on the pommel of his polished saber. An acclaimed celebrity, or so they say.

Jimmy spat. A hero at the expense of the poor, or anyone else that crossed his path.

Whitefox spoke to the king as they marched loudly enough that Jimmy caught the gist of the conversation. "Your highness, you must stop this execution."

"And why? You promised to keep these robbers under control."

"They've been under control, mostly. But you can't change an entire tribe of people in one day, or even in a month. It takes time."

"Whitefox, I appreciate your concern, but we have a treaty and it's been broken. I have no more time or patience for these people. Let this execution serve as an example."

"Your Excellency, the damage they caused can be repaired."

Valerio ordered his men to escort Elias up the gallows steps. Jimmy shifted his weight in the saddle, praying to whatever gods might be that his uncle would convince the king to stop the killing.

"Bloodshed is only going to make matters worse," Whitefox pleaded.

The king stopped at the patio and squinted into the sun. Whitefox came alongside him and gestured with broad sweeps of his hands, clearly agitated.

"Killing the Gitano's' chief will cause more harm than good. It will cause an uprising! Let me handle this. I'll work more diligently with them. Please, stay this execution. Let's give the treaty one more chance."

Jimmy nudged his mare closer to the castle steps, hoping to catch the king's response. Just as his horse inched forward, a shot rang out and a bullet ricocheted off the pedestal of the monument, chipping bits of brick that flew at Elias' guards. The sentries scattered behind the statue, jumping off the gallows, and taking Elias with them. More gunfire thundered through the square. Jimmy's horse reared, and his uncle's mount yanked her reins free from his hold, galloping out of the courtyard.

Shots rattled through the plaza. Women screamed. Top hats flew as men dodged to safety.

"Man alive!" Jimmy rode in circles, panicking, looking for cover, his horse ready to bolt. He glimpsed Whitefox ushering the king and his sons back inside. Valerio raced to his troops.

To avoid crossfire, Jimmy turned his horse toward the beach. His escape was immediately aborted by a man jumping in front of him, spooking his mare. The intruder yanked on his reins, causing the horse to stumble. Jimmy flew from the saddle and rolled behind a low adobe wall as his horse raced off. A dusty hand covered his mouth, and foul breath blew into his face.

"Shut up!" Dark eyes met his. Dirt caked on the man's skin so thick it lightened his complexion. The beads braided into his hair hit Jimmy when he spat. The Gitanos released him.

"Geno, what in the King's name are you doing here?" Jimmy choked on the dust that settled in his throat. "Why did you follow us?"

"We're saving the chief. Stay down." He jammed slugs into his pistol, peeked over the wall, and fired six rounds before he stopped to reload. Jimmy plugged his ears.

"Why? Whitefox just about convinced the king to let him go."

"Talk! That's all your uncle does. We've come for action. Getting Elias back to the island is all we care about."

"Quit shooting! Look! That cursed Commando has a gun on the chief." Another Gitanos called out.

Jimmy rolled on his belly next to three of the renegades, the stink of gunpowder still heavy in the air. The firing had stopped, and a voice called out from Square de Regem.

"Surrender, you fools!" Valerio stepped into the open and pushed the blindfolded prisoner into the plaza ahead of him. He held a pistol to his and blindfolded man into the center of the courtyard. His challenge silenced the gunfire, but a chuckle came from Geno.

"Surrender?" Geno called out; his comrades joined in the laughter.

Jimmy held his breath. They're dead! Now they're all going to hang!

Whitefox stood in the corridor, rifle cocked, and yet Jimmy knew he wouldn't shoot. They were his charges; his uncle took pride in taming the wild men of the island.

"Get up," Geno whispered to Jimmy. "Let's see whose side your uncle is on!"

"What?"

Geno grabbed Jimmy's arm and yanked him to his feet. With his pistol pressed against Jimmy's head, he pushed Jimmy into the square opposite Valerio and Elias.

"Hey 'Lisbo! Let's trade why don't we? You and I, eh?" Geno suggested. "You shoot the chief; I shoot the redhead."

The dread on Whitefox's face was a stab in Jimmy's gut.

"Everyone stop!" Whitefox lowered his rifle and lunged into the center of the square a few feet away from Valerio. King Chavez trailed behind. "No one is getting their head blown off, and no one is getting hung." He glanced at the king, who rolled his eyes.

Valerio gave Chavez a glare.

"The man is charged with armed robbery," Valerio said indignantly. "He stole from one of my officers. He's been sentenced to hang."

"He's been pardoned." The king held his head high and met Valerio's frown.

Geno chuckled and then pressed the muzzle tight against Jimmy's temple.

"What?" Valerio gritted his teeth.

"Release the prisoner." Chavez demanded. "Now! And you release that young man," the king ordered Geno. Or you'll hang."

Beads of perspiration dripped down Jimmy's face. The sun baked his forehead. Geno's tight grip on his arm hurt. If the cavalry captain shot Elias, Jimmy would die.

Heat waves shimmered over the plaza as silence settled in. Valerio pushed his pistol into Elias' thick black hair, unrelenting. He looked at Geno. Dark eyes dared him to move. Then his gaze rested on Jimmy, and he scoffed in contempt. To the king he said,

"We tried this man in a military court or law and he was found guilty and sentenced to hang."

"This one here, he's not tried at all!" Geno laughed, gaining the attention of the king, Whitefox, and Valerio. Jimmy's eyes widened when the warm barrel of Geno's gun found his neck. Jimmy turned enough to catch the wry smile on Geno's face, and a tightening clutch on his arm.

"And I have pardoned him," the king repeated, ignoring Geno.

"The scum was caught red-handed stealing from our armory!"

"Let him go." Chavez ordered.

"With all due respect, your highness, your pardon does not overrule a military judgment."

"On the contrary, I have jurisdiction over all judgments pertaining to this kingdom, both civil and military, Captain Valerio."

Valerio sneered and nodded toward Whitefox. "You favor foreigners over your own military?"

"I favor justice. And you are bordering on insubordination. Now release him immediately or I'll have you arrested."

Jimmy held his breath. His heart pounded against his chest. It didn't take much to see Valerio's inner struggle. With resignation, the commander pulled his gun away from Elias and pushed him to the ground.

One of Geno's friends raced to the chief, sliced the rope that bound his hands, and pulled off his blindfold. Elias bounced to his feet, and the two ran to their horses.

Valerio glared at Whitefox for a long moment, his face emitting enough anger to fill a hot-air balloon. "This won't be the end, Foreigner," he spat out the words. Returning his pistol to his belt, he pivoted and signaled his troops to exit the plaza. King Chavez said nothing more but turned and met his sons at the entryway of the castle.

Whitefox faced Geno, his eyes flaming. "Well? Are you going to shoot him? Or are you going to let him go?"

"He's yours." Geno said, laughing. He pushed Jimmy into Whitefox. "I think I'm understanding a few more of your tricks, but I still don't trust you. You talk too much." He tucked his gun into his belt and jogged to his horse.

"You could have been killed!" Whitefox helped Jimmy get his balance. "What if I hadn't interfered?"

Jimmy watched the renegades gallop along the beach away from Alisubbo. "Man..." Jimmy stuttered and rubbed his neck. Geno's gun barrel had left a ridged imprint on his flesh.

"You're aware that cavalry captain doesn't like me much, aren't you? Had he known you were my nephew, Valerio just may have pulled the trigger and annihilated the both of you." Whitefox snickered. "As for Geno..."

They watched the Gitanos until there was nothing more than a cloud of dust behind them.

"Unpredictable rogues. You could have been blown to pieces."

"Yeah. I guess that could have happened. Thanks," Jimmy wiped the sweat off his brow with his sleeve as he studied Whitefox, wondering if there were going to be consequences for his stupidity.

"So. Jimmy. It's a long walk home." Whitefox said. "Any idea where our horses are?"

Jimmy whirled around, scanning the surroundings. The horses were nowhere in sight.

"I'm not one to believe in rumors, but Alisubbo gets me spooked. You'd better find them lest they end up in one of the old wizard's tunnels. Eh? They say critters get lost out there in that meadow; they say Silvio puts a spell on anything that ventures into his fields."

"Right. The horses!" Jimmy scratched his head.

SILVIO

Cassie scrambled through the mass of roots as her feet slid over the damp, jagged floor. "I think maybe I made a mistake," she whispered, and reached for her cell phone. A blue error box appeared on the corner of the screen. "Out of range."

"Okay. Well!" she said. "Why tell Daemon about this, anyway? He can't do anything. I'll be okay." The rapid beating of her heart made her argument less convincing. "I'll be fine."

The tunnel grew darker as she walked save for a few specks of light that filtered through the grass above her. A spot of sunshine, and perhaps an opening to the outside world gave her hope she'd be out in the open soon where she would get reception. Perhaps she'd even find the portal before sunset.

Cassie clung to the tunnel wall and staggered over the roots and slippery moss. Soon, she heard a raspy voice above her. She froze.

"Bah! "Poor thing," it said. "Look at you. Clumsy oaf! Who are you?"

"What difference does it make who I am?" she countered.

"It could make a lot of difference! That is if you care about being you. Answer me or I'll do what I can to make you not!"

"Well, you're a nasty rascal." Cassie puffed a curl that had fallen in front of her nose. "My name is Cassandra Wilson. Who are you?"

Whoever she was talking to didn't reply.

"Hello! Get me out of here." Cassie commanded.

"Out?" The voice was now directly overhead. Two green eyes squinted at her through the entanglement of vines above. A crooked red nose appeared between them.

"Yes, out where the sun shines. This place is annoying. How do I get out of here?"

"Well!" The face disappeared. Cassie followed the rustling sound in the grass above. "Hello. Which way is out?"

A cluster of twigs fell on her head. Dirt sprinkled down her blouse and lined her collar. She brushed herself clean and snickered. What sort of foul creature is leaving her in this menacing burrow? She heard more foliage snapping above but saw nothing. Footsteps tapered off into the distance.

"Oh, great." She followed the sounds, certain that they would lead her to an exit. Eventually, the burrow widened, and the rough ground leveled out. Before too long, she stepped into a gateway of firs and maples. Long gray strands of lichen hung from the trees like the beards of old men. A squirrel rushed up a fir, chattering frantically as if announcing her arrival. Relieved that she was clear of the muddy abyss, Cassie collapsed on a moss-covered stump.

"You!"

The voice startled her.

"Are a trespasser! An intruder!" he said, though he didn't show himself.

"Intruder yourself." Cassie glared at the bushes. "Fine fellow you are hiding in the shrubberies making accusations like that!"

"Don't mock me you Mockerwerst. If you need help, ask for it or you won't get any." The scornful creature emerged from behind a tree trunk.

Cassie took a step back, repulsed by the looks of him. He was old, human by form but not by manner. His body crouched over, and despite his scraggly beard, his clothes were of exceptional interest. A robe of rich golds, greens and maroon brocade adorned his shoulders, though he also wore a cape made from twisted weeds, roots, and dying fern fronds. His shirt under his waistcoat was dusty brown, almost the color of his flesh. His face wrinkled like a dried apple, half hidden behind his long silver mane, which, to Cassie's curiosity, appeared very well groomed. He didn't have a vulgar smell about him, but a musty fragrance, like damp earth after a rain.

"Well?" he asked.

So shocked by his appearance, she had forgotten what he had said. "Well, what?"

"Do you want help? Or not?"

"I... don't know."

The man snickered and circled away.

"No, wait. Yes, please."

He faced her again.

"Please. I seem to be... lost."

30

"Lost, indeed," he grunted. "Follow me then."

"Wait a minute. You don't know where I'm going."

He squinted at her and stood silent for a moment. Finally, he said, "Neither do you."

True enough, yet Cassie was uncertain whether she should follow him.

"So if you don't know where I'm going then how do you plan on helping me get there?"

"I didn't say I would. I said, 'follow me.'"

She wanted to ask why she should follow him, but decided there was no sense arguing with the old coot. He did not give her a civil answer, he merely waddled off. As disabled as the man appeared to be, in all his crookedness, he moved quickly and without stumbling.

Cassie had a choice to make. She could stay where she was, at the edge of a dark and unwelcoming woodland with only haunting, slippery tunnels leading back to where she came from, or she could follow him. She pulled out her phone. Still no reception.

Determined to get some answers, even if they were masked in riddles, Cassie followed the silver-haired creature. He zigzagged in and out of sword ferns and bramble bushes, making it difficult to keep pace with. When Cassie hurried, she tripped over logs and rocks that cluttered the terrain. He peered over his shoulder once and slowed down enough that she didn't lose sight of him. He led her from the shadows of the firs into an open valley that spanned the horizon, dropped off into a dry riverbed and then meandered over a hill.

"Who are you?" she asked when she got close enough for him to hear.

"Silvio," he finally answered without turning around. "King of this forest." He waved his knotty arms toward the landscape they approached.

"King, eh?" she muttered as she stubbed her toe again. "Not such an impressive kingdom! Half the forest is dead or dying!" she whispered to herself, but his unhappy glower assured her he heard.

Old decrepit stumps shot up in spikes; fallen trees lay bleached white with age, dried from baking in the sun. Even the salal bent over with rust, sparse and scattered.

When Cassie stopped for breath, she had second thoughts. This is wrong. She shouldn't be following a strange old man who thinks he's a king. If only she could dial out, Dad could come rescue her. She reached into her pocket and clutched her phone, pulling it into the light. Her fingers slid over her home number, but only silence followed. The odd man glanced at her with a puzzled expression.

"Here." He pointed at a log on the ground in a clearing. "Sit there and do that."

He needn't tell her twice. Already exhausted from climbing the highlands in the heat, Cassie collapsed on the log. She brushed her sweaty locks away from her face and waited while Silvio disappeared into a ravine.

As she lingered there in that lonesome clearing, a sudden tinge of homesickness pierced Cassie's heart. The afternoon sun sank slowly, and long evening shadows covered the hillside.

Monica's mom would start dinner about now. Cassie would have been setting the table with the family. Meatloaf and mashed potatoes. Her favorite. Cassie sighed. She could almost smell the tasty meal from where she was. She tried her phone again. She even held it up and attempted to take a picture of herself, but nothing worked.

"Well, that's nice," she mumbled, and shoved her phone back in her pocket. "So where did he go? He just took off and left me here. A lot of help he is. What am I supposed to do now?"

"Sit still," a meek voice came from a thicket of thimbleberries.

Cassie jumped to her feet in surprise. "Who said that?"

"No! No! Sit!" Two voices chorused this time. At least it sounded like two, or perhaps three. "He said sit, the king did!"

The bushes next to her rustled again and a little person no taller than a yardstick ran into the clearing, waving his arms. Another creature reached out and pulled him back to his hiding place.

"No way!" Cassie exclaimed, and her face lit up. Could it be Dad's little creations? How darling! It's true! Xylon? Is it you?"

A still and silent hush fell over the forest.

"Xylon? Did I scare you? Come talk to me." Cassie searched for the little people, brushing aside the ferns, peeping around tree trunks. "You don't know me, but I know you. My dad told me stories about you. He created you when he was my age. Please don't hide from me." Cassie peeked behind a rock and under the brush. "Please come talk to me."

"Who?"

Cassie spun around and nearly bumped into Silvio. He held a black iron pot in one hand and a large wooden spoon in the other. A breeze picked up strands of his silver hair and blew it across his face so that only his green eyes showed through, and they appeared fearfully angry.

"The little man... but he's gone."

The man grunted. "Bah! They're still here. Hiding from the likes of you. Don't ask them to come out.

"Well, why should they hide? I won't hurt them."

"Maybe. Maybe not. We never know who the dangerous ones are anymore. But we know there's danger all the same." His eyes narrowed even more. He leaned closer to her, his musty breath blowing onto her chin. "How do you know about the Xylonites?" Silvio growled.

Cassie waved his smell away. "Well, for one, my dad made Xylon."

The old man froze still as stone.

Cassie laughed nervously. "He did, honest."

Silvio's eyes narrowed. "Who are you?"

"My name is Cassandra Wilson. My father's name is Ian Wilson." With Cassie's proud announcement, at least two dozen tiny people stepped into view, covering the ground like ants. Their mouths dropped wide open. They had curly red hair and quaint little beards, just like the image that had been on her phone the night before.

"My gosh," she said. "Look how many of you there are!"

Silvio took a bold step between Cassie and the Xylonites. He spread his arms defensively, as though they were his flock, he the shepherd, and Cassie the wolf. "Hogbunkers! How can I believe you 're the daughter of Ian Wilson?"

Cassie shrugged.

"What do you know about the little people?"

She scanned the throng of Xylonites who were candidly gawking at her. They were dressed in green, like gnomes in Irish fairy tales. Each wore a tunic. The men wore baggy pants, and the women wore long felt skirts with red tulips embroidered on the hem.

"Well, I don't know a lot about them." She nodded toward the little bodies at her feet. "I only know about Xylon and his missus, the characters my mom and dad made. When my father was my age, he created Xylon. And later my mom made Xylon's wife with the help of a neighbor. Dad put the little woman in the Realm and the next thing he knew there were hundreds of children running around, cutting down conks off the trees to save the forest."

Silvio scratched the chin under his beard. "You know about the Plague of the Conks?"

"I do," Cassie bragged, and folded her arms across her chest. "I'll prove to you I'm not a liar."

Silvio grunted. "Then you know about the kidnapping, the enslavement, and the voyage across the waters?"

Cassie thought for a moment. She knew nothing about that, for those events must have happened after her father left the Realm. Or else

33

he didn't know about them, either. She nodded anyway.

"Sure. Terrible times those were."

Silvio peered at her with a disbelieving eye. "Indeed." The old man set the cast-iron pot on a tree stump and gathered branches from the forest floor, breaking them over his knee. With every sudden snap, his eyes met Cassie's.

Whatever he was trying to imply by such rude gestures was not well received. She crossed her arms and watched him make his firewood pile.

"One thing I never heard of is a 'King of the Xylonites'." Cassie added with a flare of accusation. She tired of his angry stares.

"When King Ian disappeared, the Xylonites needed someone to free them, keep them hid, keep them clothed, sheltered and safe in the woods. That's what I've been doing all these years. Not my choice. Didn't choose the title either. They did." He nodded toward the little people. "Should thank me, is what you should be doing."

Several Xylonites stacked the wood in the fire pit, while one rubbed two sticks together until they smoldered and soon the kindling took to flame. Silvio put the pot next to the fire.

"King Ian? My dad's a king?"

"You're his daughter, you should know."

"Of course, I knew," she lied. "I was just surprised that someone else took over his reign."

His eyes narrowed again. "How'd you know he was king? He was gone when they crowned him."

"Then how did they crown him?" There! A little of his own riddle-making should keep him quiet!

One Xylonite reached up and knocked his fist on Silvio's knee, pulling the old man's attention away from Cassie.

"May we, sir?"

Silvio grunted, and then stared at the Xylonite for a long moment, scratching his beard. He looked at Cassie.

The Xylonite tugged at his robe.

"I don't like the idea." He walked to a stump, sat down, and folded his arms across his chest.

The Xylonite walked up to Cassie and signaled for several of his friends to gather next to him. Two ladies tugged at Cassie's clothes until she followed them to a tree stump. There, they invited her to sit down. Patting her softly with their gentle little hands, they sat next to her. The men began their story, alternating their verses in a singsong way.

"King Ian left so suddenly, his exit was so violently,"

"Our people were so despondent, in honor set a monument."

"More like a throne, I'd say."

"And every year we'd gather, to eat and drink thick lather," the man was elbowed by another. "Lager!"

Cassie laughed. The Xylonites lit up after that. Their rosy cheeks and twinkling eyes sparkled with cheer. "So, we asked the winds to blow again for the crowning of King Ian."

Cassie clapped her hands. Seeing her exuberance, the Xylonites joined in her applause and even added a jump or two of delight.

"What a cool little song!" Cassie stood, too excited to remain seated. "So he is a king?"

The little troupe bowed in unison. "The most noble and honored of all kings."

A grunt came from Silvio.

One Xylonite took off his hat and bowed to Silvio. "But you are most honored as well, Your Highness Silvio!"

"Dad will be thrilled to hear such news. I'll have to tell him when I get home." Cassie assured them, thinking that perhaps her father would even consider returning to this world. Perhaps he would bring the whole family back as well!

"And that makes you a princess." The chief Xylonite assured her.

Silvio jumped from the stump he'd been sitting on.

"That's enough of that talk! I've heard enough. Away with all of you." Silvio turned and pointed the spoon at Cassie, as though she had committed a crime. "Forget that nonsense. Pure blunder bash. Nonsense I say! You don't want to be a princess. The next thing to happen is you'll want to live in a castle!" He pointed in the direction she had seen the castle earlier that day. "You'll want to live in that castle, by the water. Foolish girl! Well, you're not alone. There are other people more powerful than you who want to live in that castle. I tell you; the walls are rotting because of it. The uprising will get you! The revolution. You'll see! Better yet, stay away from them! They'll enslave you, too, and then where will the princess be, eh? They'll tell you lies, and you'll believe them."

Cassie wasn't sure who "they" were, but Silvio's temper proved he was adamant in his accusations. She stepped back, concerned he might hit her with that spoon.

"Why do you think I'll believe their lies?" Her brow lowered in a frown. "I'm not gullible."

"Those who party in deceit are fooled by it," he retorted, ruthlessly.

"That's not a gracious thing to say!"

He whirled around and walked away from her; his silver hair shook in waves. He mumbled, more to himself than to her. "Liars, all of them... any of them. Don't get involved. Don't get involved, I tell you." He paused and looked over his shoulder at her.

"And don't tell them you're a princess."

"Who?"

He shook his head again. "Bah! They can't keep it. They don't stand a chance. The rebels will take it. The kingdom will fall, and the little people will have no allies then. They own all the magic, they will soon all the world. You'll be wise to stay clear."

"Who? What?"

Silvio spun around and walked up to her, leaned into her, touching her nose with his.

"Everything they tell you will be lies. They work for Taikus." he hissed. The air he breathed was hot and made her hair float. She had no choice but to step away from him.

"Surely someone is telling the truth somewhere," she said, unsure of how else his wrath might manifest.

"Oh yes, someone tells the truth. Does no good. But it makes no difference. Truth or not, the liars always win, they always get what they want. No matter what! I'll have nothing to do with them We'll live alone here in the woods. Me and them." He pointed to the Xylonites.

"Very well, then." Cassie breathed, happy to put an end to that conversation.

Silvio let out a disgusted grunt, returned to his campfire, lifted the lid to his cookware, and stirred the mushroom broth. The Xylonites had crept nearer to her, but when Silvio swung his spoon in the air, and began talking to them again, they scattered. "You! Don't just stand there, gather more wood. Hurry, so we can feed this nuisance before we send her on her way. Hurry."

"Excuse me?" Cassie interrupted. "I haven't been here half an hour, and I haven't bothered you any more than you've bothered me. So why do you call me a nuisance?"

"You're here, aren't you? That's enough. We'll be lucky to get away now...any of us. Don't you hear them? They're coming, and they're coming here. You're probably the one he's looking for."

"Who?"

Before Silvio answered, thunder rattled the hills. A cloud of dust rose in the west, coloring the sky with browns and reds. The sun became an orange moon that hovered over the horizon.

"Run!" Silvio shouted, sending the little people under rocks, behind trees, and into the brush. Silvio waved his wooden spoon again, this time furiously in the air, and before Cassie had time to blink, he was holding a saber longer than any she had ever seen; longer than her dad's, or even her grandpa's.

"What are you going to do with that?" she asked, eyeing the multitude of horsemen heading their way. "You're not planning on slaying all those soldiers, are you?" She snickered.

As the riders neared, the rough countryside slowed their gait. Green plumes donned the heads of fifty horses, all bays with black manes and tails blowing in the wind. The horsemen wore dusty blue coats and white sashes that reached across their chests to their waist. Decorated cords hung regally from their shoulders. Their helmets, a deep navy blue, were bedecked with shiny gold emblems on the front and a plume of golden horsehair fell from the tops of them. Handsome in their attire, they wore long white gloves that reached to their elbows. The scabbards hanging from their saddle skirts sheathed dangerously shiny sabers.

Never had Cassie seen such an impressive parade. The leader broke rank from the dragoons, slowing as he neared Silvio. His horse tossed his majestic arched neck and stepped high. Both rider and steed outshone the others. The man held his head as an officer would and looked down at them. A soldier at his side carried a map on parchment, which he rolled up and tucked into a leather case attached to his saddle.

"Ah, Silvio," the lead rider said, as his horse circled in front of them. "I mistook you for a wild hare, my dear friend. You're fortunate my soldiers weren't hungry."

"Don't threaten me, you Ransbuckle. And don't call me friend, you filthy liar," Silvio hissed.

Cassie wished Silvio would be friendlier to these handsome soldiers.

The man laughed. "Where are your little rodents today? I see you've traded them for a finer, much more attractive acquaintance." He flashed Cassie a striking smile.

Silvio glanced quickly at Cassie and positioned himself in front of her; his sword fixed as high as his aging body could hold it. "Mind your own charges you Brumsbroom. What goes on in this forest is none of your business."

The man pulled his helmet off and shook his hair; his silky black curls fell to his shoulders. Cassie stepped away from Silvio and smiled.

"Senjorita," he nodded, his big brown eyes twinkled a greeting.

He held his helmet over his heart, offering a slight horseman's bow. "The name is Valerio. And who might I have the pleasure of meeting?"

"I'm Cassandra Wilson."

Valerio sat upright and looked at the soldier holding the map. "Wilson?"

"Yes, my father's Ian Wilson, of Alcove Forest."

"Of course!" Valerio said. "Your father is a legend in these parts. I am pleased to meet you, Princess! May I introduce to you my lieutenant, Bernardo?"

Bernardo tipped his hat.

"Nice meeting you," she said.

"What would a lovely young lady be doing with this old forest gremlin on such a fine evening? Your eyesight doesn't fail you; I would hope?"

Cassie laughed and stuttered for words. No way was her eyesight failing her.

"I got lost. Silvio was going to help me find my way home, but really," she shook her head and shot Silvio with a pathetic look. "I don't think he knows how."

"Lost, are you? Why, where were you going?"

"Well, I wasn't really 'going' anywhere, so I guess I'm not really lost." Cassie back-paddled remembering her mother's warning about talking to strangers. Certainly, Mom hadn't meant dashing young officers. "I think I just wandered a little too far from home." She coughed, searching for words. "I mean I know where I am. But I don't know how to…" She tossed her hands in frustration. "My phone's dead."

Both of the horsemen and Silvio gave her a blank stare.

"It's as if your horse went lame. I mean, you're aware of all the how-tos, but just don't have the…get up and goes… I guess." She laughed at herself. "You don't know what a GPS is, do you?"

Valerio shook his head. He was still smiling. She didn't care what Silvio was doing.

"Well, Miss Wilson, or should I say, Your Highness? You're welcome to enjoy a meal with us tonight. Perhaps with a little conversation, we might steer you in the right direction?"

"Sounds lovely,"

"You're not taking anything away from my kingdom. Not a twig or a stone or a …"

"Or a pretty princess?" The horseman winked at Cassie. "Your territory is getting way too big for you, Silvio. You forget who's letting you tend it."

"It's not you. Your authority ends at Greenstay. I have a treaty with the king!"

"Your treaty will not be good for much longer, old man."

"Ha! We'll see about that! I have forces on my side!"

"Forces? You mean pixie dust?" He shook his head at Silvio, "We're not at war with you."

"I know your sneaky plans; you power hungry Gumschumker."

Valerio laughed. "I have better things to do than take over this sorry excuse of a forest. It lacks good timber though it seems we could use it for pasture. I certainly do not need to waste mine, or my soldiers' time on a disillusioned old man."

Silvio shook his fist, his silver hair flying across his shoulders. "You keep your eye off my forest. And off Alisubbo. I won't let you get one inch of this territory. You won't get past our ranks."

"Ranks? Your phantom army? You must be referring to our neighbors from the Isle of Refuge. I hardly think a handful of Gitanos and their sidekicks are a threat to my cavalry. You'd best stay on my good side if you want to see another summer."

"Bah! Another summer! Your threats don't scare me. I'm the Keeper here and the Keeper I'll remain."

Valerio turned to Cassie, and with another cordial and gentlemanly bow, as low as he could go while on top of a horse, he addressed her.

"Your Royal Highness, if your appetite calls for something more palatable than mushroom and lettuce broth, we have some fresh venison roasting on our spits tonight. You're welcome to join us. Our camp is just over the hill, and within walking distance. When you arrive, simply ask for Valerio."

"Thank you, sir." Cassie grinned, her heart palpitating, not only from the thought of savory meat for dinner, but also from being invited by a cavalry officer who was more handsome than a movie star.

"Venison sounds much more appetizing than mushrooms." Cassie hated mushrooms, especially cooked, and she never ate greens that weren't in a salad.

Valerio nodded. "Our camp will be easy to find. I'd offer you a ride, but as you can see, our troops are hot and dusty from the day's travel, and our horses weary. Head for the meadow and then follow the scent of slow-cooked meat. I hope to see you soon."

"Get away with you. Go away from here. She won't have anything to do with you and your carnivorous scallywags. Get out I say before I turn you all into toads."

Valerio laughed and rode into formation with his troops. He gave Cassie one last nod before he slipped his helmet on again. She stepped back as they passed through Silvio's camp. They rode deeper into the forest, sending the little people scurrying away from the horses' hooves. She noted their route for she planned on taking it herself in a few moments.

"Mind the fire! Go, get on with you." Silvio shooed the little people that had crept out of their hiding places. They scurried anxiously in circles.

"Pixie dust?" Cassie turned to Silvio and waited until his arms stopped swinging directions to the Xylonites. "Turn them to toads?"

He grumbled and muttered something under his breath.

"Are you a magician or something? A wizard?"

"Conjurer. Retired. I've not much magic left. A little. Almost none."

"Retired?" she asked. "Wizards retire?"

"It's a long story. I'll tell you at supper. Sit down and I'll serve you now." He waved at a stump, took the lid off his pot, and filled a bowl with broth.

Cassie turned up her nose when she saw the bubbling brew. The smell reminded her of turnips and Brussels sprouts, her least favorite foods.

"Excuse me, but I'm not eating with you."

Flames crackled in the fire pit and sent the aroma of burning pine from the smoke that hung thick in the air, a fragrance which disguised the smell of Silvio's soup. The Xylonites had pushed stumps and fallen timber around the fire to use as benches. Miniature bowls made from nutshells were in their hands and spoons carved out of twigs. They scuffled about exchanging seats with each other.

Silvio glared at her. "You're leaving? Then you won't hear the story."

"Perhaps not but thank you."

Cassie faced the forest, hoping she could find her way to Valerio's camp in the meadow. She pulled her cell phone from her hoodie and checked the screen. As much as she didn't like him, she'd love to take a picture of Silvio to prove she'd been here.

"You'll be sorry if you get involved with Valerio." Silvio grumbled again as he moved about the rows of little people, carefully pouring a ladle of soup into each little nutshell.

"Why?"

"He isn't what you think he is."

Cassie shot Silvio a suspicious look. "What do you think I think he is?"

The old man shrugged and made a funny face. "A hero, but he's not. He's evil. A rebel."

"A rebel? Well, I've been working on a term project about rebels and I realize that not all rebels were bad. Some were heroes." She tried turning her phone off and then on again, still a blank screen.

"Valerio hurts Xylonites whenever he can!"

"Why would he do something like that?"

"The forest cries at night because Valerio has the little ones hidden. He keeps them as prisoners."

"Why should I believe that tale?"

"You can hear them if you listen. Shh…" He rested his crooked finger over his mouth.

The air was still. Cassie held her breath, uncertain if what she heard was crying, but there certainly was a faint sound in the air.

"Could be crickets," she said, glancing at her phone again. If only she could get it to work. She tapped it on her knee.

"Could be. Could be crying."

"Even if it were, how do you know Valerio is the cause?"

He walked up to her and leaned close, his breath hot on her chin. "The sounds come from Greenstay, his keep, and he's not getting them out. He's keeping them as prisoners. He's a wicked man, I tell you."

"Well, if what you say is true, I'll find out for myself. I'll ask him."

"A thief wouldn't tell you where he's hid the loot any more than a murderer will tell you where he's hid the body."

"I don't know you very well, and I know Valerio less, but comparing that soldier to a thief or murderer is a bold thing to do. A villainous accusation." With her hands on her hips, she grimaced at him, but his silence stole her confidence. "Why are you looking at me like that? Are you going to hex me?"

"Why would I bother hexing you?" He gave Cassie a once over, a grin inching across his face. "Shouldn't have to put a hex on you. You'll curse yourself soon enough."

"What do you mean?"

"You'll see!"

Before Cassie could respond, Silvio opened his mouth and shouted a foul cry, sending color from his fingertips that enveloped her in green dust for only a split second. When she blinked, the dust was gone and her clothes were replaced with a skirt the same color as Silvio's eyes. A green tunic hung off her shoulders.

"There. We'll see what they do to you now."

"Who?"

"Valerio."

The blood raced to her face as her temperature rose. "You old geezer! Give me back my clothes."

"I did!" He turned his back on her and stoked the fire.

"Change them back!" she demanded.

Silvio took another scoop from the kettle and filled three more nutshells with broth. When he had finished serving all the Xylonites, they sat in a circle around the fire. The old wizard sat with them and slurped his soup. Not one of them gave her any mind after that.

If her clothes had been in a pile on the ground, she would have changed back into them. But they weren't. They were nowhere to be found.

"Fine!" A faint aroma of roasted meat came from the meadow at that moment. So tantalizing was the smell that her stomach growled, and not for mushrooms. It was time to leave Silvio and his creepy woods.

"Don't trip on your hem." Silvio laughed as she stumbled into the forest.

THE REBELS

Cassie tripped several times. The skirt hung an inch too low, catching on every splintery branch, bush, and jagged rock she stepped over. Only with luck would she reach the grassy fields and the clear skies of Greenstay unscathed.

When she stepped into the meadow, the sun had just touched the horizon, transforming all color to gray. Cassie welcomed the oncoming dark because now spots of firelight guided her course. Blue streams of smoke brought the pleasing aroma of sizzling venison, which she couldn't wait to taste.

She was well past Silvio's forest when the ring tone to her phone sounded.

"Cassie are you there? Are you alive? Are you all right? Hello!" Daemon's trembling voice reeked of panic.

"Hi Daemon," Cassie answered calmly.

"Good grief Cassie why haven't you been answering your phone? We've been worried sick about you."

"I was out of range. I'm okay. I'm about to have dinner with some awesome soldiers."

"You need to come back, Cass. Your mother will be here soon and Monica's having a fit."

"What? Mom's not supposed to be home until late Monday?"

"It's Saturday night."

"Exactly. I'll be home by Monday. I can't miss out on this, Daemon. It's the chance of a lifetime. A castle? Horses? and a camp full of cool people that are cooking me dinner? Venison roasted over an open fire! Not even you could refuse that! There's even a wizard or some king of magic maker, but he's grumpy. Oh, and Xylonites."

"You're not talking sense."

"No, well it doesn't make sense in the real world, but once you're in the Realm everything falls into place. And Daemon, it's just like we were talking about the other day."

"What were we talking about?"

"Our school project, remember? Revolution. I think I stepped into a political uprising or something. At least, that's what Silvio was hinting at. I'm about to dine with the heroes of a rebellion. I'm hoping to find out more. I'll be okay, though. I've got my phone, lots of minutes on it, and I promise I won't use it unless I have to."

"Cassie!"

"We'll talk later. I've got to go." Cassie clicked the end button, switched the setting to vibrate, and tucked the phone in her tunic pocket.

The distinct odor of horse reached her well before she arrived at the encampment. Laughter carried like an echo throughout the valley. Cassie beamed with anticipation. It would be good to talk with some real people in this alternate world. Maybe even find out who lived here, and if there really was a revolution brewing.

By the time Cassie came to the military camp, the last bit of twilight had faded. Even the pink of sunset and the thin blue ribbon on the horizon had disappeared. Stars appeared as daylight dimmed.

Only by the white in their uniforms was Cassie able to see the soldiers. They lingered near their horses, grooming them, and carrying tack into a tent. She passed several soldiers unnoticed and climbed a grassy slope toward the light of a bonfire. Two guards stopped her on the side of the hill.

"Who are you?" one of them asked as he lowered his bayonet so that it pointed at her heart.

Cassie pushed it away. "No need for that," she said. "I'm Cassandra Wilson. Daughter of King Ian Wilson. Valerio asked me to dinner."

The other man laughed curtly. He lifted his helmet and shook his hair free. "Did he now? Wilson you say? So you come from Bandene Forest all huffy and dressed like a gremlin, and expect to attend a banquet?" He chuckled and winked at his companion. "Get on, really? Mudrat clothes? That's a first! I'd like to see the Commando dining with the likes of you!" He nudged his friend and they both laughed.

"You're being vulgar!" Cassie said. "And though it's none of your business, Valerio gave me a personal invitation. I would thank you for not laughing, and take me to him."

"And get flogged? I think not. If you're so sure he wants you to join him for dinner, go find him yourself. But don't expect us to save you."

She pushed past them and came to the crest of the hill overlooking the camp. Two very large bonfires could be seen in the valley below. She counted three pavilions and four circle tents which dotted the rolling grasslands. Men smoking pipes gathered in small groups around the campfires. They were talking among themselves while several women dressed in bustle-skirts tended the fires.

Amazed at how many people were milling about, she searched for Valerio, yet she could not find him from afar. As she descended the hill, and moved in the crowd's midst, she noticed that all the people were clothed in period garb. The men wore newsboy hats, wool scarves, waistcoats with pocket watches, and had spats covering their shoes. They all had dark hair and dark complexions, an ethnic oddity compared to her father's encounter with the fair-haired Kaemperns and the light-haired people of the sea. Cassie drew closer to the fire, her own dark hair and complexion blending well with the crowd. She smiled politely at those who tipped their hats to her. With their outfits and cordial mannerisms, Cassie felt she had taken a step back in time.

"Excuse me madam," a young man stepped up to her. He was dressed in an oversized suit, a shiny tie that reflected the firelight, and which had been hastily tied. He had a cap nestled tightly on his head. Drawing a pencil from the pocket of his pinstriped waistcoat, he grasped a notebook as he approached.

"Hello," Cassie said. He seemed friendly enough. He was young, perhaps her age.

"Would you mind if I asked you some questions?" He spoke in a whisper and leaned near her ear. He smelled like horses and sweat, as though he'd been riding recently.

Curious why he was so secretive, Cassie looked around, expecting to see an eavesdropper. Although men were standing nearby, no one seemed to pay attention to their conversation. She answered him, and out of respect, kept her voice low as well.

"I guess that'd be okay."

"It's nothing personal. I just needed a few facts to take back to Alisubbo with me."

"Alisubbo?"

He gave her an odd glance, as if she should know what he was talking about.

"Town."

"Oh, yes, Alisubbo. Well, I'm afraid I might not be the person you want to talk to. I really don't know much about this place."

He laughed nervously and watched the crowd more than she. When he looked at her, she noticed his blue eyes. It impressed her he had fairer skin than the other men in camp, and he had freckles. Clearly not the same nationality at all.

"I'm sure you could give me a little information," he said.

Two men strolled between the reporter and the fire, blocking not only the light that he was writing by, but the heat as well. The reporter took her arm and directed her away from the intruders. In a more secluded spot, he came to a halt, and positioned his pencil over his notepad.

"I just need a few statistics. Like when this camp began." He wrote something on his pad and looked up at her. That was when Cassie noticed the strawberry blond curls behind his ears.

"I do not know." She laughed. "Seriously, I just got here. Maybe you could answer some questions for me?"

He seemed to be perplexed. "What questions?"

"Oh, I don't know? I've never met a news reporter before, but I think the job would be fascinating. What's your name?"

He looked over his shoulder. "Eduardo."

He didn't look at all like Eduardo, but if that was his name it would be rude to laugh. Cassie bit her lip.

"Did you just arrive from Alisubbo?" Eduardo asked her.

"No. Not from Alisubbo." Admitting that she arrived through a portal would open a door to additional interrogation, and she didn't want to draw attention to herself.

"From somewhere else?" The young man scratched his head with the end of his pencil. Again, people moved closer to them and Eduardo's nervousness intensified.

"Yes, but that's not important. What's important is that I'm here. As are you? In fact, judging from the appearance of all these people, you seem to be a stranger to Alisubbo, too," Cassie meant it as a joke, but a look of terror swept across his face.

He held his finger over his mouth to silence her.

"Me? Why I've lived in the area all my life."

"Have you? Odd, because you seem different from all these other distinguished gentlemen."

"How's that?" His smile strained.

"Well, I noticed bright red hair under your cap, for one," she said. The statement drew the attention of several people around her.

He pulled the beanie further over his ears. "Please. Can we keep our voices down?" he asked.

"Sorry."

"I just need a few statements from you for my newspaper."

"Well, I don't mind helping you, but like I say…"

"Perhaps you can give me a little blurb that will ease the mind of the residents of Alisubbo. For one, maybe you could tell me how long you've been here?"

"Me? Why only a few minutes?"

He laughed, looking into her eyes. "That's impossible. I just started talking to you a few minutes ago. There are no towns on this side of the bay from where you could arrive so quickly. If you aren't from Alisubbo, where are you from? Leinberg?"

Cassie thought about making up a story, however she feared that would get her into trouble since she did not know where Leinberg was.

"No. Not Leinberg."

"Come now, Miss," he whispered, almost patronizing. If he weren't so secretive, she would like to get to know him better. "We're on the same side of the fence here. You don't have to lie to me. It's no shame if you're from Alisubbo. Most everyone here is."

"If all these people are from Alisubbo, then I question where you're from, what with that shiny red hair!" She laughed.

With that, two men with top hats and tailored suits pivoted around, exchanged a glance with each other, and then walked toward them. To Cassie's irritation, one man now brushed against her shoulder.

"Excuse me, sir," Cassie said.

He faced her, combed the tip of his mustache with his fingers, nodded, and said curtly "Pardon me, Miss," though to Cassie that didn't seem like much of an apology. The redheaded reporter pocketed his notepad and walked away.

"You! Young man!" the mustache fellow called out.

Eduardo whirled around. He had a look of fearful surprise on his face, which made Cassie wonder what sort of trouble he had caused.

"I've seen you in camp earlier tonight. I couldn't help overhearing your conversation just now. I had no idea you worked for a newspaper. Might I ask which one?"

Eduardo's face grew beet red. He stuttered and glanced at Cassie. "The uh… Daily Gazette."

"Ah… yes, the Gazette." The mustached man waved to someone across the way and then smiled at Cassie. "Pardon me, young lady."

To her surprise, the man with the mustache reached over and pulled the Eduardo's cap off his head. The man's red hair sprung free.

"Eduardo my spat! Hello! Guards, over here!" the mustache man whistled, causing a wave of momentary silence in the camp.

Eduardo spun around, looking for a way to escape, but he was blocked by bodies now circling him.

"Let me introduce myself to you. I am Perez, the senior editor… and owner… of the Daily Gazette. We're a small outfit and I am certain I would remember hiring a red-headed reporter. Your guise, sir, has been exposed."

Two soldiers in uniform pushed through the throng until they were standing next to Cassie.

"Arrest him!" Perez ordered. "He's a spy."

"Oh!" Cassie stepped back as the soldiers moved in. They grabbed the reporter by his arms and with the crowd following, dragged him toward a large marquee. The prisoner wrestled free from one sentry and pushed at the other, but the stock end of a rifle slamming against his head aborted his escape. Eduardo cried out and fell, holding his hand over the wound, blood oozing down his face.

Cassie lost sight of him at that point because he was on the ground and the crowd pushed her aside. Seeking a clearer view, she maneuvered through the many people who had congregated, and watched from a safer spot next to the marquee. Valerio stormed out of the tent, striding past her.

"Stop this!" Valerio ordered. The crowd cleared a space, exposing the young reporter who was now on his knees. "What's the meaning of this?"

"He's a spy, sure as day," Perez accused.

Fearful of being indicted as well, Cassie inched into the shadows.

"Stand him up." Valerio approached the man when the soldiers secured him again. He grabbed the spy's chin and looked him in the eye. "I've seen you before. Where?"

The young man mumbled something that Cassie couldn't hear.

"What are you doing here? Who sent you?" Valerio asked.

He didn't answer.

"Did the king send you? No, let me guess. You're from the Isle of Refuge, aren't you?"

"I'll bleed it out of him, sir," the guard said, drawing his sword. Cassie gasped, dreading to be a witness to torture. Her outcry drew Valerio's attention, if only briefly.

"No!" Valerio commanded. "I know who this fellow is." This time, he grabbed the reporter's neck, causing the prisoner to grapple for air. "Did you ride here?"

Eduardo squeezed out a terrified yes.

"Then listen to me. I'm going to 'pardon you', just like the king did that scum Gitanos thief, but I want you to take this message to your Captain White Dog, or whatever you call him. Stay away from Alisubbo. None of you are welcome there. Not your people, or those outlaws you associate with. Do you understand?" He released his hold from the man's throat and waved to his soldiers. "Get his horse. Escort him to Pointe de Tratado."

"Yes sir," the sentry replied.

"Sergeant Bernardo!" Valerio called.

Stepping up to his commander, the summonsed officer waited for orders. Cassie recognized him. He was the man with the map; the fellow who had tipped a greeting to her. He wasn't wearing a uniform but had a velvet bolero with elegant gold embroidery and a flat brim hat.

"Take charge and get the rascal to the channel. Have a platoon follow with a munition's wagon. Once the informer has crossed the bridge, blow it up."

"Yes, sir."

For the others to hear, he said aloud, "When you release him, tell him he and his comrades are invited to stay home these next few days-"

"Yes, sir." Bernardo answered.

Valerio addressed the prisoner, his voice disdainful. "… on your island. Minding your own business."

The red head curled his lips and Cassie was afraid he might spit or provoke Valerio further.

"How much information did you gather?" Valerio asked, his voice lowered.

"Do you want to detain him for interrogation, sir?" Bernardo asked.

Valerio studied his prisoner and then glanced at Cassie. He sighed. "No. Our reputation is at stake right now. Our efforts will show fruit soon enough. Send him home. His people will be immobilized."

Bernardo waved to several soldiers, and they hurried toward the horses in the valley. Cassie watched until they disappeared over the hill, realizing that her heart had been beating rapidly throughout the entire scenario.

When she faced the fire, Valerio was staring at her. "Are you a spy as well?"

"No! Not at all!" she blurted. "I'm on your side!"

He grinned. "I knew that you were. I was only teasing. Tomorrow you and I will spend the day together, with your permission, of course?"

"I think that would be fine. I need to be back home by Monday."

He motioned for her to sit with him on one of the several logs that had been placed around the campfire.

Cassie glanced at the audience that had congregated, faces solemn and their voices low. The excitement of the spy had drawn a crowd and now that the redhead was gone, people murmured amongst themselves. Many eyes were on her as she took her place next to Valerio.

"Excitement's over. Go to your tents," Valerio commanded them. Most of the men, and the few women that had gathered, took little time breaking away from the scene. Several inquisitive glances were directed at her. The women took up the dishes and wash basins. Men emptied their flasks either by guzzling the last of the contents or splashing the liquid that was left in their cups into the fire.

Three men in civilian clothes, the one named Perez, and a woman stayed behind. They were most likely confidants of Valerio's, as he didn't seem bothered that they had stayed.

With the crowd thinning, Cassie had a better view of her surroundings. A rustic kitchen had been constructed from thin slabs of timber bound into tables. These were covered with embroidered cloth, and set with wine glasses, decanters, and tin plates. Cast-iron pots still sizzled on the coals.

The campfire seemed to settle the tension, burning peacefully, and offering warmth. Sparks floated in the air; hot embers spiraled on streams of smoke into the black beyond. Cassie absorbed the calmer atmosphere now that the crowd had dispersed. The commotion was over. In the distance, she could see the soldiers mounting their horses, but from where she sat all was quiet. The heavenly globe of darkness arched overhead like an inverted bowl, shimmering with tiny diamonds, rubies, and sapphires. She sighed, releasing the anxiety that had overwhelmed her just a few moments ago.

"I don't ever remember seeing the night sky so vast, so encompassing, and so outstanding," she whispered. Cassie felt strangely at home. She loved a campfire, and this was very much like the family outings she'd been used to. To spend such a night with a handsome officer in an unknown wilderness was an adventure.

"Hear that?" Valerio whispered.

A faint grunt repeated a rhythm from the wetlands. Cassie nodded. "It's a bullfrog. And crickets and…" And crying? Was that the sound that Silvio had described? Her brow narrowed as she studied Valerio's profile. The firelight did something wicked to the shadows on his face, but she refused to cast judgment. It wouldn't be right.

"I hear something else, too," she said.

"I thought you might." Valerio was quick to respond, as though his question about the night sounds had been a test of sorts. "Silvio is up to his tricks." He faced her. "He's evil."

"He says that about you."

"Of course he does. It takes the heat off him." He tossed a stick in the fire.

"So, what's that sound?"

Valerio shrugged. "Not sure. It could be sorcery."

"Don't you want to find out?" she asked.

"Why?"

"Well, it sounds like something is hurting out there. Silvio said it's the sound of the little people crying…"

"Is that what he said?" Valerio chuckled.

"He said you're holding them prisoner in the tunnels."

"And you believe him?" Concern darkened his eyes.

"I don't know what to believe." She watched the flames. "Silvio said some strange things. He said no one here tells the truth. He said truth doesn't really matter because liars always win."

"Silvio can deceive people with sorcery, which is why I won't go investigate those sounds."

Cassie found that interesting, remembering how, in her father's stories, her grandfather had been deceived on Deception Peak. Was Silvio the cause of all the trouble her father had faced?

"Why would he want to deceive people?" Cassie stood and walked to the fire. The temperature had dropped since sunset, and the weariness of the day made her sensitive to the cold.

"He's bitter. He's an old man. He's had a hard life and he's losing his kingdom. Everything he fought for is gone except for those little people he takes care of. I don't appreciate Silvio planting a seed of doubt about me in your mind." Valerio seemed irritated.

"That was unfair," Cassie agreed. "I told him I thought he was wrong to say evil things about you."

"Did you?" Their eyes met and he smiled. "Well, thank you." He stood and moved next to her, stretching his hands out to the flames to warm them.

"What's going on at this campsite? Why is everyone here in the wilderness?"

Valerio released a heavy sigh and slowly rotated around so that his back was to the flames. "It's a complicated story, one which I haven't the time to explain tonight. If you allow me the day tomorrow, I will tell you everything. Do you like to ride?"

"Horseback? Why, yes! How perfect!"

"Then we'll go for a ride in the morning. For now, let me introduce you to my friend Jovita. She'll make sure you're comfortable this evening."

It was then that Cassie noticed the young woman standing on the other side of the fire. Dressed in a tailored riding gown, a flat-brimmed hat tilted on her long wavy hair, she stared at Cassie, and Cassie couldn't stop looking at her. The woman's radiance was magnified by the glow of the flames. Her smile was kindly, and her eyes had a sparkle.

"And who are you?" Jovita asked after Valerio had nodded to her. He moved away from Cassie to the firewood pile and placed fresh wood on the embers. A stream of smoke and ash swirled into the air.

"My name is Cassandra." Cassie said,

"Lovely name," the lady replied. "I'm Jovita. Are you a servant from Bandene Forest?"

"No, I'm not." Blood rushed to Cassie's head. "Why does everybody think I came from Silvio's lair? It's my clothes, isn't it? Well, the old coot, Silvio, hexed me. I have nothing to do with him, though. I landed in his forest by accident and then he did this to me." She gestured toward her skirt. "I really don't know anything about him. Honest. I'm not a…"

Jovita looked sympathetic when she interrupted. "No one is accusing you of anything. And I hold no ill toward Silvio, although I may be the only one here that doesn't."

Cassie eyed the others, hoping the men in suits didn't suspect her of being a spy. Perez peered at her after scribbling something on a tablet. He tucked his pad of paper in his pocket and then poured a drink from a bottle. The other two men were deep in conversation.

Valerio squatted near the fire and stared into the flames. He looked up suddenly. "You haven't eaten yet, have you?"

Cassie shook her head, relieved that he had remembered.

"Perez, there's some venison left, isn't there?"

Perez opened a cast-iron pot and Valerio dished out a plate of meat.

"Princess Cassandra Wilson?" he bowed as he handed her the plate. "Accept our humble offer. We're most honored to have you visit with us." Their eyes met as he straightened. Cassie took the plate of food, enthralled by Valerio's chivalrous delivery. Men in her world were not so gracious. Is it any wonder little girls dream of becoming princesses?

"Thank you, Valerio," she said. She returned to the log and Valerio followed her to sit next to her. She felt the heat emanating from his woolen coat and smelled a musty perfume. Perhaps shaving cream. Mostly, his presence radiated strength and confidence. She felt safe around him, like how she felt when her father was nearby. Valerio was younger than her father, perhaps only a few years older than she was, and yet every bit a man.

The juices of the venison slid down her throat like honey. Cassie hadn't realized how hungry she was until now. She tried hard not to forget her manners, still the way she munched on the bone was barbaric. Valerio handed her a napkin. He did not stop smiling at her.

"I'm sorry. I'm hungry. I must look ridiculous." She dabbed her lips clean with the linen cloth.

"I'm thrilled that we could please you," he replied. "Eat your fill. There's more in the kettle when you're finished. Don't worry about a thing. What we have is yours." He patted her knee. "I'll have Jovita come to your tent tonight with a fresh wardrobe."

Cassie's mouth was full, so she nodded her thanks.

"I look forward to spending the day with you tomorrow. Now if you'll excuse me. I must turn in for the night." Valerio rose, dusting his hands on his trousers. He waited for her. Cassie hurriedly finished eating and then wiped her mouth with the napkin. When he offered her a hand, she accepted.

He pulled her to her feet and then gestured to the marquee. "This will be your tent, my lady. You will find bedding for your comfort. Have no fear of the night. You'll be safe with us. My men are honorable, and so am I." He lifted her chin with his thumb. So gentle was his touch it tickled. She smiled. He leaned over and kissed her forehead. Cassie held her breath and didn't exhale until they gazed into each other's eyes.

Without another word, he pivoted around in the fashion of a prince and moved into the darkness.

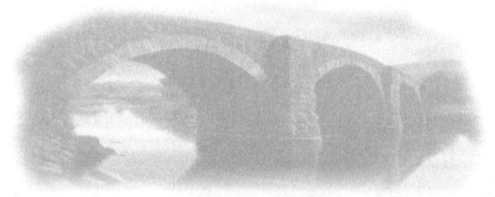

PONTE DE TRATADO

Bullfrogs chorused as the horses plodded through the thick marsh. Croakers jumped out from the cover of cattails and bulrushes, plopping gingerly into the water. Jimmy welcomed the slower pace after the long journey from Alisubbo. His gut hurt from the grueling gallop across the prairie and the steep descent from the forest. The gash on his head had scabbed over. His hair adhered to the dried blood on his temple and now flies swarmed around him. With his hands tied to the saddle horn, he could not wipe the sweat that dripped down his brow or slap the mosquitoes that clung to his wound. Valerio's troops might set him free, but they were making him suffer during the process.

His misery eased when he caught sight of the bridge, Ponte de Tratado, the ancient landmark connecting the mainland to the Isle of Refuge on the southeastern tip of the island. The bridge had been built in ancient days during the war between Hacatine and Alisubbo, and it was the only access by foot or horseback between the island and the continent. The structure now glowed in the moonlight; its mossy pillars spanned the dark waters of the swift moving channel. He'd be safe once on the cobblestone arch.

Jimmy hated to think what sort of reception he'd receive once he reached the Gitanos camp and confessed what had happened. With rumors of revolution in the city of Alisubbo, the security of the island had been shaken. The Isle of Refuge had no other allies but King Chavez. Were it not for Alisubbo's naval fleet, the rulers of Taikus would have claimed the island years ago. Political allegiance was imperative, even though the Gitanos failed to see how crucial it was to their survival. They were too happy a race, too carefree to foresee any danger.

After hearing the rumors of the unusual encampment in Greenstay, Jimmy had suspected foul play and had begged his uncle to let him investigate. Oddly, Whitefox had presumed the military exercise outside of town was nothing more than a strategic drill implemented by the king's cavalry. Jimmy was not one to argue, but he had a gut feeling that the hundreds of soldiers stationed in the meadow were more than a mere exercise, especially after seeing Valerio's true colors the day Elias was pardoned. He had planned to disguise himself, interrogate any civilians at the encampment, and bring the news back to Whitefox. Knowing the truth was the first step in assisting King Chavez. He had not expected to be caught spying.

"Halt!" Bernardo's knee rubbed against Jimmy's when the Lieutenant's mount came alongside him. The man smelled bad. They all did. Even the horses foamed from fatigue. Bernardo had driven his troops on a gruesome ride through the night. His rush was no doubt a desire to return before dawn. Even more of a reason for Jimmy to suspect an insurrection.

Bernardo drew his dagger from the sheath on his baldric and held it in the moonlight, rotating the edge with a devilish grin. "I should use this on you, brigand lover," he said. He flashed the dagger in front of Jimmy's face and let the cold metal touch his neck. "It would give no one any sorrow if I did."

"Go ahead," Jimmy dared. "Disobey your commander's orders."

Bernardo's brown eyes drilled into his. "There's a time and place for everything. I look forward to the day your time is up. Hopefully, I'll have a part in your demise." With the dagger, he slashed the rope that bound Jimmy's hands. "For now, go home. And mind your own business. There's nothing happening on this side of the water that would be of any interest to you."

Jimmy rubbed his bruised wrists and peeled the rope threads that clung to the open wounds. He was glad to be in control of his own fate again. He'd been forewarned of the dangers of spying on someone as callous as Valerio. The man could have had him executed. Why he didn't, Jimmy did not want to guess.

The sound of the channel refreshed him, and the cool starry sky picked up his spirits. He'd be home soon.

He picked up the reins that were resting on the horse's mane and smiled inwardly. The gelding was responsive, flicking his ears toward him, waiting for a command. Jimmy wiped his hair from his eyes and nodded to Bernardo. "I'll go home, but that's not the message I'm taking to Whitefox."

"Doesn't matter what you tell him."

Bernardo gave Jimmy's horse a slap on the rump. Startled, the mare bolted and galloped toward the bridge. The steady clapping of hooves on stone beat a welcomed rhythm of freedom.

As Jimmy reached the cliffs on the island, he pivoted his horse around and was surprised to see that Bernardo's men were still on the trail.

A buckboard had joined the soldiers, halted, and through the commotion that followed, Jimmy guessed their plan. Before he could do anything, an explosion rocked the earth, and then another. Half of the quaking bridge tumbled into the current. Shocked, his eyes focused on the churning waters that swallowed the rubble until the last bit of mud and rock settled. The remains were nothing but a scaffold protruding over the dark and dangerous channel. Bernardo, Valerio's soldiers, and their wagon had already vanished into the night.

The Bridge of Ponte de Tratado was destroyed. Access to the mainland by any means other than by water was now impossible. If Whitefox had plans to help King Chavez squelch a rebellion, it would not be done soon. Jimmy's shoulders sank as he realized the consequences of his failure.

JOVITA

Cassie used the washbasin on the sink outside to clean her hands and then approached the marquee that Valerio had offered her. She'd never seen a tent so large, nor so beautiful, before. Clearly an officer's temporary abode, the heavy canvas door was decorated with a large Fleur-di-lis design in red against a gold background. She pulled aside the door and stepped into a candlelit room. There in the dim light awaited an oversized bed draped with a velvet spread, two chairs, and an end table with a tatted runner. The grassy floor was covered with area rugs of the finest weave and tapestries hung from the walls. A fragrant incense of cedar permeated the chamber.

The tent was better than any motel room she had ever stayed in! Cassie plopped on the downy bed and rolled over. Above her were colorful scarves of linen forming a canopy. She wondered if these people knew she was coming, and if they had set up this tent just for her.

The vibration of her cell phone interrupted her thoughts. She answered, a bit stunned to be hearing from home. "Hello?"

"Cassie! Where in the world are you?"

"I'm in the most beautiful tent you could hope to lay your eyes on, Monica. You should see this place. I wish you would've come with me."

"Cassie! Snap out of it and come home."

Cassie sat up and scooted against the pillows. She stared at the candle flickering by her bedside. "Not tonight. I am going to sleep in this comfy bed."

"Tomorrow morning then."

"No. Actually, there's a handsome soldier that is going to take me horseback riding tomorrow."

"Oh, really?" Monica scoffed.

"Seriously." Cassie snickered.

"So, what am I supposed to tell my mom?"

"Tell her I went to Beth's for the night." Cassie fidgeted with the melting wax that formed a rim around the candle wick. It was warm and smooth, and a thin layer clung to her fingers, which she rolled into a tiny ball as it cooled.

"No! I'm sick of lying for you Cassie. And now I must go to your house and feed all your animals? And what do I tell my mother tomorrow?"

"Tell her I'm spending another night at Beth's."

"Cassie, you make me so mad."

"Chill, Mon, it's only a little while longer. If you saw this guy, you'd understand."

"What exactly are you doing there?" Monica finally broke the silence.

"Well, tonight I'm sleeping in this huge marquee, but it's more like a palace made of tapestries."

"By yourself, right?"

"Of course. What do you think I am?"

Another dead silence.

"Monica!"

"Cassie, I'm just tired of this. We were supposed to be having a weekend together. We were supposed to go to the movies. I bought a ton of snacks for afterward. We have things to talk about."

"I'll take a rain check, Mon. You know that."

"You'll be grounded for ten years."

"I'll be grounded too. We are so dead. I mean throat splitting gone. If your mother finds out about this, you aren't going to be the only one canned."

"I'll take all the blame, Monica, I promise."

Cassie heard Monica sigh and yell at her little brother to get out of the room. A door slammed.

"What do I tell Daemon?" Monica asked.

"It doesn't matter. Daemon knows I'm here. Tell him my phone only gets reception when I'm in the meadow, which is true, and I don't know where I'll be tomorrow, but I'll try to call him later in the day."

"Oh, he'll be cool with that." Monica's sarcasm dripped through the phone. "Should I tell him about your hunk, too?"

"Monica!"

"Whatever, Cassie. Daemon will not go along with this."

"What? Do you think he's going to tell Mom or Dad?"

"Yeah, he'll tell. I know he will because he's worried sick about you. He's been calling me every half hour. He'll want to get your dad to pull you out of there."

"Dad's in L.A."

"That won't not stop Daemon from calling him."

"Would you beg him to stay quiet, please? Tell him you talked to me and that I'm okay and beg him not to tell my parents."

"Whatever, Cassie. I've got to go. Stay out of trouble. You'd better be back by tomorrow night, or we'll all be swimming in muddy waters."

Monica hung up.

Cassie fell back on the bed. Monica was her best friend. She hated that she was so angry. "Maybe I should go home," Cassie said to herself. "Maybe I am going too far with this." She held the phone up, contemplating whether she should take a photo of herself and return to her world.

"If I return now, I won't be in trouble with anyone. Monica's mom could pick me up at the corner store and she'd never even guess what's up."

Cassie dropped her arms, thinking of Valerio's kiss still warm on her forehead. "If I leave now, I'll never have that adventure I've always wanted, and I'll know nothing more about Valerio, or this country, or why that man was spying."

"Cassandra?"

Cassie sat upright and slipped her camera into her pocket as Jovita entered the tent.

"I have clothes for you." Jovita set a leather case on her bed. "I have an extra riding outfit which I think will fit you. This waistcoat goes with it. And a hat." Jovita held up each garment briefly to show her. Clothes that in her world would be called antiques, but here they were clean and smelled like lavender. Embroidered with golden thread, long rows of tiny glass buttons on the sleeves, the bolero was made of finely woven wool. The blouse had a high collar made with lace, and the skirt dark and fitted.

"Oh, and boots. I'm almost sure they'll fit you. You seem to be my size."

"Those are cool. I love laced-up boots, and these are really leather, aren't they?"

"And here are your nightclothes." Jovita helped Cassie slip on the nightgown. She folded Cassie's clothes and placed them neatly at the foot of the bed. "In the morning, you'll find a wash area in the willows. You can leave the clothes Silvio gave you in the tent. I'll take care of them for you. Unless you want to keep them."

"No!" Cassie responded a bit too quickly.

"Very well." Jovita tucked Cassie's blankets in around her. "Have a good night, Cassandra. I'll come by first thing in the morning to help you get ready and to fix breakfast. We get up early."

A Day With Valerio

Waking up in a strange new world took Cassie's breath away. Dew had settled on the grass around the rugs in the tent. Flickering light from a fresh fire seeped through the canvas walls and settled on the rich and beautiful colors of the tapestry at the foot of her bed.

The artwork caught her attention for the longest time. Threads woven into the image of three tall ships on stormy seas that rocked atop waves of lapis blue and swirling cream foam. Intertwined around the ocean scene were maroon paisley bordering an intricately scaled beast with golden eyes and sharp ivory teeth. A wicked-looking creature which, to Cassie, resembled a sea serpent. The beast snaked through a golden crown inlaid with ruby red jewels. From the crown came a sword of silver which met the creature's neck, as though the serpent had been slain.

Cassie studied the tapestry as she lay in bed, curious about the story behind it. She faded in and out of sleep until she heard noises outside. The aroma of a campfire and the sizzling of food cooking woke her up.

She dressed in the clothes that Jovita had left the night before and then stepped outside into the early morning chill. The camp stirred with people.

Jovita had just pulled a frying pan off the coals. "Good morning, Cassandra," she said.

Cassie took the plate piled with venison and potatoes that Jovita handed her.

"Good morning." The two sat quietly by the campfire while eating their meal. An air of anticipation filled the valley where helmets of soldiers glistened as they saddled their mounts. Cassie eyed Valerio leading two horses over the hill. He paused before he came to them and tied the horses to a post.

"You're riding with Valerio this morning?" Jovita asked.

"Yes," Cassie answered between bites.

"Be careful," Jovita whispered.

Cassie didn't have time to ask Jovita what she meant, as the woman quickly slipped away, leaving Cassie alone to wait for her escort.

"Good morning, Princess," Valerio said. He sparkled. The sun shone on his clean white shirt framed by his black velvet bolero. The silver silk embroidery on his apparel glistened. The plume in his hat fluttered quietly in the breeze.

"Good morning." Cassie set her plate down.

"Ready?" he asked.

"I am." She followed him to the horses.

An early morning ride seemed like the perfect event to top off her visit to the Realm, after which she would go home. Her talk with Monica convinced her she'd been acting selfishly and immature.

"I wouldn't miss this for the world!"

He gave her a boost into the saddle and then led her on a trail east of Greenstay. Soon after they left camp, they veered south and crested a rise beyond which spanned a series of gently rolling hills. Oak and hawthorn trees dressed the terrain in clusters; shimmering leaves sparkled in the morning sun. The fields they cantered in were dotted with daisies, dandelions, and purple mountain lilies. Birds sang and flew in and out of the trees and across their path. They rode until the morning light stretched out over all the horizon, and shadows grew shorter. The fresh, minty air and the quietude of the place mesmerized her.

"It's beautiful here!" Cassie said.

"It is." Valerio stopped his horse and dismounted. He took her reins and offered her a hand. "Follow me," he said.

They led their horses through the grass until they came to a small creek that sprouted from a spring nearly hidden under a patch of watercress. From there they walked along the brook, which trickled quietly over rocks in its shallow bed. Soon, the flowing waters joined with another spring, and yet another until it swelled and ran quickly, saturating the soil around it and feeding the lush grass that danced in its current.

On the bank of the stream, a fallen log covered with soft moss offered them a place to rest. Cassie made herself comfortable as Valerio unfastened his saddlebags from his horse and then let the animals graze in the sumptuous pasture.

"Care for some refreshments?"

"Don't mind if I do!"

"You must tell me something about where you come from, Cassandra," Valerio sat next to her. He positioned the leather panniers in front of him and pulled out a bundle. "Sweet bread," he said, and broke off a piece, which he handed to her. "Where is this legendary king? This father of yours? Is he still alive?"

"Well," Cassie thought for a moment. "Have you ever heard of a portal?"

"Of course." He set the loaf aside and unwrapped two glasses that had been cushioned in red linen. "Some may call it a myth, but there is enough evidence to prove otherwise. I'm familiar with wizards and the evil work of sorceresses. I know there are windows to other worlds as well."

"That's interesting," Cassie said as she watched him pull a bottle from the panniers and pour a deep burgundy liquid into one glass. "You seem so indifferent about it."

"What's one form of magic above another?" He held the glass up to her and nodded for her to receive his offering. "Wine?"

She was hesitant. Cassie had never consumed alcohol before.

"No?" he asked.

"In my land, people my age aren't allowed to drink."

"Nonsense! Really? How old are you?"

"Seventeen."

"Then you're old enough to have a taste of wine in our country. Children who are younger than you drink. Sometimes when the rain floods the village, it's better to drink wine than water. Go ahead. It won't hurt you. It's good for you, in fact."

Cassie took the glass and sniffed the deep rich aroma, one of wood bark and raspberries. He watched her closely. Not until she took a tiny sip did he lift his glance from her and pour a glass for himself.

"There, not so bad, is it?" he asked.

"It's good." Indeed, the wine was sweet and warmed her inside. "How old are you?" she asked.

"Not much older than you. Is your father returning? Do you know?"

"Oh! I want him to, but I don't think he will. He promised my mom he would never come back."

"Why is that?"

"They think it's dangerous here."

Valerio gazed out across the creek. "Your father's right. The danger is insurmountable. I'm surprised he didn't prevent you from coming here."

"Well," Cassie felt the heat rush to her head. She didn't want to admit wrongdoing, but she didn't want Valerio to think her father was negligent, either. "He doesn't know I'm here."

He peered at her. "No?"

She shook her head.

A sly smile spread across his face. "A bit of a rebel then, are you?"

Cassie laughed. "I guess."

"And what drew you here?"

"I guess the fact that I found the portal. Curiosity. And then I was enthralled with you and your horses, your army, everything about this world. The beauty, the magic. I'm going home tonight, though."

"You are? Oh, that's too bad."

"Why do you say that?"

"I was hoping to get to know you better." He took a sip of his wine.

Cassie wasn't sure of his intentions, so she changed the subject.

"What about you? You promised me I could learn something about you."

"I did. What would you like to know?"

"Well, for one, why are you and your army camping outside of town? Why are newspaper reporters with you? And why did you accuse that young man of being a spy?"

"Ah. The inquisitiveness of a rebel as to the work of a revolutionary!" He chuckled to himself and held up his glass in a toast to her. She met his toast, wondering about that statement. "Before I answer, tell me one more thing about your world."

"What?"

"Is your father king there?"

Cassie laughed at the thought. "Well, I suppose he's king of our household as he's the only man in it, but he's certainly not king of our country."

"Then who is?"

"We don't have a king. We're a republic. A Constitutional Republic."

"Ah!" Valerio stood, snapping his fingers as though she said the magic word. "And why do you not have a monarchy?"

"Oh gosh, we never did. We broke away from the British two centuries ago. No one wanted a king."

He pointed at her, his eyes aflame. "You see! Neither do we!"

Cassie frowned, puzzled by his riddle. "What do you mean?"

"Our encampment is the first step to overthrowing a tyrannical monarchy. Something your people did two hundred years ago and which we should have done long before it got this bad."

"It's bad?"

"Oh, my dear lady. Yes."

"I'd like to know more. I've been studying…" she stopped herself. Telling Valerio about her homework seemed somehow inappropriate. How could she explain history to someone living in it?

Valerio was more animated now, as though being asked about his cause gave him great pleasure. He rummaged through the contents of his saddlebags and pulled out a metal case bound in leather. Inside the case was a stack of thick postcards. Scooting closer to Cassie, he presented them to her one by one. Sepia photographs faded, scratched but revealing their subjects. Each told Valerio's story in heart wrenching detail.

"These are the children struck down by famine and disease." One by one he thumbed through them. A young girl, no older than seven years, in white lace and braids, lying against a pillow, her eyes closed. Light shone on her face through a window.

"She was the first to die," Valerio said softly. "And then others fell sick immediately after. We petitioned the king and queen to do something, but our pleas fell to deaf ears." He showed her another plate; two boys propped up in a chair dressed in knee britches and embroidered boleros like Valerio's.

"Look, look at them all. There are hundreds more that were never photographed."

"When did this happen?"

"When? It's happening still. They've moved these patients to an abandoned building on the side of a hill, promising their parents they are getting medical help, but I fear it's a lie. No one knows where they are."

Cassie sensed the misery, not only of the poor victims that fell ill, but the pain of what their parents must have suffered watching their children die, pleading for help and getting none. He showed her the images one by one.

"Such innocents," she said. "Why won't they do something? Don't they have children of their own?"

"Two spoiled sons who've never walked barefoot, nor milked a goat, nor swept a street. The king's sons live in the shelter of their castle, unaware of the suffering of their people."

"I'm so sorry."

He looked up from the photographs, his eyes showing as much sorrow as she felt in her heart.

"Tell me you will never be like this. That you will never treat your subjects so inhumanely?"

"I'm not a ruler, Valerio."

"No? But you're a princess."

She nodded. "What can I do to help?"

He shuffled his photographs into their case, snapped it shut, and returned the case to the panniers. "Nothing," he said. "Come, let's ride."

They galloped home. The ride was so enjoyable that Cassie grinned the entire way. A laugh exploded from deep inside her. Her braid came undone and her hair flew into her face. She was sure she had lost the tie, but it didn't matter. She had never felt so free. Valerio seemed to enjoy the ride as well, for his stern expression had softened. When they came to the last hill before camp, Valerio slowed his horse.

"The sun is high. Let the horses walk." He waited for her to come alongside him. "I shall draw out these last moments of the day with pleasure, alongside a beautiful young lady."

"Last moments?" Cassie dropped her reins and brushed her hair back with her hands. She found the tie dangling in her hair, so she twisted her locks into a knot and fastened her hair on top of her head. She noticed him looking at her and she immediately felt a rush of heat.

"You said you were going back through your portal today."

"I did, didn't I? Well, nothing's set in stone."

"It's just as well. My men and I have work to do. Work that a lovely young lady has no business being a part of."

"Are you going to help the children?"

"Yes. Someone needs to rescue them, to care for them."

"I told you I would help if you thought there's something I could do. I could stay another day or two if it meant saving a young person's life. I'm not that much of a princess that I'm not willing to work."

He lifted his head to the wind but didn't answer and she wondered if she had somehow offended him, or left a wrong impression. Perhaps he thought she was like the rulers he was going to be fighting against, and she certainly was not! She loved children and she hated to hear that so many innocent people were suffering.

They said nothing else as they rode into camp. When they dismounted, they parted ways.

GITANOS

Jimmy reached the village when the sun was at its highest. Heat waves streamed from the dry plains, gleaming so brightly he had to squint. A few smoldering campfires sent smoke rings into the air. Bright colored blankets flapped in the breeze on lines hung between the saplings. He dismounted and walked his horse to the yurt near the creek. No one greeted him, but that's what he had expected. High noon was siesta time. The villagers were either napping or foraging in the cooler woods, away from the blazing sun.

Too proud to rebuild the castle that the wicked sorceress Hacatine had destroyed, the island people created their homes in the meadow from local timber harvested in the forests, and tanned hides. Their yurts were rustic shelters, lightweight, and easy to transport, thus accommodating their nomadic life.

The traditions of the elders gave way to progress with Jimmy's uncle and his men from the North Sea. The seafarers had a way with words and, though the Gitanos came to resent negotiations, Whitefox signed a treaty establishing legal commerce between the islanders and King Chavez. Now their homes stood as more permanent structures—their unruly lives diminishing.

Today, Jimmy would answer Whitefox for what had happened to the bridge. He tied his horse to the post outside the door, took a deep breath, and knocked. No one answered. He peeked into the yurt through the window and saw his uncle on his fleece, curled up asleep, snoring. Jimmy knocked louder.

A grunt came from within the yurt and a muffled, "Who is it?"

"Jimmy."

He waited for a response while the news he did not want to deliver gnawed at his insides. He kicked a rock and paced back and forth in front of his uncle's yurt.

"All right then, come in."

His uncle lay reposed on a sheepskin, his hands on his pillow under his head, staring at the ceiling. A robust man, weathered from living most of his life at sea, Whitefox had wrinkles that emanated experience rather than age. His topaz hair contrasted against his bronze tan, now graying in patches, giving him a resemblance to the wild animal he was named after. An authoritative character, he appointed himself chief of the island, a conqueror in his own right.

"I'm back," Jimmy said.

"Get on with it, boy. I can see you're back. You weren't gone long."

"Three days."

"Did you reach Alisubbo?" his uncle asked, his demeanor unenthusiastic.

"I did."

"Was it worth it?"

Jimmy cleared his throat. "You mean was it worth the ride?"

His uncle sat up. If the news hadn't been so demanding, Jimmy wouldn't have interrupted his uncle's sleep. The man was foul before he roused.

"I mean, was it worth the energy it took you to coerce me into letting you go?"

Jimmy's face boiled. He always turned red when eating crow and it was usually his uncle that spoon fed it to him.

"No," he mumbled.

"Speak up," Whitefox demanded.

"No. Sir, uncle, it wasn't worth begging to go, nor going, for that matter. Not with the news I'm bringing back."

"What news? Is the king all right?"

"For now."

Whitefox's blue eyes contacted Jimmy's as he swung his legs around and leaned forward. "What happened? What did you learn? Where'd you get that bump on your head?"

Jimmy touched the wound and turned away from him.

"Never mind the bump. It's nothing. Not like the news I have. The clergy were eager to tell me everything. The town is divided, and everyone is living in fear. The middle-class speaks against the king. Their views are supported by the newspapers, which have been circulating lies, inciting the commoners. It's like the plague, creeping over the city. Chavez has attempted to arrest the movement by ordering a decree that would deport hostile journalists. I'm not sure, but I think the media is using that decree to incite a rebellion of some sort. The nuns told me they'd seen riders and the king's cavalry captain head for Greenstay. They say they've been camped out there for weeks. So, I headed that way myself."

"The king's Cavalry Captain? You mean Valerio?" Whitefox asked.

"Yes."

"I thought placing troops further out of the city was just an added security maneuver of the kings."

"It's possible, except there is a slew of journalists out there camping with him."

"You know this?"

"Yes, sir. I saw it for myself. I went to the camp and tried impersonating a reporter to gather more information."

"You tried?"

There it was. The one incriminating word, 'tried.' Whitefox's eye flew open just before he jumped from his bed.

"What happened? Did you get caught? Did you get into a fight? Is that where you got that bump? What happened?"

Jimmy cringed and shuffled his weight. He walked to the window and brushed back his hair. Sweat stuck to his palms like honey. He wiped them on his pants.

"You made it to Valerio's camp and back, but you didn't find out why he's there?" Whitefox asked.

Jimmy shook his head. "They're being secretive. I guess I don't make a worthy spy."

"You must've done something right. You're still alive."

"Yeah, I'm still alive and wish I were dead."

"Why?"

"I failed. Again," Jimmy said.

"They discovered who you were?"

"They guessed where I came from."

"Great! So now it's public information that spies are infiltrating Alisubbo from the Island of Refuge." Whitefox walked up to Jimmy. "What else?"

"They don't want us there tomorrow."

"Where?"

"Alisubbo."

"That's enough information to warrant a trip. Clean that bruise, and then let's get riding. There's wash water just outside the door. We'll leave as soon as we dress it." The Boreal grabbed his belt and scabbard from the peg by the door.

"No, we won't."

Whitefox turned to him, silent. Jimmy exhaled, hoping his punishment wouldn't be too severe, although the situation in Alisubbo was peril enough.

"They blew up the bridge."

"They blew up Ponte de Tratado?" Whitefox's jaw dropped.

Jimmy nodded, the visual of the exploding bridge still fresh in his memory.

"Is it destroyed?"

"What's left hangs over the abyss like a serpent's head ready to strike."

Whitefox didn't speak for a long time. He paced the floor, stopping to tie up the window latch. He shot Jimmy a glare and then paced again.

"This is bad."

"I know."

"If they felt they had to use precious powder to blow up the bridge, they're planning something extreme. A coup, maybe. How many troops does Valerio have?"

Jimmy shrugged, still gazing out the window. "Maybe fifty in his camp. Many come and go. There's no telling how many others have been persuaded that are still in Alisubbo. There was a stranger there as well. An outsider. I don't know if she was a sorceress, a witch, a soothsayer or what."

"A woman?"

"Not a woman. More like a girl."

"What was her business?"

"I never found out. As soon as she made a remark about my hair, someone called the guards and the next thing I knew soldiers were dragging me to Valerio's tent. The commander recognized me from when we rescued Elias."

Whitefox snickered and then shook his head. "A girl?"

"It's not what you think."

"Maybe not." Whitefox gathered his armor, his knives and two of his swords along with a pistol and a rifle. "You risked your life. I'm glad you preserved it, although I'm not sure how that happened." Laying his weapons on the bed, he pulled a cloth bag from a cedar chest, stuffing it with an assortment of leather articles and clothing. It's a day's journey to the shore, so we'll need to gather everyone as soon as possible."

"Where is everyone?"

"In the woods. Scattered. You could try the ship's whistle."

Recently, the sailors from the North who had immigrated with Whitefox and Jimmy gauged every stroke of time with the blowing of the whistle, an important event while traveling on the high seas. But their life on the island demanded less discipline, so now the shrill call of the reed was used only for special occasions, or for alarms.

"We'll need more than our men. We'll need as many Gitanos as we can get." Whitefox said, lacing his moccasins.

"The Gitanos? You think they'll come?" Jimmy asked.

"They'll come. We'll take their brigantine. It's small and fast. Elias will be honored to have us use his ship. There's nothing he likes more than a voyage to the mainland and a good fight when we get there. It's in his blood. Besides, he owes me a favor. Don't forget, I saved him from being hanged not too long ago. In fact, every one of those villagers owes me. They owe King Chavez as well."

"Some of them might have enough integrity to pay their debt."

Whitefox smiled when he looked into Jimmy's eyes.

"Yes. Well, we all have our faults, don't we? Let's move!"

PERSUASION

Wool was hot in the summer, and Cassie was not used to such impeding clothing. Added to the discomfort was the dripping sweat she'd generated during the ride. Being of paler flesh, her cheeks burned from being in the sun, and already the itch of peeling skin tickled her nose. As soon as they had arrived at the encampment, Valerio had taken the horses to the valley to be groomed, leaving her to find respite on her own. There was little relief at camp from the sweltering heat. Humid temperatures inside the tent took Cassie's breath away, making the air outside a pleasant shift, if only for a moment. Had she been able to change out of her warm clothes, she'd feel better. However, Jovita had already removed the green tunic and skirt from her bedside when she slipped into the tent to check. Disappointed, she turned to leave and eyed her phone on the end table. The screen was lit, and miraculously, the battery showed a full charge.

"Well, that's good to know!" she whispered.

Cassie found the wash area near to the encirclement. Nestled in a stand of willows, a cleverly structured washroom had been built. A large enamel pitcher and washbasin were placed on a modest wooden table. Under the table were buckets filled with fresh water carried from a nearby creek. Towels, and lard soap molded around string, were pinned to a clothesline. After filling the pitcher, Cassie poured water into the basin and splashed it on her face and neck. The breeze, though slight, cooled her body temporarily, and woke her from her sluggishness. Refreshed, her mind once again whirled into motion.

Cassie had seriously considered leaving the Realm and returning home after her conversation with Monica. However, this afternoon, after her exchange with Valerio, she hesitated to make the trip so soon. The images that Valerio had shown her were troubling, and she couldn't stop thinking about them. Precious innocent boys and girls who needed someone to care for them haunted her. Not just one or two children, but an entire village had been afflicted with an appalling disease. She might not have much influence at home, with her family, or her peers, but perhaps here in this world she did. She was a princess. She had power to do something significant. Valerio had challenged her, and she was certainly willing to make a difference. If her father was in this same situation, he would have chosen to save the lives of the little ones.

"You seem to be troubled, Cassandra."

Deep in her thoughts, Cassie failed to see Jovita, or anyone else who had drifted into the camp. The woman carried a basket slung over her arm filled with mint and watercress. Her large hat shaded her face, making her blue eyes glimmer even brighter against her tan skin. Cassie hadn't noticed the color of her hair the night before, but today she saw the bronze highlights in her long wavy tresses. If she had thought Eduardo was not of the race of Alisubians, she wondered about Jovita's ancestry as well.

"I'm hot, mostly," Cassie said, taking note that Jovita wore a lightweight tea gown and looked much cooler than her.

"I can imagine! I do have other dresses you could wear. Let me get one for you."

Thrilled with the idea, Cassie jumped up and followed Jovita. She had so many questions that demanded answers she wasn't sure where to start. Surely Jovita would have more information.

"Do you know anything about the children?" she asked.

"The children in Alisubbo?"

"The ones that are ill. Do you know about them?"

"Yes, I do. Why?" Jovita lowered her voice as they approached the camp.

Valerio's saddle was slung over a bale of straw, showing that he had returned from grooming his horses. He was nowhere to be seen.

The three journalists lingered by the fire pit, even though there were no flames, and no dinner in the making. Their white shirts were sweaty, their ties hung around their necks as more of a burden than a decoration. Their caps covered their eyes as they bowed their heads in a huddle. Their discussion must have had a need for great secrecy, for they spoke so low they couldn't be heard. One of them, the little one that Cassie recognized as Perez, turned his back to her when he saw her coming.

Cassie spoke quietly as well. "They need help. I was wondering how I could help them."

"There is always a need for nurses. Did Valerio tell you about the children?"

"He showed me pictures."

"I see." Jovita set her basket on the table. "I'm not sure what he told you, nor what pictures you saw. Wait here and I'll get that dress for you."

Cassie would have liked to have followed Jovita, but the woman left quickly, leaving Cassie alone with the journalists. The men broke their huddle. Perez waved to Cassie, inviting her to join them. She obliged, cautiously.

"Good afternoon, Your Highness," he said, as she neared. "Since we'll be working together, I'd like you to meet my friends. This is Joaquin, one of my affiliates. He owns the Alisubbo Press."

"Working together?" Cassie wondered.

Joaquin was a large, stocky man with dark hair and cynical eyes. A kind smile spread across his face as he held out his hand in friendship. Cassie gave a half curtsy and let him take her hand as he bowed.

"Your Highness," he whispered.

"And this is Francis, from the northern continent of Leinberg. He's, our photographer."

There had been no reason for Perez to explain Francis' role to the newspaper. The tall sandy-haired man had his camera in his hands, and Cassie had already been staring at it.

"Your Highness," he said, equally cordial.

Cassie was distracted by his equipment and failed to offer him a genial greeting.

"May I see?" she asked.

"But of course," Francis unlatched the black leather case and out popped a shiny mahogany plate that supported the maroon bellows and its fancy brass-cased shutter. To Cassie, who loved taking photos, this camera was a piece of art.

"Few people have a camera like this one," the photographer said.

"It's beautiful!" A real antique camera, shiny and new, as if it weren't but a day old. Cassie marveled at the phenomena of living in history. "Can you show me how it works?"

"Be happy too. I'll even take a photograph of you if you like."

"Yes, yes, that would be good!" Perez interrupted, giving Cassie little time to answer.

"This here's a top-of-the-line press camera," Francis boasted. "A Panorama. You won't find another one like it in all Alisubbo!"

Cassie was quickly shuffled to the front of Valerio's tent by both Perez and Joaquin while Francis took several photographs.

"What's the commotion?" Valerio peeked his head out from inside his marquee, an appearance that sent an uncanny hush over the group. The white plume in his maroon hat was all that moved as he stood outside the door, hands on his hips, a frown on his face. Bernardo slipped out of the tent behind him.

"Just getting some images of the princess here," Perez explained.

"I see," Valerio said. The men remained motionless, as if they needed to wait for approval from Valerio. He stepped past Cassie and walked to Francis, then pivoted around. He gave Cassie an icy stare. She and Valerio had parted that morning with few words and Cassie did not know if he was angry at her or not. Judging from his glare, he was.

"I see," he said again.

Then he broke a smile, his white teeth shone against his dark skin. "If anyone is going to be photographed with the beautiful princess, I would like to be included."

"Yes, sir, of course," Frances agreed. Perez stepped out of Valerio's way and the officer took a place next to Cassie. "Does that fit well with you, Your Highness? One photograph, and then these men will leave us alone." He leaned over close to her ear and moved her chin to where their eyes met.

"I hope you will forgive me for cutting our conversation short this afternoon. In no way did I mean to offend you."

"I wasn't offended," Cassie replied.

"Good! And if you don't mind, I would be deeply honored to have Francis take a picture of us together. Perhaps we can carry on with our dialogue again afterwards?"

"I'd like that. I want to help."

"Good!" He put his arm around her shoulders, faced the camera and posed for Francis.

Cassie chilled at his touch. As arrogant as he came across, he was also caring. She smiled.

"Just one, Francis, and then be done with this nonsense," Valerio said.

The men packed up quickly. Perez gave Cassie a nod before he left the campsite with the others. Bernardo remained, although he moved quietly to the other side of the fire pit to shave.

Valerio took Cassie inside his tent. The room was lovelier than the one she had stayed in the night before. Rugs covered the ground entirely and colorful velvet pillows nestled against the canvas walls. In the center of the floor was a dark wood, hand-carved table. Its four sculpted legs were serpents that slithered upward around the blade of a whittled sword. Two chairs also bore the same design. Valerio offered her a seat and then poured a cup of tea for them both. He moved his chair close to her and sat down.

"Now, did I hear you correctly? You said you want to help?"

"Yes. I'm not sure how. I'm not a nurse, so if there's something else, I can do, please let me know. I can't go home in good conscience without volunteering. I would like to make a difference here, even if it's small."

"I see." After a long moment Valerio rose and walked to a coat tree where his wraps hung. He took something out of his pocket. An envelope, Cassie thought.

"Understand the children who are ill are imprisoned, so to speak, by the royalists. I can't, nor can any of our men, approach them. We are the enemy. They won't let us near the hospital."

"I didn't realize you were an enemy of the king." Cassie said. "You were his army I assumed."

"Appearances can be deceiving. No. I and my men have broken away from the monarchy."

"I see. Well, no one knows me here. I could go to the hospital if there was something I could do there."

Valerio laughed and shook his head as he walked back to her. "You've been here too long already, Princess. They know you."

"Are you referring to the spy?" she asked, sipping her tea.

"Yes, the spy, and the newspaper. The photographs. I don't want to alarm you. Still, if you should decide to stay and help, your only security would be to join our revolution because we can protect you. As indirect as it sounds, should our plan succeed, all the children and their parents will be on their way to good health. Then again—" He shrugged.

"What?"

"You would be safer in your world with your father."

Cassie sat upright. "I'm not worried about me," she said.

"I would, of course give you an assignment which would not be life threatening, provided you took all the precautions we lay down for you."

"I can do that." Cassie's heart quickened. He was going to include her in his plans. She was going to become part of a revolution!

"Very well." Valerio placed the envelope on the table and took a seat next to her. "This letter is a request for parlay. It has in its contents our grievances and suggested resolutions that would benefit the common people. It needs to be delivered to King Chavez."

Cassie's eye grew wide. "You want me to present a letter to

the king?" She set her cup on the table. "What about the spy and the photographs?"

"The spy will not reach Alisubbo soon. And Perez will not publish the photograph if I ask him not to." He sighed, his shoulders relaxing. "You see; we haven't proceeded yet because we weren't sure who would be the messenger. Now, having a royal princess with us, our prayers have been answered."

"They have?"

Valerio wrapped his hands around hers. "Remember, Princess, women and children are suffering because of the king and his wife. The royal house steals food from the common people. They confiscate crops and tax the peasants' farms. The entire nation is in poverty while the court feasts on foreign food. They barter in pearls and jewels, dance in gowns of silk and satin while the peasants wear rags and starve. These are the grievances in that letter."

"He hasn't heard your objections yet?"

"Not in so many words. We transcribed them this afternoon when I returned from our ride. Perez and his friends were in Alisubbo this morning. They brought back news, which I believe is the coup de grâce for this monarchy."

"Why? What happened?" she asked.

He gestured with a wave and stood again. Passion in his eyes. "The king made a decree today. Anyone who speaks against his statutes will be deported."

"They won't even let you voice your complaints?" Cassie gasped. "So, I suppose the king is targeting the newspapers?"

"Authors, journalists, men with new and innovative ideas, philosophers. No one may speak against his policies. I had a confrontation with him recently. He threatened to arrest me. Me! The commanding officer of his cavalry because I spoke for justice while in public."

"What did you do?"

"I had no other choice. I submitted. But I knew we'd be vindicated soon. With your help, we can move forward. Our women and children have become pawns under the monarchy. There isn't anyone who can speak for them except passionate people in prominent positions. People like you and I."

Cassie sprang to her feet. "This is exactly what I've been telling Daemon about the turn of the century and here I am, fighting for human rights and for liberty! You've totally convinced me." Cassie said.

"I can't tell you how grateful I am."

There they were again, those exceptionally handsome brown eyes fusing with hers. A chill raced up her spine.

"I guess we have something in common, don't we?" she said.

"We do. I'm so thankful that you've come to us. Your arrival is truly an act of Providence."

"I guess stumbling through Silvio's tunnels wasn't an accident."

He touched her cheek and spoke with a quiet voice. "What a surprise that a Wilson came to visit our country. You bear a royal name unlike any other." He took her hand in his. "You will make your father proud."

Cassie's breath felt like ice in her chest. She swallowed.

"Tell me something, Valerio. If you're against monarchies, wouldn't you be against me, too? Being a princess and all?"

He laughed. "Our people resist the monarchy of Chavez. Not your father's, or yours. Is that what you think? That I include you, along with my disdain for the Crown of Alisubbo?" Valerio took a deep breath. He frowned and then walked to the door, opened the flap, and looked outside.

"I was not always an enemy of the King. I was, in fact, an officer in the Royal Guard. My father served under King Chavez for many years. He was a righteous king, at first. Power, and then position, got the better of him. He used to be fair and just, but the last few years have seen a sharp decline in his character."

"Why, I wonder?"

"Foreign influence." He dropped the door flap and pivoted to face her, rage stirring in his eyes.

"He sought council from other nations, from the Gitanos and the Boreals who rule over them, when he should have confided in his own men. His interest in his subjects lessened. He made promises he did not keep. Promises..." Valerio's voice trailed, and he looked away. When he caught his composure again, he continued. "... that in the end, killed my father. I couldn't watch the decay of the kingdom any longer. I had to break away even though it caused much turmoil in my heart." He glanced at Cassie, tenacity in his eyes. "I couldn't abandon Alisubbo. I had no choice but to gather like-minded soldiers that would help the commoners. I am now a leader of the rebel cause, taking two-thirds of the royal cavalry with me. So, I'm not alone."

"Wow, the king's army has turned on him? That says something about his character. He must be horrible."

"Yes, well, you can see that if I tried entering the city to bring him an appeal, according to this new law he enacted, he would either deport me or hang me for treason."

Cassie shuddered at the thought. "What about all these people that are with you? Surely the king wouldn't arrest them."

Valerio laughed. "My friends? Perez? He owns the newspaper. These other civilians are journalists. The king knows everyone here. They will all enter the city soon in protest, but they can't approach the king as individuals. They've been silenced."

"I see."

"A Princess from another country has bargaining power." He took her hands in his again.

"I see your point. Taking an appeal to the king, though? I'm not sure if I can do it."

Valerio squeezed her hand and took a moment to study her before speaking.

"Why not? You won't be alone. I'll ask Jovita to accompany you. You'll be perfectly safe. Remember, you're royalty. Chavez and his wife spend many hours with foreign diplomats."

"But appearing before a king? I'm afraid I have no training."

"Then we'll arrange it so you don't have to go directly before the king. I'll send you to the Duchess of Leinberg. She can give the missive to Martim, the prince, and in that manner, it will make its way to the King. That would be much more personable."

"And who is this duchess?"

"An enchanting woman whom I once desired to marry." He fixed his eyes on her hands, stroking her fingers gently. His voice softened. "Unfortunately, her father and Chavez betrothed her to his youngest son, Martim. Nothing the King does is with integrity, I'm afraid. To think of all those years of service to him, defeating the enemy in battle, earning a medal for my courage, and watching my father die." A note of bitterness seeped from his eyes.

"I'm so sorry." When he didn't continue, Cassie searched for comforting words. "That must have been tragic."

Their eyes met and he stroked the side of her face again, this time rubbing her skin with the back of his fingers. He spoke so softly she could barely hear. "Perhaps he did me a favor by betrothing the duchess to his son."

"What do you mean?" Cassie asked.

"You're much more mesmerizing than the Duchess. You're a princess, innocent, neutral, pleading for the rights of the commoners. I think even the king's heart would melt at such a notion. It's only a small favor ... for such a mighty cause. And it would mean so much to me."

Cassie shivered from the chills his breath caused. His touch shouldn't feel that good. She tried to move, but he held her wrists and leaned forward. His lashes tickled her cheek as he neared. He kissed her gently, his lips pressed ever so softly on hers.

When he drew back, she sighed.

"I'll take your message to the duchess," she whispered.

CONSPIRACY

That evening, as Cassie donned her nightgown in the privacy of her quarters, her hands trembled. Something deep within her spirit stirred. Deciding to remain another day, when she knew her mom would be home, and she wouldn't be there, was not the only thing that bothered her.

Jovita came to the tent as she had the night before.

"Cassandra? May I come in?"

"Please do." Cassie eagerly welcomed the woman's presence. She felt safe around Jovita, as though the woman had some sort of stability, and wisdom from which she could glean.

Over her arm Jovita carried a linen clothes bag. "Valerio tells me I'm to ride with you to the castle tomorrow."

"I would really appreciate it!" Cassie said.

"I have a formal gown for you, one that will be appropriate in the presence of royalty." She gently lay the bag on the bed and untied the leather lacing, revealing the most beautiful dress Cassie had ever seen. Embroidered stars of golden threads were set against a sea of maroon silk, which shimmered in the candlelight. Jovita drew the gown carefully out of the valise, ironing out creases with her hand, and gently pulling the fabric away from the enclosure until it was free.

"That's amazing," Cassie said.

"Valerio has panniers for your horse. Keep it in its bag until you get to the castle, and please be careful with it."

"Of course." While quietly admiring the dress as it lay across the quilted spread, Cassie wrestled with how to express her thoughts. "Am I doing the right thing?"

"I'm no judge of your choices, Cassandra."

"Don't you have any advice, though?"

As cold as the woman's answer had been, her eyes showed compassion, sympathy almost.

"The only advice I can offer you is to show you what I know. Tomorrow I will."

Cassie watched as Jovita wrapped the dress back into the valise and tied the lacing. She hung it over a chair. Pulling the sheets of the bed back on the bed, she nodded for Cassie to lie down.

"We'll have to rise early. Get some sleep, little angel. You have a long day ahead of you." She smiled and combed back Cassie's hair, kissing her on the forehead once she tucked her in. Jovita smelled sweet, like roses, and her gentleness calmed Cassie's spirit.

The cool of the moonlight replaced the warm light in the tent after Jovita snuffed out the candle. But a gold aura shone around the woman as she stood at the door.

"Jovita," Cassie whispered. "You're glowing."

"Cassandra," Jovita returned, her voice barely above a whisper. "You'll not be able to go home until this is over."

What? Cassie's eyes widened as she heard the tent flap fold behind Jovita. In a panic, she reached for her phone on the end table. It was dead.

She sunk back into the pillow. Even if she didn't want to return home, it upset her she couldn't. Trapped now, she tossed from one side of the bed to the other. Dark images of an unknown future haunted her. What had she gotten herself into? Would she ever see her mom and dad again?

The worry that tormented her manifested itself as a nightmare when she finally fell asleep. In her dream, she ran through a long narrow room with white walls, ornate pillars, and deep mahogany antique furniture. She flew into a musty chamber, dark and hollow, past a giant stained-glass window. From there, she slipped into a moldy tunnel with walls so close, cold, and damp she could taste the grime and mildew. She ducked and crawled, fleeing from something.

The beautiful dress that Jovita had given her snagged on the rocky floor and tore. Slick moss stuck to her hands, and her hair fell from its braid and clung to her shoulders. She heard dogs outside barking as though they wanted to tear into her. They burst into the burrow. Just as one of them got his teeth around her heel, she woke.

Sweating, Cassie tossed the blankets back and stared at the tapestry. Moonlight filtered through the canvas walls, shining eerily on the woven serpent's teeth. The air was muggy. The sound of wind whistled in the tie-downs and the tent flapped against the textiles. Cassie turned around and closed her eyes. Soon, she drifted into a dream state again.

The stained-glass window shone vividly. Its light radiated Jovita's profile, and Cassie thought she saw wings on the woman.

"Run quickly," Jovita said as she removed a painting from the wall and pushed a small wooden door that opened into a secret stairwell. "Through the tunnel to the stateroom, past the doors and into the field. Keep running until you know you are safe. Do not turn back."

Cassie woke again, this time she purposely held her eyes open. She was too afraid to doze off one more time. She smelled smoke and through the tent walls, saw shadows of men moving around outside. The campfire had been ignited, and the fragrance of hickory seeped into her bed-space.

"I tell you, Perez, publishing this editorial about the new security law was exceptional. If the commoners don't sympathize with our cause now, they might never. Pity that guns were outlawed. That will make our efforts more difficult."

Perez spoke softly; Cassie held her breath to hear.

"Perhaps, perhaps not. With an angry crowd, we'll have more locals on our side. Besides, the king has cut his own throat announcing the deportation of radicals. Do they think only the newspapers are outraged at the handling of the state's affairs?"

"I don't know. I don't understand why he has so much support. Unless the commoners are completely blinded by foreign royalty."

"And if that's the case, we have something of our own to satisfy their taste, don't we?"

"What a sly fox you are? You'll have to let me borrow some of your copy to run in my little newsletter once you finish printing. Not for any monetary purpose, mind you, but because your words and illustrations carry so much ...depth."

"You may take anything you wish. Just be certain that what I've said about the principles of liberty and equality remain intact." Perez offered.

"Of course. It's those words that are so daunting. There couldn't be a more solid advocate for the cause of the Republic than you, Perez. With the help of the Prime Minister, our success will be won overnight. By Monday, we'll have a new government." Joaquin's voice sounded confident.

"When he returns home, King Chavez will find he has nothing left." Perez agreed.

"Indeed," the other man chuckled. "Nothing indeed! I'll see you in the morning."

"Good night, Joaquin."

Cassie sighed. The men seemed to know what they were doing. Allowing them to use her photograph to help the cause was the least she could do. Maybe this wasn't going to be as hard as she thought. Maybe it was going to be just as Valerio said. Cassie will deliver the Appeal for Freedom to the duchess, who will give it to the king's son. The king, though a reluctant monarch, will grant their request. With the help of Valerio's people, the children will get good medical care, and she'll be back home before the week is out. Hopefully, Dad and Mom will forgive her for the delay once she tells them about the children she saved.

***

She awoke to the fragrance of salt pork frying in a skillet, and the sound of Jovita moving about in the tent. Cassie could see a golden sunrise on the horizon through the open flap.

"Time to rise." Jovita laid out Cassie's riding skirt and shirt and helped her prepare for the day. When Cassie's hair was neatly styled on top of her head, Jovita added a broad-brimmed hat, shaking with plumage, atop her bouffant. She handed Cassie a hand mirror.

"Look how lovely you are. Breakfast is almost ready." She helped Cassie put on her tailored bolero over her waistcoat and stepped back. "Yes, you look fine. Come greet the day! Breakfast is ready."

The fresh scent of early morning greeted Cassie when she stepped outside. Jovita handed her a tin plate piled with venison and potatoes. They sat quietly by the campfire with their meal, watching the stars fade into dawn. An air of anticipation hovered over the valley where helmets glistened as soldiers saddled their mounts. Valerio walked up the hill to them, leading two horses.

"Are you ready?" Jovita asked. Cassie nodded, wiping the last of her breakfast from her lips.

When Valerio reached them, Jovita took the reins of the gelding and mounted it. Valerio led the dapple gray mare to Cassie. When she reached for the saddle, he placed his hand on hers.

"Wait," He leaned over her, his breath warmed and cooled her neck at the same time. She pivoted around to find the depth of his eyes on her. "I have something for you."

She swallowed. Is this going to be a habit, that every time he looks at me, I'm speechless?

His hand reached for her waistcoat. His fingers pulled open a pocket and slid something inside. "It would be wrong for such a sweet, innocent princess to be without protection."

Cassie froze when she saw the handle of a Derringer nestled against her blouse.

"You know how to use a gun, don't you?"

"My dad taught me a lot of things. How to shoot a handgun was one of them. But you promised there wasn't going to be any violence."

"I said we weren't going to cause any violence. What happens after the letter is delivered depends on King Chavez."

"And I thought possession of firearms had been banned in Alisubbo."

He grinned, but didn't comment on how she might have picked up that bit of information. "You are not a citizen of Alisubbo. You're not under their laws."

"I don't want to get caught doing something illegal even if I am exempt. I'd have to prove I'm not a citizen. I can't prove anything."

"You won't have to prove anything, my dear. No one will arrest you. I promise."

"You can make a promise like that?"

"You forget; I know every soldier in Alisubbo by name. Follow instructions, and everything will be fine. There's no need to be afraid."

"Then why do I have to carry a gun?"

"My, but you are a rebel, aren't you?" He shook his head and smiled as if laughing at her. Cassie frowned at the reaction. "Because the king still has soldiers, and they're fully armed. I'd be a fool to send you without defense."

"I will not shoot any soldiers of the king."

Valerio touched her face in the same fashion he had the night before. "Perhaps then you'll shoot the king?"

"Don't be absurd."

"I'm teasing you." He kissed her on the forehead. "Please, just carry it. You may be glad you have it at some point. It's small enough to keep concealed. The appeal is in your pack. There is also a package in your saddlebags. Once you arrive, Perez will take that off your hands."

"Why can't Perez take it there himself?" she asked.

"Perez will be searched. He's a journalist, remember?"

Cassie gave him a questioning look. "So, it's something illegal?"

"Cassandra, rebellion's illegal. But it must be done to free the people. Don't worry about politics. It's not your concern. If you do what you're told, everything will work out fine. Deliver the appeal to the duchess. Make sure she reads it before she takes it to the king. That's all you need to do. The citizens of Alisubbo are depending on you."

"How do I find the duchess?"

"Jovita will guide you. Once your message is delivered, Perez will escort you back here. Stay by him. He may have a little mission in town you can help him with. I'll see you when you return. Then we can decide how you can help the children."

She gazed at him, puzzled.

"Or I'll help you get back to your home and to your father. Whatever you wish."

"When?"

"If all goes as planned? Soon. Very soon. I'm looking forward to your return."

Valerio gave Cassie a boost in the saddle.

"Have a pleasant ride," he smiled and patted her horse on the rear.

MEDIO

A s she rode, a thick fog rolled in from the sea, and she felt the dampness of the mist settle on her skin. The scent of the morning campfire still saturated her clothes. It was a pleasant smell; the fragrance of winter firs, like when Dad fired up the old wood stove on frosty autumn mornings.

She got a lump in her throat.

Mom would come home from her conference in San Diego with a present for everyone. She always brought something back when she went on trips. What would she say when she finds Cassie gone?

What's her dad thinking?

Cassie looked up the hill toward the meadow where she had first entered the Realm.

"This way," Jovita turned on a trail east, away from the grasslands. The horses walked steadily into the forest fog. Every step took her farther and farther away from the portal, away from home and deeper into the woods. The day before, her cell phone had kept her connected to her friends in the real world. Today she was robbed of that assurance. Now, with this fog with no way to go home and a loaded gun in her pocket, trouble hounded her. Real trouble.

"For the sake of the children. That's why I'm doing this, Jovita. For the children's sake," she said.

Jovita did not respond. All Cassie saw of the woman was her back, her flat brimmed riding hat, and her braid.

"Jovita, Valerio promised he'd help me get back home. Do you think he can?" Cassie asked. Jovita still didn't answer, although Cassie was sure she had spoken loud enough for her to hear.

"Jovita?" Cassie prodded.

Jovita looked over her shoulder and reined her horse to a halt. She waited for Cassie to come alongside her and then spoke in a gentle but firm voice.

"Whatever happens will depend on the choices you make, Cassandra."

Cassie sank back in the saddle. She had made a choice already. Now it was time to stand by her decision.

As the morning wore on, they came to the forest edge. The fog cleared, opening to a vista of ocean, mountain ranges, and the village Cassie had seen earlier, only now she was much closer. White-walled houses with red-tiled roofs nestled against the hills in rows. Below the township, on the cliffs that hugged the water, was a large square of structures and in the center, a plaza. The castle upstaged everything surrounding it, standing regally on top of a high bank. Below, waves beat against the white sandy beach, and not far offshore in the turquoise waters moored a three mast ship.

"Whose ship?" Cassie asked.

"That's The Felicia, named after the queen. It belongs to the royal family."

The trail veered away from the coastline inland and down a shallow canyon where the forest thinned to scrub cedars and sage brush. Soon they came to a stone building that hugged the cliffs. The building resembled an ancient hotel towering three stories high. Ivy covered pillars marked its entrance, the large windows reflected the sun, and whitewash peeled away from its exterior.

"Our first stop, Cassandra," Jovita said.

"What is it?"

"It's the Sanatorium de Alisubbo. At one time, it was a health spa for the kings and queens and their royal guests. Today it functions as a hospital for people with terminal illnesses—mostly children. The building was donated by the queen."

"Friendly gesture," she snickered under her breath. "You're allowed here? I thought we were the enemy."

Jovita ignored her, yet Cassie could tell by her expression she was disturbed.

Once the trail leveled to a stone walkway, their horses' hooves clapped noisily up to a stable gate made of old wood bleached by the sun. Large knotholes interrupted the smooth weathered shine of the entry, and a brass latch sealed it shut. Wildflowers adorned the yard; an array of yellow, white, and lavender blossoms peeked through the rocks that were assembled artfully into a pathway. Jovita dismounted.

"You'd think for a hospital someone would take care of this place."

"Alisubbo lacks the funds." Jovita answered.

"The king could sell his ship." Cassie said, though she wasn't sure to whom.

"Cassandra, please heel, and pay attention."

Cassie slid off her horse. Sore from being in the saddle, her legs buckled under her, and for a second, she had forgotten how to walk. They tied their horses to the gate stake with lead ropes and walked around the barn entrance to another stone walkway which led to a long, dark hall. The ominous tunnel was a sharp contrast to the flowery path that led up to it. Surrounded by a mass of concrete, its appearance reminded Cassie of a mouth to a dark and damp cave. When they stepped into the corridor, she was sickened by the stench of antiseptic lotions and the stink of decay. She held her breath and gagged once. Jovita seemed unaffected by the smell.

At the end of the hall, a stairwell ascended to the floor above. Another led downward toward a dark passage into the mountain. When Cassie leaned forward to see past the last bit of light on the descending staircase, Jovita touched her arm.

"Come away from there. That stairwell leads to the catacombs. A resting place."

"A resting place? Like a grave?" Cassie asked, wide-eyed as she gazed into the dark hollow.

"Follow me." A ray of sunlight lit the wooden rungs under her feet as she held onto the wobbly handrail and climbed the switched-back stairs. On the third level, she heard voices interrupted by fits of coughing. When Jovita opened the door, sunlight burst from the entry and into a bright solarium that overlooked the ocean vista. Along the wall facing the windows, children rested on wrought-iron beds. Simple spreads of white linen covered them, and large white pillows propped up those who were awake, so that the daylight shone on their faces. Nurses with white aprons and small pointed hats moved about from bed to bed, giving medicine and meals to the children. Several Sisters of the Order were there as well, unpacking fresh sheets from a basket.

Cassie stayed by the doorway. The whole scenario left her in shock. Jovita hadn't warned her she was coming to the very hospital that Valerio claimed was hidden. How did Jovita know it was here, and why hadn't she told Valerio? Cassie kept her eye on the woman as she strolled down the hall, suspicious that perhaps she was a spy, or worse a double agent.

Violent coughing from a child on a bed at the end wall interrupted her thoughts and sparked her into action.

"This mustn't be!" she mumbled, and moved swiftly past a nurse, bumping into her tray, and accidentally joggling the contents of a teapot.

She rushed past Jovita, who whirled around as she sped by.

At the foot of the young patient's bed sat a woman. At first, Cassie supposed she might be the child's grandmother. However, the woman was dressed too elegantly to be a peasant child's relative. Her dress was silk, pale green, and jewels tatted into lace adorned the neckline. Her hat was extraordinarily large, with more plumes than an ostrich boasts. She held a cup for the child, perhaps a taste of medicine, but the young girl, no older than seven years, could not stop coughing. The child collapsed against her pillow, gasping for breath.

Before Cassie reached her, Jovita took her arm and pulled her to a stop. Cassie spun around and their eyes locked.

"That's Angelique," Jovita cautioned. "She's been here the longest. And the woman on the bed is Queen Felicia."

Cassie's jaw dropped. They watched the two. Angelique's coughing eased and the queen tilted the cup and fed the child her medicine. When Angelique sank back on her pillow, the woman looked remorsefully at Jovita. She had large brown eyes and black hair that draped over her forehead, swooped up again over her ear and disappeared under her hat. "Jovita, my dear, I'm so glad to see you again," she said.

Cassie was stunned that the queen would address Jovita in such friendly terms.

"Your Majesty, I bring alarming news. Can we talk?"

"Save it a moment," the queen warned, and then peered at Cassie suspiciously. "Who is your companion?"

"Pardon me, Your Majesty. This is Princess Cassandra, daughter of King Ian of Alcove."

Cassie was at a loss for words as she realized Jovita had betrayed both her and Valerio. The queen held out her hand and Cassie did not know how to receive her greeting.

"Cassandra, Your Royal Majesty Queen Felicia." Jovita leaned over and whispered in her ear. "Touch the queen's hand. Show respect."

Cassie did as she was told but gave Jovita a scowl.

"A pleasure, my dear. Though we never had the good fortune to meet your father, word of the foreign king and his adventures have graced our ears for many years. I trust your absent father is well?"

"He is, Your Majesty." Cassie could somehow speak without stuttering.

The queen studied Cassie for a long moment, and Cassie, her. Here she was, face to face with the woman whom Valerio condemned and how true his words were ringing in her ears. The facility they were in was a poor excuse for a hospital, while the queen wore expensive silks and satins.

Queen Felicia turned to Jovita, "I find it hard to trust anyone, anymore, Jovita. Lies and rumors infest our entire country. And now I hear gossip about insurrection. When will it end?"

"I'm aware, and I worry about your safety," Jovita said.

Cassie shot Jovita a fleeting scowl.

"My family is fine." Queen Felicia nodded toward the children. "How can Carlos and I continue with this project with so many people working against us? I'm tired of politics. Every cent I spend in this Sanatorium is used as a dagger against my family. I swear the press seeks our ruin. If it weren't for the journalists, we'd have employed villagers to work here. But ideology and political musings have hampered human need." The queen rested her gaze on Cassie.

"Aren't politics and human need the same?" Cassie asked. "They should be!"

The queen sat upright but did not answer Cassie's question. Instead, she picked up a newspaper that was on the foot of Angelique's bed and handed it to Jovita.

"Did you see this?"

"I've seen it." Jovita answered.

"May I?" Cassie asked and took the newspaper.

"My hands are tied. I can't do enough for these children, and yet the more I do, the more hostile the rumors become."

Cassie wanted to shout at the woman that it was her own fault; that she should have helped the poor children sooner, that disease follows poverty and if the royal family spent their money on their kingdom and its people instead of her wardrobe, or her husband's boat, maybe these kids wouldn't be dying. She held her tongue, though. Valerio had given her explicit instructions, and if she gave herself away, she could ruin the opportunity of a parlay.

She opened the paper instead. The first name Cassie recognized was the editor's. Perez. She read aloud. "Royalty Rebukes Poor, Entertains Enemy: Bans the Press". When she glanced up from the paper, she studied Queen Felicia's eyes.

"Lies," the Queen said, the word barely audible.

Cassie bit her lip, set the paper back on the bed, and walked away before her anger became obvious.

There was no ignoring the children. None of them could have been over thirteen years of age. One child was so lethargic that Cassie barely noticed him sunken into his sheets. Sweat drenched his hair. His beautiful dark eyes and long thick lashes seemed out of proportion to his thin face. He stared at her and whispered something when their eyes met, but Cassie couldn't understand him. She walked to his bedside and took his icy hand in hers.

"You're not from Alisubbo," he repeated.

What a pathetic sight, a child so young to be in such a state. He had dark rings around his eyes, his tear ducts were red. His skin was a deathly gray, his lips chapped. His lanky body sunk under the covers barely visible.

"No. I'm not." Cassie answered. The sight of his sickness made her shudder.

"Where do you come from?" he asked.

Cassie flashed a look at the queen. She leaned over and whispered in the boy's ear. Her breath must have tickled him, for a slight smile curled his lips.

"Seattle," she said.

"What a grand name! Is it far? I would very much like to go to Seattle with you," the boy pleaded. Cassie was at a loss. Though near in tears, she returned his smile. He wasn't ever going to Seattle. He may never leave this hospital alive.

Cassie nodded. 'Okay," she said. "I'll come back for you on my way home."

He nodded and mouthed the words, "thank you." When he closed his eyes, his body relaxed. Cassie hoped he had only drifted off to sleep.

She turned to Jovita. "Why did you bring me here?" She frowned at the queen. "Is this the best you can do for these children?"

No one answered.

"How is this place helping anyone?" Cassie's question was directed to the queen, who did not defend herself/ The entire hospital fell silent. A Sister of the Order walked up to her and cleared her throat. She looked first at Jovita, and then the queen, and then her eyes met Cassie's

"I'm not sure who you are, young lady, but your tone is disrespectful. Aside from being impudent, this chatter is also against the law."

"Sister Ann, that's fine," the queen interrupted.

"But the king's decree says…" the nun started.

"I know what it says, and I'm letting this slide. Cassandra is from a foreign country. She doesn't know our laws." Queen Felicia stood. Her eyes were like Cassie's grandmother's on her mom's side. They had a placidness about them, and a sparkle, as though no matter what crossed her way, she would maintain her dignity. If Cassie weren't so angry about the condition of this sanatorium and these children, she may have liked the queen.

94

"What decree?" Cassie asked, although she knew well.

"The Prime Minister has outlawed derogatory criticism against the king's policies and his reign," the nun answered.

"Only temporarily," the queen interjected. "Only to establish peace. Prime Minister Torres acted outside the will of my husband, but that is a matter I should not be discussing here. It is the king's responsibility, and he bears the burden."

"Peace? How can you ask your people to be peaceful if they can't speak the truth in front of you? What kind of place is this?"

The nun shook her finger at Cassie. "You stand before royalty. Hold your tongue."

"How can I hold my tongue? If poverty is the reason for this disease, then it should be addressed openly so someone can do something. There's wealth enough in your country from what I can see. It should be distributed so that these kids don't die!" She held her breath. When no one responded, she pulled Jovita away from the nurses and the nuns, and so that the queen couldn't hear, to the back wall near Angelique's bed. The queen retreated to the other end of the hall.

"Why did you tell her she's in danger? I thought you were on Valerio's side and wanted to rescue these children!"

"No Cassandra, you're assuming things."

"You're wrong about having to rescue us from the queen," Angelique interrupted them. As ill as she was, her voice had a tenacious quality to it, as though what she said was more than an observance, but a passion. "You're wrong about the queen. She's our friend. She cares about us. She would do nothing to hurt us, and it's not her fault that we got sick."

"I'm sure she cares in some ways," Cassie returned.

Angelique waved for her to come by her bedside. Cassie clasped the little girl's frail hand. Angelique wasn't cold like the little boy, but warm and feverish.

"You're pretty," Angelique said. Her gaze did not stray from Cassie's.

"Thank you," Cassie said. There was something consuming about the way the child looked at her, as though just setting her eyes on a princess would turn her into one. Cassie smiled at her and squeezed her hand.

"I'd love to be a princess. To dress in beautiful clothes, ride horses and travel this world. Not everyone is as blessed as you." Angelique's eyes were brighter than they had been earlier. She tossed her hair over her shoulder.

"I know," Cassie said, immediately being reminded of her own

95

thoughts that afternoon. "I'm more fortunate than many people."

Angelique nodded in agreement. "Not everyone can be a queen."

"No, they can't."

"It isn't the queen's fault we're ill. She's already done everything she can. And Prince Marques is finding a cure for us, he promised. And Prince Martim comes and plays violin for us sometimes. They are good people. Like family." Cassie exchanged looks with Jovita.

Angelique coughed and held her finger up for them to wait, not that Cassie would have left her.

"Queen Felicia spends time with us. She doesn't have to, but she does. She loves us. In fact, she's going to pick flowers this afternoon with me. Will you come?"

"She's going to pick flowers with you? It's weedy out there and she has a very expensive dress on."

Angelique shook her head again. "Queen Felicia dresses up for us every day. She says we're special to her, so she wears her prettiest clothes. She takes me to pick flowers whenever she comes, and she will this afternoon too. You should come with us."

Picking flowers was not on Cassie's agenda. Even though she would have loved to stay with Angelique, there was urgent work to do elsewhere.

"Angelique, we're leaving for Alisubbo this afternoon. But we'll be back soon." Jovita tucked the covers in around Angelique's chin and kissed her on the forehead. "Enjoy your day with the queen. She'll need lots of flowers to give the king and Prince Marques."

"I know. Queen Felicia told me how much she misses them. We're going to pick the biggest, prettiest bouquet ever! I can't wait to see their faces when they see the bouquet!"

Jovita patted the girl's hand and left Angelique's bedside and addressed the queen quietly. Cassie followed.

"Excuse me, Your Majesty, but I have pressing news. I came to deliver a warning to you, Felicia. I've reason to believe that Valerio is planning an attack on Your Majesties as early as this afternoon."

"That's not what Valerio said." Cassie balked at that announcement, but neither the queen nor Jovita seemed to hear her.

Queen Felicia showed no surprise; still a wave of concern darkened her eyes. "So. It's true then. He is a traitor." Her eyes lost their glow, and she stood quietly for a long moment. "My husband was warned, but he refused to believe that Valerio would turn against him."

"You must flee, Your Majesty. He has an army with him. Go to the Ilha de Consolo. Don't return to Alisubbo."

"Wait!" Cassie interjected and gave Jovita a dagger eye. "Valerio has given me an Appeal for Freedom to bring to the Duchess of Leinberg. I'm sure that if the king consents to the simple terms he's laid out, there won't be any fighting."

"An Appeal?" the Queen asked. "That doesn't sound like Valerio." Queen Felicia gave Jovita a questioning glance.

"Cassandra carries a sealed note addressed to the duchess. That's all I know." Jovita said.

"I have my doubts Duchess Elizabeth will receive your an…appeal, Princess. But if you think it wise to continue to the castle, then do what you must." She addressed Jovita, "We won't run, my friend. The kingdom is in our charge, and we will stay with it until the end. I'll wait here for my husband and my son and pass the warning on. Take the princess to the castle so she can deliver her message. I suppose we should give Valerio the benefit of the doubt. Perhaps he's asking for amnesty."

Cassie took a breath to argue, but Jovita touched her lightly on the arm. "Yes, Your Majesty."

"I'll have someone escort you to the village. Take my buggy," the queen offered.

"And you?"

"Angelique wanted me to help her out of bed to pick flowers this afternoon. I don't mind staying here until my husband arrives. I'll ride back in the landau with my family. Sister Ann will drive you into Alisubbo." The queen took a deep breath and looked Cassie straight in the eye. "I hope your heart softens a bit toward us. I respect your father and all he's done for this world. I would hope to feel the same toward you." With that, the queen exited the room.

Cassie didn't speak again until the queen was well out of earshot. "What's happening Jovita? Valerio promised this would be a peaceful march."

Jovita walked hastily down the stairs and headed for the barn. Cassie hurried alongside.

"You're going to be meeting more of the royal family when we get to Alisubbo. I can't tell you what to do, or what to think, Cassandra. What I can say is this. Keep your eyes and ears open and try to be respectful. Now get your things from our horses and take them to the buggy in the stables. I'll find Sister Ann and hurry her along."

The double doors were open already and sunlight had filled the stalls, illuminating the straw floor. The odor of hay and manure hit her as soon as she stepped inside. A servant had just finished hitching a very large chestnut horse to the buggy. He bowed quickly when Cassie entered.

"She's ready for a ride, Miss," he said. Slinging a lead rope over his shoulders, he picked up a bucket. "I gave your horses some grain and fresh water." The man nodded to a stall where the horses that she and Jovita had ridden were kept. The tack had been removed and set on a couple of hay bales.

"Where are the panniers?"

The man nodded at the bales. "Everything is as it was, simply removed from the horses in order to care for their needs."

Cassie waited for the man to leave and then moved swiftly. She checked the saddlebags, making sure the dress and the letter were there. She slipped the letter in with the dress. Unlacing the saddlebags from the saddle, she swung them over her shoulder and grunted at the weight.

"Your gift to Perez, eh? Don't worry mister Valerio. Your secret's good with me," she said to herself as she flung the bag into the buggy and jumped onto the back seat. "But only if you show me what it is!"

It took great effort to pry the black case from its snug fit inside the bag. Once freed, she pulled the valise on the seat next to her and unsnapped the brass latches. Upon viewing the contents, she instantly wished she hadn't.

A disassembled rifle had slipped neatly into separate compartments lined with blue satin. Clearly not a military weapon, for the etching on the ivory plate on the stock bore someone's name. Cassie had no time to read it. Jovita and Sister Ann entered the barn. Cassie snapped the case shut, squeezed it back into the saddlebags and nestled everything under the seat before they were near enough to see what she had done.

"Are you ready, Cassandra?" Jovita handed her a straw hat. "Wear this instead of that wool one. It's much cooler and the brim will keep the sun off your face. It's a gift from the queen. She says your cheeks are burning. I believe she is correct."

Cassie took off the plumed hat, put on the straw one, and tied the scarf. "That was kind of the queen to worry about my sunburn," she said.

"Watch your tongue," Sister Ann reminded her.

"My apologies," Cassie said. "I didn't mean to sound snarky," she added under her breath.

As Sister Ann hopped into the carriage, Jovita led the horses they had been riding to the back of the buggy and tied them with a lead rope.

The nun looked over her shoulder and studied Cassie.

"I would hope the comfort of the queens' buggy will prompt you to penitence, Your Highness. The queen has returned your rude comments with acts of kindness. Let that be a lesson for you. And may the good Lord forgive you!"

Cassie shuffled in her seat and turned away.

"I have never in my life heard anyone talk to royalty the way you did today," the nun grumbled as Jovita climbed onto the seat next to her.

"Is everything well with you two?" Jovita asked.

"Fine," Cassie said the same instant Sister Ann responded with a 'yes'.

One click of her tongue, and the gelding moved toward the open door, setting the buggy in motion.

ALISUBBO

So, what if there's a gun in the case? It's none of my business, and I shouldn't have looked. Cassie leaned against the soft leather buggy seat and watched as the countryside passed by. Indeed, the queen's gift was a welcome relief. Cart travel was more comfortable than a long ride on the back of a horse. She tipped the wide brim of the hat that Jovita had given her so that the shade covered her eyes and nose. Cassie wished she had brought her sunscreen as her nose burned and her cheeks had already started peeling.

Adjusting her waistcoat, she patted the pocket where the gun was nested, making sure it was secure. She'd feel better just tossing it out of the buggy, but decided against doing so. It was a gift from Valerio. Still, she wasn't certain she could ever use a gun on another human being. Her father, a dedicated bow hunter, cared little for firearms, though he owned several old rifles that belonged to her grandpa. He taught her to shoot all kinds of weapons, but his words of warning stuck with her.

"Learn to shoot one accurately, for your own safety. But remember, handguns invite trouble."

"I don't need any trouble! I think I'm already in enough of it!" Cassie whispered to herself and glanced at the two women on the seat ahead of her. She considered telling Jovita about the guns and then thought better of it. Valerio trusted her. He'd been open with her and had asked her to trust him. She knew his plans. Jovita was secretive and seemed to work against Valerio. For that reason, she kept silent.

Maybe it was fatigue, or maybe it was the dust that followed in their wake, which made her sleepy. Added to her weariness was an overwhelming sense of homesickness. She wished her dad was with her. She lay her head back against the seat and just watched the world pass by. The golden rock formations of the hillside baked in the sun, the vista, the smells of the sea coming from the shores below the great cliffs made her sleepy.

***

The clap of horses' hooves and the vibration of the buggy on rougher ground woke her later that day. They had reached the city. Long shadows stretched across the cobblestone road, blocking the heat of the day. The road was extremely narrow and meandered between towering apartment buildings made of adobe. Porch railings were draped with laundry. Flower boxes beautified the windows with hues of colorful geraniums, cascading like ribbon over their sills. The alleys bustled with people, mostly children and their pets. Barefoot, wide-eyed, and dark-skinned, the junior residents bore a resemblance in ethnicity to the children in Medio. They were healthier, and yet just as thin.

Sister Ann sat stately on the driver's seat, commanding the gelding with only a grunt in her voice, or pull of the reins. Not once did she speak to either Cassie or Jovita.

The longest and narrowest alley they moved through opened to a large square of majestic buildings. When the buggy rolled out in afternoon daylight, the heat hit Cassie's face like a blast from a furnace. Jovita tapped the nun on the shoulder.

"Please stop before we reach the castle. I won't be going any further."

Sister Ann nodded, but Cassie sat up in alarm as the buggy came to a halt. "What do you mean? You're not coming to the castle?"

"I've come as far as I can, Cassandra. The letter was given to you to deliver. It's up to you from here on."

"What? What am I supposed to do? Where do I go? How do I even get in?"

"Sister Ann will take you into the palace. Be respectful. Keep your opinions to yourself in the presence of royalty. Queen Felicia was very kind to let you speak to her the way you did in Medio. I would hope you temper your mouth a little better from now on."

Jovita stepped out of the buggy and untied her horse. "If I were to stay, I would interfere. That's not my place." Her eyes looked deep into Cassie's. "Your father's love is with you, my child. Make him proud." Cassie opened her mouth to protest, but Jovita smiled and held her finger over her lips. "I'll see you later," she said.

Cassie's shoulders sank. Jovita's departure meant she would have to face the royal family alone, and she wasn't sure she was ready.

As much as she hated Jovita leaving, she couldn't help but admire how beautiful the woman was on top of the dark bay mare, her gown and veil draped over the horse as royally as any princess. Graceful and confident, Jovita rode up the road that they had just traveled. Suddenly, she disappeared. Cassie gaped in amazement. The woman hadn't turned a corner, nor did she become lost in a crowd. She just vanished instantly.

"I have an errand in the chapel across the street that I need to tend to before we enter Square de Regem. Wait here! Stretch your legs if you like, but don't get lost. I've got arthritis in my knees and I can't be stumbling all over the city looking for you."

"Yes, ma'am."

The nun slid from the buggy, pulled a rope from under the seat, and tethered the gelding. Her walk was labored as she limped across the brick driveway. Her gray muslin habit reflected the sun almost as vividly as the white-washed walls she retreated to. The nun opened the dark hardwood door of the chapel, crossed herself, and entered.

The structure was a close resemblance to the old missions Cassie had seen on her trips to California. Bleached under a blistering sun, the chapel boasted a tall steeple and an old iron bell. Climbing rose bushes clung to its walls and porch railing, budding with bright red blossoms. Cassie could smell the fragrance from across the street.

She slumped low against the leather bench, hot and dusty from traveling all day. Sweat plastered her hair against her skin. It wasn't until she removed the sunhat that her head cooled.

"This is indeed a poor village," she whispered to herself. The tall apartment buildings that at first glance seemed clean and presentable had rickety stairs with railings that were broken or non-existent. Porches had roofs that needed repair. Garments that swayed in the breeze on clotheslines were stained and tattered. Even the lone mongrel dog she saw roaming the alley was skinny and half-starved. Chickens patrolled the streets, and she even saw a pig rummaging through a pile of garbage.

Just when she was wondering where all the people were, she heard laughter. A group of children raced past the buggy and dodged behind the chapel. Soon screams over-powered the merriment. Cassie panicked, jumped from the carriage, and broke into a run toward the crowd of youngsters.

"Don't do that to him." A young girl hollered as she flung her arms at a cluster of boys huddled in a circle. Her colorful skirt rustled, her bare feet kicked up dust as she thrust her hands wildly, hitting only air as the boys dodged her attack. One boy spun from the group and made a face at her, inciting her hostilities even more.

"No!" she screamed.

"Get away Carmen." An older boy pushed her.

Cassie approached the children at that moment and as the child fell backward, she bumped into Cassie. If Cassie hadn't had such quick reflects and caught the girl, she may well have landed in the dirt.

"Hey!" Cassie scolded. "What's this all about?"

"Please," Carmen twirled around and tugged at Cassie's skirt. "Save it, please! They're going to kill it."

"What? What are they going to kill? What's going on?" Cassie asked.

"Look!" Carmen pointed. There was nothing to see except the backs of several youngsters crouched low, their heads bobbing up and down as if playing some sort of game. Cassie pushed past the children until she saw the object of their attention.

Amongst an array of little brown toes, skirts, and pant legs, was a small mammal. A prairie dog of some sort, though Cassie wasn't sure, since she'd never seen a prairie dog that young. The pathetic little creature spun in a circle, its mouth opened in panic, and foaming from dehydration. It hissed and spat at the sticks the children were using to torment it.

"Stop, all of you." Cassie exclaimed, working her way into the circle. She pulled one poker away from a boy and slapped the other sticks with it. "Just stop this!" When the commotion quieted down, she quickly took her riding gloves from her pocket, slipped them on her hands and stooped to the ground.

"Look at him! He's terrified." With some coaxing, Cassie calmed the kit enough to pick it up by its neck fur. She held it close to her and stroked its back gently. "Why are you torturing such an innocent animal?"

Without an answer, one by one, the boys threw their sticks on the ground and raced through the alley, laughing. Cassie was left with five young girls and a toddler by her side.

"Is it a prairie dog?" Carmen asked. She stood as tall as Cassie's waist, wearing a brightly colored skirt, turquoise blouse, and several scarves around her neck. Her black hair was tied in back, her skin olive and smooth. Thick lashes framed her dark eyes.

"Yes." Cassie answered.

"Prairie dogs eat chickens," she said.

"Sometimes they do," Cassie said. "But you can train them not too. Just feed them like you would a kitten. Your name is Carmen?"

"Yes." She pointed to the other girls. "These are my sisters, Graca, Marta, Rosa, Veronica, and our little brother's name is Marques. He's named after the Prince Royal."

Each of the children blushed and smiled.

"I'm pleased to meet you. My name is Cassandra. Do you live

around here?"

"We live up there, in the top building. That was my older brother, Deniz. He thinks he's smart because he's thirteen now. Those were his friends. They're always mean to animals. My sisters and I like to take care of animals, though." Each of the girls were reaching past Cassie's arms, stroking the baby prairie dog that snuggled close to her. "Are you going to keep it?"

"Do you want to take care of it?" Cassie asked.

Carmen nodded.

"What about your brother?"

"If we take it to the house, Mama won't let him near it. He teases, but he's still a good boy. He does what mama says."

Cassie let the girls cuddle the prairie dog. They kissed it and handled the creature with such affection she could hardly tell them no. "Let's let him calm down a little, and then you can take him to your apartment."

"Are you going to Square de Regem for the parade? To see the king and queen when they come?"

"I'm pretty sure I'll be there." Cassie said. "When is it?"

"We don't know yet. But our whole family will go. Mama's going to dress us up in our Sunday clothes." Carmen wore a broad grin. "We love to see Queen Felicia. She's so beautiful. Our family knows her."

"You know her?"

Carmen nodded proudly. "She comes to our house to give us things. Soon she'll be giving us shoes. When Graca was sick, the Queen took her to the hospital on the mountain. Now look at my little sister. She used to cough all the time and some days she couldn't get out of bed. But now she's like the rest of us. Getting fat too!"

Graca hid behind Carmen as the other girls giggled. None of the children were close to being fat, but Cassie didn't argue with her.

"Queen Felicia would help anyone; all you must do is ask. If she can't come to you, she sends the nuns. Do you need help?"

"Help? No. Well, maybe sometimes I do."

"You should never be too proud to ask for help. That's what Mama says. Everyone needs help sometimes." Carmen stepped back and let the other children get closer to the prairie dog. "If you don't you should help others then. I will. I'm going to be a nun when I get older and work in the hospital. I can't wait to help people."

Cassie sat next to the children on the ground and leaned against the walls of the chapel. The alley was much cooler than if she had still been in the buggy roasting in the sun. She held the trembling kit in her arms while the girls stroked it. When the prairie dog finally stopped shivering, it closed its eyes. Cassie handed the kit to Carmen. "You can start by helping him. He needs your love."

Carmen gave Marques' hand to Graca and took the little creature, touching her cheek to its fur. It was then that Cassie saw Carmen's older brother watching from the corner of a building.

"Take the kit home. If you treat him right, he'll be a good pet for you."

"I will," Carmen promised as she stood. "Thank you." She led her sisters and the toddler across the road.

When they were out of earshot, Deniz approached her. "You gave the animal to them?"

"You should be kind to the prairie dog. He could be your pet. Too."

He didn't answer, but held out his finger toward her. "What's that?" he asked.

Cassie looked down at her waistcoat and her insides turned sour. The pistol had inched its way out of her pocket during the commotion. She tucked it back into its sleeve and rose to her feet, straightening her dress. "Nothing." She hurried back to the buggy.

She didn't have time to see if Deniz followed her. Sister Ann was already picking up the reins. Cassie hopped in and leaned against the back seat, adjusted her hat, and checked again to make sure her pistol was tight in its pocket. When she glanced over her shoulder, Deniz stood in the corner, watching them travel toward Square de Regem and the castle. He then ran back into the alley. Cassie wondered what he might think, where he might run, and who he would tell. Surely, he was old enough to know about the ban on weapons. Here she was, caught red-handed by a child.

It was high noon when they reached the gardens. The buggy rolled around the stone architecture that graced the square, and a giant bronze statue of a horse and rider that marked center. Carved pillars formed archways at the entryway, providing shaded corridors that bordered the plaza. The blaring white of limestone radiated the heat of the day. Sweat dripped from every pore of Cassie's body.

"Who's that?" Cassie asked Sister Ann as she squinted up at the statue.

"That statue? A king highly esteemed by his people."

"What did he do to deserve such a remarkable monument?"

The nun shook her head. "I'm not sure. He lived in the same era as a great artist, I guess." She laughed. "I'm just teasing you," she said when Cassie sunk back into her seat. "That's King Roberto, a brilliant warrior who defeated the wicked Hacatine in ancient days."

Sister Ann pulled the horses to a stop in front of the castle and applied the brake. They were met immediately by a palace soldier dressed in full uniform. His helmet reflected the sunlight, and a white plume danced above his head. His uniform fit snugly around his chest, the trim sparkling silver in its woven design. Bright buttons adorned his coat, and white gloves reflected the sun as he reached out to her, offering his hand to escort her from the buggy. Another soldier in the same apparel took the reins from Sister Ann.

"Thank you," Cassie accepted the help. The soldier bowed.

"Your Royal Highness."

No sooner had she touched solid ground than Perez, Francis and Joaquin appeared along with several other civilian men dressed in top hats. Francis had his camera in hand and began taking photographs of her, the carriage, and the surrounding crowd. Sister Ann got between the camera and Cassie.

"None of that!" she said, but no one listened to her.

"Your Highness!" Perez tipped his hat in greeting and gave her a devious smile as he elbowed his way through the throng. He gave Cassie a wink. "May I have a moment of your time?"

Sister Ann nudged Cassie. "Get into the palace as soon as you can and don't mingle with the likes of him. He's a scoundrel. He'll twist your words and hang you with them," she complained, giving Perez an eagle eye.

But it was too late. Perez and his journalist friends ignored the nun and encircled Cassie. Francis took photographs of the insignia on the buggy. Perez stepped close to her, his questions pouring out faster than Cassie could think. Their hovering irritated her as she was already hot and unsettled from the long and dusty ride.

"Word of your arrival has spread," Perez said, jotting down his comments. "Would you like to make a statement to the good people of Alisubbo concerning the purpose of your visit? Is it a royal party? I noticed that you traveled in the Queen Consort's carriage. Has she afforded your costly trip from lands far off? If so, why? What's the occasion?"

The crowd of reporters laughed, their faces eager. Perez waved to a man lingering in the distance and then leaned over her shoulder and whispered in her ear. "Just give us something we can feed on, dear. Something we can spin from."

Cassie glowered at the man. She might not be a friend to the queen, but she wasn't going to lie for a newspaper either.

"No one's paid for my trip, Perez. What are you saying?" It was then that she saw Joaquin pull the saddlebags out of the carriage.

"Wait!" Cassie whirled around to Sister Ann. "My clothes are in there." The nun already reached for the pannier, but she was intercepted by a stranger and unable to stop Joaquin. The journalist removed Cassie's valise, threw it over the side of the buggy, and then dodged into the crowd with the saddlebags. No one stopped him, though everyone congregated around the buggy had to have seen him.

Perez shook his head. "That's not what we want to hear," he complained under his breath. "Surely you can think of something to say about the queen... something derogatory?"

"Not really. I've been getting to know her, and I don't think she's all that bad."

He raised his brow and puckered his lips. "Shh. Now mind your manners," he said and under his breath he whispered, "Don't bite the hand that feeds you."

"What are you talking about, Perez?"

"The mission. Don't oscillate from the cause here. Remember? Liberty and equality for all?" He laughed, but his eyes scolded her with a condescending air.

"I'm not here for a party, though I see you're having one. And where is Francis going with my things?"

"Ow! Feisty," Perez made a face, ignoring her question. Francis was gone.

"Come, your highness," Sister Ann grabbed her arm and tugged her toward the door where the guards stood at attention, waiting for their entry. Much to Cassie's chagrin she followed, though she would have loved to have stayed and exchanged a few more words with Perez.

"Go on." Sister Ann hustled her into the castle. "We'll get your bags inside. Change into something more appropriate. And please do wash."

CASTLE ROYALE

Cassie soon forgot the commotion outside once she entered the cool interior of the castle. White marble floors laced with gold, silver and granite flecks tiled walls enameled with floral patterns shepherded Cassie through a corridor of incredible beauty. The artwork took Cassie's breath away. The ceiling arched over her like a cathedral, adorned with magnificent fresco designs, and accented in intricate patterns of gold leaf. Painted angels hovered over her as lilywhite cherubs trumpeted her entrance into the palace. The edifice was exactly what Cassie had imagined a castle would be. For no place in her world could modern artisans emulate those who mixed talent with magic, artistry with alchemy. Indeed, more than human hands contributed to the palace construction, and Sister Ann made certain Cassie heard the story.

"These halls were fashioned by the hands of wizards and sorceresses when our nation was at peace with the land of Taikus."

"I've heard of Taikus," Cassie said, remembering stories her father told her of Taikan warriors. "I never knew you had been at peace with them."

The brilliant map on the vaulted ceiling above her told the story. Swirls of gold enveloped the globe, painted in vermillion, aqua, and chestnut, while a scarlet dragon guarded the northern continent, and an emerald serpent lurked below the atlas. Sister Anne walked swiftly, her footsteps echoed through the hall. Cassie held back, hoping to absorb the elegance of the décor before her dreams were interrupted.

"When kings ruled the island, we were friends. Long before King Chavez reigned here in Alisubbo, Taikus had a civil war. The wise ones were exiled, and evil came to power. We were attacked because of the queen's imperialism. But we defeated the enemy, though with many consequences. Hence, war continually looms over us, and will do so until a righteous ruler comes to the Island's throne again."

"So, the queen still rules?"

"No. Not Hacatine. She was defeated, and rumor has it she died. But the crowned king has a troublesome personality. Some say he's a madman, and there is cause to believe the rumors are true."

They came to a double door that creaked as it opened into a bedroom. The room was curtained in pinks with rose patterned wallpaper and a canopy of satin draped over the bed. Cassie couldn't have asked for a more exquisite bedroom.

"This is your quarters. The private room is through those doors. Thanks to King Chavez, and his recent trip to the southern province of Berdau, you'll find hot water at the turn of the knob. Show gratitude. The project was labor some. And when you're called for, make haste. Tardiness is not tolerated." She leaned into Cassie's face. "At all."

Sister Ann lay Cassie's valise on the bed. "Don't speak until spoken to, and especially not before you're formerly introduced. You'll be in the presence of Prince Martim and Duchess Elizabeth. She's the one you're supposed to deliver the message to, from that insufferable rebel, Valerio, if indeed that's your intent. But not until an appropriate time." She leaned even closer to Cassie. "If it were me, I'd toss the wretched scroll in the fire pit and be done with it. You'd be better off going back to where you came from without mentioning that man's name!"

She walked to the window and pulled back the drapes, letting a gust of sunlight into the room. "Sister Bernadice will be here to fetch you for dinner. I'm returning to Medio this afternoon. So much work to do!"

Cassie stepped back and cleared her throat, choosing to ignore the hostility in Sister Ann's advice.

"And when is an appropriate time?" Cassie asked.

"Sister Bernadice will announce your arrival and inform the duchess that you have a message for her. The duchess will let us know when she wants to see you. Thank the Holy Saints, you're now out of my charge, for I doubt I can handle the consequences of any trouble you might cause! Now, get presentable. With God's grace, your smell will be washed away with soap, but just in case it isn't, you'll find a spray of Couer De Jeanette, a new fragrance from Lafende on the dresser. Wear it." Sister Ann waved briskly under her nose.

"I beg your pardon!" Cassie said. "Considering these heavy riding clothes, the raging heat outside, and the fact I was on top of a horse all morning, it's not my fault I stink."

The nun's eyes flew open.

"Smell… bad…" Cassie corrected herself.

"Make sure you remedy the situation before Sister Bernadice comes to take you to the duchess. Please." Sister Ann left the room, waving away the smell.

***

The silence, the soft light in the room, the sweet scent of lavender from her bath, solaced Cassie. Clean and refreshed, she slipped the gown over her head. The fabric fell gently over her body and fitted itself over her form perfectly. The deep burgundy of the dress complimented her complexion. The swooping neckline showed off her delicate shoulders, and the lace swept gracefully up to the velvet choker, accenting the youthfulness of her face. She unbraided her hair and let her dark curls fall down her back.

Transfixed by the princess standing before her, she lifted her chin, seeing herself as a new person. She was now Cassandra, Princess of Alcove: her Royal Highness. Wow!

As she admired her dress in the mirror, Cassie discovered a secret sleeve lined in leather at her waist, the same shape as the pocket in the waistcoat, a perfect compartment for the Derringer. The convenience of which had to have been planned.

Startled by a tap on the door, she slipped both the pistol and her cell phone into the pocket.

"May I come in?"

Before Cassie could answer, Sister Ann entered with another nun. "Cassandra, this is Sister Bernadice. I wanted to introduce you before I left for Medio."

"Hello," Cassie felt awkward as Sister Ann shuffled around the room, setting things in order, pulling a hairbrush from a drawer, and placing it on top of the dresser, straightening a mirror, and setting a candle on an end table where Cassie could find it.

"I supposed my work is done here, then." Sister Ann turned to Cassie. "Keep your temper in check. I would be disheartened to hear any more unfavorable reports of your behavior. After all, I'm the one who brought you here. I'm responsible."

"You've scolded me once already. I think that was sufficient. I promise I'll be on my best behavior now."

"Good! See to it you respect the throne," she retorted.

"Oh, I'm sure this lovely young lady has nothing but kind words to say to everyone. I'm looking forward to getting to know her!" Sister

Bernadice smiled kindly at Cassie.

"I'm glad you're tending to her now. She's tried my patience and has added to my time to confession.

"Go take care of your business. I'll introduce the young lady to castle etiquette."

"Very well," Sister Ann left, closing the door behind her.

Cassie was refreshed enough from the bath to let the nun's criticism shackle her good spirits. Less than pleasant farewells to the nun played out in Cassie's mind, but she spoke none of them.

The Sister who remained had a smile completely opposite of Sister Ann's uninviting attitude. Nothing in this woman's eyes suggested judgment. Instead, the petite nun, dressed in the same sort of habit Sister Ann wore, had a gentleness to her; her facial expression was one of wisdom and patience.

"Whatever did you do to ruffle Sister Ann's feathers?" Sister Bernadice asked. She chuckled.

Cassie laughed. "Nothing. I just told the queen what I thought."

"I see."

"Sister Ann thought I was being disrespectful, but I see it as being honest. Someone needs to be honest around here."

Sister Bernadice mouthed an 'oh.' She helped Cassie with the buttons on her gown.

"I assume your active mind gives you better insight than those of us with older, and subsequently feebler intellect, might have?"

"I don't know about that. I just have opinions."

Sister Bernadice laughed. "We all have opinions. However, we don't always see all sides of the story. When you deliver your letter of appeal, just remember that a smile is much more impressive than a frown."

"Impressive? Who am I supposed to impress?"

"Well! For one, you will eat dinner with Prince Martim who is acting king while his Royal Majesty is away on business. Duchess Elizabeth is his fiancé. Regardless of your opinions, your message will have greater impact if it is delivered cheerfully and respectfully. "

"I didn't mean to be rude."

"Of course not. There. All buttoned!"

"When do I deliver this letter?"

"I'll send word to Elizabeth now. Perhaps she'll have time to receive you before dinner."

Sister Bernadice stepped out of the room, and guided the heavy oak door shut, giving Cassie one last smile as if to say things would be all right. Cassie knew better. When the latch clicked silently, sealing her aloneness, Cassie groaned. She'd feel better if this was over with. Never had she been more exhausted, and more anxious, than now.

No wonder the reflection in the mirror startled her. No longer a teenager finishing high school, here she was, a lovely princess in a stunning castle. What girl her age wouldn't love to be in her shoes?

Unfortunately, Cassie was quickly finding out that worry and dread came as naturally to the office of royalty as curtsies and hand kisses.

Cassie sorted through the dirty clothes on the bed, the wool skirt which now looked more like a horse blanket than a gown, and her waistcoat. She found the letter and slipped it into her pocket that already concealed the gun and her phone.

Someone tapped at the door.

"Come in."

Sister Bernadice peeked into the room. "I just caught the duchess in the hallway. She'll see you now."

***

There was a hallowedness that Cassie sensed when she entered Duchess's Elizabeth's bedroom. Perhaps because of the splendor of the décor, the polished cherry wood furniture, the powder blue velvet of the davenport and pillows, the matching canopy over the bed, or the illustrious duchess herself. Cassie was awestruck. Lace curtains kept the room cool from the heat of the day and cast a soft, romantic light throughout the chamber.

The Duchess was at her dresser, pinning a black box hat atop her golden hair. Cassie walked into the room, struck by the oil paintings on the wall, and the Victorian era photos on the dresser.

"Thank you, Sister, you may leave us," Elizabeth said. Sister Bernadice bowed and shut the door. "I was told you have something for me."

Cassie found speaking difficult. "Yes, Your Highness," she stuttered, her eyes resting on both her reflection in the mirror and the image of the duchess.

"I thought you were princess?" she laughed.

"Yes, I suppose I am."

"Well, Princess, you have a higher position than I, so there is no need for you to address me formally. However, to be politically correct, were it not for the hierarchy, you would call me Your Grace, not Highness.

113

Because you're a princess, you can just call me Elizabeth."

Cassie laughed nervously. "All right. Then you can call me Cassie."

"Cassie? That's an odd name. Somewhat juvenile." Elizabeth tucked her hair into the hat and fastened her hairdo with a pin. She looked over her shoulder at Cassie.

"It's short for Cassandra."

"How old are you?" she asked.

"Seventeen."

"Then I shall call you Cassandra." She rose from her chair and turned to face Cassie. Her complexion was delicately pale, not like someone ill, as Cassie had seen at the hospital, for there were no dark shadows that hollowed her skin, but smooth like porcelain. Her cheeks were warm pink, and her eyes were blue like a Steller Jay; a blue repeated in the color of her earrings, and in the fan that she held. "And what do you have for me?"

"A letter. It's only partially for you. You're supposed to deliver it to the king."

"Partially for me? I have to share it?" her smile was mocking. "From whom?"

"Valerio."

The name had the impact of a thousand arrows bringing down a stag. Elizabeth's eyes flew wide open, and she froze. Cassie had not expected such discord. The duchess opened her fan and waved it in front of her face. Her cheeks grew brighter than rouge, and Cassie thought her entire head would turn red. Elizabeth lifted her chin.

"Pardon me, I was not expecting this."

Cassie slipped the letter from her pocket and handed it to her.

The duchess moved toward the window and tore the letter open, as though she couldn't wait to read its contents. So excited was she that a piece of the envelope fluttered to the floor. Out of place in this perfect velvet room, the stark white scrap of parchment, which now rested on the lint-free carpet, symbolized a much larger transgression. A broken heart, perhaps? This was the woman Valerio had been in love with.

"Where did you get this?" she asked. Her voice trembled.

"He gave it to me."

"You were with him?"

"Yes, your Grace," Cassie said. How vividly she saw him in her mind just then. His smile, his kiss, his aggressive touch, and then guilt swept over her.

"I thought he was away on a military assignment."

"I don't know about that. He was in a camp with some soldiers and some civilians."

Elizabeth walked about the room, fanning herself and still blushing, but more from anger as the frown on her face emitted hostilities. "Civilians? Like yourself?"

"Well, no, not like me. Citizens of your country. There were some journalists too."

Elizabeth strolled to the open window again, and this time she closed it.

Cassie shifted her weight; the lack of communication frustrated her. "I know this appeal might be a little confusing, but I can assure you, he doesn't mean any harm to anyone. He just wants… "

Elizabeth reeled around to face her. "Appeal? What are you talking about?"

Cassie snickered. "The letter that's in your hands. The Appeal for Peace. It's for the king."

Elizabeth laughed and hesitated before she spoke. "He told you what this was?"

"Well, yes." Blood rushed to Cassie's head in a wave of embarrassment. "Is there some mistake?"

Elizabeth shook her head. Her slanted smile mocked or pitied her. Cassie couldn't decide which, nor which would be easier to accept. The duchess walked to the mirror and Cassie followed her every movement with her eyes. Elizabeth's attitude changed as she composed herself.

"It's very strange that Valerio would tell you about the contents of this letter. Business of the Crown is just that. Private."

"I'm sorry, I didn't know." Cassie was curious as to the content of the letter. How much of what Valerio told her was true?

"This parchment is no more for your eyes than a sugar cube is for a drowning cat!" Elizabeth stared at Cassie's reflection in the mirror.

Cassie, too stunned to talk, glared back. Finally, with a frustrated breath she broke the silence. "I don't know what to say. All I know is what he told me."

"There are questions that we both have, then. Start by repeating to me everything that Valerio said to you."

Everything? Cassie rolled her eyes. No way she could remember three days' worth of conversation. And even if she did, why should she even tell this woman? Elizabeth should be concerned with bringing the letter to the king.

Cassie cleared her throat. "He said this letter was an Appeal for Peace and that you would take it to the king personally. He didn't say it was private."

The duchess paced back to the window, stopping to study Cassie as she passed her. There was no doubt from her expression that she was disturbed. She read the letter again.

"In your own words, what would you say Valerio is preparing to do?"

"Do? I don't know if he is going to do anything. I'm just here to deliver a message."

Another grave silence followed. Elizabeth folded the letter, closed her eyes as though praying for strength. "How long have you known Valerio? What's your relationship with him?"

Was she jealous?

"I only just met him. We don't really have a relationship-at least I don't think so. I came from another world, Elizabeth. I plan to go home as soon as I can," Cassie assured her.

"I see." Elizabeth tucked the message in her bosom and took a deep breath. She faced Cassie straight on. "May I suggest that you tread lightly during your stay here, for however long that is? For your own safety."

"I don't understand."

"No. Of course not. How could you?" With that, Elizabeth walked out of the room, brushing past Cassie as she left.

MARTIM

After the odd confrontation with the duchess, Cassie strolled through the hall and entered a stateroom lined with books. Hand carved, the elaborate bookshelves reached to the ceiling and were filled with volumes of leather-bound journals, tomes with gilded pages, and other unusual works in all shapes and sizes. Near the window, a ship's wheel made of polished cherry wood hung on the wall. The lace curtains floated gently over a brass nautical compass, which rested atop another bookstand and housed oceanography journals and logs which were stacked on top of each other. Charts and maps penned in ink were framed under glass. Next to the compass was tinplate of a middle-aged man. He wore a uniform decorated with many medals and medallions. Because he had the look of nobility, Cassie thought it might be King Chavez. She studied the image for a long while, wondering if he was as evil as Valerio had suggested. The man looked serious, perhaps arrogant.

"But what can you tell from a photograph?" she whispered to herself. "I'm no judge of character!"

The room was furnished with a high-backed sofa; deep burgundy velvet, and its arms were hand carved with an intricate design. A tapestry hung on the wall behind it, and the davenport faced another window that overlooked a patio outside. Above her, a gold candelabra hung with delicate crystal prisms that cast rainbows around the room. To the right, near a roll-top desk, stood an ebony grand piano.

She would have browsed through the books longer were it not for the sound of stringed instruments coming from the floor above. Queen Felicia had mentioned her son played the violin. Could the music she heard be that of the prince? Curious, she walked down the hall to the circular staircase and followed the melody to the second floor.

"Now, quickly, in time, like this," she heard a man's voice say. The soft tapping of a shoe, and then the sound of several stringed instruments

117

in harmony, led her to the open doors of a brightly lit den.

The walls were painted in pastel yellows and pinks, sheer curtains draped from the ceiling, covering six slender windows. An ornate gold-framed mirror hung over a fireplace, and next to the hearth sat an older gentleman in uniform. His skin was olive color, his beard salt and pepper, and his face leathered with age. His uniform boasted medallions and ribbons, more military honors than Cassie had ever seen. His eyes were closed, his lips turned in a quiet smile, and he nodded to the rhythm of the music.

On the other side of the room were the musicians. Standing was a young man maybe a year older than Cassie, his chin nestled against a violin. He slid his bow across the strings with both strength and grace. The rich sweet sound of his instrument filled the room. His body moved in time, his dark hair bounced freely as he nodded at the teenage girl playing harmony on a second violin. Two young boys in suits and ties accompanied them on cellos, their instruments adding a deep melodic voice to the song.

"Now," the violinist said. With that cue, he and the girl plucked out a light melody, the music so enchanting that Cassie swayed with the beat.

"That's good, that's good," the dark-haired man said, eyeing Cassie in the mirror. Lifting his bow, he nodded for the children to cease playing. "Excellent. The queen will be pleased with how much progress you've made, and she'll be tickled to see you again."

The children set the instruments on stands. Cassie stepped into the room to let them by, however the smallest boy stopped and turned to his teacher.

"Your Highness," he said, tears in his eyes.

The prince kneeled to his height. "What can I do for you, Mr. Abilio?"

The boy wiped his nose with his sleeve, and the prince quickly unleashed a hankie from his pocket.

"No, no, no. Here, let me."

"Will mama get to see me play?"

"Yes, of course." The prince wiped the boy's tears. You'll be in the courtyard. Your family has been invited, even your sisters and your brothers. We'll have delicious teacakes and lemonade for everyone. And a special treat for you when it's over."

The boy nodded, but tears still flowed down his cheeks.

"What is it, young man?" The prince drew him to his knee.

The child shrugged, and then mumbled, "This collar hurts."

The prince laughed, unloosed the boy's tie, and unhooked the top button of his shirt.

"There!" he said. "I never cared for starched shirts either. You're not required to keep your collar tight. If anyone gives you any guff, tell them to see the prince." The boy threw his arms around his teacher, who patted him on the back gently. He stood. "Now, freshen up for dinner. No more formal practice. Next up, the concert when the king and queen return. Amanda, if you practice at home, work on your wrist position." Amanda nodded.

"What about us?" the boy with the loose collar asked.

"You're good. Just exercise your fingers and keep them agile."

"How?"

Martim thought for a moment. "Marbles! That will do the trick, and here, to help you..." He strolled to a cabinet near the man sitting down and opened a drawer, pulling out a bag bulging with small round objects. He handed it to the older boy. "Share, now!" he instructed.

"Yes, sir!"

The boys ran to Amanda, and she took the youngest one's hand. "Thank you, Your Highness," they said in unison. Amanda greeted Cassie with a nod when she walked by.

The prince faced Cassie. His smile was captivating as he bowed low. "You must be our guest!"

She curtsied. "I'm so sorry," she stuttered. "I didn't mean to interrupt."

The older man in the corner opened his eyes. "Oh, goodness!" he said and stood, bowing cordially. "Pardon my manners. I must have dozed."

"We were done with practice, anyway," the prince waved off her apology. "And it's their dinnertime. You are Princess Cassandra, from Alcove, I was informed?"

"I...yes."

"I'm Martim," he pushed his hair behind his ears. "Martim Joaquin Martinez Amiens Santos Chavez, second son of King Carlos Chavez." He laughed. "But call me Martim." He nodded toward the older gentleman. "And this is Maestro Pedro Sanchez."

Cassie returned his greeting with a curtsy.

"He is the Crown's rapier Maestro, taking a repose."

The man chuckled. "I enjoy listening to you play, Martim. And it's my pleasure, Your Highness."

"The pleasure is mine," Cassie said. Her eyes returned to Martim, a very personable young man with a bright smile. She wondered why she wasn't advised to give him the letter. His attire was simple, not one that she would have expected a prince to wear. High buttoned trousers and a brocade waistcoat. His sleeves were rolled up informally.

He smiled shyly. "Please come sit with me. I'm eager to get to know you." His movements were graceful as he escorted Cassie to a parlor chair. Both he and Maestro Sanchez waited until she was seated before they, too, sat down. Martim leaned over toward her. "Tell me, what brings you to our wonderful kingdom?"

Cassie felt heat rush to her head. She did not want to discuss why she was here. "I would feel disrespectful discussing business so soon," she suggested. "Especially after hearing such wonderful music. You play the violin beautifully." Cassie folded her hands on her lap, suddenly conscious of the gun in her pocket.

"Thank you," he blushed. "I've been playing since I was small. Please forget the protocol. It's a thing of the past. I don't worry about formalities. They stifle a person's friendliness and inhibit creativity."

"I'm not fond of them either." Cassie agreed, not that she even knew much protocol or anything about formalities. She quickly changed the subject. "Angelique told me you play music for the children at the Sanatorium."

"You met Angelique?" He sat upright and glanced at Maestro Sanchez. "You were in Medio?"

"Yes. I met your mother." She stopped, alarmed by the prince's anxiety. Something was wrong.

Martim hesitated to speak. Sanchez was wide awake now and leaned back in his chair. He twisted his mustache, observing Cassie as though he expected her to say more. Martim finally exhaled. His gaze drifted to the doorway and down the hall. "The ones you saw today are only a few of my students. The loveliest thing about the children is that they're here. They've been healed and are no longer suffering in the Sanatorium." Martim faced her, his dark eyes serious. "They've a special place in my heart. They come alive when they play music, they laugh, they love. It wasn't always that way for them."

"I see that they care for you. You've given them a special gift." Cassie checked her heart rate, remembering her mission. She delivered the letter, and now she's waiting for Perez to come and get her. In the meantime, she mustn't forget why she was here, or to whom her loyalties were promised. Even though the children at the castle seem well cared for, there are many more dying of disease. Do not be fooled, she warned herself, no matter how charming he is.

"I try," he whispered. "Although I know it's not enough." He tossed his hands. "It's all I know to do right now. Marques and my mother are working hard to find solutions. In a matter of time, they will have either the most beautiful hospital ever built, or they will find a cure for the disease. I hope the latter comes first."

She studied his eyes, looking for the depth of his sincerity. He couldn't be that saintly, not from what Valerio said. "I do too."

"So, tell me about yourself. Your family is legendary in these parts. I must admit I was surprised to hear of a visitor from the other side of the ocean. What brings you here?"

Cassie froze. "Oh! Well," she started. "My father thought it was time to contact his kingdom again, and he sent me." Oh, nice, Cassie. She investigated Martim's smile and felt two feet small. Here she was worried about his sincerity when she herself was lying. She'd never been a spy, or an agent in a rebellion before. She feared she was failing miserably. This was the other side of the fence, the royal family that mistreated their subjects. These were the crowned heads that Valerio appealed to. What should she say? She cleared her throat. "I came here by mistake, really. You might say I got lost."

The prince laughed, but there was a question in his tone. "You're lost?" Cassie nodded. "You didn't come here as an ambassador of your father's?"

"No. Not really. My appearance here was a mistake. I fell into Silvio's tunnels, and then…" she dared not mention Valerio. "Well, I just ended up at the Sanatorium and your mother sent me here with Jovita and Sister Ann." She shuddered.

It was his turn to be speechless, and he added a royal flare to his bewilderment when he sat upright in his chair. He still smiled, but Cassie felt an immediate distance grow between them in the silence that followed. "Perhaps you'll remember things better after you eat," he said.

"I'm sure that will help. It's been a long day."

He stood and bowed cordially, as did Maestro Sanchez. "I must excuse myself." He nodded to Maestro, who then stood. "I have matters to tend to."

Cassie rose and curtsied. "It's a pleasure meeting you."

"Please join me and my fiancé, Elizabeth, for dinner. Soon, on the veranda." He bowed again and left with Maestro.

Did I ever mess that up?

Island Departure

Jimmy stomped on the embers that had popped out of the pit, snuffing the hot coals into dust, until even the smoke had ceased. His act was more a release of anger than to prevent a fire. He heard every word that Whitefox and Elias were saying. He wished he could burst into the conversation, but he knew full well that both would bark back. It was not his place to argue.

Geno and the other Gitanos sat quietly, drinking their coffee. Jimmy peered at Elena, who had been ignoring him all morning. She rolled a cigarette, twisted it tight, and licked the ends. Their eyes caught hold of each other and he swore he saw a faint smile. He returned a quick one.

"Come on Elias, you've had time enough to think about it. Any more wasted hours will be the death of someone," Whitefox reasoned.

"It takes time to sort these things," the chief said, pouring another cup of hot brew into his tin cup.

"We've wasted too much time already. Valerio is planning his raid on the castle if he hasn't yet done so. Who knows what murderous schemes he is carrying out?" Whitefox grabbed a piece of firewood from the pile.

Elias laughed and shook his head. "What's that to us? Do you see anyone here concerned about who dies in Lisbo? That's their business."

With an angry groan, Whitefox heaved the firewood farther into the woods. "Curses, Elias! King Chavez is your friend."

Elias spat on the ground.

Geno tossed the contents of his cup into the ashes, and grumbled, "C'mon 'Fox, what sort of friend is the King? He was going to hang Elias. That's no friend!"

A chorus of complaints came from the discontented men and women who were sitting around the campfire.

Jimmy slapped his cap against his leg and scowled at Elias.

"If I remember right, Valerio was the one fixing to hang you, and his troops were the ones aiming to shoot you."

"Valerio is not the king. A king calls the shots," Elias returned.

"All right!" Whitefox contended. "What if Valerio kills Chavez and becomes king? How will you save yourself then? The man is rotten, Elias. If he crowns himself ruler of Alisubbo, who knows what will happen to your family, and to all your people? Who knows what will happen to this island?"

The group of Gitanos grew silent. It seemed to Jimmy that Whitefox's words were sinking in until Elias shook his head.

"Can't risk it. Can't risk our people getting involved,"

Jimmy threw his hat to the ground, drawing everyone's attention to him. Elena leaned over the fire and let the end of her cigarette smolder on the coals until the paper curled, and the golden shreds of the tobacco sparkled with heat. She took a puff, stood, and walked leisurely toward Jimmy. She handed him the stogie. No matter how angry or upset Jimmy was, Elena always seemed to take his anxieties away. He took a puff and gave it back.

Whitefox's voice shattered the silence.

"What do you mean you can't risk it? Every time you raid Alisubbo you're risking your people's lives. Now you can change things. Stand up for the king. Right your wrongs."

"What wrong?" Elias asked.

"Oh, I don't know. Stealing. Raiding."

"No wrong done in feeding the children or getting pretties for the ladies. We're just taking care of our own, is all." Geno said.

"What? With stolen goods?" Whitefox argued.

"I don't know what you want, 'Fox." Elias mumbled.

"I told you. We want to use your boat. We want to sail to the mainland and defend the castle."

Jimmy took another puff of the cigarette when Elena held it to his lips. He looked up, hoping for a positive answer. Elias tilted his head and surveyed each of his men. They seemed indifferent, waiting perhaps for the argument to end, waiting for instructions, perhaps. Gitanos were hard to read.

"Nah," the Gitano chief said.

"Come on, Elias," Jimmy blurted. "My uncle rode all the way to Alisubbo on horseback to save your hide. You could at least return the favor. If you don't want to come, then let us borrow your boat."

"No one borrows my boat." Though he was a small man, he stood up to Jimmy and puffed out his chest. What Elias lacked in size he gained in support from a dozen hard hitting men who'd back him with their lives. They were all giving Jimmy an eagle eye.

Elena moved closer to Jimmy at that moment, took another toke, and tossed the cigarette on the ground. She blew her stream of smoke at Elias.

"You should go," she said. Her voice had authority. All the men looked up at her.

"What?" Elias asked.

"You should help the king. We've lived a long time on the island in peace. No one bothers us unless you boys go to Alisubbo. You cause trouble there and the king has saved you many times. Whitefox has saved you. If things change on the mainland, if Valerio becomes king, then who knows what will happen? Can you tell me what kind of future he'll give us?"

"No," Elias admitted.

"No? Well, there's your answer. You don't know. But I read the cards this morning. I tell you. You should go."

"You read the cards?" Jimmy asked. She nodded. Geno tossed a stick in the fire and looked up at Elias. The cards meant something to them. Not abiding by the cards' wisdom was tempting fate. Elias spat again.

"Show me!" Jimmy whispered to Elena. She motioned for him to follow her to her tent. No one else stopped them. Not his uncle, who still paced from the campfire to the woodland edge and back again; not Geno who poured himself another cup of coffee and leaned against a stump, blowing the steam into the morning air; and not Elias who pulled a cigar from his pocket and lit it with a piece of firewood.

"Where'd you get the stogie?" Geno asked him.

"Valerio," Elias said with a grin. Whitefox whirled around and glared at him.

Elena took Jimmy's arm. "C'mon. Let's go."

Fragrant incense was so heavy in Elena's tent that Jimmy found it difficult to breathe. He coughed and waved at the air in front of him. A green hue permeated the atmosphere, a mysterious aura that suggested magic. Elena motioned to Jimmy to sit on the sheepskin in the center of the tent and placed a shor-legged table in front of him. She lowered herself across from him, fixed her skirt around her so that she sat comfortably and set her cards on the table. Her eyes were deep when she looked at him, like the blackness of the channel at Point de Tratado. He smiled at her, and she winked at him.

She dealt five cards face down in a circle. Slowly, and one by one she flipped them over. Each of the five cards had pictures of soldiers holding a rifle in a firing position. Elena held the deck out to Jimmy.

"Pick one."

Jimmy chose a random card, which Elena set face down in the center of the others. "You watch," she said. She slowly turned the center card over. On its face was a king. His beard was long and silver.

"Chavez?" Jimmy asked.

Elena shook her head. "Maybe. But this is a call for help. Look." She waved away the smoke. Jimmy coughed. "This is the green-eyed king."

"So, who is that?"

"I think it's the Shaman." She stared at the cards.

"Who?"

"The wizard."

"Silvio? Why do you say that?"

"Look how this smoke is green. See? It's never green. Elias and Whitefox need to go see the Shaman."

Jimmy studied her, wide-eyed. "It's never green?"

"No, and it's been doing this all afternoon, every time I read."

He jumped up. Jimmy might have experimented with fortune telling before, but he knew better than to impede magic, especially legendary magic from a patriarchal wizard.

"We'll be gone within the hour. No one will want to be left behind once I tell them about this!"

"No! You can't go too?"

"C'mon Elena. You know I'm my uncle's partner. I travel everywhere with him."

She stood. Jimmy walked over to her, took her hands, and gave her a kiss. After that, he was out the door.

"No, Jimmy! Not you!" Elena called after him.

DINNER WITH THE PRINCE

The banquet table wasn't long, like the royal dining halls she had seen in movies and storybooks. She was glad they were eating in a more modest atmosphere. Wrought iron framed the ornate ceramic-tiled tabletop, and matching chairs were on a veranda overlooking the courtyard. The cozy patio was surrounded by flowerpots filled with orchids and other blossoms. The flowers emitted sweet aromas and added to the allure of the evening.

Martim had been waiting for them. His dark hair was parted in the center and curled neatly behind his ears. He wore a black woolen suit and a golden ascot that was tucked into his waistcoat and fastened with a jeweled pin. His expression was solemn as he bowed cordially and took Elizabeth's hand.

"You look lovely tonight," he whispered.

"And you are as handsome as always, Your Highness," she said as she curtsied. She cleared her throat. "We have a guest, the Princess of Alcove."

"We've met." He clicked his heels together in military fashion and then bowed.

Martim pulled a chair out first for Cassie, and then for Elizabeth. Once they were seated, he took a chair next to the duchess. Cassie sat across from Martim.

Servants, who had been waiting at the door, then brought food to the table; a cuisine more splendid than any Cassie had ever seen. Even the production screenings her father took her to in Seattle hadn't catered like this. Petite sandwiches with savory trimmings and unusual flavors presented on snowy white pedestals. Cold and creamy soups in colorful ceramic tureens with matching ladles. Huge olives stuffed with garlic cloves and spiked by toothpicks with colorful paper fringe coiled at the edges.

There were platters of fresh vegetables, creamy dips, and fruits dipped in butterscotch and chocolate all laced with shredded coconut and apple bits.

Cassie assumed that Martim and Elizabeth would be preoccupied with each other, so she gave the luncheon her undivided attention, without worrying about regal etiquette or manners, being ignorant of both. Elizabeth gave her a disapproving eye once, but the duchess offered no helpful advice.

"You're unusually quiet tonight Elizabeth," Martim said.

"I'm sorry." Elizabeth sounded weak; her voice trembled. Cassie took a moment away from her feast to observe the duchess.

"What's on your mind?" Martim asked.

Elizabeth glanced at her. It was the letter; Cassie was sure of it.

"I think I may be homesick, that's all. I'm still grieving over my mother's death. And, well..."

"I'm truly sorry about the betrothal, Elizabeth. I might still persuade my father against it. I don't want to see you suffer."

"No, Martim."

Martim set his napkin on the table. From the way he moved, Cassie wasn't sure which of the two was more uncomfortable. "Let me talk to my mother. She'll understand," Martim offered.

"No. I'll be fine. Please. Let's not talk about it now. We have a guest."

A moment of silence passed. Cassie was the only one enjoying the food. The duchess had not even put a single morsel on her plate, and Martim, apparently losing his appetite, set his napkin on top of his perfectly good strawberries. After a moment of awkward stillness, and Cassie, trying to chew as quietly as she could, the duchess scooted away from the table, and stood.

"Please excuse me, Your Highness. I feel ill." Without waiting for a reply, she left the room.

Martim rose as Elizabeth walked out. He bowed slightly and then gestured toward the door. "I beg your pardon, Cassandra but..."

"That's fine," Cassie said. She watched him leave the dinner table and hurry down the hall after Elizabeth.

Cassie wondered about the letter, and the duchess, as she finished dining. An Appeal for Peace couldn't possibly be that troubling. You'd think she'd be happy, Cassie thought as she popped an olive in her mouth.

***

Late that afternoon, as the shadows grew long and the sky darkened, Cassie waited impatiently for Perez to appear somewhere in the castle, hoping to make her departure plans. She'd like to be back at Valerio's camp the next day. Traveling by herself would be out of the question, as she did not know how to get back to Greenstay, nor did she have a horse or buggy. She needed his help. Her job was complete; the letter had been delivered. She was ready.

She considered looking for the journalist, and went as far as the castle garden, for she did not know where he lived or where his office was. Cassie strolled through the courtyard in hopes she'd find a servant who might give her directions; however it was soon clear she was completely alone. As evening fell, she finally saw someone lighting the gas lamps along the walkway. She hurried to talk to him, but his job was finished before she reached him, and he disappeared through a gate at the far end of the garden.

The scent of lilacs, roses, and heather filled the evening air. Annuals were in full bloom, and ivy trailed over trellises and lamp posts. The garden enclosed by the palace, and though there were windows overlooking the courtyard, only one window showed light.

From that window also came the faint sound of a violin. Assuming it was Martim who was playing, she drew nearer and sat on a bench not far away, under the open screen to listen. She could see Martim's silhouette through the curtains, his violin nestled against his shoulder, and his bow in hand. The song he played was sweet and melodious. Pleasing. A gentle reprieve from the tensions of the day.

Soon, a breeze picked up. She shivered. She was tired and cold, and unsuccessful at finding someone to take her back to Valerio's camp, so she returned to her room.

Morning Troubles

Someone knocking on her door woke Cassie. Before she answered, or put on a robe, Sister Bernadice rushed into the room and stood at the bed for a moment, her hands folded in front of her, while two servants who had followed her in, pushed open the curtains, and took clothes out of an armoire and laid them on her bed.

Cassie, puzzled at the expression on Sister Bernadice usually happy face, sat up.

"Breakfast?" she asked.

"Oh, that would be fortunate for you if we were waking you up for breakfast! No, my dear. The prince has called for a meeting with you in the library," the nun responded. "I'll wait in the hall while you dress. Please hurry." She exited with the servants and shut the door behind her.

Cassie dressed quickly, making certain she had her revolver and her cellphone tucked into her pocket. When she opened the door, not only was Sister Bernadice waiting for her, but there were two guards as well. They stood erect, their chins high, their stark white baldrics and gauntlets bright. They each carried a rifle. The blood drained from Cassie's face, and her heart skipped a beat.

"What's wrong?" she asked.

"The prince has some questions he needs to ask you. That's all I know."

As they made their way down the foyer, no one spoke. Only the gentle whoosh of Sister Berndice's habit, and the sharp click of the soldiers' boots on the marble floor, resounded through the corridor.

When Cassie reached the library, Elizabeth was there waiting. She didn't speak, but her expression mirrored the same fear and bewilderment Cassie was feeling.

The soldiers opened the double glass doors and marshaled the women inside. Sister Bernadice did not follow. Instead, she took Cassie's hand and squeezed, crossed herself, and left.

Martim stood by the fireplace in his uniform. His coat was

unbuttoned, and his collar loose. His appearance showed he lacked sleep, as his hair was uncombed and his eyes were sunken and red. His friendly grin was gone, replaced with a stern frown that made him look years older than he was. Maestro Sanchez leaned against the wall near the window. The morning light cast a golden glow on his pressed uniform. He was not unkempt like Martim, and yet his frown was equally chilling.

Martim nodded to them as Cassie and the duchess stepped inside. The guards closed the door.

"Ladies," Martim greeted in a cordial tone.

The air of formality thickened. No one offered them a seat. No one even spoke for the longest while. After studying both her and Elizabeth, Martim paced from the fireplace to the window and back again. His steps were slow and deliberate. Cassie watched him, controlling her breathing so that she didn't faint, for her heart thundered.

"I've had some disturbing news late last night," he said, his glance moving between her and Elizabeth. Cassie caught the duchess looking at her.

"Marques was nearly assassinated Thursday evening."

Elizabeth gasped. Cassie's eyes widened. Martim observed their reaction, his hands behind his back. He then exchanged glances with Sanchez.

"Oh, Martim. I'm so sorry. What happened?" Elizabeth asked. She moved toward him, but he stepped back.

"A sniper. Someone stole into the stables, made themselves quite at home. It appeared he had camped in the hayloft where he waited until my brother took his valise to the carriage. They fired four shots in the dark. Luckily for Marques, his coat saved him. If my brother hadn't been so quick on his feet, and keen witted, he would have been killed. Marques dodged away in the nick of time. Perhaps he heard breathing in the loft or something, I don't know. I'm not convinced Valerio doesn't have a sharpshooter in his clique." Martim transferred his glare to Cassie and there he settled his focus.

"That's horrifying!" Elizabeth said.

"Yes. Horrifying. Fortunately, he carried on. A bit shook up, I imagine, as we all are. He continued his journey with my father as though nothing had happened. For some odd reason, I didn't learn about the attack until yesterday. I'm in charge of my father's kingdom in their absence." He became candid at that moment and loosened his collar even more.

"Equally horrifying! The son and acting-king are the last to hear about an attempted assassination. And to have the news presented to me as an afterthought by the Prime Minister, two days later, no less!"

Maestro's cough was a stern interruption, which quieted Martim's temper.

"But that's not your concern."

"Did they find out who did it?" Cassie asked.

Martim's stare pierced through her like a dagger. He didn't answer but continued with his discourse.

"It's been brought to my attention that an insurrection is stirring in Alisubbo." He switched his focus to Elizabeth, and paced over to her, his hands behind his back, his voice admonishing, "The instigator has been identified as someone we all know. And love." The last words were emphasized, stretched with cynicism and disdain. Whether he meant to hurt Elizabeth, or if he were digging for a reaction, Cassie couldn't tell, but she immediately felt sympathy for the duchess.

"Martim," Elizabeth pleaded.

"The scoundrel is not working alone. No one could plan an insurrection by himself. Valerio has too many followers to do this solo. How many men and women...?" He paused as he gave the duchess a critical eye. "... how many he's gathered in the name of treason is not known, nor are his plans known."

"I have nothing to do with this. Please believe me," Elizabeth begged. "I have no relationship with him anymore."

"You were seen talking to Bernardo Thursday morning."

"Martim, it's not what you think. Bernardo stopped me on my way to the stables. I spoke only a minute with him."

Martim raised a brow.

"You must stop this, Martim! Before you let your imagination carry you away, I have a confession." She struggled for words as she reached into her corset. Her hand trembled. She was on the verge of tears. "If I had seen this coming, I would have said something. If I had known what he was, I would have reconsidered my feelings toward him. I did not know he would turn against you. We grew up together, all of us. He was your brother as much as he was mine. How could I possibly know treason was in his heart? Ever since I received this letter," she held the envelope in front of her. "I've been tormented by the truth.

Cassie gawked. It was the same letter she brought.

Martim took the envelope, giving pause, his countenance softened by the tears that streamed down Elizabeth's cheeks.

"Please forgive me for waiting so long to give this to you. I didn't know. I love your family and would do nothing to wrong you or harm you."

133

"What is this?" He pulled the letter from the envelope.

"It's a request from Valerio that I leave you and join him. I did not know it was related to an insurrection."

Martim unfolded the letter and walked to the window. When he finished reading, he handed it to Sanchez. After studying the parchment, Maestro raised his brow and cast Cassie and Elizabeth a stern glare.

"When did this come? By whose hand was it delivered?" Martim asked.

Elizabeth looked at Cassie. There was no need to say anything else. Martim took the newspaper that Sanchez had tucked under his arm, unfolded it, and walked toward Cassie. His face was filled with pain, hurt, and betrayal. He held the paper up in front of her. There, under the headline, was an image of Valerio, his smile daunting, his arm around Cassie. They looked like a happy couple rollicking in their rebellion. Cassie's heart skipped a beat and her breath left her.

"You brought the letter? A plea for Elizabeth to leave the castle?"

"No. I mean yes I brought it, but I didn't know that's what it said!"

"I don't suppose you knew that the Gazette was taking a photograph of you with the insurgent, either."

"Well, I knew but…"

"What exactly does Valerio have up his sleeve?"

"I don't know."

"What were you doing at his camp?"

Sanchez moved from his spot by the window and put his hand on Martim's shoulder. "Martim this is urgent. Take care of these women quickly and let's secure the castle."

Martim pivoted to Elizabeth.

"I trust your innocence. You have been a friend to our family too long, and your father has been a loyal colleague to my father. I'm saddened by your relationship with Valerio, but what he does is not your fault. We're betrothed to marry, and I will stay faithful to that vow." He strode to the door and swung it open. Pointing to Cassie, he signaled the guards.

"Come now and arrest this woman. Search her for weapons and then take her to the garrison. Call the troops and secure the castle. Make haste. Send armed riders to meet my father's landau."

"I'm not a part of this. I did not know what was in that letter. He said it was an appeal for peace. That's all I know! I swear!" Cassie implored.

"And the photograph?"

"It's all a mistake! I can explain."

"Very well. You can explain to my father when he returns."

Martim gestured to the soldiers to proceed. They searched Cassie and found the gun. Martim's face paled. Cassie had never seen a more accusing look than the one he gave.

"Get her out of here!"

The soldiers took Cassie by her arms and escorted her through the long corridor of the palace. Martim, Elizabeth, and the royal guard followed them to the door, gathering more soldiers as they walked.

Once outside, the heat of the day blasted in Cassie's face, adding to the flames of terror that burned inside of her. They parted ways; she being dragged toward the garrison on the other side of Square de Regem. Martim, Elizabeth, and their royal guard turned down the road toward the sea to meet the landau at its entrance to the square. A crowd was forming in that direction and would soon border the path on which the king and queen, and their son, Marques, would travel.

The soldiers strong-armed Cassie up the cobblestone street into a business section of the town. They did not continue to the garrison, but they stopped and released her, much to Cassie's surprise. The tallest of the two leaned over and whispered in her ear.

"Being as you're part of the coup, my lady…"

Before she could argue, he put his finger over his lips.

"You are released!"

He handed her the revolver that he had confiscated earlier, as well as her phone. "Go! Do what you came to do!" The soldiers dispersed, leaving Cassie stranded, confused, and surrounded by a horde of civilians hurrying to the plaza. The swift current of bodies forced her down the hill and back toward the castle.

"The audacity of the king, to dissolve the parliament!" A cry rang out. A wave of shouts followed.

"He's no patriot at all, if you ask me, nor does he have our interests at heart."

This wasn't an audience gathered to greet a king. These people were angry. They waved their fists in the air and shouted obscenities. A mob. The throng grew dense. The headlines that Cassie had read at the Sanatorium had become a call to action, as they waved newspapers violently above their heads.

"End tyranny!" a man shouted, prompting a chorus of similar slogans.

Cassie didn't want any part of this horde. She gathered her strength and cut through the mass of bodies and maneuvered her way to a sidewalk café. There, she regained her balance and caught her breath. The flock of discentents continued to the square to await the royal family.

It was then that Cassie saw Perez walking with Joaquin.

"Over there," he waved to several men in suits and pointed at the statue in Square de Regem. He gave one man a friendly slap on the shoulder and sent him into the crowd. Perez caught Cassie's gaze, winked at her, patted his hip, and then nodded.

She spun in a circle, looking for help. This couldn't possibly be what she thought it was. Perez nodded toward the road where the crowd was assembled and patted his hip again. Cassie turned her back to him and covered her mouth. She remembered Valerio's words.

"Perez may have a little mission in town you can help him with before you leave."

Oh my God, no! She glanced back only once, and that's when she saw Perez holding the rifle with the ivory nameplate on the stock. The same rifle she had delivered. Someone was going to get hurt. She scanned the crowd, looking for the king's soldiers.

Both a rumble and cheer came from the plaza in the direction Martim and Elizabeth had gone. The royal landau had entered the square. Horses with plumes on their heads towered above the swarm, and a rifleman sat next to the driver. Cassie could barely make out the king, but the feathers on Queen Felicia's hat were visible. The vehicle barely moved due to all the people surrounding them.

Children laughed and cheered; their voices were heard clearly over the noise.

"We love the Queen!" they shouted. She saw Carmen and her family on the street, dodging in and out of the multitude toward the carriage, waving joyously. Sister Ann, Sister Bernadice, and several other nuns stepped out from the chapel.

Cassie crossed the road, keeping a keen eye on the man Perez had sent to the statue. He seemed innocent enough, standing in the monument's shadow. He glanced at Cassie and nodded.

Several royal guardsmen stood near the road, and she hurried to them. "Sirs, please, something's wrong."

One soldier broke his stance and smiled at her.

"There are men here with guns. Something's wrong. Look over there." She pointed at Perez and whispered in the soldier's ear as he leaned over to hear. "He has a rifle," she said.

"Yes, ma'am. We have it covered. It'll be fine. Extra security," he told her. He stood at attention again. Cassie's gaze raced across the other guards' faces. She wondered if they were just oblivious to what was happening, or if they, too, were part of the conspiracy.

As the carriage advanced, soldiers continued to clear a path, scooting the crowd to the side. The closer to the castle that the landau came, the louder everyone cheered and the thicker the horde grew. Cassie was near enough now to see the procession. A team of large, elegant horses which pulled the coach wore white plumes on their heads; their manes and tails were braided with ribbons. The black bed of the carriage shone like obsidian. The tall, slender wheels were decorated in green and gold. Two coachmen sat high on a skirt of brilliant green, tassels hanging from the hem; their helmets glistened and flashed in the sunlight, the white of their sashes sparkled. The carriage jostled and rattled slowly on the cobblestone road.

She had a good view of the king. His white uniform embellished with shining gold medals sparkled in the sun. The plume on his helmet rustled gracefully in the breeze. Nestled comfortably next to him was Queen Felicia. She waved to the crowd; a loving grin stretched across her face, a bouquet in her hand. Cassie recognized the white and purple blooms she held as those that grew by the Sanatorium. They must be the flowers she picked with Angelique this afternoon. She looked so eloquent, so regal, and so vulnerable.

Marques the Prince Royal, a stately young man, older than Martim, also in uniform, sat across from his parents.

When the carriage pulled into the plaza near the castle turnabout, Martim left Elizabeth's side and jogged beside the landau. He waved at his mother, and she blew him a kiss. He touched his brother's hand. Marques nodded a smile.

Martim smiled, and then his face turned white in horror the moment a loud pop rang out from behind the landau.

Shocked and confused, Cassie struggled to understand what had happened when the crowd ceased cheering, and instead dispersed in panic. People fled from the carriage and that's when Cassie saw the king lying against the Queen, blood gushing down his throat. The Prince Royal pulled his gun and fired at a man climbing onto the back of the landau. Another crack of gunfire, and blood seeped from the king's chest. Queen Felicia held his head on her lap.

Martim ran faster as the carriage picked up speed. He tried to jump in, but the wheels now spun too fast. He raced alongside.

Cassie ran to the motionless soldiers standing guard in front of the castle doors. "Stop them," she yelled. "Save them! Do something!"

Gunfire sounded several times again from the crowd near Cassie as the landau approached the center plaza. Marques fell over, bleeding from his chest and head.

"No." Martim's ear-piercing cry wailed over the turbulence. He lunged into the landau and lifted his brother in his arms, pulling him to his chest. His brother's blood soaked his pure white gloves and the front of his coat. "No!" he cried out again.

Cassie's heart broke.

An assassin leaped onto the back of the landau; his gun aimed at Martim. The queen turned. With the flowers in her hand, she swung at him, hitting him in the face. She pushed him off the back of the landau.

More shots peeled through the plaza. People ran through the street in every direction and alongside the horses. Soldiers raced toward the landau with their bayonets. Who the soldiers were chasing, Cassie couldn't tell. Many men in uniform did nothing. The royal family was defenseless, being picked off like targets at a shooting range. Someone had to stop it.

Cassie panicked when she saw Perez walking calmly toward the landau, his rifle at his side. The horses had broken into a canter; the wheels raced over the cobblestones directly toward them.

She turned to the soldiers again and pointed at Perez. "Stop him!" When they did nothing, she pivoted around, running to Perez, she screamed. "No!"

Perez kneeled on one knee and aimed his rifle at Martim.

"No Perez, stop," she pleaded. Perez acknowledged her for only a second. He lifted the scope to his eye, rested his elbow on his knee, and cocked the gun.

Cassie drew her pistol from its sleeve. She aimed for the shoulder that steadied the journalist's rifle. Her hands shook. She fired. The revolver recoiled. Blood flew from Perez's head as his rifle and her pistol discharged simultaneously. The journalist fell over. The landau bolted past her, horses galloping. Martim collapsed on top of his brother in a pool of blood.

"They killed my king," someone yelled above the roar of the crowd. "Over there! Look! She has a gun!"

Soldiers rushed at her. She dropped the pistol and soared past the guards into the castle.

ESCAPE

Her heart pounded so hard she could barely breathe. Still, she sped down the hall. Cherub statues flew past; large oak doors with golden handles blurred by. Lacy windows, the grand piano, the bookshelves unnoticed as she tripped on her dress. The hem tore. Nothing mattered but flight.

Her mind whirled in confusion. She saw blood; the king's blood dripping down his broken neck, Marques' blood pouring out onto Martim's snow white gloves, Perez' blood shooting across the plaza. The torment of those images crawled through her stomach like a thousand worms, boring through every organ, eating deeper into her heart, and ending with the horror of having killed someone: a person, a living human being. Bile poured into her throat, and she swallowed.

The halls of the castle were empty. Everyone was outside. They all had heard the shots. The entire village saw the king and his son die. Perhaps Martim had died. She hoped not.

Cassie dashed past a kitchen, a mop room, and the servant's quarters. She dodged through a door and down another hallway. There's got to be a back exit to the palace. There's got to be an escape. She came to a stairwell. The thought of being trapped in a basement terrified her, so she raced to an exit leading to the outside world. Pushing the screen door open, she stumbled into a small alcove, a nook of a courtyard garden cramped by thick rock walls.

She didn't see the other entrance in the bushes across from her, not at first. Not until she flew around the garden bed did she notice the sun's rays fall on a wooden crucifix hanging over an old wooden door. A cluster of olive trees camouflaged the ancient structure.

The sounds of men running through the halls where she had come drove her onward. Hounds barked; their howls echoed in the marble halls.

She heaved the door open. Her body flung to the ground as it gave way. Quickly she pulled herself up and slipped inside, closed the door, and lowered the wooden latch into its slot in hopes it would keep the hunters out long enough for her to find an escape. She peeled moss from the floor and the walls and shoved it under the door, trusting the stink would deter the hounds.

That done, she perused the primitive chamber she'd take refuge in. Little more than a cold and dark cellar, smelling of rotten wood, the old chapel reeked of abandonment, as if men had left it to erode with the mountainside it was built on. The only light streamed from a stained-glass window high above, illuminating a spiral staircase to a loft.

Here was Cassie's haven, a depressing black hole in a forsaken realm. It might as well have been a dungeon. Cassie fell to her knees and covered her face with shaking hands.

"Dad!" She doubled over in grief. Oh, if only she were home, and this had merely been a bad dream. She reached into the pocket of her once lovely dress and grasped her cell phone. She had little hope it would work and she was right. The screen was black.

Canine scratched at the threshold of her shelter; men rattled the door.

Oh my God! Cassie held her breath. This will be my death, my end, and Mom and Dad will never even know what happened to me. They'll never find my body. I'll lie massacred by an unknown army, in a moldy little chapel, in an unreal world!

With one last dodge for cover, she climbed the stairs and sat on the loft across from the window, her elbows on her knees, hiding her head in her hands, hoping the soldiers would go away, yearning that she'd wake up from this nightmare. She braced for death.

To her relief, within a few minutes, her pursuers gave up and soon there was no more grating at the door, nor any voices outside. She brushed the curls that clung to her face. Guilt ripped at her heart.

What had she done?

Why did I even come here? Why did I enter the portal? If I hadn't, the king would still be alive. Queen Felicia would have tea and lemonade with her two sons while listening to the children's chamber music.

No punishment for what she had caused would be severe enough. She should have a public hanging. All the children in Alisubbo would suffer because of the king's death, because of Marques' death. There would be neither hospital nor any cure for the disease that plagued the city. There would be no more music.

Silvio was right all along.

"Those who party in deceit are fooled by it."

What a fool I've been!

Her own dishonesty caused her to believe Valerio. Her own lies brought her into the Realm. Lying to my teacher and lying to Monica's parents. I should never have come. I should have listened to Monica and Daemon. Now it's too late. People are dead; honest people who didn't deserve to die.

Cassie covered her face again. She hated herself. She shouldn't have the comfort of tears even though they rolled down her face before she could wipe them from her eyes.

Sunset cast its light through the stained-glass of the church window. Cassie would spend the night in this moldy little hideaway. Maybe forever. Maybe she'll never see another human being again.

She walked to the window and peeked through the glass. There she saw the steep cliff that made the chapel's foundation. Far below, a ship moored out at sea, the last rays of day settling on its masts. A peculiar square-sheeted vessel sailed toward the mainland. Closer, a dingy rocked on the rising tide near the shore below, pointing to a path which vanished into thick brush and up a bank. Cassie walked down the stairs and returned to a pew where she sat down again. It didn't matter what was outside because she'd never get out there again. The hounds would find her and eat her. The soldiers would shoot her. Besides, she didn't have a right to escape. She had blood on her hands.

Just as the last rays of daylight bid its farewell, the image of the Christ child in the window glowed. A red scarf was wrapped around his innocent body. His mother watched over him.

"I'm so sorry," Cassie whispered. "I miss you, Mom. I wish I were innocent."

Above the Madonna stood an angel, now lit like a torch from the radiance behind it. Cassie stared until the image faded into the night. Her wings covered the whole arc of the window, scalloped delicately with a wrought iron border. Her dress was made from dark, cobalt blue tiles. A gold halo circled her head. Cassie blinked. The angel's face seemed strangely familiar. Then, when the image should have been completely darkened because nighttime had come, the angel burned with brightness. Cassie recognized the face.

"Jovita?" Cassie whispered. The angel's hands stretched out at her sides, the right hand flat with her palm up, as though it beckoned Cassie nearby. The left hand pointed gracefully to whitewashed walls and a landscape painting that looked somewhat like the country back home.

Cassie remembered the dream!

"Jovita's an angel! That's why she disappeared, and that's why I had that dream. It was this place that she took me to."

Cassie raced back up the loft stairs to the painting, and carefully lifted the frame from the wall, uncovering a dark hole.

From outside, Cassie heard a loud whistle, and then an explosion. The ground shook, loosening dirt from the wooden beams above her. When she looked out the window, she saw a flash of a light spark from the sea, another rumble, and another blast, this one so close she heard walls crashing.

They're bombing the castle!

If Jovita were the angel in her dream, then this would surely be her escape route. She crawled into the dark hole and carefully hung the painting over the entry behind her.

The Brigantine

ook, Uncle!" Jimmy said, pointing to rockets that sped over the water into the twilight sky, ending with a brilliant flash on the crest of the bluffs. "That ship is blowing up Alisubbo!" He gawked at the scene both amazed and terrified. Explosives were alien to the Boreals. Even the destruction of Pointe de Tratado hadn't been as impressive as what he was witnessing now.

"Rotten Libos. They'll blow up my ship, too. Curse be to you, 'Fox! You've led us straightaway into a trap," Elias grumbled. "Why I let you lead me, I will never know. You say you know what you're doing, and you don't."

The rumble from the blast reverberated through the water, rocking the small sailing vessel with unexpected force. Elias wheeled the helm of the brigantine so that the bow of his vessel faced the rolling surf.

Whitefox slid his spyglass closed. "Not what I was expecting either, Elias. Believe me, I don't want this ship to sink any more than you do. Bear southwest and take her to the Bandene shore. We're late. Whatever damage Valerio planned is already being accomplished. Jimmy, call all hands to the deck, bring in the jib and the main."

"Row, sir?" the boy asked.

"Until we reach the shoreline current, yes." Whitefox said with a nod. "That will take us quietly to the coast."

Yes, sir." Jimmy jumped from the poop deck and paused next to Elias, surprised by his laugh.

"You'll pay better this time, 'Fox, eh?" Elias said with a gruff voice. A red glare lit the sky. "If not, my men will have a little fun at your expense."

"Your pay will be good. Just stay with us," Whitefox said. "Follow my lead into the forest. From there, we'll sneak into Alisubbo and find out what's going on."

"Sneak?" Elias's white smile glowed against his dark skin. "You promised a raid. What now? We are packing arms just to hide in the bushes like rabbits. Show me the fight!"

"Get on it, Jimmy!" Whitefox ordered, slapping his nephew on the shoulder. Jimmy jumped. Elias's black dreadlocks flew wild when he faced the boy.

"Get on it, kid!" he said, mocking Whitefox.

Elias was short, but not without muscle and an intimidating mannerism. Jimmy could never tell what the rogue was thinking, for the man always smiled, showing only half a row of teeth. A wild native of the island, the Gitano chief was cunning and extremely intelligent, a beast his uncle swore to tame. Jimmy secretly hoped that would never happen. He admired Elias just the way he was.

"Yes, sir," Jimmy saluted. Elias nodded.

With the sails in, the Cradle drifted toward the mainland, just as Whitefox had predicted. The bombings had stopped. Once during the night, they heard a round of gunfire, but it ceased shortly after it had begun.

The Cradle reached land in the deep of night. Whitefox called the crew on deck, where he handed out pistols, sheaths, and swords. He then opened a duffle bag and unpacked a pile of dark leather masks.

"Everyone will wear these," he said.

Jimmy took his mask and slipped it over his head, strapped his sheath around his waist, and stuffed as many daggers as possible into his belt along with several pistols.

He looked up when he heard laughter. "What?"

"Everyone has to disguise themselves," Whitefox said to Elias. "You and your men especially."

Elias shrugged. "My men laugh at you and your nephew."

"Laugh now. Fine, but what happens if we're ambushed? There's no telling what allies Valerio has. What we're doing is for the good of the island, your people and mine. Because of that, we keep our identity hidden. At least for now."

"Good?" Elias chuckled. "Good is the look on Valerio's face when I slit his throat and he knows it's me! That will be good."

"No, Elias. Not if we're going to save Alisubbo. For all we know, the king is dead. Judging from where those bombs landed, they've attacked the castle. If you rush in there like savages, shoot, kill and steal, it will gain you nothing but a noose. If that's what you want, fine. If not, follow my lead."

Elias glanced at his men.

"Think of the influence Valerio will have if the king is dead. He was going to hang you, remember? And then he was going to blow your brains out. I'm sure the Commando hasn't changed his plans. He may even have some new form of torture for you."

Elias picked up a mask and signaled with a wave for his men to do the same.

"Though he'll probably recognize you by your attitude." Whitefox muttered under his breath. He tossed a black hooded cloak to Jimmy. "And you keep that red hair in check, boy!" he said.

"Yes, sir." Jimmy answered.

THE DARK SIDE

Cassie felt her way into the dark void, feet first, hands slapping against the walls. She trembled whenever another blast rumbled the earth. The air turned cool and moist. So moist that her legs buckled under her, and she slipped, injuring her back and tailbone. Crawling would be better, though the grade was steep. Her dress soaked up the slime and smells of the channel as she inched downward. The dark gave no promise of an end.

As the tunnel grew more vertical, control yielded to gravity. Her hands slid along the walls; her chin scrapped against the cold stone. She skidded down the wet rock completely helpless, rolling through murk, her hair sopping up moss and pebbles, accelerating as she plunged into complete darkness.

Her fall ended with a tumble onto soft ground. Terror ceased when she realized she was still breathing, still alive, and that she had landed outside under a starry sky. She felt no pain. Spitting stones from her mouth and blinking dirt from her eyes, she sat up. A rising moon illuminated the landscape, which seemed peaceful.

The bay was only a few yards below her now. The dinghy she had seen earlier still bounced gently on the waves. The bombing had stopped, and a bullfrog bellowed in the reeds nearby as if nothing had ever disturbed the night. Stars glittered through the smoke that had settled on the sea. The navy ship had disappeared, but the royal sailing vessel was still moored in the waters, ringlets of moonlight dancing on its form.

Cassie's heart still ached from the sorrow of the assassination and her body from the fall. Stones and slime stuck to her torn hands and face. Washing in the inlet seemed the right thing to do. However, when she rose, she heard voices on the bank across the bay. She squatted in the brush.

"Careful, come this way," a man said. Moonlight glinted off his helmet.

Cassie held her breath, wondering how they had tracked her here so soon.

"Take his pack. Easy. Watch his arm, lest the bleeding starts up again," another soldier cautioned.

The troops she heard emerged from the woody trail. Two military men assisted an injured man to a stump, seated him, and waded out into the marsh to pull the dinghy to shore. Though his face was in the shadows, Cassie recognized Martim by his clothes. His arm was wrapped in white bindings that glowed in the moonlight. His body lifeless, as though only semi-conscious. The queen came into view. She draped a coat over Martim's shoulders and kneeled next to him, holding his wounded body in her arms. Relieved that Queen Felicia and Martim were alive, Cassie grieved for them as she watched.

The splash of the tide against the dinghy, and the resonant clap of the two soldiers lifting Martim into the rowboat, interrupted the silence of the night. After the queen boarded, one soldier pushed the dinghy afloat and then stepped into the boat. Silence resumed. The boat glided along the shore, halting in the shadow of low hanging willows. The oarsman looked toward the hill above Cassie.

She followed his gaze and froze. A group of armed men, their silhouettes backlit by moonlight, paused on the bank above her. Three soldiers and two civilians with spyglasses searched the sea. The Felicia was out there, no doubt the destination of the exiles. The enemy had to have seen it. Martim's party would never make it to the safety of their ship, and if Martim and his mother were spotted trying to escape, Valerio's men would gun them down.

Remorseful of the trouble she had caused the royal family, and for deceiving Martim, Cassie made a choice. She owed her life to them, for she had a hand in the king's death. She stood. With one last glance at the boat, she stepped out into the open and tripped on her skirt. She grunted. She hadn't been heard, so she stumbled on purpose again and muttered, allowing her voice to carry.

"There! That's the one that killed Perez!" A soldier on the hill pointed at her.

In a second, a gunshot broke the quiet. A bullet hit a tree near her head. Cassie picked up her skirt and ran toward the trail, glancing over her shoulder. The assassins had taken the bait, giving the royal prince and the queen an opportunity to sneak away to *The Felicia*. The guards were in pursuit. Like dogs on a chase, the entire group of scouts stumbled down the rocky cliff after her.

She saw the dingy pass briefly into the moonlight, and then circle the bend on its way out to sea.

She screamed, keeping her pursuers' attention away from the water.

If the troops were wrestling their way down the hill, their aim would be clumsy, and their attention drawn toward her.

Cassie scrambled across the bank, slipping steadily until she reached the trailhead. A volley of shots flew in her direction, but she hit the ground, miraculously avoiding them. If the rebels reached the trail soon, she'd be killed. Her only chance of escape would be the marshy thicket by the mire. She pulled her skirt up and tucked the hem under her belt, then ran like the Seattle teen that she was, putting distance between her and her stalkers until she reached the bottom of the hill, and then she dodged into the brush.

Cassie wished she were wearing her blue jeans and sneakers. Her pumps had split at the seams and her feet bled from scrapes she had gained in the tunnel. Her dress and bloomers were a mess. Branches had already torn, pulled, and knotted her hair. She bent low and found it easier to maneuver through the foliage on her belly. Fortunately, her red dress was now so muddy that leaves and sticks clung to it, camouflaging her.

She froze as the men neared. Their boots beat heavy on the earth, breaking branches as they walked, canteens rattled, and ammunition belts flapped against their waists. Nearer now, they slowed, as if they sensed her presence. The smell of their perspiring bodies reeked through the marsh. They poked at the weeds, their boots too near her head. How long it would take them to notice she had dodged them she didn't know. Nor could she decide whether to grapple through the bramble or stay put. If they didn't find her now, they may return with hounds, and that thought sickened her. There would be no escaping a pack of dogs here in the bog.

She held her breath as they searched. So close were they, she could have tripped them. By some good grace, however, they kept on, and Cassie breathed again. When the soldiers were no longer audible, she crawled through the bramble, hoping to put as much distance between her and the hunters as possible.

IN THE DARK

Jimmy shuffled nervously behind Whitefox as his uncle knocked softly on the old wooden door to the chapel. He was glad he and his uncle went to Alisubbo alone. Elias and his men were not capable of being discreet. However, that left Jimmy to be the lookout in a town creeping with Valerio's troops. A role which was both exciting but dangerous. Another confrontation with Valerio, however, was not something Jimmy craved.

"They would have answered by now; don't you think?" Jimmy asked, referring to the clergy. He adjusted his mask and dropped his hood further over his head.

Whitefox knocked again. "Unless they thought we were Valerio's men. If anyone has information about what's going on here, it will be the nuns. Let's hope they haven't been arrested, being so loyal to the Crown."

"We're going to get caught if we loiter," Jimmy treaded nervously across the back porch, certain he'd seen movement in the shadows.

"Let's go, then." Whitefox jumped off the steps and hugged the darkness as he inched toward the street.

"Where to?"

Whitefox paused for a moment. "Queen Felecia has friends in those apartments. She did ministry work there. They might let us in if we can convince them we're allies."

Jimmy peered from the alley to the row of apartments across the street. To get to the residences they'd have to jog over the wide cobblestone road, now lit by the moon. An unsafe feat, Jimmy feared, for he heard the jangle of approaching troops as Valerio's men marched. Pressed tight against the wall, he and his uncle waited and watched as a company of foot soldiers passed.

An order rang out, a dog barked, the soldiers turned north, and then all was quiet.

Whitefox peeked around the corner, glanced both ways, and dashed across the alley. He slid into the shadow of a backstreet. Jimmy stepped cautiously away from the chapel, then sprinted, stubbing his toe on a cobble in the road. He grunted, setting off another howl from a family canine. Whitefox grimaced when Jimmy stumbled to his side and caught his balance by grabbing his uncle's coat.

From where they hid, they could see the three doors that faced the wooden porch on the upper level, marking the entry to separate homes. There were no pedestrians. No light in the windows beckoned visitors, which to Jimmy seemed odd as the hour was not late. The only creatures shifting about in the night were three swine rummaging through a tipped over garbage can several apartments away. Whitefox ceased cowering in the dark and walked up the stairs. Jimmy followed, dodging the laundry that hung low over the balcony railing.

"Who there?" Someone answered Whitefox's quiet tapping.

"Friends of the queen." Jimmy's uncle spoke low, targeting his voice into the seam of the doorframe. "Allies."

The door creaked open a notch. All Jimmy could see was a small person's eyes darkened by shadow.

"We need information. Can you let us in? We mean you no harm."

The door shut again, a chain unloosed, and when the two stepped inside, children raced from the living quarters to a bedroom. A middle-aged woman was seated at a table, her dark complexion radiant in the dim lantern light. A young girl shut the door and linked the chain behind them.

The woman spoke in a language Jimmy was unfamiliar with, gesturing with her hands to a bench along the wall.

"Mama says to sit down," the girl said.

Whitefox sat, but Jimmy stood, taking in the dimly lit décor of the room. Two lanterns burned on the table: the smell of kerosene thick in the air. The burners on a woodstove against the wall still glowed from the fire within while an enamel pot simmered and steamed on top. Behind him, he noticed a blanket tacked over the windows. The girl moved to the table and sat next to her mother. The woman spoke in her language; the girl translated.

"My mother wants to know who you are."

Whitefox cleared his throat. "Tell your mother that we are allies of King Chavez. We came by boat from the Isle of Refuge." He waited while she translated, whispering to her mother. The woman nodded but did not take her eyes off of Whitefox. When the girl once again looked at him, he continued.

"We received news that there might be trouble, but our men could not come directly here. The bridge at Pointe de Tratado was destroyed, so our journey was delayed. Tell her we are here to help the king but don't know the situation at the castle."

151

The girl translated. The mother nodded but didn't speak.

The girl then spoke. "My name is Carmen. You're too late to help. King Chavez is dead."

"They killed him?" Jimmy exclaimed. Remorse overwhelmed him, his hopes crippled. He felt responsible. The bridge would still stand if he hadn't been caught spying. Had the bridge not been destroyed, their army might have arrived at Alisubbo in time to save the king.

"Carmen, my name is Whitefox and this is my nephew Jimmy. Can you tell us anything else? Anything at all? We're here to help your people."

"It's too late. There's nothing anyone can do now. Valerio is in the castle, so you better not go there. He has hundreds of soldiers patrolling the streets."

"Where are the clergy?"

"Valerio's soldiers went to the chapel during the bombing and took everyone away. We don't know where they are. You'd better go. It's not safe for you to be here. They'll arrest you, too."

Jimmy pivoted, anger mounting. He lacked religion, having left his pagan culture in the northern lands. Still, he'd nothing but respect for the nuns that served the royal family. They had always been pleasant and peaceful people.

"Why?" he asked.

"Jimmy, sit down," his uncle said.

"Where are Marques, Felicia and Martim? Were they injured?" Jimmy asked.

"The Prince Royal Marques was killed. Queen Felicia and Martim escaped, I think. That's the rumor. They say the soldiers are looking for them. They've knocked on all our doors and searched our homes. I don't think they were found. There's no sign of Maestro Sanchez or the Duchess and her father, either. It's all lost. The people mourn. Our hope is lost."

"I'm sorry to hear of your misfortune." Whitefox offered. The girl nodded, but aside from her words, she braved showing any emotion.

"Are there any men that have taken leadership for the royalists here?"

Carmen shrugged.

Whitefox rose and bowed cordially to Carmen's mother. "Tell your mother that if she knows of any men willing to defend the city, we have a camp in Bandene forest and are gathering troops."

Carmen relayed the message, but the woman only shook her head and whispered something to her daughter.

"There is nothing you can do. My mother says you should go

152

home."

The girl escorted them to the door. Jimmy was lost for words as he eyed the children in the other room peering at him on his way out. The family's plight would not be a good one, not with a military rule and the tyrant Valerio controlling their fate.

Jimmy hurried down the stairs behind his uncle but kept silent. So many thoughts haunted him. The king is dead. This was not something that could be easily dismissed. Their men could fight. But if Alisubbo didn't have a successor to the throne why risk lives? Jimmy wondered what his uncle would decide to do. At this moment, a discussion would be fruitless, and dangerous. He kept his musings to himself.

By the time Whitefox and Jimmy returned to camp, they expected the Gitanos to be asleep, but the fearless nomads had a bonfire crackling on the beach. Flames burned high, illuminating the shore and parts of Bandene Forest with a brilliant glow. They were laughing and singing in the night.

"What in the world do they have to sing about?" Whitefox grumbled to Jimmy. He tossed his gloves on his bedding and stormed to the fireside. Elias, Geno, and several other men were sprawled out on the sand, joining voices in song with a sound more obnoxious than musical.

"Is this your idea of being discreet?" Whitefox interrupted. "This fire can be seen all the way to Alisubbo, you know."

"They should know we're here. Let them come to us!" Geno said with a laugh. "We'll fight them!"

"We're not ready to fight them. Not until we know what Valerio is up to."

"I'll tell you what he's up to. No good!" Elias snickered.

While Whitefox argued with Elias, something caught Jimmy's eye. On the other side of the bonfire was a lone figure resting on a piece of driftwood. Bent over, oblivious to the loud, jovial outcries of the Gitanos, the man was quiet. He must have sensed someone looking at him, for when the breeze blew the smoke aside, he twisted his head enough to make eye contact with Jimmy.

The wizard, Silvio.

Jimmy had never met him before. He had always wanted to. Geno once described him so vividly there was no mistaking the decrepit old man. His silver hair and thinning beard reflected the firelight. His wrinkled face was cemented in a scowl.

"Put the fire out, Geno," Whitefox ordered.

"No," the Gitano said. He glanced at Silvio. "We're having an important meeting."

"A meeting? With whom?"

"With our Shaman." Elias nodded toward the old conjurer.

"Silvio?" Whitefox whispered.

"Yes, 'Fox. We know this forest. Silvio is our patriarch. Only one of his kind anymore. Where do you think we get our powers from, eh? Bandene is a sacred place to us." He nodded toward Silvio. "And Silvio our elder." His grin broke the rigid air. "He always gives us good advice. And magic."

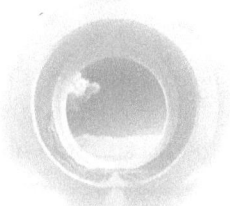

A Magical Journey

With mosquitos biting her face, her hands, and her legs, and flies buzzing in her ears, thorns digging into her flesh and tugging at her tangled hair, Cassie grappled through the marsh. Her back ached from the fall through the tunnel, and the once regal gown now wound in shreds across her body so that she had to unwrap it continuously in order to move. Mist crept through the dark, which cloaked her from her enemies, but also seeped through her skin and chilled her bones. Her body convulsed with shivers from the damp night air and from exhaustion. There were no tears left in her, only despondency.

With the last bit of energy consumed, Cassie rolled on her back. Leaves from the brush hung low over her head, Clouds had touched the earth in a thick fog. There was no beyond. Cassie was at her end. Everything was spent.

She had made her choices and failed miserably.

With her eyes closed, she drifted into unconsciousness, hoping eternity would accept her pitiful soul, because as far as she could see, there was no purpose for her existence but to grieve.

She was certain death had claimed her when her body floated across the earth. Though she scrapped against the sticks and stubble, she felt no pain. She was numb. The bushes sped by like the haze of smoke from neighborhood wood stoves seen through dirty windows on a school bus. People moaned as she passed them, probably her mom and dad when they found out she had died. She spiraled down a cylinder of darkness, although she wasn't dizzy or sick. She felt surrounded by joy, snatches of songs ringing of freedom and happiness. Yes, she was dead. The world would no longer have to suffer from her inadequacies. Goodbye Cassandra Wilson, Princess of Alcove Forest…

"Cassandra Wilson, Princess of Alcove Forest." Small hands slapped her cheeks.

Princess Cassandra," a meek voice tickled her ear.

"Is she awake?"

"Not yet. Keep working."

Eyes glistened in the dark, prairie dog eyes, moms and their kits, and then her head pushed through a net. As it came apart, its cords wrapped tight around her body. She spun and spiraled faster, twirling through space. Prairie dogs hung onto the streamers of netting attached to her, gripping with their teeth. Little hands reached out and touched her. "You saved us, you saved us," they cheered as they grabbed on to her skirt, spinning violently around as she sailed like a cannonball through the dark. Wind passed through her hair, and water washed her face.

Cold water.

Cassie coughed. The water trickled down the sides of her cheeks, into her nose and the side of her mouth. She blinked. The sun was so bright she closed her eyes again to avoid the pain.

"She's awake, she is. Look, she's awake." A chorus of a hundred voices rang in her ears all shouting in triumph. Feet ran across her body. More water splashed on her face.

"Enough with that. Let her get her senses."

Cassie recognized the gruff voice, and when she blinked again, the green eyes and red nose of Silvio shielded her from the sun's glare. His silver hair tickled her face.

He shook his head slowly, and in a disgruntled manner muttered, "You are a wreck of a Princess. I told you they'd destroy you." He straightened his crooked body as much as he could and waddled away.

Cassie tried to move, but little people tugged at her dress and kept her pinned down. "Stop, we're not finished," a Xylonite woman shouted.

From the corner of her eye, Cassie noticed the women repairing her gown. Some of them held quills in their mouths and pinned the rips, while others wove gold threads in and out of the fabric with pine needles. The men had sponges made from mushrooms stuck to the end of sticks that they used for mopping the mud and blood from her face, arms, and feet. Tattered string resembling a fishing net lay in a pile behind them.

Cassie let the tears ooze from her eyes. She didn't deserve to be treated kindly. Someone lifted her head onto their lap and gently brushed her long, dark curls.

Jovita.

"What happened? How did I get here?" Cassie asked.

"Silvio brought you here after his return from Bandene. It's a good thing too. Between the suction of his magic and your spinning, Valerio's nets were destroyed."

"They were?" Cassie looked into her eyes.

A smile glistened on the angel's face. "They were. You rescued the little people who were trapped. You even freed their prairie dogs. Everything is fine now. You're safe."

Cassie swallowed. "Everything's not fine. I should be dead."

"It isn't for you to pass judgment on yourself," Jovita answered. "There is still much work to do."

Cassie shook her head. "I can't do anything."

"Oh, but you can. You can save the king."

"The king? The king is dead."

"Martim," Jovita said. "He is king now."

Unspoken words passed between them. Martim was alive, in exile, and Jovita hinted that Cassie save him? She's crazy if she thinks I can do any such thing!

"You saved King Martim's life. Twice," she whispered.

"I only did what I had to do to make up for the damage I caused." Cassie's voice was equally soft.

"And you've saved us, too," someone added.

Cassie lifted her head. Seated comfortably on top of a curiously bridled prairie dog was a different Xylonite. Though he was thinner than the others, he was dressed legally, in a uniform of red and blue. He held his shiny brass helmet tucked under his arm. A miniature saber hung at his side. His beard sputtered unevenly from a wrinkled face, reminding Cassie of a dried-up pear.

"Were you one of Valerio's prisoners?" she asked.

"Was. Not anymore, thanks to you!"

"Who are you?"

"Xylepher is my name," he bent over in a bow atop his mount.

"Can I get up, please?" Cassie asked the women Xylonites that were still brushing her hair and mending her dress. They quickly gathered their quills. The ones that sat on top of her jumped to the ground and they all backed away. Cassie sat up and placed the skirt around her so that they could continue their work. Her gown was already mended significantly.

"I don't know you."

"No, but you know our forefathers."

"I do?"

"Xylon's soldiers. Though they didn't start off being soldiers. They were tree climbers, conk cutters."

Cassie remembered the stories and she smiled. Her father had drawn more tree climbers just the other night. "You come from the tree climbers my dad made?"

"We do! We've been warriors ever since Xylon made us soldiers. We're good ones too! Best soldiers in Bandene Forest if I say so myself. We've got our enemy on the defense. He's afraid of us, Valerio is, and with just cause." Xylepher stuck out his lower lip past his gruff red beard and narrowed his bushy eyebrows to a scowl.

"You see," Silvio interrupted. "I was right. They were the ones trapped, imprisoned by that Ramshackle Valerio. He kept them locked up, all of them." He waved his arm toward a crowd of tiny soldiers mounted on prairie dogs all dressed like Xylepher.

"Well, if Valerio knew you were here, why didn't he imprison all the Xylonites?"

The little man grunted. "Oh, the forest people are nothing to Valerio. But us soldiers are a mighty force. We could destroy him!"

"You could?"

"Maybe you will," Silvio whispered.

"Miss Princess, we owe you for our lives. You saved us, you did! For that, we will help you fight to win back the kingdom. No one wants Valerio on the throne of this country. He's a..."

"A Blastbonker." Silvio offered. "No good through and through. Evil, I say." And he said it extremely close to Cassie's face. She put her hand over her ear.

"He is," she agreed.

"Bah! Not so entranced by that Mind-boggler now? Well, you learned something, then."

"I learned something." Cassie stood, tugging her dress away from the seamstresses, who packed up their quills and thread and scurried away. Cassie faced the soldiers that had congregated next to her.

"I'm sorry, guys. I'm not going back and fighting anyone for the throne. Coming here was a big mistake. I've ruined everything. First, I lied to Queen Felicia, and then I lied to Prince Martim and his fiancé. I didn't listen to Silvio. Instead, I believed Valerio. I wasn't thinking and it caused a lot of problems. Maybe I didn't have a huge part in the rebellion. And perhaps the king and his son would have died even if I hadn't been there. Still, I helped Valerio's cause and that makes me just as much a tyrant as he is."

Cassie turned to Jovita. "You told me to make my father proud, and all I did was shame him. He wouldn't have approved of what I did. He doesn't even approve of me being here."

Jovita started to speak, but Cassie pivoted around, facing the army.

"Besides, Martim would never believe I'm on his side. He had me arrested once. He thinks I'm one of Valerio's spies, and I'm ashamed to say that I was. No way would he let me fight for him. He'd be too suspicious of me. It just won't work."

"You could convince him of the truth," Xylepher offered.

"I'm afraid not. I did my damage and it's over." She looked at Jovita. "I need to go home. My parents are probably worried sick about me, and I don't want to hurt them any more than I already have. Really, Jovita, please just let me go home."

"I can't forbid you from doing what you want to do, Your Highness," Jovita answered softly and laid the brush on the blanket next to her. She stood next to Cassie.

"You'll be making another mistake." Silvio grunted from his stump. "Just one mistake after another. Go on. Go home. You couldn't make a right decision if you wanted to."

Silvio's words pierced her heart.

"You're right then," Cassie said, her voice hoarse and cracking. "So why would you even want me here if I can't make a right decision? I'll just ruin everything for all of you."

The old conjurer shot her a glare. "Go home."

"Let's not be angry and argue amongst ourselves," Jovita interrupted. "We all want the best for our world. Please understand, Cassandra. Silvio and these men and women are desperate. With Valerio as dictator, they risk losing their homes and even their lives. The man has had his eyes on this forest for many years. I'm afraid if King Martim is not returned to the throne, more calamities will befall this country. But you're right. It's not your concern, nor is it your responsibility. You have the option to stay or to go home."

"I'm sorry, Jovita, I just don't think I can do anything. I've messed too many things up already."

"Come walk with me." Jovita stood, giving Silvio and the little people a warning eye not to follow.

Before Cassie took her hand, she looked at the crowd of pale and saddened Xylonites. Their faces were long in pouts, their eyes weepy and their shoulders slumped. She had never seen such downcast expressions. It was as though she was abandoning them. Cassie sighed.

"I'm sorry," she pleaded. "There's nothing I can do!"

The forest was especially beautiful this morning. Wildflowers sprinkled the ground like confetti, yellows, pinks, and blues. A robin called from high in the glistening firs, answered by its mate. Cassie breathed in the healing menthol of the evergreens. It was a lovely day, though the heaviness of grief still weighed on her heart.

Jovita didn't say anything on their walk. She simply strolled through the forest, her feet as silent as a hare as she walked around stumps and stepped over logs. Cassie followed close behind. When they arrived at the forest edge, Jovita stopped. The meadow was alive with color, and the sun so bright Cassie had to squint.

"Home calls for you." For the first time, Cassie saw the sky sparkle in Jovita's blue eyes as though heaven itself took refuge there. "Answer."

Cassie fumbled in her pocket for her cell phone and found it just as the ring tone sounded.

"Cassie?" It was Dad. His voice was the most pleasant sound in the entire world for all time. "Cassie? Are you there?"

"Dad?" she whispered.

"Oh baby, you're alive!" his sigh of relief stung Cassie. In that one phrase, she heard the agonizing worry that must have consumed him and Mom all this time. "Are you all right? Where are you? Come home, baby."

"I'm ready, Dad."

"Your mom called. She thought you were at Monica's for the weekend."

"I know. I'm sorry."

"You know I was in L.A. on business, don't you? I made my trip short to come home to look for you. Your mom's extremely upset, and I can't say I've been handling your disappearance very well, either. But we aren't mad at you. We want you home. Are you okay?"

"I'm okay."

"Daemon told me how you got in. I wish I'd been here sooner. I would have warned you. The Realm is no place for you, not alone. We never meant for you to run away, Princess."

Cassie was silent. Dad calling her Princess struck an odd chord on her heartstrings.

"Cassie?"

"I'm here. I didn't run away. I didn't mean to hurt you."

"I'm getting in the car right now and I'm stopping at Daemon's. Your phone camera is working, right? You'll be able to get back?"

"Yeah," she looked at Jovita. "Yeah, it will work."

"How long will it take to get to the portal? A half hour? Behind the school, right?" her dad asked.

"Probably. You must crawl under a fence."

"I'll call you when we get there. Are you in a safe place now?"

"I'm safe now."

"Maybe I'll have Daemon call you while we're on our way."

"Just... just you call me back, Dad. I don't want my batteries to die." Cassie wasn't ready to talk to Daemon.

"I love you, Princess."

"I love you too, Dad. I mean I really, really love you."

"I'll see you real soon."

"Dad?"

"What, love?"

"Would you bring me a clean pair of jeans?"

"Sure, hon."

"And my black tee."

"I'll get mom to find it for you."

"Not the gray one with the heart, the black one, and my hoodie and my sneakers and some socks."

"Can't you change at home?"

"I can't crawl under a fence in a dress."

"I'll see you soon."

She turned off her phone. "They're on their way," she said to Jovita. "I'm supposed to wait until they get to the woods."

"Did you want me to wait with you?"

"I think maybe I should wait alone. I need to think about things. I need to say goodbye to this place."

"I understand."

Cassie watched as Jovita stepped quietly back the way they had come. "Jovita?"

The angel turned to face her.

"I'll miss you."

"I'll stay in touch."

"Will you?" Cassie fumbled for words. "Will you make sure I'm okay while I sit here? I mean, will you watch over me, you know, like angels do, so nothing else bad happens?"

She smiled. "Always."

"Thanks."

A Dragon?

Cassie sat on a lone log half hidden in the grass overlooking the meadow and waited for her last half-hour in the Realm to pass. The morning sunshine comforted her. The song of a lark set her mind to rest.

She took solace from the warm breeze that tickled the grass and made the wildflowers jiggle. Yellow, purple and white; the same flowers that grew on the mountain by the Sanatorium. She picked a white one and twisted it in her fingers. She thought of Angelique in her white hospital gown, and her beautiful dark skin against the white pillow that she lay her head on. Angelique would no longer walk alongside the Queen to pick bouquets. What would become of Angelique now? she wondered. Would anyone take care of the hospital on the hill? Or will all the sick children be sent home to suffer their illness in silence?

The delicate stem bent, the petals fell apart, browned and smudged. Cassie released the remains and watched them fall beneath the dancing blades of grass by her feet. Just as the blossoms had fallen from the Queen's bouquet during the assassination. Just as the queen's husband, her son, and her dreams had fallen, broken and bleeding.

"Why am I so lucky?" Cassie asked herself, squinting at the sky. The majestic white clouds floated overhead on their hasty venture to nowhere. "I can walk away from all this untouched. Go back home. Back to school, as though nothing happened. Why?"

Cassie looked out across the meadow to the sea. In the distance, the stone Keep of Alisubbo shone against the turquoise waters. Somewhere out there were two very, very sad and damaged people. She'd probably never see them again. If only she had the chance to tell them how sorry she was. As bad as she felt, her pain couldn't compare to their agony. "I guess I'm not going home untouched," she said.

Her ringtone sounded.

"Dad?"

"Daemon."

Cassie sighed. "What?"

"We're here."

"Where's my dad?"

"He forgot your backpack in the pickup. You know, Cass, you epically failed this time. You made your folks go freakin' crazy."

"Shut up Daemon. Why do you do that? Like I really needed to feel worse than I already do."

"Well, are you coming back?"

"Yeah, when my dad gets there," Cassie said. Daemon could have very easily made her change her mind.

"He's here." Static followed as their phone changed hands. Soon she heard her father's voice.

"Cassie? Your mom didn't find the black t-shirt, so I brought you the gray one. Are you ready?"

"Dad, can you ask Daemon to go away somewhere?"

"He's okay. He's…"

"Please. I only want to see you, no one else." A muffled sound, a silence, and then Dad's voice came back.

"He's waiting in the pickup. I'm ready for you."

Cassie held her phone up to her face, inhaled deeply, and lowered it again, looking out over the green meadow, the shimmering forest, the sea, and the castle. Before any more feelings of remorse could creep back, she focused the camera again, clicked the shutter button, and stumbled into the dirt hole where her journey had begun.

Her father lifted her to her feet. When she looked into his eyes, everything inside her exploded. He held her and stroked her hair; his caress soothed her trembling body.

"It's okay, baby. It's going to be fine. You're safe now."

They stood there in the woods, father and daughter holding each other. Cassie didn't know what to say, and she didn't want to let go, either. She held his shirt with her fists, absorbing his smells, his strength, and his parental care, as her tears dampened his chest. She wanted to be safe. She wanted to be Cassie the high school senior, only child of Abbi and Ian Wilson, residents of Seattle, Washington, USA, Earth a.k.a. Real World.

Finally, Dad held her away from him, leaned over, and tried drying her eyes with his palms.

"Where is my backpack? I need to change my clothes," she sniveled.

"Where did you get this dress?" Ian asked. "Incredible."

Cassie wiped her mouth, her nose, and her cheeks with her hands and her arms while her father looked for something in the pack that she could use as an alternative.

"I have to tell you everything."

"Wait until we get home." He handed her a bandana and she blew her nose and dried her tears.

"No. I don't want to tell mom what happened. You're the only one who would understand. Mom hates the Realm. She wouldn't get why I even went there."

"Oh, Princess, give your mom credit. She loves you."

Cassie settled in the dirt, and Dad kneeled next to her. "I know she loves me, but she won't understand. She didn't understand when you were there. What makes you think she'd understand what happened to me? Besides, it's all too horrible."

"Your mom was afraid for me, that's all. And there were other issues too."

"Well, if she knew what happened this time, she'd croak." Cassie held her head in her hands. She had wanted her homecoming to be an awakening of sorts, expecting the horrid memories to disappear. She expected peace. But the images of blood, and tunnels, and death still tortured her vision. Her hands wouldn't stop shaking.

Ian sighed and waited. "I have as much time as you need," he offered.

Cassie tried to compose herself. "Did you know you are a king?" she asked, wiping her nose. Chills raced through her body as she looked her father in the eyes. Her fears had been completely unfounded. His eyes spoke of nothing but a father's love.

He shook his head.

"The Xylonites crowned you an absentee king, and your name is known throughout the entire Realm, in foreign lands you never even knew existed. You're a legend and a hero."

He said nothing, so Cassie went on. "But there's one part of the Realm now where I don't think they consider you a hero anymore."

"Why is that?"

"Because of me." She bit her lip.

He laughed in disbelief. "Oh Cassie, you couldn't have done anything that bad."

Cassie moved away when he touched her shoulder. She didn't want sympathy. She didn't deserve it.

"And even if you ruined my name as a king, it doesn't matter. I won't be going there again. Being in the Realm was too hard on your mom. She almost left me because of that world. I swore never to put our relationship in jeopardy again."

165

"You're so honorable. You mean what you say, and I so admire you for that. I wish I could be that good. I wish I weren't so stupid."

"You're not stupid, Cass."

"I was. I believed a liar, this awful man. Valerio. He made me think he liked me, and then he used me like a pawn in a chess game. I didn't mean anything to him. He made me believe I was doing something good, and it turned out to be part of his plot to assassinate the king and his family."

Ian turned pale. "Did he do anything to you? Did he hurt you?"

Cassie shook her head. "No, nothing like that. He never touched me. Well, he kissed me, but I didn't kiss him back. But it didn't mean anything. He was in love with the duchess, and the whole reason he sent me to the castle was to get her back. He told me I was taking an Appeal of Peace to the king. Boy, was I ever stupid to believe that story! But that wasn't the worst. I did something awful, something horrible."

Dad took her hands and held them tight. "You don't have to tell me if it's too hard."

"No, I have to tell you." She swallowed. Cassie breathed deep, winced as she looked into his eyes, certain he'd hate her forever, and then blurted out. "I killed someone."

Cassie feared her father's reaction, but all he did was sit in front of her, his eyes searching hers. Maybe he hoped he hadn't heard correctly. Maybe he was waiting for her to explain.

She whispered, "I can't give you a reason because there isn't any excuse for killing someone."

"Were you in a battle?" He finally asked, his voice cracking.

"No. Well… in a way. They shot the king twice as if being dead wasn't good enough the first time. And then they shot his oldest son. And then Martim, the younger son, jumped on the carriage and I had seen nothing so sad in all my life when he held his brother's body and cried out. And then this man, his name was Perez, walked out as plain as day with his rifle, and the soldiers did nothing, Dad, they didn't do anything! They just stood there. It was evil. It was like they wanted them all to die. The king's own soldiers. Perez kneeled on the ground and aimed his rifle at Martim. He was going to kill him, too. And then he would have shot the queen."

Cassie caught her breath and wiped her face again. "I met her. She's a sweet woman; she hurt no one. She didn't deserve to see her family die like that. She's just like us trying to do the right thing, and to see her kids grow up, and to save the sick kids at the Sanatorium. Without her, those kids won't get healthy again. I couldn't watch them kill the whole family.'"

She blew her nose and lowered her voice. "I had a gun. The man,

Valerio gave it to me. I think he wanted me to be an assassin too, but he's crazy. I never agreed to anything like that. When I saw Perez holding up that rifle, I was only going to shoot him in the arm or something, you know, to stop him. But I didn't... maybe it was the recoil, I don't know." She held her face again and her hands muffled her words. "I shot him in the head."

The temperature rose, heat hung stagnant under the trees. Gnats buzzed around her face. Cassie leaned against a fir tree; her face buried in her hands.

Dad finally touched her shoulder gently and whispered. "You saved a man's life. The queen's son, you say?"

She nodded.

"You saved a king's life."

Cassie looked up from her tears. Dad stood, reached over for her backpack, and set it at her feet. "Are you going to change your clothes before you go home? You don't have to. You look pretty in that dress, you know."

"I want my real clothes on, Dad. This isn't me."

He looked around, his hands on his hips. "We're kind of out in the open," he said.

"I can slip my jeans and t-shirt on under my dress. I'll be discreet."

"I'll wait in the truck with Daemon."

Her father walked down the trail as Cassie shuffled through her pack, disrupting several paper bags, a canteen, a hoodie, a flashlight, Dad's spyglass. What's this? Why were these things in her pack? She found the neat little pile of clothes at the bottom.

It felt good to be in blue jeans, a t-shirt and hoodie, with sneakers and soft socks that kept her feet comfy and protected her bruised toes. She folded the dress and put it in the pack. Looking briefly down at the trail her father had taken. The leaves of the maples shook in the breeze and beyond the trees, the red of her dad's truck glistened in the sun.

Modern civilization was there waiting for her. A few more steps and she'd be riding home to all the conveniences her world offered. Her life as a typical American teenager waited for her. Why did she hesitate?

"I can't," she whispered, and then sat on a stump next to the fir tree. Something kept her from walking away, even though she knew Dad and Daemon were waiting for her.

Alisubbo haunted her. She smelled it and tasted it. If she walked into the real world, that episode of her life would be over and for some peculiar reason, she didn't want it to end. She couldn't let it end. If life in

Alisubbo was unsettled, her life here would be unsettled. She'd never be able to separate herself from the trauma that was happening there.

"Are you ready, Cass?" Her dad walked back to her, yet Cassie remained motionless. "Are you ready?" His voice was softer this time.

She shook her head.

"What is it?"

She shrugged. "This isn't right, either."

When their eyes met, there was a connection with her father that Cassie had never felt before, as though he understood this unsettled feeling in her heart. As though he felt it too.

"You're reconsidering," he said. He didn't mean it as a question. He said it as fact. He knew. "Those people mean something to you, don't they?" he asked.

Cassie nodded.

"Did they say they needed your help?"

She nodded.

Her father sat down next to her and picked up a twig. She watched him as he peeled the bark away. "I know what you're going through," he said. "They called you Princess, didn't they?"

"They called you King Ian."

"You know, when I first entered the Realm, I hated the place. Your grandpa disappeared. I thought he was dead, and I had to come home without him. I'll never forget how much it hurt. Still hurts sometimes, you know? Wondering how he's doing. Your mom saw me through all of that. She felt the pain as much as I did. Three years of living in the real world wasn't enough to wash the memories away. I had to return."

"To find grandpa. I can understand that."

"There were other reasons too, and the longer I waited, the harder it was to control. It became an obsession. The day I opened the door to dad's abandoned house, and saw his computer, I couldn't stop myself. Your mom tried to talk sense into me. I didn't listen. Only one other time did I return, and that was to rescue your mom." He breathed a quiet laugh. "She ended up rescuing me, and then we were done. We could come home."

He tossed the twig on the ground and spoke so low that Cassie could barely hear him. "Cassie, do you need to do something in the Realm? Did you leave things open-ended?"

"Yeah. I sure did," she said.

"Then I understand where you're coming from. I guess it's like there's a dragon you must wrestle with."

Cassie nodded again, wiping her face with her sleeve. "A dragon.

You could call it that."

"What are they asking of you?"

She shrugged. "They want me to bring back Martim from exile."

"Do you think you can do it?"

"There's an army that is supposed to help me."

"An army?"

Cassie saw a hint of pride in her dad's smile.

"Xylepher's army. They don't want Valerio to declare himself king. He scares everybody," she added. "If that wicked man takes over everyone will suffer. The citizens of Alisubbo, the children in the hospital, the clergy, the little people. Valerio's a tyrant. But I can't go back and help them without your sanction," Cassie added. "I can't be there while you and mom are brooding over me. I need you to be happy that I'm... that I'm doing whatever it is they want me to do."

Dad sighed, filling the quiet with his breath. "I know this sounds trite, but I understand," he said. "I understand because that's exactly how I felt. I needed my Dad's blessing. When we were finally reunited, he gave it to me. What we did together after that was amazing. There's something remarkable in store for you. I wish I could go with you."

Cassie searched his eyes. "Why can't you?"

"I gave your mother my word to never return, at least not without her permission. I could ask, I suppose..."

"No, Dad, don't. This is my mess. I must fix it." No way did she want her mom to know. "I learned my lesson. I will not lie to anyone ever again. Never. I won't sneak around ever again, either. Or borrow things without asking."

"You've learned your lesson well and took a big step already by telling me what you did, Cass. It's difficult to confess to something of that magnitude. Do you need some armor? A sword to take with you?"

Cassie shook her head. "They fight with guns. It's a time warp, like the turn of the century."

"Interesting." Her father frowned. "I wondered why you didn't come across the dragon's lair. It must be a different portal, a different chamber you went through."

"It was nothing like the tunnel you experienced."

"Good. At least you won't be fighting a dragon."

"They don't want me to fight at all. They want me to find Martim and convince him to return to Alisubbo. That might be hard enough because he thinks I'm a traitor. Anyway, that's what Silvio said."

"You met Silvio?"

"He's now the acting king of the Xylonites, because you aren't there. I think with Silvio and Xylepher, we can succeed, as long as King Martim consents to return."

"It sounds as though you'll have support. But remember, Xylon was a computer character. The Xylonites have limited intelligence. You might have to take the lead."

"What? Lead an army? I'm not a warrior like you."

"No," her father smiled. "I don't think anyone expects you to be. They expect you to be yourself."

"Well, I'm great at that. Which would be fine if I weren't such a dork."

He gave her a hug. "Have confidence, Cassie. Gather your courage. You can do anything you set out to do if you have the right attitude. You might need my help, so I expect you to keep your phone on. I put an extra battery in your pack, along with a flashlight and a couple of other things. Waterproof matches. They came in handy for me when I was there."

Cassie gawked at him. "You put all those things in my backpack because you thought I would go back?"

He laughed. "I had a sneaky suspicion you might change your mind about coming home."

"Why did you think that?"

He ruffled her hair. "You're a lot like your dad, you know. Draw me a map before you go back, and Daemon and I will come up with a battle plan for you. Keep your phone on and stay connected."

Search for the Wizard

When Cassie returned to the Realm, the air smelled fresher, cleaner; the scent of dew on the grass, wildflowers, bulrushes, and forest flavored the air in a way it hadn't before. She had gained a new life, as though she received an 'A' on her math exam or turned to a new chapter in her favorite book. A burden had been lifted from her shoulders, for she knew what she was doing this time, and this time she would make her father proud.

An experienced Realm traveler now, Cassie found her way to the forest without falling into the underground burrows. The sun was high, a dazzling ball of warmth. She couldn't wait to find her friends to tell them she had returned.

When she stepped into the shade of Bandene Forest, pine needles crunched under her feet, and though neither Silvio, Jovita, or the little people were where she had left them, she was certain they couldn't be far away.

The deeper into the forest she walked, the balmier the air became. Cassie stopped and took her canteen out of her pack. Sweat and dirt tickled her shoulders and her hair stuck to her neck. She sighed as she looked around, wondering if Silvio and his friends had taken refuge from the heat in a cool burrow underground.

She swallowed a gulp of water, sponged her head and unwrapped the sandwiches her father had packed. Peanut butter and raspberry jam. She took a bite and washed the morsel down with water. While she was eating, she heard the rumble of horses and saw a cloud of dust rising from the north. Who would ride in these woods but Valerio's men? She panicked and scrambled to the safety of a thimbleberry thicket, dragging her pack along with her.

When the dust settled, seven of Valerio's soldiers dismounted.

"Don't leave a rock unturned," one of them said to the others." With that order, the soldiers walked their horses slowly through the woods.

They kicked over rocks and stumps and mumbled profanities under their breath. Luckily for Cassie, they were headed away from where she hid.

"Where could the rascals have gone?" A soldier stopped, pulled off his helmet, and wiped the sweat from his brow.

"You know darn well they ran into the tunnels. Where else would they be?"

"If you're so sure they're in the burrows, why doesn't Valerio know?"

"He knows. He doesn't want any stragglers, Juan," another soldier laughed as he pulled out his canteen. "Besides, Valerio says this exercise is good for us. Keeps us healthy."

Juan spat on the ground. "From what he's making us go through, I'd say he wants us to hate the varmints. He ought to smoke them out of their holes."

"He will. I think he was hoping for a prisoner or two."

Juan mounted his horse again. "We've been gone long enough. That silver haired devil is nowhere to be found and neither are his mud rats. I vote we go home, and let Valerio burn the forest. He can shovel coals into the tunnels to drive them into our clutches."

"You're joking! What would we do with prisoners? I say roast them alive in their burrows and be rid of them." Leather saddles squeaked, and spurs chimed as the men mounted their horses. They rode through the woods toward Valerio's camp, talking casually, laughing occasionally.

Cassie must do so before the soldiers return. She pulled her cell phone from her pocket. "Dad."

"How's it going so far? Did you get your sandwiches?" Her father's voice was relaxed.

"Dad, I haven't found Silvio yet, but some of Valerio's troops rode by and I overheard their conversation. They say they're going to burn the forest and smoke Silvio and the Xylonites out of the burrows."

There was silence on the other end.

"Did you hear me?" Cassie asked.

"They mean business. Cassie, find Silvio. Warn him. Lead Silvio and the Xylonites to the edge of the woods near Alisubbo so they can join forces with any troops you can round up from the city. They should be close enough to the sea there if they need to escape a fire."

"I don't know where Silvio is."

"I realize that. You've only been in the Realm for forty-five minutes. Don't panic. You'll find him. Come on babe, have confidence. It isn't going to be easy. You'll have to get tough! But you've done it before. You were strong when the king was assassinated. Just remember why you're there."

"Dad!"

"Princess, what do you want me to do?"

She thought for a moment. I want you here. But no. This was her responsibility.

"You're right. I can do this! We'll talk later."

She lifted her backpack on her shoulders again, wondering why she had even called her father. She was fine. She had food, water, a cell phone, and her Dad's confidence. There was shade in the forest where she could avoid the heat. An occasional fly sped by her nose, and she had to swat a mosquito or two, but otherwise the walk was enchanting. Trilliums dotted the forest floor, ferns played strobe light with the sun.

She stopped occasionally to catch her breath, or glance up at the blue sky and the tips of the firs that now swayed in an afternoon breeze, or to peek around the corner of a stump in search of the chattering squirrel.

"Where is Silvio?" she asked the little creature that scooted in front of her. His black eyes were wide and alert. Cassie laughed. "Ok, never mind. Squirrels don't talk."

The animal raced up the trunk of a cedar tree and disappeared.

It was then she saw a set of small blue eyes hiding amongst the ferns. She paused, still like a stone, and watched. The eyes didn't move. At last, she whispered.

"Please find Silvio and tell him Princess Cassandra has changed her mind and she's come to find the king. Please hurry. We don't have much time. I'll wait here for your answer."

The eyes disappeared.

Cassandra sat on a rock and waited. She opened her backpack and took out the remaining sandwich, but froze when a cold metal object slid across her shoulder.

"You!" a man said.

Cassie dropped her lunch. The saber's blade, the glint of its golden guard, the dark leather glove of its bearer slowly circling in front of her, held her motionless. An intimidating character, his blue eyes framed with a leather mask all but covered his face. Cloaked in a leather tunic, linen pants tucked into knee-high moccasins, and around his waist an arsenal of weapons; daggers, fighting knives in sheaths, and a pistol. A black cloak draped his shoulders, and a hood covered his hair.

He stopped circling her once he was in full view. His blade was now at her throat.

"Who are you?" she asked.

A muffled laugh came from behind his disguise. "I get to ask the questions little miss, being as I hold the edge. And since I already know who you are, we'll skip the introductions."

"I don't know you," Cassie didn't mean for her voice to shake, but the point of his sword was now pressed tight against her neck.

"Good!" He grinned. "So, tell me why you're in these woods."

"My name is Cassandra Wilson, Princess of Alcove Forest."

The point of his blade lifted her chin as it slid up her throat.

"Princess? Is it? Isn't that sweet?"

She swallowed; the sword now pinched her skin. Any closer and she'd be bleeding.

"Why would I be impressed that you're a princess?" he asked.

"I'm not sure you would."

"It doesn't. Besides, I know that you're lying."

"I'm not."

"No? What sort of princess would visit a rebel camp and turn against a king?"

"I... well, that was a mistake."

He pushed the point deeper into her flesh and Cassie winced as it pierced her skin. She felt a tiny flow of warm liquid trickle down her neck. If she moved, she'd be dead.

"Ah! A mistake? Now we're coming to an agreement," he said.

So, he's not one of Valerio's men. Then who is he?

"Please. I can explain. I'm friends of the king, really, I am. Put down your weapon so we can talk."

The man held his sword unwavering. "I don't believe you are friends with the king. I believe you'll say whatever you think I want to hear to save your skin."

"You're wrong. I'm telling the truth. I made a mistake, but I learned my lesson. Whatever I've done in the past, I won't do anymore. I have come to help Martim," she said, trembling. "I'm waiting for Silvio to call for me. Honest. I'm not a spy or an enemy or one of Valerio's pawns. Honest!" It was getting harder to talk. The pressure of the blade pressed against her throat. "Please don't kill me."

"The king is dead."

"I know." Cassie trembled. She was defenseless against this man. One wrong move and her life could be over. "I'm supposed to bring Martim back to Alisubbo to reclaim his father's throne."

The sword inched deeper; the blood flowed faster. "You lie. I should kill you and be done with you."

"Take me to Silvio. He'll tell you I'm not lying."

"Come now!" A Xylonite interrupted the two, waving from behind the ferns.

The man slowly withdrew his sword and returned it to its sheath, pulling a dagger and a cloth from his belt. He tossed the linen at Cassie. She held the rag to her neck to stop the bleeding.

"Follow him."

"This way," the little soldier said.

With one hand still dressing her wound, she grabbed her pack and swung it over her shoulder. She stumbled over the fern bushes as she tried to keep up with the light-footed Xylonite and hold the cloth to her neck at the same time. The man trailed her, and every few steps she felt the tip of his dagger at her back.

When the Xylonite halted at a hole under a cedar root, she hesitated. "Is Silvio in there?"

No one answered. The Xylonite jumped into the hole and disappeared.

"See for yourself," the masked man said.

She gave him a dirty look before she slid into the burrow. The hole wasn't high enough for her to stand up in, so she ducked to get through the passage. Had she waited a second longer, she would have lost her guide, for the Xylonite rushed away through a tunnel that veered around a corner. The masked man nudged her, and stayed close as a shadow, the edge of his blade at her waist.

"Your Majesty!" the Xylonite exclaimed when they came to a room carved into the earth and lit by a candle. Two chairs twisted from willow branches, a rug woven from bulrushes, and a log table furnished the chamber.

"He does a good job, doesn't he?" Silvio grunted from the shadows and gestured toward Cassie's captor.

"Who? This masked man?" Glad that Silvio was at least talking to her, Cassie dropped her shoulders and breathed. Silvio's chamber was lofty enough for her to stand.

"He's scaring the living daylights out of me! Call him off!"

"Call him off? Blastbonkers, I'll not call him off. This one's my bodyguard, presented to me by the Gitanos! He's doing exactly what he's supposed to do. Good work!" he added to the masked man.

"You shouldn't be talking to her, Silvio. She's an insurgent," The bodyguard said. "She was in Valerio's camp before the coup. Give me the word and I'll dispose of her."

"Dispose of me?" Cassie looked over her shoulder. When he pulled his mask off, she huffed. He was none other than Eduardo, the man Valerio had arrested the night she arrived in the Realm.

"Oh, my gosh! You're the red-headed spy at Valerio's camp! That explains everything!"

"A spy for the king!" he retorted as he shook off his hood, releasing his red hair. "Jimmy Rutherford's the name! And proud to be a king's man! The question is, who are you a spy for?"

"I'm not a spy. I was at Valerio's camp, but I only ended up there by mistake. I'm not a rebel. I volunteer to persuade King Martim to return to Alisubbo at Silvio's request."

She turned to the wizard. "Tell him it's so Silvio."

Silvio grunted.

"Silvio!"

"Bah. What good are you? You left. Deserted us. Far as I'm concerned, you are a spy," Silvio glared, green magic emitting from his eyes.

"That's not true, Silvio. You know I'm not a spy. I only left you because I thought there was nothing I could do to help."

"Nothing? There probably isn't anything you can do, you sorry excuse for a princess."

Jimmy grabbed Cassie's arm and pressed his dagger against her back. "Give me the word."

"You'd do that?" Cassie asked, wild with rage and fear both. "You'd let him kill me, Silvio?"

The old wizard waved Jimmy back with his hand.

"Not kill, too messy. No. Could use a moral lesson, maybe."

"What sort of lesson?" Cassie said.

"Think about it, Silvio," Jimmy said. "Don't act rashly and don't feel sorry for her. If she's a spy and if I let her go, she could do even more damage. If that happens, my uncle will kill me."

Silvio bowed his head and shook it, his silver hair rippling like wind in the grass.

"Spy? No telling what she is. Bah! Stumbled into my tunnel, turned her nose up at my dinner. Went clambering through the bramble after that Bushbungler Valerio."

Jimmy grabbed her arm again.

"Silvio, please have a heart. You even admitted that I rescued Xylepher from the tunnels."

Silvio looked up, his green eyes wide with surprise. "That's it. You did. And then Xylepher asked you to get the king from exile and you wouldn't."

"I had to go home first."

He scowled. "Why?"

"I had to talk to my dad. I've come back now to help. I promise." She struggled against Jimmy's hold. "That is if you'll call this brute off of me."

Silvio waved again. "Bah. Let it go."

Jimmy released her, reluctantly returning his blade to his belt.

"Thank you!" Cassie said.

"Do you need my help anymore, Silvio?" Jimmy asked with a tone of annoyance. "Because I'm supposed to rendezvous with Geno this evening."

"No." Silvio waddled into his dark corner and mumbled. "Go on. Everyone go! Leave me alone. Go do your business."

"Send a Xylonite if you need me," Jimmy turned to the entryway, but not without first giving Cassie an accusing glare. "Just so you know, you haven't proven your innocence to me. If you turn out to be a traitor to the throne, I will kill you. And that's a promise!"

Speechless, Cassie watched him crawl out of the hole. "How many of those guys do you have?" she asked Silvio when he was gone.

"Why should I tell you, eh?" Silvio looked at her with those big green eyes of his. The lantern light in the burrow glowed on his face and cast an eerie shadow. "Give me a reason to trust you?" he said. "You abandoned us."

"Oh, come on Silvio. I wasn't gone for more than a few hours. Besides, you need me. Valerio and his men are swarming all over the woods right now. They're talking about burning the forest and smoking your tunnels to drive you out in the open or cook you alive inside them."

He stared at her, as frozen as an old tree trunk dying in the woods.

"I saw my Dad when I went home. He gave me instructions on how to help. I'm to lead you and your troops. He said to gather everyone, Xylepher, the Xylonites, everyone, and travel to the end of the forest, around the city of Alisubbo."

"Burn the forest?" Silvio stood, petrified.

"Wait for me there and I'll go into the city and find recruits to fight with us and I'll send them to you. And then I'll find Martim and ask him to lead us."

The old conjurer didn't blink. The eerie light still cast its shadow, and the green eyes still stared.

"Silvio, wake up. We need to go, and we need to go now!"

"Do you know what that means? Burning the forest? It is the doom."

"No, it isn't. We'll try to stop him before that happens."

"You cannot stop him. How? Who's going to fight him?" he finally asked.

"There will be an army."

Silvio glanced toward the ground behind her where several of Xylepher's soldiers stood. "Go get your men," he ordered.

"But the stampede?" they whimpered.

"Go."

They ran.

Silvio called out after them, "On mounts, and head for Alisubbo, but don't leave the woods."

"Yes sir, yes, sir."

"Scared they are. Attacked by soldiers not long after you left. We ran, or they did rather. These old knees won't move like that anymore. The Xylonites scattered everywhere. It wasn't easy finding everyone. It's too hard. I'm done." He cowered closer to the wall. "I'm retired."

"Retired? Well, I have my faults, too. But in these circumstances, I will not let my faults be obstacles."

The tunnel filled with Xylonites and prairie dogs pushing their way out of the crawlspaces that intercepted Silvio's chamber. The musky smell of the varmints was so thick that Cassie gasped for air. "We need to go. Now." She reached for the ledge above and climbed out of the hole onto the forest floor. "Are you coming Silvio?"

His head bobbed above the horde of Xylonites who were also climbing out of the hole, scurrying for hiding places in the forest. Miniature men, women and children dressed in green. The little ones climbed on the shoulders of the taller ones, while everyone jumped and shimmied up the sides of the dirt walls. After them came a Cavalry of mounted soldiers. The prairie dogs charged through the opening, forcing Cassie aside. When the Xylonites vanished into the woods, she peeked back down into the hole. Silvio combed his beard with his hands and shuffled across the room. He trembled and for a second, Cassie felt sorry for him. She waited, thinking maybe he was looking for his pack or something.

"What're you doing? Let's go."

He glanced around and shook his head. "I'm retired. I'm not doing this."

"Silvio!" Cassie sighed. "Xylepher and his troops are well ahead of us already. If we don't catch up, they won't have a leader. Plus, we need the help of everyone you know. Even those…" she hesitated at the thought of being on the same side of the war as the redhead. "Even those masked men however many there are."

"Do it then."

"Silvio, we need you. You're the king."

"You don't understand. The king is dead. It's the end. The doom. My magic was stolen so consider it over. No more king of the Xylonites. Silvio will die now."

"Not true! You used your magic on me!"

Silvio snickered and shook his hand at her. "That thing I did with your clothes? Elementary. That was no magic."

"It was a lot more magic than I've ever seen. What about the green that seeps out of your eyes? What's that?"

"Remnants. That's all. Now leave me alone."

"Your remnants may be more powerful than you think. Even a trace of magic would be of use. I won't leave you alone. We need you. It's nobody's end, no one's doom. There's hope for us. You have the blessing of King Ian Wilson. I bring it to you personally."

Light from the sun behind her threw warm rays on his wrinkled face, revealing a tiny tear that slid down his cheek.

"A blessing? From King Ian?" he asked with a quivering voice.

"The very one. His Royal Majesty." She reached out her hand. "Come on Silvio, it's not that bad. We can do this. We can bring Martim back to Alisubbo and restore the throne. We can drive Valerio and his rebels out of this land forever."

"We can?"

"We not only can, but we will."

"You won't run away again?"

"You have my word."

OUT OF THE WOODS

C'mon Silvio!" The Xylonites traveled twice as fast as Silvio and Cassie. Already they were well out of her sight. She worried what the little people would do once they reached the end of the woods; if they'd get lost, or worse, if Valerio would find them. Still, there was no way Silvio could keep up, and she couldn't leave him behind. The crippled old man was less than his spirited self. His crooked form waddled from side to side as he stepped cautiously over logs and carefully maneuvered around boulders. As if he had that sort of time to spare! Cassie wanted to run.

"They're most likely in Alisubbo by now," she complained.

"Who?"

"Everybody! Xylepher, all your men, the prairie dogs."

Silvio let out a disgusted grunt. "Let them go. More suited for the city than you are!"

"What do you mean?"

"You can't go into Alisubbo looking like that," he said.

"You are not putting a skirt on me again!"

"You look like a court jester in that outfit."

"I do not. People in my world wear these kinds of clothes all the time."

"Whose world are you in now?"

"It doesn't matter. I can't move around in a skirt. It's too cumbersome. If it makes you feel better, I'll pretend I'm a boy."

Silvio stopped and looked at her, his mouth puckered.

"Don't you dare," Cassie warned. "Look, let's make a deal. I'll let you put a tunic over my clothes. No skirt. I'll keep my blue jeans and my sneakers. Sort of like a modern-day Robin Hood. But you must promise to return my T-shirt when it's time to go home. This is my favorite T."

He started mumbling odd words; phrases that were even more peculiar than his occasional expletive. Surely, he was casting a spell.

"You can even put tulips on the hem... Silvio!"

Green dust spiraled out of his eyes and instantly wrapped around Cassie. When the dust settled, she had a lightweight tunic tied with a belt and sheath, no tulips. Her blue jeans and sneakers were still intact. He nodded a smug little smile and walked on.

"Thanks Silvio," Cassie said. "And this empty sheath? What's this?"

"Might need it."

"Need what?"

"The saber. It's special. Went through many battles. More than you can ever imagine. Bah, you, of all people. Why should you get it?"

"What?" Cassie asked again, but gasped when the sheath filled with glowing green dust that twirled powerfully until a saber materialized. Cassie took hold of the guard. It was as real as any sword she had ever touched.

"You might need it. Don't use it unless you need it."

"Okay."

"Used to be my father's. Been in some terrible battles. Terrible. Lost it for a long time. Xylonites found it for me." The old conjurer turned his back to Cassie. "You do not know who I am," he grumbled as she walked alongside him.

"No, I don't, and I admit it was mean for me to leave the night you were going to tell me. I would love to hear your stories, Silvio."

"Well, are you ready to listen now?"

"I am."

He shot her a suspicious look.

"I'm ready to hear everything you want to tell me. I would love to know more about wizards. My father was curious to know more about you, too. Besides, we have something in common."

"Bah!"

"We're on the same side of the war, aren't we?"

He grunted. "Are we?"

Cassie scowled, uncertain what he meant. He couldn't possibly still think of her as a traitor, could he?

As they walked deeper into the woods, the forest darkened. Trees reached above their heads, long swooping branches, and huge red trunks hid the sky. The sword ferns they had passed earlier gave way to mosses, and vines that crawled along the forest floor clung to everything in its path. Thick lichen hung in shreds from fallen limbs, and dainty white flowers laced the ground. A cool air filled her lungs; there was a salty tang to it.

"We're near the sea, aren't we?" she asked. Silvio grunted again.

Cassie eyed the Xylonites up ahead, standing still as statues at the end of the woods. When she came to the overlook, she understood why. The magnificence of the vista took her breath away. Sea gulls called out over the turquoise waters. Spray from the waves crashed against the bluff below and cooled her face. To her right were the cliffs of Alisubbo.

"Out there," Silvio's skinny, crooked arm reached out, and his knotty fingers pointed to a purple landmass on the horizon. "That's where I once lived. Taikus is the name of that island; after the first ruler. A great wizard, he was." Silvio's lips quivered. Maybe the spray in the breeze dampened his face or it might have been tears from a longing in his heart.

"It's dear to you." Cassie stated, assuming she read his thoughts.

"Dear? Bah! A shattered rock in the water." He faced her with a wicked frown. "Shattered I say. The ocean should swallow it, I say. Evil." He leaned closer to her. "Evil."

"Well, I guess that's why you aren't there anymore."

"Better to never have been born, then to be from there."

Cassie studied Silvio's grimace as he looked out across the ocean. His melancholy spooked her. He was usually grumpy, but she'd never seen him as despondent as he'd been today. Valerio's war may have frightened him. But as they gazed out across the water, to the island the wizard called Taikus, Cassie wondered what tragic story lay behind those eyes of his.

"Do you want to talk about it?" she asked, willing to console.

The sea pounded against the bluff, and a lone seal barked. Silvio shook his hair. "What good would talk do? It took half of my life away. More, even. It's gone now, my youth. I was never young like you. Those years were robbed from me." He gave her that eye and she shuddered. "Old, always. Like a tree. Like the old cedar tree. Because of a burning forest. That's why."

That explained his terror. Cassie understood now. "I'm sorry that so much trauma happened to you. At least you got away from the island."

"Got away? From there? Bah, what do you know? Got away? I never got away. It came with me. It's here, now, standing next to you." He faced her with that piercing look of his. "The sword from a spoon, the clothes from my eyes, it's all Taikus. And it's here with me. I'm retired, I tell you. I've done this for too long. Shouldn't have brought it with me. Should have left the devils to fight their own war." He looked out into the distance again, his eyes traveling as far as the horizon. "Their war without end. They don't die, not there. They hate forever. And they have my soul, the king does."

"The king of Taikus has something of yours?"

Silvio nodded.

"Maybe we can get it back, if it's that dear to you."

He glanced at her. "You don't get back what they steal."

"Things can change."

He grunted. Cassie was determined to pull him out of his gloom. "Look, you survived. You don't live there anymore, even if you lost your youth. You should tell me what happened. Maybe I can help. Maybe my dad can help." Cassie suggested.

He let a long moment of silence pass, and then he bowed his head. "My mother sent me away, in a skiff with three friends. Tried to save me from Hacatine. Bah. There was no saving me. No saving any of us. Bandene beach was as far as we got and then the ocean swallowed up my friends. Two of them anyway. The other walked away. My mother shouldn't have sent the magic with me. I would have been better off. She would have been better off. You would have, everyone."

"Did you ever see your friends again?"

He shook his head. "I was afraid. I ran. That wicked queen fused me into a tree. That old cedar fed me. Kept me alive. For too many years I lived in the branches, the bark, and lichen. I saw it all, everything that happened in Alcove Forest. I saw your grandpa and your dad when he was your age."

"You did?"

"Until the night your father came to fight. Then the magic happened. Children held the power in their hands. Kaempie's power. I recognized him, his spirit."

"Kaempie?"

"My friend. The older one. And then I fell out of that old stump. That's what it did. My dear friend's magic released me."

Cassie was speechless. Her father had told her he had seen a strange old man appear from the stump they used as a cache for their armor the night he rescued her mom. But he never went into detail. "Then it was you my dad saw."

"Looked right at him. Saw right into his eyes and then he lowered his bow."

Silvio shuddered so hard even his hair trembled. "Your father, the king, left the day the dragon tore out of here and nearly took Alcove Forest with him. But it wasn't the end. More like the beginning. The pirates came back. Slaves they made of the Xylonites. Wrenched my heart to see it. Bah, you think the little people could take care of themselves. Eh?" He glared at her.

"Not hardly," she answered.

"Not hardly," he repeated cynically. "Not hardly? Ha! I snuck aboard their stinking ships. I freed the little ones with my magic. Made them tunnels to hide in. Then your father returned, got in trouble, nearly got killed. Me and the old Magic Thief had to save him. And there you stand talking to me about your father fixing things? Bah. Not even the greatest magic can save our world now. No. We're doomed. It's the end. It's done now. It's over. I'm retired. I won't do that anymore. It turns ugly. Don't ask me."

"The magic turns ugly. Is that what you mean?"

He pivoted around and waddled back into the forest.

"I need to go into Alisubbo tonight," she said, following him until he sat on a log. Xylepher stepped into view. Everyone was with them, camouflaged in the bushes, and resting.

"Do it then."

"From there, I'm supposed to find the king." Cassie cleared her throat. "You're being kind of difficult, you know." She set her backpack down and put her hands on her hips.

He grunted.

"I don't know where the king is," Cassie explained.

"Then how will you find him?" Silvio asked, drawing on the ground with a stick.

"You're supposed to tell me."

"Don't know. Don't know where he is. The island most like."

"Taikus?"

"Pfft. Taikus. No, not Taikus. Refuge. The Isle of Refuge. That's where they go when they're running."

"OK. So where is this Isle of Refuge?"

He nodded. "Everyone knows the Isle of Refuge." He pointed toward Alisubbo. "It's out that way. Past the city. In the water."

She looked where he had showed, but only saw rooftops peeking through trees. "What about a boat?"

Silvio squinted at her. "I don't have a boat."

"Can you make one for me?"

"What? Use my magic?"

"Well, yes," she said.

"Listen, will you? I said I'm retired."

"I heard you. But that doesn't help our mission. I guess I'll have to give up asking." Cassie wanted to slap him.

"I guess you will," he retorted.

"And then nothing will be done. Your homes will be destroyed;

Valerio will be your king, and me? I'll go home."

He grimaced, but by the slump of his crooked shoulders, Cassie realized he had given up.

"He'll burn the forest, you know. Tonight," she added.

His lower lip quivered.

"Do you have any other place you can live? There must be someplace." Cassie said.

The only answer he gave was the dubiety in his eyes. He tossed the stick and hunched over, hugging his arms and rocking on the stump.

Cassie picked up her backpack and stepped well away from Silvio's pouting figure. She wasn't sure what to do, except to continue her plan to find Martim. Maybe someone in town knew where he was. Whatever her options, she needed to get away from Silvio or else her own mood would fall into the same miserable pit of discouragement as his. The Realm's fate weighed on her shoulders. She needed to stay strong.

Cassie pulled her phone from her pocket and hit redial. Her father would give her the encouragement she needed.

"Cass?" the voice on the other end inquired.

"Dad?"

"Daemon."

"Where's Dad?"

"Your Dad went home. This is my cell."

Cassie looked at her screen. She'd been redialing Daemon's phone when she thought she'd been calling her father's.

"What's up? Are you okay?" Daemon's voice was gentle, like her dad's had been.

"Yeah." She hesitated, not sure if she wanted to tell Daemon her troubles. She heard a noise in the background. "Are you playing a video game?"

"Yeah."

Cassie sighed.

"Go ahead, I can talk," he said.

"Things are not going as planned. Silvio isn't giving me very good directions on where Martim might be. He says an island somewhere. He says everyone knows where it is and then he points toward the ocean. Duh, like I couldn't have figured out the island was in the ocean."

She waited for Daemon to finish shooting zombies on his big screen TV.

"Well, someone in Alisubbo might know where it is," he replied after a few moments.

Cassie was quiet. Maybe Angelique was back home, or maybe she could look up Carmen and her family. They might help her.

"Yeah," she agreed. "Maybe someone else can get a boat for me, too. And maybe they can fight a war for me, too."

"Maybe."

Daemon was as much help as Silvio. She was about to hang up.

"Cassie."

"What?"

"Who do you have on your side? How many people?" he asked.

"People? I don't have people on my side. I have computer characters about the size of a Chinese string bean on my side. I have a crooked old Conjurer and... oh, yeah, the feisty Foreigner who hates me. I guess he's kind of like people. Except I'm not so sure I'd want to run into him again. Yeah, he's on my side. Behind my back, even, ready to stab me."

"Foreigner?"

"A masked man who's really a red-headed punk dressed in leather and carrying a saber that he's too careless to be wielding! He cut me, like you even care."

Daemon laughed. "Masked, like Zorro?"

"No. Like a zombie."

Silence.

"Okay, like Zorro," she said, wishing she could get his full attention.

"Cool."

"Thanks Daemon. Talk with you later, if I survive."

"Wait. What are you going to do?"

"I'm going to rescue the king. What do you think?"

"How?"

"How should I know?"

"I'll call your dad."

"Thanks, Daemon. You're a lot of help, but I can call him myself."

"Cheer up, Cassie. It's going to work out," Daemon said.

"Whatever. Watch out for the zombies. They might get you."

"Not a chance. I've beaten this game three times already."

"Good for you." Cassie hit the 'end' button on her phone. "You're a zombie, Daemon!" She dialed her dad's cell. It was busy.

Once she tucked her phone away and zipped her pack shut, she threw it over her shoulders. Glancing at the frightened eyes of the little people, she turned down the dusty trail leading to Alisubbo.

She had wasted too much time in Bandene forest. The sun was setting, and Alisubbo was still a great distance away. She liked the idea of finding Carmen, however after dark it would be more difficult than in the daylight. Banging on people's doors in a city under siege was not something she looked forward to. Even less asking about an exiled king when she had never established trust. She hadn't forgotten that it was Deniz, Carmen's brother, who saw her with a gun when guns were outlawed. Not to mention her photograph with Valerio's arm around her plastered on the front page of the Daily Gazette!

The trail meandered in and out of the forest on the ridge of a mountain. There were several clearings along the way where Cassie could look out over a vista of the ocean and beyond. After that, the passage dove into the deepest part of the woods.

The shadows danced like ghosts, haunting the encroaching night, making the woods unnerving. She kept her eyes glued ahead of her and finally, after hearing unfamiliar sounds in the brambles, she broke into a jog.

She came to the last overlook in time to watch the sun slip below the horizon. From here, the trail wound inland. A dark twilight crept over the earth, making her entry into the thicket more treacherous than before. She stopped briefly to pull the flashlight from her pack. Her heart raced. One more call to her dad might help calm her nerves. No one answered.

"Be tough, Cassie," she repeated her father's words as she bounced the backpack in place and adjusted the saber Silvio had given her. She shone the flashlight into the thicket at every snap of a pinecone or rush of a bird. The nocturnal wilderness had come alive. And what that meant for her, she tried not to imagine.

An owl hooted from the trees, and then another. Bats charged from nowhere, almost colliding with her head. Glowing eyes disappeared into the brush, and they were not the eyes of Xylonites.

"They might be raccoons," Cassie said to herself, hoping that the sound of her voice would intimidate any real predators. But as she stumbled over roots and dodged branches that hindered her passage, a musky scent engulfed her. The scent of animals. She moved faster, having the uncanny sense that something or someone followed. She looked over her shoulder, but she could see nothing in the dark.

The trail turned sharply to the right and descended into a steep passage surrounded by thick brush. She hurried. Fear and gravity moved her. To her left, she saw two dark figures from behind the trees. They kept pace with her. She broke into a run. Her white sneakers barely touched the ground in flight, but the hunters followed and matched her speed. In her haste and panic, she tripped and slid down the hill. She swung her arms over her head to protect herself as she fell. When she landed on her face in a thicket, her nose hit against the roots of an old tree. Her heart raced. She waited for the thrust of a weapon. None came. With her head buried in the dirt, she held her breath. Someone kicked her legs.

"Get up," he said.

Cassie brushed the hair from her eyes and blinked the dirt off her lashes.

"That's her, Geno," another man said. Cassie recognized the voice. Jimmy! Not him again!

"This one?" Geno pushed her toes with his foot. "She's the one you saw with the Commando?" He was heavier than the others and wore beads in his hair. His face was masked, his eyes dark. He didn't wear a cloak. His shirt was opened in front and strings of beads rattled against his chest. Besides his saber, two knives and a machete were tucked into his belt.

"Why are you stalking me?" Cassie sat up.

Jimmy snickered and pulled his mask off. "Where do you think you're going, traitor?"

"I'm going to Alisubbo, and I'm not a traitor."

"You're not going anywhere," Geno snapped, drawing a dagger from his belt.

"What's this?" Dreadlocks with his foul breath came from behind the two. "You're venturing into the city at this hour? Alone." The man laughed. His smile shone in the dark.

"I am." Cassie scrambled to her feet, resting her hand on the hilt of Silvio's saber. The gesture drew a chuckle from the Geno. She frowned.

"If you had any idea where I got this you'd mind your manners," she warned.

"That's Silvio's sword!" Jimmy said. "How did you get it?"

"He gave it to me."

"Ah, then you must be special, eh? To carry a magic sword! What do you think, Elias? Eh?" Geno asked.

"Very special," the man with the dreadlocks reached out to touch her cheek.

She slapped him, causing his smile to broaden.

"As much as it pains me, I'm on the same side you're on, so keep your evil thoughts to yourself." Cassie said.

"Are you?" Jimmy asked. "Prove it. And settle your debt."

"What are you saying? What debt?"

"The bridge."

Cassie's mouth dropped. "What?"

"Pointe de Tratado."

"I do not know what you're talking about."

Jimmy pushed past Elias and moved close to her. His smell was of leather. Dirt scattered over his freckles, but the color of his eyes was crystal clear. "You aren't under the wings of Silvio now, lady. So now you can answer some tough questions. If you're an ally, then why did you blow my cover at Valerio's camp? Valerio's men followed me and bombed the bridge. If they hadn't, we would have arrived in Alisubbo in time to save the life of King Chavez. So, you're either a liar or a fool. Which is it?"

"I didn't know," she whispered, swallowing her tears. "I was a fool."

Jimmy set his jaw, nodding ever so slightly. "So, what dumb mistake are you going to make tonight?" he asked.

"None. I hope. I'm supposed to find King Martim and ask him to come back."

"By yourself? That's stupid."

"Well, there isn't anyone here offering to help me."

"Hey Geno, do you want to help the little miss?" Elias asked.

Geno laughed. "Let's help her get to where she needs to go, yes."

Jimmy's gaze was set on Cassie. She stared back at him.

"Leave her alone," he said, turning to the others. "Whitefox said no personal vendettas. Let's not spoil the siege." He turned back to her. "I don't trust you. You're slime. If it weren't that you have Silvio's sword, I wouldn't be walking away right now. You know that don't you?"

She nodded.

"You had better not foul up this mission."

"Yes, I know," she choked on the words.

Jimmy turned away from her. "Let's go."

"You're leaving? I mean, can you at least tell me where Martim might be?"

"Check the Rockwall Castle," Geno said.

"Which is where?"

"The Isle of Refuge, our home. It's always been a haven for exiled royalty," Jimmy answered.

Cassie snickered. "Well, if he's hanging out at your place, why don't you ask him to come back?"

Jimmy shook his head. "We aren't there, for one. For another, someone must muster an army." He sneered. "You'd better come back with a king. My threat holds true."

"Yes, sir!" Cassie whispered as she watched them walk away.

THE REPUBLIC OF TYRANNY

The trailhead from the woods ended where an alley in Alisubbo began. Certain she could find her way to the chapel by keeping her eye on the tower, she adjusted her pack, fixed her sheath around her waist and began her walk.

Several soldiers crossed her path, but she leaned near to the wall and kept in the crevices and corners of dark buildings to avoid being seen. She was hidden well until a dog caught her scent. He charged at her, his ears stretched back, his teeth bared. He barked. She tried hushing him, but he scrambled back and forth in front of her, growling and yapping in a horrible fit. A door from across the way opened and called the animal and he left. Cassie slipped around the corner to avoid a confrontation. She inched her way down the hill to the main cobblestone road Sister Ann had taken her the day she first arrived in the city.

The night was quiet; the village hushed. The moon shone on the street as bright as day. Square de Regem was in full view. The mounted soldier statue proudly sparkled under the stars, and the unseen ocean beat its constant rumble as background music. The chapel was easy to see, and Cassie meandered through the street toward it, but as she neared, she noticed the door off its hinges and one of its walls damaged.

There was no need to go there. From the broken window, and debris outside, the chapel had clearly been abandoned. Instead, she crossed the street and skulked up the rickety steps to Carmen's apartment. Not knowing which door belonged to the family, she tapped gently on the center door and heard feet running about inside the apartment to her left. Cassie knocked on that door, and when there was no answer, she knocked again.

"Who is it?"

"Cassie," she whispered. When there was no response, she said, "Princess Cassandra."

She heard a chain unlatch and immediately Carmen opened the door, grabbed her arm, and pulled her inside.

"You returned!" the girl gasped. Her sisters and brothers peeked out from the bedroom. Carmen shooed them back. "What are you doing here? Do you know how dangerous it is to be out past curfew?"

Carmen led Cassie past the table and stove into a small room lit by candlelight. Several adults sat on chairs, and Deniz stood behind them. There was no couch. The room had the stench of a building that housed too many people for too long; a warm, rotting odor mixed with the smell of wax burning. The windows were covered with blankets.

Bedding was sprawled across the floor, but the children were hardly settled down except for the toddler, Marques, who lay asleep.

Carmen spoke to her mother in another language. The woman smiled and nodded, addressing Cassie with a thick accent. "Pleased to meet you," she said.

"Her name's Maria," Carmen told Cassie.

Cassie nodded a greeting and then the mother's smile disappeared. "Carmen calls you a friend, but you are the girl in the photo with Valerio. What do I believe?"

"Mama," Carmen protested.

"No, it's fine," Cassie told the girl. "I made a foolish mistake. He lied to me, and I believed him, but I have since seen my error and have returned to make things right."

There was a long silence. Deniz took a seat next to his mother and the look on his face softened. Cassie hoped they would believe her.

"I trust you," Carmen said. "I don't trust Valerio or the men who write that paper."

Carmen's mother nodded. "It's good," she said. "It's risky for you to be here. Don't you know they will take you away like they did the nuns?"

"They've arrested the nuns? Sister Ann?"

Carmen nodded. "Sister Ann, Sister Bernadice. The priest. All the nurses."

Cassie's heart leaped into her throat. Those poor people! This news brought even more urgency to Cassie's mission.

"I've come back to find recruits. Are there any men or women you or your mother know who would fight? There's an army congregating, and they need recruits."

"Two men were here the other night. They asked the same thing."

"Two men? Who?"

"One of them introduced himself as Whitefox. The other Jimmy."

"Jimmy?"

"Do you know them? My mother thought they might be spies."

"No, they aren't spies. They're allies of the king. Did they ask you to send volunteers to the woods?"

Carmen nodded.

"Good. That's good. I'm going to bring back His Majesty the King."

Carmen gasped again and clasped her mouth. "Prince Martim is still alive? There is hope, then? We need him. You know the children from the Sanatorium were all sent home?"

"No." Cassie. "I didn't know. I'm so sorry. That's horrible news, but I suspected that would happen."

"With the nuns gone there's no one to tend to the children and the old people. The plague has gotten worse. Mama keeps us inside so that we don't get sick." Carmen took Cassie's arm, "Come. I want to show you."

"No, Carmen, don't go out." Maria called her daughter as Carmen pulled Cassie out the door and onto the porch.

"Angelique lives here with her grandfather. I visit her every day. Come. She is asking for Queen Felicia, maybe you can talk to her and make her feel better."

Carmen knocked quietly on the door next to hers, and then opened it, pulling Cassie inside with her. The two walked past an old man who sat at a round table lit only by a flickering candle. "It's us, Grandpa." Carmen addressed him and rested her hand on his back. He nodded.

"He's blind," Carmen whispered in Cassie's ear.

They stepped into a small bedroom where the open window allowed the moon's rays to shine softly on a girl propped up on pillows. Cassie recognized Angelique. Even in the eerie glow of moonlight shining through the window, she appeared thinner and much paler than she had been at the hospital. Her dark hair stuck to her forehead in ringlets from the sweat that beaded on her brow.

"Carmen," the girl began, but her voice tapered into an uncontrollable cough.

Carmen sat on the child's bed. "Angelique, you remember Princess Cassandra?"

Angelique nodded, attempting to speak, but only able to release a series of hacks.

"You don't need to say anything," Cassie said. "Sit quietly."

"Where is Queen Felicia?" Angelique asked.

"I don't know yet, but I'm looking for her. When I find her, I'll tell her you're waiting to see her."

Angelique nodded and mouthed the words thank you as another

coughing spell took her breath away. Carmen rose and pulled a bottle from a drawer near her bed.

"Take this Angelique."

The medicine soothed Angelique's cough. Carmen helped her lie down and tucked the blankets around her chin. "We need help, Princess Cassandra," Carmen whispered.

"I know you do."

The two stepped quietly past the sleeping grandfather and walked outside.

"How do I get to the Isle of Refuge? Is it possible to get there before dawn? Do you know of any boats that I might use?"

Carmen shrugged. "Maybe the dinghies the fishers pull up on the beach. They'll let you use one if you tell them what you're doing."

"You're sure?"

Carmen nodded. "The king helped the anglers. He always paid extra for their catch. He helped all the working people to stay in business. No one knows how they'll make a living now. Don't fear the people who live on this side of the city. The ones who overthrew the Crown are not the poor. The rebels never go to Mass. They don't work with their hands either; they work with their mouths. Mama said so. They gossip and write lies in their newspapers. That's why we know the photograph was a lie about you. We've seen worse." Carmen whispered. "Wait!"

She ran into her house as Cassie lingered on the stairs. The girl returned with a paper sack.

"This is so you'll have something to eat on your trip. Now go quickly before the soldiers see you. Watch out. They patrol the streets all night long."

Cassie started down the stairs when Carmen called in a whisper to her, "Go that way." She pointed to an alley behind the chapel.

Following Carmen's direction, Cassie soon came to a sandy beach on which were scattered skiffs and rowboats turned upside down and on their sides.

Protecting the shoreline were rock piers protruding far into the sea, a breakwater Cassie presumed, creating a safe harbor for small vessels to moor, or beach. The shoreline was a campsite for anglers. Campfires sizzled with dying embers, the smoke from which hovered over the sleeping bodies that were strewn across the sand in among the boats.

Cassie took her sneakers and socks off and tucked them into her backpack. She placed the paper sack Carmen had given her in another compartment. As she meandered along the shore, she looked around for someone, anyone, who might be awake and keeping watch. Shadows and moonlight played tricks with her eyes, but she soon made out the form of a body rolled in a blanket near a pile of nets. Uncertain what sort of reception she'd receive, she held onto the hilt of her saber and shook the man awake.

"Sir," she said, quietly. "Excuse me, sir."

He sat up, a look of confusion on his face. He was a powerful man, his face gray in the moonlight. "What?" He rubbed his eyes.

"Please sir, I'm sorry for waking you. I need a boat. I'm a messenger for the Crown and I need to get to the Isle of Refuge immediately."

The man blinked and squinted at Cassie. "Pretty young lady, you are," he said. "Am I dreaming? You're not a mermaid, are you? What would you be needing a boat for?"

"No. I'm a person. I'm on my way to find the king."

"The King? Oh, dear lady the king is dead."

"No. The new king. Martim."

"Shh." His voice quieted. "Oh, my good heavens, it's true then? He's alive? You know where he is?"

"I think I do. I need a boat to find him. I also need someone to give me directions. I believe he is in exile on the Isle of Refuge."

The angler rubbed his ruffled hair and pointed. "The Isle? Nor', nor 'east from here. You'll be there before dawn if you row with the tide." He let his blanket fall to the ground and led Cassie to a small boat near the water. "This is my crabbing dinghy. I'll let you use it. Anything for the King. Will you both be coming back in it?"

"If we have to, yes." She hadn't given any thought how she was going to return.

"Well, don't worry about bringing the boat back if you find another way. Pull it past high water and I'll find it. You're going to fetch the king? He's going to liberate us from these liberators, I hope. Tell him to hurry. Alisubbo is in worse condition than it ever has been. That scoundrel has done more damage than a storm to an unsound craft on the open sea, and he's been in control for less than a week."

"I'll tell him. If you want to help the cause, there's an army forming south of town in the forest. They need recruits, so if there's anyone else you might round up, please do."

"Yes, ma'am." The man gave her a quick salute and helped her put the dinghy into the water. "She doesn't tip unless you stand up in her. Be careful disembarking. Blessings to you, and God be with you."

"Thanks." Cassie said, as he pushed the boat into the water.

THE ARMORY

Crawling through tall grass behind the castle's walls was difficult enough for Jimmy, but to avoid bullets in the process made it nearly impossible. Whitefox and the Gitanos had found the tunnel to the armory but had been spotted by Valerio's soldiers. A dusty battle ensued.

"Cover him, Geno!" Whitefox hollered from afar.

When a volley of gunfire resounded, Jimmy jumped up and rushed to the dugout, dancing over bullets as he tumbled into the hole and landed at Geno's feet. Explosions from the Gitano's rifle rung in his ears.

"Hey, Red," Geno greeted him. "It's about time you joined the party!"

"I had to find Silvio," Jimmy growled as he got up. "Heard tell Valerio was going to torch the forest."

"Even more reason to kill the man," Geno growled, his teeth barred.

Whitefox waved to Jimmy and then disappeared into the tunnel.

"You've been missing all the fun. This is what it's about, man!" Geno said, reloading his rifle and shooting another round. "Whoop! Look at them!" he laughed and wiped the dirt from his mouth with his sleeve. "I haven't had this much celebration since our raiding days."

Jimmy peeked his head out of the hole and whistled. Valerio's men had just dismounted and released their horses, sending them galloping through the fields. They now crawled in the grass opposite them but unlike the Gitanos, their plumed helmets gave them away.

Jimmy laughed. "What idiots."

"How many are out there now?" Elias asked.

"At least twenty. Ha! You'd think we were shooting turkeys with all those feathers they're wearing!"

"It's about time we use our skills in this war," Elias agreed as he ducked into the damp earth, his own gun empty. He ran to the other side of the tunnel, pried open the ammunition box and grabbed a couple of wooden cases filled with shells, tossing a new rifle to Geno. "Are you hitting anything?"

"Heck, I don't know. What difference does it make? Whitefox says it's not important." Geno emptied his gun, firing in rapid succession. Smoke filled the tunnel.

Jimmy coughed.

"Can you see Whitefox? What's he doing?" Geno asked, nodding toward the dark passageway. "Can you see anyone?"

"Digging. Jimmy, get down there with him. He calls for you!" Elias answered after peering into the tunnel. Shots from another section in the meadow drew their attention.

"Rondo broke ground, as planned!" Geno announced.

"Barbeno should pop up east of us soon. Keep shooting. Go, Jimmy!"

Elias maneuvered himself next to Geno and took aim. "Never mind Fox, I don't mind picking off a couple of those turkeys."

Jimmy left the Gitanos and raced down the dark tunnel, following the sound of picks and shovels. As soon as he reached his uncle and the Xylonites, Whitefox grabbed his arm.

"Hold still," he said. He lifted Xylepher onto Jimmy's shoulders.

"What?"

Whitefox guided Jimmy to a section of the tunnel where they had been digging.

"Just stand there."

Xylepher stabbed at the dirt above him with his shovel, rocking Jimmy's shoulders.

"Hey, watch it, you're poking me in the eye," Jimmy said, pushing Xylepher's foot out of his face.

"Whoa, there big guy, you're throwing me off balance," the Xylonite returned. He grabbed a bundle of thick red hair as he teetered.

"Ouch!" Jimmy complained.

Xylepher repositioned himself and tapped the shovel against the earth. A clod of dirt fell, landing on Jimmy's head and filtering into his eyes, his nose, and then his mouth.

Jimmy spat. "Man!"

"Okay, nephew, when they're done digging, you'll have to climb into that armory and work fast." Whitefox came up behind him, leading several other Boreals, powerful men, their shirts off, ready for work.

"Me? Why me?" Jimmy eyed the others. "Ow. Dang it, Xylepher, stop pulling my hair."

"You're the skinniest." Whitefox's smile spread across his face. "And none of these little guys can lift those crates."

"Well, what about those big guys standing next to you?"

Jimmy paid little attention to the Xylonites staring at him. Shirts unbuttoned, hair sticky with sweat, they had worked all morning digging strategic pits to shoot from to divert the enemy. Having raided one smaller cache already, the little people watched the last and most important excavation, the one that would take them into Valerio's main armory. Several of the little people bridled the prairie dogs. Soon, they'd all have to stampede out of the tunnels and race against the powerful magic of Silvio.

"I'd say you're the strongest too, but I'm not so sure you'd win at arm wrestling any of those Gitanos." Whitefox added.

"Which brings up the question of why they get to shoot guns, while I get to do acrobatics with a midget."

"Watch who you call a midget!" Xylepher complained, tapping him on the head with his shovel.

"You both want to see me suffer," Jimmy winced.

"We're all paying our dues, Jimmy. Our men have been tossing ammo boxes all day. I bet anyone of them would trade places with you."

Jimmy turned his head as well as he could and eyed the group of workers standing next to Whitefox.

"Really? Want to trade?" he asked. Their grins answered him.

"Steady," Xylepher complained. "Quit moving around. And don't look up. We're breaking through. A little more... Yes!" He thrust his shovel at the ceiling of the tunnel and a mass of dirt fell from above, covering Jimmy with black soil, stones, and bits of wooden debris. Whitefox and the others jumped away, laughing.

"We're there. Help me up. I'm going in." The little man said. "Lift me up!"

"Nope. Xylepher, Jimmy's going in. I need you to jump on that prairie dog of yours and ride. Get out of these tunnels and tell Silvio we're ready. By the time you deliver the message, we'll have the boxes stacked."

"Drat it then, all right. C'mon guys." Xylepher said, jumping to the ground. He waved to his troops, who were already mounted. "We did good. The mining is over. Let's ride!"

Jimmy shook the dirt out of his hair and shirt, stepping away as the pack of prairie dogs and their riders headed for camp.

Everything was working perfectly. Whitefox slapped Jimmy gently on the back. "Get up there. We need to work fast."

Jimmy had never seen the building from the inside before. The abandoned adobe structure rested near the eastern border of the square. Ivy covering the outside kept it well hidden from public view. Valerio had been using this room as a cache for his armory. Xylepher discovered the hideout on his espionage excursion the night before. Luckily for the royalists, it was accessible through Silvio's tunnels.

"Hurry Jimmy," Whitefox whispered.

He could hear gunfire from inside the building much clearer than underground. A bullet even nicked the wall. Jimmy ducked.

"Those Gitanos are nuts," he said, leaning over the hole they had dug. "They're shooting at everything!"

"Jimmy!" Whitefox said.

"What?"

"Start pushing boxes into the tunnel. We don't have a lot of time."

"Boxes! Right!"

The crates were stacked shoulder high, lined against the walls and piled in the middle of the room. They were lightweight enough to slide into the hole, especially when other Boreals jumped into the cache to help him. But the number of long wooden boxes was overwhelming.

"You want all of them?" Jimmy asked when the center pile had been moved.

"Yes." Whitefox peeked up at him. "All of them."

"What we have isn't enough?"

"Jimmy, whatever we leave, Valerio is going to use against us. So, you tell me."

Jimmy's shirt was soaked from sweat, but the three of them worked relentlessly. When the cache was emptied, he collapsed on the floor, swinging his legs over the shaft.

"Look out!" Someone from the burrow shouted. Jimmy jumped, but when he landed, he wished he hadn't. Green dust spiraled toward them, illuminating the dark channel with an eerie substance that traveled at an alarming speed.

"Man alive!" Jimmy exclaimed. "What is that?"

"Silvio's magic, blast it," Whitefox said and grabbed his arm. "He was supposed to wait until we got out of here. C'mon. Run!"

"I thought Silvio lost his magic?" Jimmy stumbled after his uncle, yelling over the sound of the wind that swept into the tunnel.

"Right!"

REFUGE

Cassie didn't have the energy to search the island for the missing king that night. She pulled the dinghy out of the water and up the bank. Smells of seaweed and ocean refreshed her enough that she walked along the beach, looking for a place to sleep. Judging the reach of high tide by the line of flotsam, she collapsed next to several driftwood logs that offered shelter from the wind. With her head on the cool sand, she gazed at the coast, hypnotized by the constant motion of the waves, and how their ripples glistened in the moonlight. The relentless rumble of the breakers lulled her to sleep.

In the morning, a call from a seagull woke her.

"What?" she laughed as the bird flapped its wings and soared away into the seascape.

The tide had come in, causing the dingy to bound on the surf. Had she woken any later, the boat would have slipped out to sea. Cassie hurried to rescue the skiff, wading knee deep into the foamy water. She tugged the craft ashore again. This time she secured its bowline to a stationary piece of driftwood and yanked the knot tight.

She grabbed her pack and mapped out her surroundings. The island, in all its seaside beauty, was a lonesome place. Save for a gull or a hawk in the sky, sand crabs scurrying away from her toes, and an occasional hare disappearing into the dunes, it isolated her from friend and from foe. Little wonder that this block of land surrounded by a vast ocean was considered a refuge. Or was it a prison?

Fir trees on the bluffs in the distance were weather-torn, misshapen and stripped of their needles. The boulders Cassie passed by were scarred with sand-filled holes, eroded by the wind. Grass grew in swirling patches of dunes cut out by the sea, and the salty breeze lifted the coarse white earth, blowing it in circles around her feet. Low clouds rolled in from the ocean, obstructing her view of far-off shores. Cassie shivered and pulled her hoodie from her pack.

It took a good part of the morning to climb up the gently sloping headland. The sand had turned coarse and scratched her soles, so she stopped to put on her shoes and socks. Looking out over the choppy sea, she wondered how she had rowed so far. Alisubbo was now a purple mound on the horizon, and the castle but a white dot sparkling through the fog. To the south, the wind had pushed the hovering clouds apart to reveal a three-mast ship moored near shore. The king's ship! A sign that Martim may indeed be here. Perhaps she'd find a footpath from the beach that would lead her to his asylum.

The shoreline eventually ended in enormous cliffs that Cassie had to climb. She blazed a trail to the top and then hiked along the rim, keeping the sea to her right. The terrain grew rockier and steeper. Soon she heard rushing water and came to a steep and an impassable canyon. Standing on the edge of a precipice, she surveyed the wild river below.

She walked along the gorge in search of a crossing with no success. Instead, she journeyed parallel to the river, into a forest of knotty pine, peculiar rock formations, and prickly scrub brush. The sparse foliage offered little shade, exposing her to both sun and wind-burn. The depth of the canyon lessened until she came to a tributary, a shallow creek that could she could easily ford. She filled her canteen, scooped the cool fresh water onto her face, and drank from her cupped hands. From there, she corrected her course, although she was now much farther inland than she had originally intended.

By the time she crossed the creek, fatigue overwhelmed her. She stood still amongst the trees and watched an eagle soar high over the grassy meadow that stretched past the woods. Hot and tired, the climb and the search for a crossing had taken all her energy. She collapsed on the ground, shuffled through the contents of her pack, and retrieved the flatbread and cheese Carmen had prepared for her. When she finished eating, she laid down and, though she didn't mean to, she fell asleep.

In the late afternoon, she awoke to a faint sound that whispered in the breeze.

"Odd. Am I dreaming?" Blinking at the sunlight that peeked through the treetops, she listened carefully. It can't be. Music?

Not the song of a bird, though it was just as sweet, nor the whisper of the wind, though it was just as light. It was the sound of a violin.

Oh, my gosh. That has to be him! Cassie collected her things and stuffed them into her pack, which she heaved onto her back. When she stood, she noted the direction of the music. Certain of the direction she should go, she hurried into the grasslands.

An old fortress stood nestled in the weeds; a stone ruin that had been a grand castle in its time. Built by the queen of Taikus in Silvio's tale, this stronghold had been destroyed and yet some parts of it seemed to be fully functional. What was once a tower had collapsed, leaving huge bricks, rubble of cut rock, and half-standing pillars scattered across the meadow, with spikes rising high above the grass. Crumbled walls protruded from the earth, hinting at legends of grandeur from another age.

Cassie followed the melody to one of the castle's chambers. Reluctant to interrupt, she slowed as she neared the alcove, and stopped next to a gap in the stone wall, which must have been a window years ago. Despite the curious remains of the structure, the music had Cassie's undivided attention.

A single stringed melody resonated from the violin, first a painful, sorrowful refrain; then as gentle as a tender kiss.

She leaned over the stones and gazed into a room vacant of any furnishings. A single ray of light shone into a corner and rested on the back of a young man. His uniform torn, his arm that held the violin wrapped heavily in bindings. He had been critically wounded, yet he displayed no sign of physical pain. Engrossed in his song, his body moved to the rhythm of the music. Chin nestled on the instrument that had become a part of him, hands too large for the slender bow, fingers trembled across the strings in complex chords. The instrument was his vocal, singing a ballad too pure for the human voice.

Cassie watched, transported in time and space by the sound of his melancholy. Every note he played, every move he made, told his story. It sang of his patriotism; it cried in agony at the death of his father and his brother; it mourned the loneliness of exile.

His long, dark hair danced with the swaying of his body. Tender for a moment.

Then violent.

He could have been wielding a sword, fighting a battle that raged within his own soul. The violin resonated with a barrage of harmonious discord throughout the empty halls. Through the wrenching pulse of the music, his song was grief.

Finally, the quiet, euphonious cry of a single string ended the chorus; a complete circle to where it began.

Cassie closed her eyes. The agony that had been in him rushed through her veins. He had spoken in a voice with no words. She turned to face the sun, leaned against the cool stone, and slid to the ground, overwhelmed by his song.

Here was the young king, so close and yet so unapproachable. When the music stopped, she waited, wondering what she should do next, not wanting to startle him or enrage him.

He thinks I'm an assassin. How will I ever convince him otherwise?

She stood and gathered her courage. His back still turned to her, head bowed; his instrument lay across his lap. He sat in silence.

Cassie didn't move, nor was she willing to take her eyes off of him. "That is the sweetest, most heart wrenching music I have ever heard in my entire life." Though she spoke in a whisper against a background of silence, he had to have heard.

He turned to face her.

"It comes from the despondency in your heart. How simply awful you must feel." Cassie's eyes filled with tears for him.

"I didn't realize I had an audience."

Cassie said nothing.

His face grew stern. "You... you're the Princess."

"Please forgive me for the trouble I've caused you and your family."

"You saved my life."

That shocked Cassie.

"The night of our escape. You risked your life on our behalf." Martim wrapped his wounded arm in the sling that hung over his shoulder.

"You saw me?"

"I saw everything. You stood in the moonlight after you had fallen, your dress torn. You called out and distracted the soldiers, affording us an escape. Were it not for you, they would have shot us. I worried they had killed you."

Cassie wiped the tears from her cheeks. "I think someone in the heavens was watching over me. I thought I was dead, but I escaped through Silvio's tunnels. And you are safe, too. I'm glad. So very glad."

He nodded, but there was sorrow in his eyes.

"Come to the entryway, and I'll let you in."

The heavy door creaked on its hinges, and Cassie stepped into a dark hallway. Torches lit their path as Martim led Cassie into the depths of the ancient castle. They moved from the room with the cathedral window where she had found him playing the violin, to a larger room. A dining hall where daylight shone through several arched windows and onto a large oak table.

"Please make yourself comfortable." Martim walked to the fireplace, where an iron kettle rested near the embers.

"Are you alone here?" Cassie asked as he poured the tea.

"By alone, you mean...?" He nodded for her to sit, and he took a chair across from her.

"Is there anyone to help you? I mean to take care of your wound or bring you food? Is your mother here?"

"Did you see our ship?"

Cassie nodded.

"The servants stay on board. They transport supplies, cook meals and bring them to me. I've asked them... that is, I've told them, I want to be left alone." He fell silent.

"I'm sorry I interrupted you."

"Might I ask what you're doing here? I find it peculiar that a young princess is wandering around on the Isle of Refuge by herself." His expression sobered. "You are by yourself, are you not?"

"Yes. I am. And I'm here because I 'm looking for you."

He stared at her, his dark eyes discomforting. Cassie brushed her hair behind her ears and waited for him to speak, uncertain whether he trusted her. It seemed doubtful.

"Well. You found me. Now what?"

Cassie cleared her throat. "Alisubbo wants you back."

Martim raised his eyebrows.

"Valerio has taken siege of the city, but it's not what your people want. They want you. They want their king and your mother."

Martim stood and walked to the window. She looked past his shoulder. Clouds traveling north grabbed the pinks and oranges of a setting sun.

"My mother has sailed to the northern lands to live with my aunt and her family. She will never return to Alisubbo." His words were final, the air stiff as Cassie tried to think of a response. "Nor will I. In the coming months, I will join her."

He's leaving? He can't leave.

"Where is Elizabeth?"

A long, painful moment passed before he answered.

"The last I saw of Elizabeth was the moment my father was shot and I jumped into the landau. I believe her father rushed her away from the crowd and took her to safety. As he should have. How could he allow her to marry the son of an assassinated king?"

"I'm so sorry," Cassie offered, but she knew it wouldn't comfort him. He nodded, his back still turned to her.

"I don't blame them." He took a deep breath and exhaled slowly. "My father and brother are dead. My mother has fled. My fiancé is..." he choked on his words. "Gone. I can't return home. There's nothing left for me. Everything I ever loved has vanished. And so, for now, I've chosen solitude." With a whisper, he added, "And it all happened so suddenly."

The linen napkin Cassie twisted now resembled a choked heron. She wondered why she even came. "I guess I should go, then."

"Where to? It's almost nighttime."

"I have a dinghy on the beach I can sleep in. Somewhere out there, though, I have no idea how to find it again."

He breathed a laugh. "I didn't mean to make you feel unwelcome. Stay the night, stay two, or stay a week. It would be a crime to turn you away after you saved my life. Maestro will take you to where you need to go." He faced her with a stern and sorrowful air. "I am grieving. For me, to return to Alisubbo is not an option."

She looked into his dark, sad eyes. "I have things to tell you," she whispered. "But they can wait. It was a terrible thing that happened. I'm so sorry for any part that I might have had in your misfortune."

The silence was pressing. Martim changed the subject.

"Please. You are welcome to stay. The castle is yours, what's left of it. The destruction is from another war." he waved toward the door as an offering. "But…"

"I'll leave you alone." Cassie rose.

Martim escorted her back into the hallway. "You will find bedrooms at the end of the hall. Choose any you wish. The servants serve a fine breakfast each morning in this dining room. I might join you. Are you hungry now?"

"I have food in my pack. I think I'd like to be alone as well. It's been an arduous journey."

"I understand. Rest well."

Cassie walked alone through the corridor to the bedrooms, one on each side of the hall, and one at the end. The doors were slightly ajar, so she peeked in each of them. Though not furnished as elaborately as the castle in Alisubbo, all three had beds that looked comfortable.

The smallest room had a southern window that opened to the fragrance of wildflowers in the meadow. Perhaps the view would lift her spirits. She unpacked her things and laid the burgundy dress on the bureau, a gown she should wear the king's presence, yet it brought such horrid memories, she feared it would bring the same to him.

As she watched the sun sink behind the horizon, the smell that filtered into the bedroom was no longer sweet. Smoke. Fresh pine and cedar smoke. It was then that she eyed a puff of gray cloud floating on the wind, turning pink and gold as twilight neared.

Cassie ran through the hall and out the door. Martim stood on a rise in the meadow facing southwest, watching the smoky cloud as it grew in intensity, now hanging across the horizon like a torn blanket. He said nothing. He nervously rubbed his wounded arm and repositioned the sling around his neck.

"Valerio is burning Bandene Forest," she whispered.

They watched the flames rise in the distance until the sky grew dark and the air chilly. Finally, Martim pivoted to face her, his expression cold.

Without a word, he returned to the castle.

PERSUASION

Even though breakfast was laid out before them with royal fineries, steaming plates of food covered in silver trays, crystal goblets of juice, and china teacups brimming with hot coffee, Cassie didn't have an appetite. She could tell Martim was only going through the motions of hospitality. He walked with the servant to the door and whispered in her ear.

"Yes, Your Highness." she said, glancing at Cassie. With a curtsy, the woman backed out of the room.

Martim returned to the table and took his seat. Handing a basket of bread to her with his good hand, he then served himself a small portion of food.

It seemed forever to Cassie before either of them spoke, and when Martim finally broke the silence, his voice cracked, so he cleared his throat and tried again.

"Did you sleep well?" he asked.

"No." Though Cassie had been exhausted, her worry over Silvio and the Xylonites had kept her tossing and turning during the night. She had barely slept at all.

Another silence. Cassie thought perhaps Martim was as weary as she. From the way he kept rubbing his arm, it appeared to be hurting.

"Was Silvio in a safe place when you left?" he asked.

"Silvio was at the edge of Alisubbo with his troops when I left. We both had been alerted that Valerio might burn the forest and try to smoke the Xylonites out of the tunnels. Silvio had given up. He wasn't even going to run. He wanted to stay and die, but I convinced him to get to safety. They fled to the edge of the forest and now he and his army are waiting for you just outside of Alisubbo."

"Waiting for me?"

"They trust you'll come and rescue them."

His dark eyes met hers for only a second. There was a grimace on his face, but he quickly hid his emotions by taking another bite of food.

"All of Alisubbo waits for you." Cassie set her fork on the table. "You are loved, Your Highness. Valerio's republic is not a republic of the people, only of traitors."

Martim shook his head, wiping his mouth with his napkin. "They have the Royal Navy, the castle, the armory. Only a handful of soldiers remained true to my father. What could I possibly do?"

"You have sympathizers in the village willing to stand by your side. You could go back and fight to recover your throne. Lead those men and women who are ready to follow their king," Cassie said. "They're without a leader."

"I was never trained to be a king, Cassandra," he whispered. Martim rested his fork on his plate. His expression showed extreme discomfort, whether from his gunshot wound, his troubles, or everything that had suddenly befallen him. He looked especially vulnerable. He also looked young. He was only a year older than she was.

"Marques should have been the king after my father's death. He was educated in political matters. I was not. Marques' eldest son would have inherited the throne, had he a son. I wasn't raised under the assumption that my family would be slain. In this circumstance, I would be crowned king, yes, but…" His voice tapered; his eyes grew red as he blinked.

"Sometimes we're called to do things we don't ever expect to do," Cassie said, not sure how to encourage him. "I mean, like I never expected to come into a different world and be in the middle of a war."

She stared at her scrambled eggs, remembering her journey.

"No one warned me I'd be stumbling into a revolution, nor losing my heart to a hospital filled with sick children. I had never visited ill people before, and to see all those kids—" she shuddered, thinking about the dying boy. Their eyes met. Cassie withdrew her glance and buttered another piece of bread.

"I didn't think I would ever, ever kill someone."

She froze, wondering if Martim knew she had fired a gun the day of the regicide.

"You killed someone?"

Cassie dropped her bread onto her plate and leaned back, watching her hands as she twisted the napkin on her lap again. "I shot Perez."

"Perez, the journalist?"

Cassie nodded. With an elbow on the arm of her chair, she covered her head with her hand, hoping Martim wouldn't see her tears. "He was the one who shot you. If I hadn't fired that pistol, you would have been dead," she muttered.

When she composed herself, she went on, avoiding his eyes, "And I didn't think I'd ever have to run like a criminal through beaten down chapels and into creepy dark tunnels. Or stand in front of flying bullets."

Martim moved in his chair.

"I'm not brave, and I'm not a hero, that's for sure. I whined and cried the whole time. Just like I'm doing now. I doubt I would have volunteered if I had known all this stuff was going to happen. I certainly didn't expect to crawl through bramble and brush and tear my pretty dress, all the while getting chased by soldiers and their horrendous man-eating dogs." She breathed a cynical laugh.

"If I had known that I would have stayed at home and studied for my geology test or… finished my term project."

After wiping her eyes with her napkin, Cassie took a deep breath and glanced at Martim, his face filled with sympathy.

"I'm not telling you this for you to feel sorry for me. I'm just saying that sometimes we end up doing what needs to be done even if we don't want to, or expect to, or even if we don't think we're capable."

She put her napkin on the table. "Like, it wasn't really my idea to walk halfway across a hot deserted island to find a king only to hear him say he…" Cassie stopped. She had already said too much. It wasn't her intent to make him feel any worse than he already did, nor to be disrespectful. "I'm not any better than the next person. That's all."

"You're a child," he breathed. "What you've experienced is beyond your years, Princess Cassandra."

Cassie sat dumbfounded. "That's not the point. You're experiencing more than you should be, too. But…"

Martim waited for her to finish. She swallowed, hoping to gather courage. "I guess what I'm trying to say is we're not done yet."

He sat back in his chair and gazed out the window, rubbing his wounded arm.

"I know it's not how royal people do things. This request is abrupt, but the situation is urgent. I know you care for the people in Alisubbo. I know you do. Valerio has made a mess of things. He's burned the forest, destroyed the chapels, and imprisoned the clergy."

"He's imprisoned the clergy?"

Cassie nodded.

"What is he thinking?" Martim spoke more to himself than to Cassie.

"The children at the sanatorium. They've been sent home. They will not get better."

"The children have been taken from their beds in the hospital?"

Cassie nodded. "I saw Angelique last night. She's home with her grandpa. He's blind. He can't take care of her! She's in a dark room, coughing. She's not doing well. She asked me where your mother was, and I didn't know what to tell her."

Martim's face reddened, and he threw his fork on the table. "How could he do something like that?" His chair tipped as he stood; he caught it before it fell.

"He's not only a traitor to you and your family, Martim, he's destroying everything your family has done." Cassie followed him with her eyes as he paced the floor.

"After my father spent so much time getting him that position in the Royal Guard, encouraging him. Awarding him medals, promoting him. How could this have happened? Why? Why did he betray Alisubbo? Why did he forsake the children?"

Martim winced in pain and held his arm.

Cassie had no answers; all she could do was watch as he grappled with the pain.

"How can I fight a war with no army? It would be suicide to step foot in Alisubbo again."

"You have an army." Cassie said.

"Who? Silvio and the Xylonites? What can they do?"

"A man named Whitefox and the Gitanos spent the night recruiting men from the city. They were supposed to rendezvous with Silvio's troops at the eastern edge of the forest."

"Whitefox! He's there? Are they armed well?"

"Sabers, daggers. Some machetes. I don't know about guns."

"Swords? Swords are useless against powder. Valerio has the entire armory, including my father's naval fleet. Do you know what that means?" He paced again and then stopped. "How old are you?"

The question surprised Cassie. Her eyes met his. "Seventeen."

"Seventeen?" Martim cleared his throat. "You think I should take the advice of a seventeen-year-old girl and march back into that disaster? Should I lead this supposed army of Gitanos, strangers, and little people to certain death? They couldn't stop the enemy from burning the forest. How are they going to defeat Valerio when an endless number of guns and ammunition are at his disposal? Bombs? The Royal fleet? Hundreds of troops? It's preposterous to even think we could win."

Cassie shrugged; her face flushed. "I don't know. Use your own judgment. But I know what my dad would do."

211

"Your dad?"

"Dad would fight. It wouldn't matter how many people joined him or how many people were against him. If he couldn't find anyone, he'd go it alone. He'd fight to the death to save the people he loved."

Martim sighed. "I don't think you understand war, Cassandra, nor your father's good intentions. He wouldn't lead men into a battle they were certain to lose. A righteous king loves his army as much as he loves his cause. If he were an honorable warrior, he would first have a strategy."

Martim walked back to the window.

"I can't believe Valerio moved the children out of the hospital."

Cassie stopped responding. Perhaps if Martim mulled over what she had told him, he would change his mind.

"If the clergy are imprisoned, there are no nurses to visit the patient's homes, either. You're right. The situation is urgent. I wish I knew what to do."

"Do you want to be alone to think about it?" Cassie asked.

"No." His response was short and quick. "No. Stay here. Let me talk to you. Let me talk through this." He paced again. "There are other factors. There's a common enemy."

"A common enemy?"

"The island northwest. Taikus. If the king of Taikus thought we were divided, or weak, or worse that Silvio was defeated, we could never stay their hand against us."

"Silvio mentioned Taikus. Who is this king?"

"King Ivar is his name. My father told me he was a madman. The island itself is a mystery made up of sorceresses and wizards who wield magic. I know Silvio experienced the evil that breeds on that island first hand. When Queen Hacatine was alive, she invaded this island. My ancestors showed their power against her many years ago, and drove her back, but the battle was not easily won. There was another confrontation recently on the shores of Bandene in which Valerio's father died. Alisubbo was a powerful nation when we were united. Now we are not. If the king of Taikus knew about the coup, he would surely take advantage of our distress."

Cassie waited, hoping his silence meant he was thinking of a plan.

"Perhaps we could go back to Alisubbo secretly and see what forces Silvio and the Foreigners have gathered," he said.

"We could." Cassie agreed, her heart beating faster.

"I've had some military training. Not enough. This is huge. But Maestro Sanchez is with me, and he's been in many battles. I refuse to ask him to engage because of his age, but he could give me his views, help me chart a strategy."

"Where is he?"

"He's aboard The Felicia." Martim looked at her wide-eyed. "I can't do more than what is humanly possible. Men die thinking they're more powerful than they are. I will not discharge a foolish command and risk lives because of inadequacies and poor planning. I've had training from the best, but I'm not experienced in combat. I've never actually fought in a battle. But we may have some recruits who have. Men in Alisubbo, or these Boreals. Perhaps there's a king's soldier or two left that are still loyal?"

"We're going back then?"

Martim spoke softly. "Not to win a war. It's doubtful we have an army strong enough to overthrow Valerio. Still, I'd be satisfied freeing the clergy and remodeling my ship into a hospital for the children. That I would die for."

Cassie nodded, teary-eyed. "You're already a hero."

"We'll return to Alisubbo, then. My servants are keeping the dinghy on shore until noon. I thought I might send you to The Felicia this morning, but as it is, I'm going with you. Pack your things, young lady. We'll be sailing."

"Yes, Sire, Your Most Faithful Highness!" Cassie nearly tipped her chair over as she jumped up and raced to the door.

THE SAILING

Martim offered his hand to Cassie as they climbed from the dinghy up the ladder and on board the sailing vessel. A crew of strong young sailors saluted them as they passed by, a line of servants bowed, and Maestro Pedro Sanchez stepped up to Martim and embraced him.

"Martim, my boy, it's good to see you out in the fresh air. I've been worried about you."

Martim blushed and stepped back. "Maestro, you remember the Princess of Alcove, Cassandra Wilson?"

"Ah yes!" Maestro Sanchez bent low in a royal bow. "The young lady who came to visit the castle. And how did you find your way to the Isle of Refuge?"

Before Cassie could answer, Martim returned the crew's salute and took Maestro's arm, hurrying him across the deck to the hatchway and down the stairs. "We need to talk," he said. He motioned Cassie to follow.

Amazed at the simple beauty of the cabin, Cassie couldn't peel her gaze from the bulkheads and furnishings made of rich pecan polished to a hand-rubbed sheen. Cabinets and cupboards were placed strategically in the cabin to conserve space. What caught Cassie's attention from the moment she stepped inside was the collection of swords on a wall rack above the portholes. Shiny blades with ornate markings, jeweled bells, gold guards, and tooled sheathes radiated in the ambient light that filtered through the room.

"Cassandra, Maestro Sanchez has been a soldier in my father's infantry for many years, having won the highest of honors with his service. He's trained both my brother and me in the art of rapier, saber and other weaponry."

"I'm honored," Cassie said.

"I'm hoping he might give you a few pointers as well." Martim nodded toward the sheath strapped to her belt.

Cassie blushed. "I suppose I ought to learn how to use it. Dad taught me how to shoot a gun and string a bow, but we did no fencing. I was going to take it as an elective in school next year."

"So, you plan on doing some fighting Your Highness?" The maestro's eyes twinkled as he patted Martim on the back. "How is the arm?"

Martim shrugged. "I guess it's getting better. It still hurts."

"Let's look. Being alone on the island with a gunshot wound was never a good idea. You're a stubborn man, Martim. I'll get the nurses down here."

"Can we talk first?"

Sanchez took time to study his eyes and then glanced at Cassie.

"I ask for your advice." Martim explained. "Cassandra brings news from Alisubbo. The city is suffering."

Maestro ushered him to the table, making certain the wounded king was sitting before he answered.

"We can talk while they dress your wound. On this ship, I'm the captain, son." He walked to the door and spoke to the servant that stood guard.

Martim shuffled nervously on the seat, and Cassie watched sympathetically. Obviously, his wound bothered him, and his pride fought to conceal the pain. He peered up at her. She was staring. His face flushed and he looked away.

Maestro Sanchez lifted Martim's coat from his shoulders and removed his shirt so that the sunshine rested on his arm. Cassie moved aside so that the servants could set a basin of warm water in front of him. They unwrapped his bandages. When a foul odor filled the cabin, Cassie turned away. Martim grimaced when they applied the poultice and dressed his torn flesh.

"If you don't keep it clean that wound will never heal." Maestro moved closer to inspect the swelling. "I've seen better than this end in amputation." His eyes rested on Martim's, though the prince tried to avoid them.

"Don't let your grief destroy you, son. It was a terrible thing to see your family die like that, but life is still going on, and you're a part of that life, an important part."

Martim blinked and looked out of the porthole. Maestro walked back to the table and sat across from Cassie. The two nurses finished dressing Martim's wound, slipping on his shirt, and wrapping his coat over his shoulders. When the three were alone, the only sound was that of the ship creaking.

Maestro broke the silence. "So, Martim, what's happening in

Alisubbo?"

"Cassandra has brought word of the damage Valerio has done."

"And is still doing," Cassie interjected.

"Tell me what you know, young lady?"

"Well, for one, the children have been sent home from the hospital. They're dying because no one is taking care of them. The nurses have been arrested and taken away from the city."

The old man groaned and bowed his head.

"The church is in rubble. The nuns have been imprisoned."

Maestro winced, opened his eyes, fixing his gaze on Martim.

"Bandene Forest has been burned," Martim muttered and stood.

"Yes, I saw the smoke last night. Pity to lose the little people and the old wizard." Maestro said.

"Silvio wasn't in the woods. Thank goodness for that. He, the Xylonites, and the Boreals are regrouping near the border of Alisubbo, waiting for…" Cassie stopped, aware her next words were presumptuous.

Martim finished her sentence. "For me."

"You're going back?" Maestro asked. They stared at each other, the seasoned warrior and the young king. Much was said in that moment of silence. Maestro Sanchez rose, opened a cabinet over his head, and pulled out a chart that had been rolled into a scroll, which he laid across the table.

"Cassandra, show me where Silvio and his army wait; to the best of your knowledge."

Cassie studied the map until she understood it. She pointed to a cluster of firs sketched on the parchment, which signified the forest along the beaches southwest of Alisubbo.

"Then that's where we'll moor. We can set sail along the coast of the island, but we cannot hit open waters until after dark. It will be too obvious where we're headed, and the last thing we need is to have Valerio's navy attack our only ship or raid Silvio's camp." He rolled the map and returned it to its cupboard. "In the meantime, Martim, have you been training?"

"Not a morning has gone by that I haven't trained, sir."

"Good. We'll bout. It'll sharpen your senses and get your mind off your despondency." He turned to Cassie. "And you can watch. After which, I'll give you some pointers. Valerio may have guns, but his weapon of choice is the sword, as is his second's, Bernardo. I don't doubt the man will try to get in some hand-to-hand combat before this battle is over. You'll need to defend yourself or else he may choose to capture you and use you for leverage. That would be most unfortunate."

217

"Me?"

Maestro Sanchez winked. He chose a rapier from his rack and motioned them out the hatchway and onto the deck where he stopped and gave orders to the crew to set sail.

Cassie enjoyed watching the sailors shimmy up the ratlines to loosen the sails. In constant motion, they called to one another, tossed lines in one direction, and pulled on others. When the wind grabbed hold of the sheets, it took her breath away. The ship cut through the water, and she leaned starboard to breathe the salty sea air, her hair flying across her face. The sensations were so exhilarating she couldn't help but laugh.

"Are you coming?" Martim asked, jolting her from daydreaming. She faced him and met his smile. What a beautiful smile. His dark eyes caught the sun, sparking a rich amber color. There was peace on his face that she hadn't seen before. A warm feeling settled in her heart as she followed Martim and Maestro down another hatchway under the deck at the bow to a room with a no furnishing save a bench, and a wooden floor polished to a sheen.

Hooks hung at the entrance where coats and armguards swayed with the motion of the ship. The quilted jacket that Maestro chose was black with a circle embroidered over his heart. Martim picked out a jacket for Cassie, and then one for himself.

"Wear that arm guard, Martim. To protect your wound."

Martim obeyed. He slipped on the leather guard and winced as he tried to tie the lace with one hand. Cassie tied the knot and their eyes met.

"Thank you."

She took a seat and watched the two salute one another. Their sparring took them back and forth across the deck. Metal against metal, the clang of bells and boots pounding the floor.

Maestro stopped.

"You're training for war, Martim. Aim for the vital areas."

They continued. Martim was agile on his feet, his lunge aggressive, his stance extremely graceful, accurate with his sword, displaying the utmost precision with a flick of his wrist.

"Enough?" Maestro asked, showing concern when Martim reached for his wounded arm.

"No. I'm fine," Martim argued.

"As you wish. We'll continue then."

"I'm finding it hard to get in," Martim complained.

"Of course. You're using the same moves repeatedly, which makes it easy for me. You've not fooled me at all. I can see every move you make before you make it. Feint, son feint!"

Martim nodded, this time circulating his tip ever so slightly as he lunged, disengaging Maestro's parry.

"Yes!" the trainer encouraged as the point touched.

Several more rounds and they had exhausted themselves. Martim took a seat next to Cassie, panting and holding his arm again. Cassie untied the laces and removed his guard.

"You do well." Maestro told him. "I can see you've been practicing with your blade as religiously as you practice your violin. You've become a master at both."

Martim laughed as he caught his breath. "Coming from your lips, Maestro, that is indeed encouraging."

"Your footwork and accuracy are astounding. I only wish you would think more seriously about your target."

Martim's smile faded.

"In battle, the intend is not to maim, but to kill. If he's alive, your opponent will attack. Your target must be a major artery." He touched his rapier to Martim's neck, his upper arm, and his abdomen. "If not, the heart. Think survival."

Martim nodded and gazed at the ground. Cassie sensed his anxiety and wondered if Martim felt the same way about killing another human being as she did. Then her memory ignited, and she saw Perez dying. She looked out the porthole, as if she needed to hide the image she saw in her mind from the people she was with.

"Cassandra," Maestro gestured for her to stand. "Let's see your weapon."

She drew it from her sheath and relinquished the saber into his strong, weathered hands. He inspected her weapon, taking care to examine the weld of the blade, the strength of the hilt, and the weight of the pommel. "This is a lovely blade. How did you come by it?"

"Silvio. It came from the green dust that shot out of his eyes and ended up in a sheath around my waist."

"Curious way to gain a weapon," he chuckled. "I wonder about its history. The old wizard is a legend, you know."

"So, I'm finding out," Cassie replied. "I'm also curious whether it has any mystical properties of its own!"

Maestro laughed. "It may have. Yes, Silvio has some unusual attributes. One thing I know. The old man's sorcery works at his command. The problem is you can never tell what he's thinking." He stepped away and slashed the saber through the air.

"Since it's a saber, it isn't handled as a rapier."

"No?"

"Strength in a saber is its edge, not its point." He stepped into the middle of the room and slashed the air with a swift, deliberate swing. "The side of the blade makes the cut. Though you can use a rapier's edge, with a saber, it's the only means of attack. It's designed primarily for the mounted Cavalry. Your enemy, Valerio, was the Cavalry's captain, you know? This is the type of blade he uses. It demands distance. A deadly weapon in the right circumstances, but would take great skill to battle against a rapier. There are those who have gained that skill. Valerio is one. I know how he fights. I trained him." He winked at her and gave it back. "Just be careful. You might ask Silvio when you see him if there's magic that comes with this gift."

"I'll do that." Cassie said.

"And as promised, I want to show you a bit of self-defense. Just in case."

Cassie looked at Martim and then back at Maestro again.

"I suppose I will need to be ready for anything and everything. That is if we're going into a war."

"My dear, you were once at Valerio's beckoning. He will not be easy on you. He will view your shift of loyalty as an act of treason. And so will his men."

Cassie inhaled. The thought of Valerio taking a personal vendetta out on her was sobering.

Maestro stationed himself next to her.

"The feet will be your saving grace. Be light on your feet, eager to lunge but ready to retreat. Step with me." He took Cassie through the steps. Advance, lunge, and retreat, over and over until she picked up the rhythm and could do the steps on her own. Then he stood opposite her, and when he advanced, she retreated.

"Very good. Practice those steps until they become second nature to you. Keeping distance will be imperative. Practice with Martim if you must. Remember, with a saber, you must prevent your opponent from coming in close. Always use distance to maintain the advantage.

"Can I ask you a question?" Cassie said.

"Yes, ma'am," he answered.

"You told Martim to feint. What does that mean?"

"Ah! Good question. In a duel, you must out-think your opponent, not out-muscle him. Feint means to fool him with trickery to perform a successful attack. You make him think you will do one thing, when you really mean to do something else."

"Oh! I see," Cassie said, returning his smile and not understanding how she might be clever enough to do that.

After lunch, Maestro Sanchez left Martim and Cassie, excusing himself to his cabin. Cassie sat on the deck and soaked up the sun. The ocean breeze was cool, the water turquoise. She pulled out her cell phone and to her surprise, got reception.

Martim sat next to her. "What's that?" he asked.

"Oh, it's a talking device; a common invention in our world. Part of our culture, sort of, I guess."

He leaned over and took a closer look.

"I can tap certain numbers here. Depending on who I'm calling, everyone gets their own set of numbers. I push this send button and the person on the other end will answer theirs, if they have one of these, and then we can talk."

His breath tickled her neck, and she lifted her head to see he wasn't looking at her phone. He was looking at her.

"Whom do you want to talk to?" he asked.

Cassie shut off her phone. "No one," she said. "I mean, no one in the other world, not right now, anyway."

The sea air blew her hair in her face, and he laughed when his hair blew across his eyes. He didn't touch her, though she wished he had. But she felt confident about being next to him. They strolled side by side on deck. Martim pointed out significant spots along the coast and told her some of the island's history. The two visited with the crew. Later, they stood at the stern and watched the ship's wake as the vessel skidded through the water. Listening to the sound of the sails, the wind whistling through the lines, and the call of the gulls was healing for Cassie. She hoped it was healing for Martim, too.

The sun fell to the horizon all too soon. Cassie heard Maestro giving orders to the crew. With a loud whip of the boom, the sails caught the wind again, and the ship came about. She thought she should help, but when she turned to leave, Martim took her hand and held her back.

His touch gave her shivers. His hands were warm, his hold tender but firm.

"Cassandra," he whispered. "There may never be a chance for us to enjoy each other's company again. Danger waits in Alisubbo. Neither of us knows what the future will bring, so I want to take the time now to thank you for what you've done."

Cassie looked into his eyes.

221

"You've saved my life twice, and you've given me hope. You've pulled my head out of a shell of self-pity and despair." He paused. "You are very young, though I'm not much older than you. And you're from another world. You'll probably want to return to your family soon." He touched her face and stroked her hair. "But if things were different, if they ever are different, I…"

Cassie felt her eyes fill. She swallowed.

"I hope to spend more time with you. I would want to know you better."

"I feel the same way, Martim."

"Would you mind if I held you?"

Cassie shook her head. Their bodies pressed against each other. He was warm, perhaps a little feverish, and still had the odor of antiseptic. She was careful not to touch his wound.

She laid her ear against his chest and listened to his heartbeat, holding him tight and enjoying the comfort she found in his strength. He caressed her, resting his chin on her head. His fingers stroked her curls. Their embrace was cloaked in the colors of sunset.

"Thank you," he finally whispered and stepped away. "You're a beautiful girl. You will be a lovely woman someday. I hope I know you then." His thumb wiped the tear that had trickled down her cheek.

"Come, let's join Maestro Sanchez and our crew. We'll be mooring soon. Reality awaits us."

FEINT

Clouds drifted in front of the moon, darkening the skies, and offering perfect camouflage for the small boat that drifted on the surf. Maestro rowed silently, allowing the movement of the waves to rock the dinghy ashore.

"How's your arm, Martim?" Maestro whispered, helping Martim out of the boat.

"It's still attached," Martim answered, adjusting the sling.

Once in shallow waters, all three of the passengers stepped into the tingling cold water and pulled the vessel onto the sand. There was no way of knowing where Whitefox and the Royalist army might be by now. However, Maestro had mentioned he was familiar with the Bandene shoreline. So, when they landed, Cassie pulled her backpack from the boat, and she and Martim followed Maestro Sanchez inland toward the bluffs.

"Where do you think we'll find Silvio and the Boreals?" Cassie whispered.

"If they're near, they're more likely to discover us." was Maestro's quick reply as he held his finger over his lips. "Stay together. I hope that our allies, and not the enemy, will find us first. But one never knows."

"Yeah… here's hoping," Cassie whispered. "What if we run into Valerio and his men?" She shuddered, moving closer to Martim. "Do you have a gun?" she asked.

"I do." Martim answered and then glanced at her. "Don't worry. You're in excellent hands. We'll find our allies."

She wasn't so sure he could keep that promise. Still, his words were comforting, and all she had to cling to for the moment.

Every so often, the moon appeared from behind the clouds, offering a glimpse of what Cassie thought might be a trail. She stumbled once, twisting her ankle. When she leaned over to rub her foot, a small dot of white near to the ground caught her eye. She gasped.

"What?" Martim asked.

"Look!"

Eyes peered up at them from behind a boulder.

Maestro bent low in the direction of the miniature faces and whispered. "The king is here."

The eyes disappeared and soon two of Xylepher's soldiers waved from the brush.

Martim ushered Cassie ahead of him and Maestro fell behind. Cassie tried to keep up with the soldiers, but they were quick and scurried in and around rocks, making it near impossible for her to follow. When the men disappeared into a crevice, Martim called to them. "Slow down," he said in a hushed voice. "Find a way that is large enough for us to pass."

"You're almost there, sir," one Xylonite said, nodding toward the cliffs only a few feet away. They climbed the last rise and ascended into the mouth of a cavern.

"Wait here," the soldier said and darted away into the dark hollow beyond, leaving the three alone.

"It seems safe enough," Cassie said as she retrieved the flashlight her father had packed. When she turned it on, Martim spun around, a look of surprise on his face. She laughed. "You never saw one of these before, have you? See here. It's like a pocket torch."

She flashed the light in Martim's eyes. Not to be rude or mean, but to tease him. He was always so serious.

Martim covered his face. "What is that? Let me see it."

Cassie took the light off him and danced the beam around the cavern walls. "Never! Unless you take it from me, you will never see it!"

She paused, waiting for his reaction. He turned to her. She grinned and then he lunged for the flashlight, but Cassie was faster. She ran past Sanchez, shining the beam down a cave. Martim was close behind.

"Hey, you two!" Maestro called as she whizzed by, but she was having too much fun to stop. The look on Martim's face was delightful. He chased her. She glanced over her shoulder one too many times and tripped. Martim caught her with his good arm and kept her from falling. He didn't let go, but held her, panting and laughing. She couldn't free herself from his grasp, nor did she want to. She backed up against the cave wall and held the flashlight behind her back.

"That's not fair, you know. You're taking advantage of my disability!" He pressed against her to hold her still with his body while he reached for the flashlight with his good arm. Cassie enjoyed the closeness, and she presumed he did too, as neither of them were giving in and they both were in good spirits.

"I'm sorry, Your Highness. What disability was that?" she asked.

224

"You have two good arms, Cassandra. Please may I hold it? I just want to see its magic."

Cassie quit fighting. When she felt his hand on the flashlight, she released her hold. "Then it's yours. However, I must be honest with you. It's not magic. It's science."

"Then you have me even more curious. Science I can understand. Let me see how it works."

She relaxed as he pulled the flashlight from her hand. "This turns it on and off." Cassie showed him how it worked, and then she took it apart for him.

"These are batteries?" he asked. "We have batteries, but they are much larger. Alisubbo should know about this!"

"Then you should tell your kingdom!" she said.

They were close to each other, in body and mind. Cassie felt a kindred spirit in Martim as though she'd known him all her life, as if he was the one she'd been waiting for. There was nothing about his actions that showed he felt differently. His smile, the gentleness of his eyes when he searched hers, the way he talked barely above a whisper as though his thoughts were for her only.

He capped the flashlight, turned it on, and directed the beam around the cave, stopping when it lit up a stack of ammunition boxes.

"Holy cow," Cassie said.

"You two young people are much too robust for your own good!" Maestro Sanchez said as he appeared in the tunnel. He stopped short and whistled low. "And it appears our allies have been equally enthusiastic!"

The beam of light caught an ensign on the box. "This is my father's arsenal! I thought Valerio would have owned all of this by now."

"Shine your light this way."

Martim directed the ray further down the tunnel where rows upon rows of ammo boxes were stacked one upon the other.

"My word!" Martim whispered. "Does he have any weapons left at all?"

"Not much, save for his hand weapons." Whitefox stepped from the darkness. "Though I suspect he isn't aware of his loss yet."

When Martim acknowledged his presence, Whitefox bowed. "Your Highness," he said to Martim. "This is only one of our caches. Others hold more weaponry than what you see here, guns, powder, and ammunition."

"Whitefox! What a pleasure to see you! "This is remarkable, simply remarkable," Martin Held out his hand in greeting. "You pilfered all of this?"

"We did, sir. We also gained access to the castle with the help of the townspeople. We've boarded two of the king's battleships. We are currently preparing to attack the flagship. We wait for your permission to proceed."

"You may proceed. Is Valerio on board?"

"We don't believe so."

"Have you any idea of his whereabouts?" Martim asked as the cave filled with Whitefox's motley army. Hooded men entered first, and then men more colorfully dressed, led by the two cocky Gitanos that had been with Jimmy in the woods. 'The smiling ones', Cassie had called them. She caught herself sneering when they glanced at her, but when she recognized Jimmy, she looked away entirely.

The men bowed to Martim. A few younger men stood by the entrance of the cave. One caught her eye. He was thinner than the others, and seemed awkward, as if he didn't belong. All the Boreals wore clothing made of leather. They had belts loaded with weapons that were strapped around their waists. They all wore black masks and some of them, like Jimmy, had cloaks. She could feel their eyes on her, despite their disguise. It wasn't easy avoiding a roomful of stares. She moved closer to Martim.

"Your Majesty, all we know is that when we drove him out, Valerio made camp somewhere in the hills of Medio, near the Sanatorium above the city," Whitefox began. "It's been a hard battle until yesterday, when we could finally reclaim a good portion of the weapons the enemy had stolen. He still has troops at the armory, but there's no armor there." Whitefox grinned. "Not sure if he knows it yet."

Martim nodded approval. "You've done well, Whitefox. My apologies for being so late to arrive."

Whitefox shrugged. "I understand your circumstances, Martim. I wish we had arrived in time to save your father and your brother."

Martim looked away for a moment. Cassie could tell by his stance that the mention of his family reignited his grief. Martim cleared his throat. "Excuse me," he whispered.

"I'm sorry," Whitefox apologized.

"Had the bridge not been destroyed our men would have been here before the coup. We could have prevented the bloody murder." Jimmy said under his breath, his eyes set on Cassie. She shifted her weight, guilt eating at her.

"You have something to say?" Martim asked.

Jimmy's eyes jumped from her to Martim.

"If you have a comment, or information, speak up," Martim

226

prodded.

"Your Majesty, there's a female in our midst who identified me as a spy in Valerio's presence, which prompted the demolition of Pointe de Tratado and…"

"Sir," Martim said harshly, surprising even Cassie by his tone. "You will implicate no one here for my father's death, least of all the Princess of Alcove. The only hands stained with my family's blood are Valerio's and his insurgents. Do you understand that?"

"But…"

"Jimmy, be quiet." Whitefox said.

Martim stepped between Cassie and Jimmy, blocking the red head's accusing glare. "If you have a problem with Cassandra, then you have a problem with me. We can settle immediately." He tucked his coat behind his rapier and with his good arm, grasped its pommel.

Jimmy's eyes grew wide, his face red. "No, Your Majesty, of course not. I don't mean any harm. I apologize."

Not until Martim finally stepped away from Jimmy did Cassie breathe again. Martim looked over his shoulder at her and then addressed the crowd. "There will be no more divisive talk among us," he said, and returned to Maestro's side. "What has happened has happened. The criminals will pay. Not another word of accusation. Is that clear?"

The assembly mumbled in agreement. Jimmy stepped into the shadows.

"Whitefox, what you and your men have done so far is ingenious. How…?" He motioned to the piles of ammunition stacked along the walls.

"Some of us acted as decoys, drawing the enemy's fire while we located the munitions. We used Silvio's tunnels to access the cache from underneath. Once we knew where the guns were, the Xylonite dug in, and our men lowered the boxes into the burrows. Silvio used his magic in those channels, creating a vacuum that transported the ammunition here into the caves. The whole thing has been a breeze," he laughed. "No pun intended."

"That's brilliant," Martim said. "Simply brilliant. I appreciate your dedication, Whitefox. I understand why my father regarded you so highly."

"Your Majesty, we're relieved that you've returned. If an heir to the throne lives, we will defend the Crown." Whitefox said.

"I am humbled." Martim returned quietly. "As for Valerio's schemes, Cassandra has brought word the clergy has been imprisoned."

"We think Valerio is holding them at the Sanatorium close to where he camps. We're uncertain exactly. Our spies haven't been able to get close enough."

"We need to locate and rescue them," Martim told Whitefox. "The longer they're in captivity, the less chance they have for survival."

"Yes, sir."

"Is the castle secure enough that you could spare some of your men to find the prisoners?"

Whitefox looked at his friends, uncertainty in his eyes.

"If Valerio and his officers weren't guarding the prisoners, we could send out a search party. Though we've confiscated these weapons, we do not know what personal arms they carry. If we're discovered, and a battle ensues, even if we won, I'm certain he'd use the prisoners as leverage."

Martim thought for a moment. "Of course he would."

"I bet they're hidden in the catacombs." Cassie blurted, surprising everyone. "There's a stairwell that leads into a deep passageway under the earth. I think it's where they buried the children that died in the hospital. Jovita called it a resting place. It'd be easy to hide people there."

"We could raid their camp..." Whitefox suggested.

"No. That would endanger the prisoners." Martim interrupted. "We need to pull Valerio out of hiding and then attack him."

"It's improbable." Whitefox said. "Valerio doesn't fight with his infantry."

"Improbable but not impossible." Martim argued confidently. "I wager I could draw him out of his rabbit hole."

Maestro opened his mouth to say something, but Martim continued.

"What is the one thing Valerio wants more than anything?"

"The throne?" Cassie asked when no one else answered.

"Exactly. And who's standing in the way of that?"

"You?" Cassie asked, not sure of what he was thinking.

"No, Your Majesty, don't risk your life," Maestro said.

"I'll be safe, Maestro. If I'm the decoy, half of our men will rescue the clergy, and the other half can protect me." Martim said.

Maestro straightened, anger reddening his face. "That's ludicrous. I won't have it."

Martim's eyes widened.

"Forgive me Your Majesty, but without you there is no throne."

"My dear master and Maestro at Arms, do I need to spell it out for you? If Valerio and his troops are occupying any part of Alisubbo there is no throne. He won't relent until I'm dead. And I will not stop until he's defeated."

Martim's zealous words resounded through the cave. Silence

followed. Cassie swore she heard everyone's heart beating, though it was hers that pounded in her ears.

"Martim, don't," she said, touching his arm.

"Princess Cassandra," Martim snapped, his voice strangely distant. "It's not appropriate for you to include yourself in the discussion of military maneuvers with a king and his army."

Cassie's mouth dropped. Who was this talking? Had power gotten the best of Martim already? She stepped back, and felt the size of a fire ant, for she burned as hot as one. She peered at the surrounding men, relieved that no one had paid mind to the rejection except for one skinny Boreal who tilted his head in sympathy and winked at her through his mask. It was the sort of look her father would have given her. Embarrassed, Cassie turned from his gaze.

"I'll go into Alisubbo. You can provide an escort." Martim announced to Whitefox. "Publicly. Everyone will see me. I'll reclaim my father's throne in public. The Valerio's soldiers will retreat and bring word to him. Valerio will come see for himself that I've claimed my father's throne. I assure you. I know Valerio. He'll come. When he does, your men will be at his camp to save the prisoners."

"Your Majesty, send someone in your stead into the streets. Let them be in disguise, in your clothes." Whitefox begged.

Martim shook his head. "Neither Valerio nor his men would be fooled by such a trick."

"So, what would prevent him from using the prisoners as hostage for your life at that point?" someone asked from the crowd.

"He could and no doubt would." Maestro Sanchez protested. "He would ask us to exchange your life for theirs. He doesn't respect your position, Martim, and he knows how you feel about the Church. He would assassinate you on the spot."

"Perhaps if your appearance wasn't a public display?" Whitefox suggested. "If you entered the city quietly and allowed Valerio's men to think they were sneaking up on you, overheard you making plans to return to the castle at night?" Whitefox shrugged his shoulders.

Martim stood silently for a moment, rubbing his arm under the sling, surveying the group that stood anxiously waiting for his response.

Martim didn't rub his arm unless it hurt. Cassie sensed he was in pain, fatigued from the long boat ride, and not healing as he should from that bullet wound.

"He's not thinking right," she whispered to Maestro.

"Sneaking into the castle might work," Martim agreed.

"It would be easier to protect you. Innocent people won't be put in jeopardy." Whitefox added.

"True." Martim paused. "But what guarantee have we that Valerio will come? The miscreant didn't show up to assassinate my family. Why would he show up to assassinate me?" Martim paced a short distance. "There's one way to guarantee his appearance. I will send him a personal invitation."

Maestro cleared his throat. "Begging your pardon, Your Majesty... but you're not well. This talk is irrational. You may be feverish. Let me take you back to the ship and we can speak privately."

Martim ignored Maestro. "Valerio needs to be confronted. I will challenge him to..."

"No!" Maestro interrupted. "Get that notion out of your head!" He took Martim's good arm and coaxed him deeper into the cave, talking silently, but Cassie, being near, heard everything.

"I can fight Valerio, Maestro." Martim said.

"And he can cheat and have his men kill you."

"A gentleman's challenge."

"And what gentleman will you be fighting?"

"How else will we draw him from his hole? We must free the hostages."

"A trade, a blasted trade, Your Majesty, your life for the prisoners? What good is that if you're dead? Listen to me. It won't work, Martim. We'll think of another way. We'll sleep on it. Come back to the ship with me. I want to dress that arm again."

"Stop." Martim brushed Maestro away. The order was loud enough to make Cassie jump. Everyone in the room gave them their attention.

Maestro drew back.

"I am not a child," Martim insisted.

"You are the king, Your Majesty. The only one we have." Whitefox explained. "It's our duty to protect you. Should you be slain, everyone's efforts will be in vain. There is no other heir."

Martim studied the men that surrounded him. "You are correct. I am your king," he said slowly and deliberately. "And therefore, my decision is final."

Cassie held her breath. Maestro groaned and turned away.

"Is it a republic that you want? Would you like to take a vote?" Martim challenged. "Or do you believe in our Monarchy? I'm assuming the reason you are here is to defend the throne. Therefore, let the throne decide." He took a breath and glanced at Maestro. "If not a duel, then we wait. On the ship if you so desire." He added the last quietly to Maestro as he rubbed his arm again.

"Yes, Your Highness." Maestro said, sighing. "Thank God."

"Valerio is already using the prisoners as leverage, but he's lacking ammunition, and he's in a secluded area. His food and water supplies will run out within a week if we keep him blockaded from the city." Martim nodded to Whitefox.

"See to that. As far as the prisoners are concerned, I'm going to trust that he wants them alive. They'd be no use as hostages if they were dead. Everyone is to stay quiet and on guard. Only return fire in defense. If Valerio's men have not seen our ship already, they will at dawn. I don't doubt that if he doesn't already know I'm here, he will know soon. Perhaps he's waiting for us to attack. We will secure the navy flagship that he captured and then wait for his next move."

Martim smiled at Maestro. "Feint," he mouthed. Maestro raised his eyebrows and then returned the grin with a nod.

The Challenge

At the break of dawn, Cassie woke to the rocking of the ship and a low rumble echoing across the ocean floor. She jumped from bed and peered out the porthole. Though barely able to distinguish the vessels in the dark until their own explosions illuminated them, she remembered Martim giving permission to take the navy cruiser. The explosions ended as dramatically as they had begun. A white flag of defeat rose from the mast of the sinking ship. The bombing ceased.

Cassie dressed quickly and climbed through the hatchway, zipping her hoodie over her tunic as she jogged up the stairs. The brisk air, the smell of smoke from gunpowder, and burning ships reached her when she stepped onto the deck. She nodded a good morning to the crew and then made a dash for Martim's cabin. Maestro strode out the door as she arrived.

"We've taken the cruiser," she said.

He nodded, but there was no celebration in his eyes.

"Is something wrong?"

Maestro looked at her, his face full of sorrow. He didn't answer, but turned and climbed the hatchway, leaving Martim's door slightly ajar.

When Cassie stepped into the king's room, a faint ray of morning glistened through the porthole, beaming at Martim's figure, still under the covers. Cassie's heart jumped to her throat. He should be up.

At the head of his bed stood Jovita.

"No!" She cried out in panic. "You're not coming to take him?" Cassie ran to Martim's bedside. "You can't have him."

"Cassandra, that's not why I'm here." The angel smiled. "He needs a healing touch. I'm here to help."

Martim's face was cool, his skin pale. His eyes twitched when Cassie touched his hair and pulled a strand away from his brow. She kneeled over him and whispered his name. He opened his eyes; dark circles shadowed them.

"Cassandra," he whispered.

"What happened?" she asked. "You were fine last night."

"I'm fine now." He shivered. "It's just a reaction... or something."

"A reaction to what?"

"To lead?" He laughed softly.

Cassie smiled, but there wasn't any gladness in her heart.

"Get better, Martim. We need you."

His continence turned grave when he looked at her. There was no sparkle in his deep brown eyes, only pain and despair.

"Why? Because I'm king?" he scorned. "Because I hold a title no one else can have?"

"No."

"No?" His brow rose.

"I don't care if you're a king or not. What I care about is you being alive, healthy, and strong. You need to get better because you're Martim, a wonderful caring person who feels deeply about those he loves."

She held her breath, waiting for his reaction, hoping her words impressed upon him how much she cared.

"You couldn't mean that. My station in this world is what's important. Not who I am as a man. What difference does it make to anyone who Martim is?"

When she frowned, he looked at her.

"I wouldn't lie to you," she said.

"No. You wouldnt lie. But...," he said. "Really?"

"You are a good man, Martim. Not everyone can make that claim."

"Well, that's the nicest thing anyone has ever said to me."

She stroked his hair, worry overwhelming her.

"You're going to get better, Martim. Jovita's here. She's going to help you, but you must want to get better." Cassie pulled the blanket close to his neck and felt his forehead. "You're cold. I'll get you another fleece and maybe have the ship's cook make you some hot soup. That'll be good, won't it?"

He nodded.

"Did Maestro change your wrap?"

"He did."

"Good. So, you wait here." Cassie hesitated, leaned over, and kissed his cheek.

He grabbed her hand. "Cassandra."

She settled next to him again, waiting for the words he struggled to say.

"Yesterday in the caves. I was wicked toward you."

"You weren't wicked. You were only taking charge of your army. I had no right to interfere."

"No! I shouldn't have talked to you like that. I returned your kindness with cruelty. I embarrassed you in front of all those people. I'm so sorry."

"Please don't apologize, Martim."

His words of confession scared her. People confess when they're about to die. She squeezed his hand.

"It's not me," he said hoarsely.

"What do you mean?"

"What I had to do last night. Making decisions that will affect the fate of our country, that affect people's lives. Deciding whether they live or die. I can't do it. It's not me."

"You did fine."

"No." His voice tapered; he winced in pain. "You don't understand. It was all a show. I was trying to be someone I'm not."

He spoke so softly that Cassie had to lean closer to hear him. Sweat seeped from his pores, and his fingers that lay limp in her hand felt clammy in her grasp. He whispered in her ear. "I don't want to be king."

Cassie spoke just as quietly. "That's no reason to give up being Martim!"

She kissed him again and laid her head on his chest. "Don't give up. Please don't give up."

Martim's breathing quieted, his heartbeat slowed, and his eyes closed. Cassie stood. Jovita came up to her and rested a hand on her shoulders. "Let him sleep. He needs rest and care. He'll be himself again, soon."

***

Three days went by, and The Felicia remained moored off the coast of Bandene Forest. Maestro Sanchez went ashore often, so Cassie visited Martim alone for long hours at a time. At his request, she read his father's books on oceanography and marine sciences to him. She tried to understand them, but when she told Martim they didn't make sense, he translated their complex ideas into simple terms. Other times, she sat and watched him sleep. She dozed on the bench next to the porthole, unwilling to leave his side for fear his condition might worsen if she did.

Cassie helped Maestro dress Martim's wound. She had grown

braver and could now watch the changing of his wrap without turning away. Though the wound still appeared swollen and extremely painful, the constant care Maestro gave resulted in a more rapid healing. Whatever infection had been threatening his life soon disappeared. By the third day, both Martim's color and strength returned. When the week was over, the king was on deck again.

One week to the day from when Martim first woke up with an infection, Maestro returned in a dinghy from shore. Cassie watched him climb the ship's ladder and beckon for Martim. As they spoke, their body language graduated to fierce agitation. Martim threw his coat on the deck with his good arm, and then pointed toward land.

"It's settled," he said.

Maestro grabbed Martim's shirt, spun him around and shook him. Cassie couldn't hear their words after that, for though they both appeared angry; their faces were so near to each other that their conversation was inaudible. Martim, red-faced with wrath, pushed himself away from Maestro's grasp.

Though she wished they had, neither of them called her over to explain what had transpired.

Martim retrieved his coat and raced down the hatchway to his cabin. He quickly returned with his uniform jacket on, the left sleeve hanging over the sling that supported his injured arm. Buckling his sheath around his waist, he adjusted his rapier into place. He waved to several crewmen. Though Maestro attempted to stop him, Martim stepped down the ship's ladder into the dinghy. Three sailors followed and rowed him toward shore. Maestro called for another boat to be lowered.

Cassie raced up to Maestro.

"What's happening? Where is he going?" Cassie asked, running up to him.

When Sanchez turned his back to her and moved toward the ladder, she followed. "Maestro Sanchez where is Martim going?" she asked again, tugging on his coat.

He brushed her off. "It's not the business of a young lady. This is a man's affair," he mumbled.

"Hog wash." Cassie yelled, stomping her foot.

Maestro spun around, surprised.

"I have risked my life for him, Maestro. You must tell me where he's going."

Maestro took a breath as he waited for the men to launch the second dinghy. "We have been successful in starving Valerio out of his hole. He's arrived at the castle with the prisoners."

"Well, that's a good thing!" Cassie sighed. "They're alive and accounted for."

"Oh yes. Well, he has his entire army waiting in the plaza with a flag of truce, however he's not succumbing to anyone's terms but his own."

"How was he allowed into the plaza?"

"He outnumbers us, Princess. Even with Whitefox's men and all the Gitanos by his side, we don't hold a candle to his army. We may have more guns, but we need men to operate them. It's little wonder Valerio gained access to the plaza. The prisoners are no safer than they were."

"What's he planning on doing, then?"

"He's proposed a contest. He challenged Martim to a duel. Today, at noon, in Square de Regem."

"What? That's absurd. Martim can't fight."

"That's what I told him."

"How could Martim jump into a duel like that?"

"Because of Valerio's terms, of course. If Martim fights him and wins, the prisoners will be released. If he refuses the duel, or loses, or if the Royalists try to free the prisoners, they'll be executed in the square."

Cassie gasped. "How wretched! No wonder Martim was fuming."

"Oh yes, not without reason! However, I was hoping to rein in his anger. It will affect his handling of the blade. I'm sure Valerio won't fight fair."

"We've got to catch up to him." Cassie said.

"That's what I'm attempting to do."

"I'm coming with you."

"You're not."

"You are not keeping me here." Cassie said.

"I'm an old man, your Highness. I cannot look forward and backward both at the same time. I cannot keep my eyes on the king ahead of me and the Princess behind me. Do us both a favor and stay here." Maestro stepped down onto the ship's ladder.

"If I don't come with you in that boat, then I'm swimming ashore."

He stopped and glared at her. "Don't do this to me," he begged.

"I won't be a burden to you, I promise. I can't stay here, Maestro, I can't. I'll be a help to you. I'll do everything you say. I promise."

Maestro sighed heavily, taking a long moment to respond, and then he sighed again.

"Very well. Grab a couple more pistols from my dresser. I have two tucked in my belt already. And get your saber. Perhaps if we see Silvio, he will explain its magic to you."

IN QUARTATA

Besides a few Xylonite women cleaning the breakfast dishes, the Royalist camp at the beach near the caves was empty. Willow branches bent from the clotheslines that hung from them and blankets swayed in the breeze. Smoke from dying embers curled into the air. Cassie trudged up the beach while Maestro Sanchez secured the dinghy.

"Everyone went to Alisubbo," one woman informed her. Cassie paced back and forth, waiting for Maestro to join her.

Everyone?" She looked toward the caves.

"Except us. We're the only ones here. There's a lot of excitement going on. They say the king will claim his throne today."

"Is there a trail up that way?" she asked.

"It's a steep one if you take the hillside."

With a glance over her shoulder at Maestro, Cassie hastened toward the cliffs.

"You slow down, young lady," Maestro called out to her.

"Please hurry," Cassie said.

"Come this way. I know a shortcut." He waved to her.

Cassie followed Maestro along the shoreline until the sandy beach met the cliffs of Alisubbo. He paused for a moment, searching the rocky incline for the trailhead. It was a short but steep climb to the crest of the hill. Whether they would get there in time, Cassie wasn't sure. The duel was scheduled for noon, and already the sun was high.

As they started the ascent, Maestro's pace slowed, signs of fatigue becoming more apparent with every step. Sweat streamed down the side of his sunburned face and he wiped it with a hanky.

"Are you alright?" Cassie asked concerned for his health, but impatient. He nodded, too short of breath to give a reply.

As the trail leveled and vegetation gave way to thick brush and cork trees that offered shade, small cottages marked the outskirts of the city. Though the streets were quiet at the edge of town, as they neared the marketplace, more and more people congregated in the alleyways, roads, and housetops. Once near the castle, passing through the mass of onlookers was impossible.

"There's no way we'll get to the Square in time." Cassie complained.

"Follow me." Maestro led her behind the crowd to an alley which was bordered on one side by a drop off; a steep bank that overlooked the ocean. From there, he turned down a trail where branches hosting boughs of ivy arched over their heads. They ventured behind the servant's quarters, the castle, and the other structures that formed the plaza. Maestro opened a screen door and ushered her down an arcade that ran parallel with the castle walls. When they reached the end of the corridor, he stretched out his arm to stop her. They had come to the plaza.

Valerio's troops occupied Square de Regem, dressed in starched cavalry uniforms and golden plumed helmets. They held their bayonets across their chests, intimidating the crowd away from the courtyard.

In the center of the square, in the shade of the giant stone horseman, Valerio's tall figure was easy to spot. He stood calmly, talking with Bernardo. Beyond him were the nuns and priests who were barricaded by a host of guards, roped together like animals. Sister Ann and the other clergy stood in the scorching sun, their faces already sunburned, dirty and distraught.

"Oh, my word." The blood rushed from Cassie's head. The sight of their plight sickened her.

"Martim will free them," Maestro assured her, touching her shoulder gently and whispering in her ear. "That's what he's come to do. Right now, he needs a second. That will be me."

Cheers and applause interrupted them as Martim appeared on the beach to the east of the square, escorted by the three sailors that had rowed him to shore. Cassie could see him perfectly, pulling the sling off his shoulder and adjusting his sheath securely on his belt. Even though the wound was healing, Martim still favored his hurt arm. Sword fighting would not help his recovery.

"Stay here." Maestro said. He walked to the plaza only to be intercepted by one of Valerio's guards. After a brief confrontation, the soldier allowed him to continue to Martim.

Cassie watched, wishing she were with Maestro. Determined to draw near where the duel would be fought, she stepped from the shade of the colonnade into the heat that beat on the veranda. She was ready to confront the enemy.

Valerio's uniform reflected the brightness of the day. His stance was equally brilliant in that every move he made reeked of over-confidence and arrogance. That smile Cassie once deemed handsome, she now saw as evil. Demonic. Cassie clenched her saber. She silently wished she'd taken more lessons from Maestro.

Valerio's mounted cavalry stood sentry over the south of the square, plumes dancing on the heads of their steeds. It wasn't long ago the finely outfitted dragoons held Cassie's admiration. Now the sight of the rebels repulsed her.

"Murderer", Cassie thought, disappointed Valerio couldn't read her lips from where he stood. Their eyes met, though. He leaned over and whispered something to Bernardo. Valerio's contorted smile beamed across the courtyard. Bernardo laughed and glanced her way. Cassie flushed with anger.

Inching her way toward Maestro and Martim, she found a shady pillar to lean against. There, she would have an unobstructed view of the duel. She watched Martim as he and Maestro walked up the hill.

"Where is your sling?" Maestro asked, matching Martim's pace. They stopped in the shade next to Cassie.

"The sailors are watching my things for me. I'll be fine. I'll be much more comfortable with my left arm loose and I won't look so vulnerable."

Martim's glare went past Maestro's shoulder, but Maestro stepped into his line of vision.

"Look at me, Martim," he said. "Look at me! Your life, and the life of those prisoners depend on you. Don't let your anger dominate this duel. You are an honorable swordsman, keen witted and fast on your feet. He is a brute. Play by your rules and you will win. Play by his and he will kill you."

Their eyes locked. Maestro straightened.

"Don't forget what I've taught you. This is what you've trained for. It's your music. You practice violin for the concerto, the symphony." He nodded toward their opponent. "This is your overture."

"I'll do as you say, Maestro," Martim said, though the tone was not convincing.

"Yes? Good, then. And remember the last piece of advice I gave you?" Maestro asked.

"Which was?"

"Kill him, Martim."

Martim did not respond.

"The prisoners are depending on you."

Martim glanced at Cassie.

"Please be careful," she said, her heart pounding. She took his arm and made him face her.

"You're here because you love these people. You want the best for them, and for the children. That alone makes you a better man than he is. You said once that a righteous king loves his army as much as he loves his cause." His eyes penetrated hers, as though he was absorbing her every word—as though her tenderness was taking the fear and pain from him.

"These people are both your army and your cause. You are that king, Martim. Your father would be proud of you."

At that moment, someone from Valerio's party shouted, "It's noon. Let the duel begin!"

Maestro stepped away from Martim, taking Cassie by the arm as he did.

Valerio strolled casually from his circle of friends toward the center of the plaza. Martim drew a deep breath and entered Square de Regem. The sun beat on both their backs and reflected off the cobblestones of the courtyard. The bronze statue of the Kingly rider hovered over them.

People sat on rooftops, peasants, soldiers, journalists, women in fancy clothes. Hundreds of people lined the streets. The entire population of Alisubbo had come out to watch! A child's muffled cry in the distance broke the stiff air. Perhaps it was Carmen's little brother Marques.

In the shadows of the colonnade across from Cassie, a Boreal dodged out of sight. Two Gitanos crouched low in the shadows. She breathed a sigh of relief after seeing them. If there were a few, there had to be more. Valerio would not get away with playing dirty.

Silence fell over the square.

So much of Alisubbo's future weighed on this duel: the lives of the prisoners, the sick children, the government, Silvio's forest, the kingdom. Maybe even the entire Realm.

The steady clicks of boot heels on stone resonated through the square as the two men slowly circled each other. Everyone watched. Everyone in Alisubbo would see someone die today.

Odds in this duel were in Valerio's favor. He was older than Martim, broader in the shoulders, with a much longer reach, seasoned in battle and not afraid to kill. The saber was a deadly weapon in his hands. Martim hadn't even been in a battle. Though trained by the very best, his bouts with Maestro Sanchez could hardly count as experience compared to a deadly confrontation such as this.

As she watched Martim step closer, and closer to his rival, guilt overwhelmed her. She was the one that had persuaded him to come back to Alisubbo. He could have stayed in exile and lived to a ripe old age.

The Gitanos would have taken him in. If something awful happened to Martim, she would blame herself.

Valerio's grin spread across his face. His voice resounded across the square. Every man, woman, and child heard his mockery.

"Where are your men, Martim? I don't see your army." He held out his hands. "Or will the pretty little princess pick up your pieces and claim your throne when you're dead? I see you've given her a sword!" He laughed again.

Cassie boiled inside, comforted only by Maestro's hand on her shoulder.

Martim said nothing. With his torso proud and his head high, he stood elegantly. He took another step closer to his opponent.

Valerio faced his audience and pointed at Martim. "Look at him! So pathetic! A naïve young prince who's never even seen a battle. He struggles for identity, and do you think he'll find it in such a cold and ruthless world? With his mommy and daddy gone, what's left for him? Revenge?"

To Martim he said, "I almost feel sorry for you. Almost."

Martim drew his rapier.

Valerio chuckled. "Almost." He pulled his saber from its sheath.

Cassie held her breath and covered her mouth, fear clenching her heart. Afraid to look, yet afraid to look away.

Circling again, Valerio's wrist danced. His blade caught the sun as it spun over his head, bouncing sporadic flashes across the square. Not once did his grin falter, as though he enjoyed every moment of this prelude, as a cat enjoys stalking its prey.

Martim remained silent, rotating as an axis to Valerio's antic, any emotions concealed. He pressed his wounded arm close to his side.

Once they had inched two swords distance from each other, Martin presented his rapier en guarde. Valerio stopped circling but played with his saber, whipping it in the air and over his head.

"Frankly, I'm surprised at you, Martim," he said. "Coming back to Alisubbo as if it were your home. As if the throne belonged to you." He snickered. "Didn't the mudrats tell you? Your rights to this country died with your father and your brother. It was only by accident you didn't die with them. But we'll take care of that today."

"You're a murderer," Martim said with a hiss. "You will pay for your crime against these people. And against my family."

Valerio laughed. "Will I? And who will see to that? The struggling boy king? The commander of no army?" The rebel held his sword in salute. "Don't even think you will go out in honor, fool. You will grovel for your life like a wild boar at the end of a chase; your veins will empty on the stains of your father's. When you are dead, Alisubbo will have no throne. These people you're so concerned about will be set free. Finally, after how many years of tyranny?"

"You are the only tyrant this city has ever seen."

Valerio's face turned red. He lunged, slashing Martim's torso, but Martim dodged and parried, binding Valerio's saber as the rebel advanced.

Freeing his sword, Valerio beat on Martim's blade. And then again and again. The bell on the rapier sparked, the sound of metal against metal droned through the courtyard as the two engaged. In the bashing, the saber's edge sliced Martim's wrist, and he retreated.

Blood soaked Martim's glove. Cassie buried her head in Maestro's shoulder for a moment before her eyes were drawn again to the dueling swordsmen. If only there were a magic spell, she could call out to protect him. Where are Silvio and his wizardry when you need them? Where is the magic of the Realm?

Ignoring his wound, Martim advanced, tipping his blade to every slash of the rebel's saber, the sound of their weapons ringing through the plaza.

Valerio struggled to distance himself to get a full swing at Martim, but the king kept a forward pace. Having no room for attack, Valerio thrashed at the rapier's guard with the front of his blade, cutting the king's hand again. But this time, Martim backed his opponent into the wall of the monument. Valerio lost his balance and jumped sideways. Martim drove his blade toward Valerio's chest, but Valerio parried and disengaged.

Martim parried his opponent's riposte.

"Feint, Martim, feint," Maestro whispered only loud enough for Cassie to hear. She wrung her hands.

Rotating around each other, Valerio's back was now turned toward Cassie. Tucked in his belt under his right arm was a dagger. She looked at Maestro, wondering if he had seen the weapon, and then she moved toward the duel, hoping to warn Martim, somehow. Maestro pulled her back.

"Stay," he ordered.

"But..." she panicked.

"I see it. But distracting him in the heat of engagement could cost him his life," he whispered. "There's nothing we can do."

Their swords locked above their heads, each of the men struggling to gain strength over the other. Their faces red with energy, sweat beading from their pores, veins in their necks protruding, they pushed against each other. Valerio grasped the saber with both hands, using twice the strength of the wounded Martim; he gained control, sliding his blade along Martim's rapier. With a powerful thrust, he knocked the guard into Martim's face.

Martim fell.

Valerio thrashed at the fallen king, splicing strands of his hair and coat as Martim rolled from the attack, and lifted himself up enough to drive his blade into Valerio's thigh.

The rebel groaned in agony. Martim staggered to his feet.

With a fresh breath, rage spewing, Valerio gathered his strength and lunged. Martim parried, their weapons entangled, their bodies pressed into each other. Valerio slammed his weight against Martim, pushing him against the statue wall. Once Martim was pinned, Valerio reached to his belt with his left hand, and slammed the dagger into Martim side.

The cry pierced Cassie's ears. She screamed. Valerio withdrew the bloodied lance and stepped back. The young king doubled over.

"No," Cassie struggled against Maestro's grip.

Her cry had won Valerio's brief attention. He scoffed a devil's grin. With his saber in one hand, the dagger in the other, he moved toward the slumping figure again.

Cassie struggled to free herself from Maestro's grasp.

"Do something!" she demanded.

With pompous arrogance, Valerio swung his saber over his head and then wailed at the prince. Martim unexpectedly uncurled and raised his rapier with lightning speed, slicing Valerio's left hand, spewing blood across the plaza. The dagger flew, clanking on stone as it bounced on the ground.

The rebel cried out in pain and anger. He paused and inhaled with his teeth barred. Then, like a wild and furious animal, he ran again at Martim, the saber catching flashes of sunlight as he held it over his head, his momentum deadly.

"No!" Cassie inhaled her fear, too afraid to close her eyes and yet dreading what she might witness.

Martim staggered. He stood erect and stretched out his blade, taking a quarter turn to the inside just as Valerio's blade came down. Valerio missed Martim's chest by a hair's distance. His body followed the force and weight of his sword, the energy too violent to stop. Having missed his target, the rebel fell on Martim's sword.

The impact forced the king backwards. When Martim gained his balance, he yanked his rapier from the dying man and swayed, weak and bleeding. Valerio collided with the ground in a pool of blood.

Maestro ran to Martim and caught him before he collapsed.

"Take me to my ship." Martim breathed heavily.

Cheers rang through the plaza. People swarmed around the fallen rebel as his loyal followers carried Valerio to a horse.

Cassie glimpsed Jovita in the crowd, and assumed she'd come to Martim, but she didn't. Instead, the angel maneuvered her way through the crowd toward Valerio, and Cassie wondered why.

A deafening sound rumbled in the world around her. Still, the noise was only a distant hum in Cassie's ears. Overwhelmed and shocked by how brutal the duel had been, Cassie was oblivious to the mob. She worried about Martim's injuries and hurried toward Maestro and those that carried the king away from the city, down the beach and to the dinghy.

Before she caught up to them, the unexpected ringtone to her cellphone startled her. She stopped, hoping no one else heard, and reached into the pocket of her tunic. When she answered the call, she saw Daemon's number.

"Cassie," he said, frantically.

"What?"

"Look behind you."

Cassie turned to the thunder of horses galloping toward Martim's entourage. Bernardo, leading Valerio's mounted troops, their sabers drawn, slashed at the footed Boreals who tried to intercept them. Geno, Elias, and Whitefox ran in response. Smoke from their guns clouded the air.

"Maestro, Martim!" Cassie screamed,

She shoved the phone in her pocket and pulled her pistols from her belt. Bullets made little impact on the charging horde. Dust flew into her lungs as the herd neared, carrying the smell of horses, gunpowder, and human sweat. The thunder of the stampede drowned out her screams.

A flash of metal flung at her. She jumped back, but the horseman circled and charged at her again. Cassie's guns were empty. Fumbling to draw her saber, as the horseman's blade came down, a masked man parried it from the ground, knocking Cassie off balance as he shoved by. She fell. Her rescuer leaped on the assailant's horse. His hood sailed off his head, his red hair flew. He pushed the rebel out of the saddle and claimed the steed as his own.

Cassie spun around as another horseman fast approached. She drew her saber from its sheath and swung the sword with all the force that her body could conjure.

Green powder burst from the saber and shot like a comet into the sky, splicing the air in half. Wind raged, enveloping Valerio's horsemen with a magical funnel that swallowed them, sucking them into the air. Breathless, Cassie watched as the eye of the tornado opened, a void hollow which darkened the sky above Alisubbo. Out of the chasm, fire spat; and then the dragon appeared. Its wings spread and breath were as petrifying as the abyss it flew in. Its scales iridescent green, it's horned head and marble eyes terrifying as it spat fiery wrath.

As quickly as the magical storm had appeared, the portal closed, leaving only a filtered stream of green particles floating in the air, and a quiet Realm below.

Frozen, she stood gawking, as did Maestro, Martim, and the sailors. All Alisubbo fell silent.

Jimmy pulled his mask from his face. "Did you see that?" he asked, breathless. "That there was a legend. That there was Old Stenhjaert, sure as I'm a redhead!" He trotted his stolen horse up to her, his hair glowing in the sunlight. "Looks like we took care of them, all right?" he added.

In the distance, the prisoners had been released. Whitefox and his men were already disarming the remaining foot soldiers. The spectators filled the square and streamed toward the beach. Many of the people cheered, celebrating and hailing Martim as king.

"Quickly, Maestro, please get me to my ship." Martim pleaded, bloody and weak. His aides carried him briskly to the beach and lifted him into the dinghy. Before Cassie could reach them, the lone figure of a crooked old man came waddling from the forest edge.

He cleared his throat. "I'll take that now," he said, his knotted fingers reaching for the saber.

"Silvio. your magic came through!" She was elated to see the wizard again. When she handed him his sword, their eyes met, though he looked away quickly. She thought she had seen a tear.

"So did you," he mumbled. "Now get out of here. Go on."

She wanted to spend more time thanking the old coot. He had lost a lot in this war and had risked even more. Leaving him behind without showing her gratitude didn't seem right.

"Silvio," she started before he could make his way back into the woods. He stopped and peered at her with one green eye open wider than the other.

"Thanks for letting me use your sword," Cassie said.

He grunted and flicked his fingers at her. Her tunic disintegrated into green dust, leaving Cassie in a gray t-shirt, the one with the hearts.

The old conjurer looked long and hard at her before he grumbled in a low and crotchety voice.

"Nice T."

He shuffled his way back into the forest.

Cassie turned back to the beach just in time to be saluted by Jimmy.

"Nice work, Your Highness," he said. With a nod, he turned his horse and loped toward the square, intercepting a crowd of people swarming to meet Martim.

"Go back to your homes," he called out. "The king will return when he recovers. Go. Go home."

Slowly, the crowd dispersed and cleared the grounds. Silence returned, but this time fear did not hang over the plaza as it had earlier. This time, the air was filled with the peaceful and gentle lull of the breakers, and the call of a seagull.

"Coming, Cassandra?" Maestro asked. Martim was secure in the boat, his wounds being tended to. The sailors were ready to push off. Maestro held out his hand as an invitation to join them.

"I'm coming." Cassie said.

Now that the excitement was over, Cassie took another look at her cell phone and wondered about Daemon's call.

THE CROWN

I t's as beautiful as it was when Jovita first gave it to me," Cassie whispered, realizing what a wonderful job the Xylonites had done mending her dress. She admired the handiwork in the mirror Martim had his crew bring to her cabin. She pushed her hair behind her shoulders and stared at her image.

I'm not the same person I was before I came here. I feel so much older. How will I ever face my friends back home?

There was a knock on Cassie's cabin door, though it was already slightly ajar. Martim peeked around the corner.

"Are you busy?"

"Come in." Cassie said, watching his reflection as he slowly approached her. Their eyes met in the looking glass; their figures gilded by the morning sun that seeped through the window. He in a kingly uniform, a white sash reached from his shoulder to his waist adorned with medals and medallions that glistened when the light hit them. A rapier hung at his side. He pulled a necklace from his breast pocket, pushed her hair aside and slipped it around her neck, fastening the clasp. His touch sent tingles through her body when he lifted her hair back over her shoulders and combed it gently with his fingers. Cassie had never seen such a beautiful piece of jewelry, a true heirloom, probably belonging to a long line of queens.

"It's the most beautiful jewel in the world!" She touched the stones and reached for his hand. He clasped hers eagerly, the warmth racing from his palm to hers.

"You are the most beautiful jewel in the world." He leaned over and kissed her hair; his breath tickled her ear. She smiled.

"Thank you," she said, unable to hear herself for the pounding of her heart.

"If only I could keep this moment in a time capsule or take it home with me. Today is a special occasion, Your Majesty. It's your homecoming."

He didn't return her smile.

"And mine," she added, bowing her head.

"Let's not talk about that right now. Let's enjoy our moment," he whispered.

He offered his hand and escorted her out of the cabin to a dining table on the upper deck of The Felicia. The air was cool. A slight breeze announced the morning with the salty scent of the sea. Golden hues of sunrise sparkled on the water while pinks whisked across the scattered clouds. Cassie couldn't remember a more colorful dawn. Nor did she want the sun to climb any higher lest this moment end.

She took a deep breath and then sat in the chair that Martim held for her. He poured two cups of coffee, seating himself across from her and then fixed his gaze on the ocean. Before the swelling of emotions took her some place she didn't want to go, she unfolded the newspaper and read the front page.

"Look what your subjects say about you, Martim!" she said, and then read aloud.

"For three weeks, King Martim has been undergoing intensive care on his personal yacht. During this time, the grateful clergy, having recuperated from their ordeal at the hands of the ruthless rebels, have organized a working detail with local citizens and former servants. They have been busy repairing and cleansing the castle, removing the destruction this unfortunate war had caused."

She looked up at him. "Wow, that's cool! They're remodeling!" Cassie said. He nodded solemnly. She continued.

"After the Coronation and in honor of our newly crowned King's return today, the children, who studied with him, will perform at three o'clock for His Majesty, in private, in the castle chamber room, and then again at six o'clock for the public in the garden. Banners are flying throughout the town, in celebration of King Martim's return. Free food and beverage will be offered throughout Alisubbo for the entire day."

Cassie set the paper down. "This is really thrilling, Martim. The whole town is throwing a gigantic party on your behalf. They love you so much."

Martim sipped his coffee.

"I don't deserve treatment like that."

"Why do you say that?"

"I'm not the king my father was. My father was brave. He knew there was a rebellion brewing and yet he never once cowered, but rode openly through the streets, fearless. In our citizen's most desperate moment, what did I do? I fled."

"And you came back."

He laughed cynically. "Not on my own."

"And you fought a duel on behalf of your subjects that could have meant your death."

He turned away.

"You deserve to be loved and they love you." She folded the paper. "You should be happy. At least try to smile. Things are returning to normal."

"Are they?" He set his cup down. "Cassandra, things will never be normal for me. And this royal treatment is not what I want. I've told you that before. I have a duty to my country to serve as king, but it isn't my heart."

"I know." Cassie's manner softened. "You're a humble person, a student of music and a lover of children."

"I miss my family. And I'm going to miss you."

"I'm sorry about your family, Martim. If only I had magic like Silvio, I would flash a saber across the sky and change everything that happened."

"Even Silvio can't do that, Cassandra."

He was right. Those kinds of things don't come undone. Death is final, not only in the real world but in this one too.

"I wish I were older, because then I wouldn't have to go home. I could stay with you."

"And that can't be changed either, not now. No. You need to go home," he blurted. "Your family needs you. And as far as helping me, no one aside from Maestro Sanchez has done more for me than you."

"Well, from what I can see, others are trying their best to help you, too. They're celebrating your health and your return. They want you to know they love you."

"I'm aware of their loyalty and am humbled by it."

Cassie felt awkward trying to think of something to say to cheer him on. Perhaps in time, he would get used to the idea of leading his people. She knew she wouldn't be around then. Her mission was complete. Alisubbo has its new king. There's nothing left for her to do except what would be done today.

It had taken well over three weeks for Martim's wounds to heal, and he had refused to go anywhere with a black eye, claiming it obstructed his sight and would be counterproductive having a king bump into things in public.

"Tell me something, Cassandra. Before we meet the public, before our lives are no longer private, tell me some things about your world."

Cassie set her cup down. "Like what?"

"What is it like where you live? The people, what they do, how do they think, who are they? Tell me about the young men my age in your world. What is their life like?"

The question surprised Cassie. "Why?"

He shrugged. "There's a way about you I admire, envy almost. A freedom. You're carefree, headstrong. That's a good thing. I wonder if everyone who lives in your world is like you. I wonder if I'm that much different from your race."

She thought for a moment. "Well. Most guys your age are still going to high school. They'll be graduates this year, except the more intelligent ones, like you. You would probably already have some college credits, if not a degree. Some guys your age would be working."

"What, besides school do they do? What sort of recreation?"

"Football or soccer. A lot of them have computers and play computer games." Immediately, she thought of Daemon. "Actually, the nerdy ones play computer games."

"Nerdy? Computers?"

"They're gadgets, like my phone only bigger. Nerdy is an affectionate name we call people who don't get away from their computers very often."

"What else?"

"Well, some of them drive cars… motor coaches only faster. Some boys have girlfriends and go on dates."

"You mean courting?"

"Yes."

He was quiet for a moment. "Do they court you?"

"Not yet."

His face turned red, and he looked away. "I'm sorry. That was intrusive."

"Some of them play the violin, too," she added.

He faced her.

"That shocks you. Martim? You're not any different from anyone else. You are in different circumstances. If a normal guy from my world who had your intelligence and your passion were given the chance to lead a country, he would. It would be an opportunity of a lifetime for him, especially if he could help people."

A morning breeze picked up, and the ship rocked gently. Cassie held her coffee cup steady. Martim once again fixed his focus on the sunrise.

"I'm giving the ship to the clergy, you know, for the children. As a Sanatorium."

"Maestro told me. That's very generous of you."

"It's the least I can do. My mother and my father were just as generous. Unfortunately, they were sorely misunderstood."

"It didn't help that lies were being spread about your family."

"No. But being royalty has risks."

"Is that why you're hesitant to be king?"

"Not at all. It's the loneliness that scares me. Being untouchable, that's what scares me. It's not my idea of a happy life." He gazed her. "And what about you, Cassandra? What will you do?"

"I need to finish school."

"I'll miss you."

Cassie felt tears breaking through. She fought them back. "You'll be too busy."

"No. I won't. I will take time out each day to sit and think of you."

Cassie bit her lip.

"And I will ask Jovita to bring you back here when you're ready."

Martim stood and gestured for her to rise. When she did, he drew her to him.

"There are few things that are deep and beautiful in my life anymore," he said softly. "Waiting for you will be a pleasure." He wiped her tears. "Crowns and scepters shine on the surface but mean nothing to me. I almost wish I could run away from all this and go to your world." He touched her hair with his lips. "Go to college or play soccer."

She smiled with her head buried in his chest, not wanting to let go.

"But I can't. There are a few things that I look forward to here. I'll be sailing The Felicia occasionally, taking the children for brief excursions out to sea. That will lift their spirits. They can learn to sail as they heal. We have a forest to replant, so Silvio and the Xylonites will have a home again. Perhaps we'll build tiny houses for them and make them more comfortable. A bridge at Pointe de Tratado needs rebuilding. There's work to be done. Maybe after we finish, you'll be ready to come back."

Maybe.

"Come, let's go reclaim a throne and get on with our day."

❋❋❋

The sailors rowed the dinghy to shore as Cassandra nestled in Martim's arms. The gunshot wound had healed completely, but the dagger wound was still bandaged. The gash on his forehead was only a scar now. His strength had carried him through the worst and for that, Cassie was glad.

A carriage waited for them on the beach, along with the militia, men that had remained faithful to Chavez. Maestro was the first to greet them. His face was red. Either it was sunburn or emotions, Cassie couldn't quite tell, but when he shook Martim's hand, he pulled the king to his chest and embraced him.

"Welcome home, Your Majesty! Son!"

"Thank you, Maestro."

The carriage entered the city with hundreds of people on the street cheering, singing and throwing confetti. Cassie laughed with excitement. When she glanced at Martim, he wasn't watching the festivities, he was watching her.

"Our wedding will be this sweet," Martim said.

That was the one thing she was hoping Martim wasn't going to say. How could she promise him anything like that? And how could she break his heart if it didn't work out? They had already agreed that after his wounds were healed and he returned to Alisubbo, she would go home.

She missed Mom and Dad terribly. Even though she loved the Realm and everyone in it, and even though her heart beat wildly for Martim, Cassie wasn't ready to think about living in this alternate world, much less marriage. Still, the more Martim looked at her with those loving eyes, the harder it was for her to stand by her decision.

Cassie tucked her cell phone in its pouch that was strapped around her waist, checking to make certain it was secure throughout the day.

***

The crowning of the king came first. The ceremonies were not nearly as long as she thought they might be. Cassie stayed in the audience, admiring Martim from afar. He might not want to be king, but he sure looked handsome on the throne!

At noon they stole away to the children's concert. Martim didn't hold back his excitement at being with the children again. They swarmed around him like bees around a honeycomb. Angelique was there. Maria had bundled her up in the family's best quilts and carried her to the castle. Her smile warmed Cassie's heart. Carmen brought Martim his violin and he played music with the children.

Afterward, Martim and Cassie strolled in the garden. They ate crumb cake and drank punch with the guests until the day dimmed and the shadows lengthened.

The Boreals honored Martim and his Coronation, though they didn't mingle with the other guests. Martim approached their group in the garden.

"I thank you personally for your help." Martim said. "Your bridge will be restored as soon as we are able."

"Thank you, Your Highness." Whitefox said. "And our men will help with the building." Whitefox nudged Elias who nodded, grinning.

Martim turned to Jimmy. The red head had Elena at his side. "You saved Cassandra's life. For that I am indebted. There's a place for you here in the Royal Cavalry should you wish to enlist."

"Wow!" Jimmy's mouth dropped and he straightened his back and saluted. "Yes sir, Your Majesty. Thank you!"

"You see?" Elena kissed him on the cheek. "What did I tell you? The cards were right. Good things are in store for you."

"Your nephew is a courageous fellow," Martim said to Whitefox. Jimmy's face burned redder than his hair.

"I must admit, Jimmy, it's been a stormy encounter with you. But I'm glad things turned out the way they did. Especially the part where you saved my life!" Cassie said.

"Thanks, Your Highness. I'm sorry about the…" Jimmy motioned to his throat.

Cassie laughed. "I'm over it." she said.

"I look forward to our alliance." Martim said and bowed cordially to Whitefox, Elias and Geno. "And to trading with your people, Master Elias. You have earned a fair wage in gold for your help in this battle."

Elias smiled widely, his broken teeth glistened. He nudged Geno and the two raised their cups. "Hail the King!" they said in unison. The men of the Isle of Refuge left shortly after that, and Martim guided Cassie out of the garden, past Square de Regem, and onto the grassland.

"Walk with me?" she asked.

"May I?" He raised his violin.

"I would love it."

Cassie took Martim's hand and led him through the meadow. It was safe to wander through Greenstay now. Maestro, serving as temporary minister during Martim's healing, had persuaded Silvio to seal the tunnels that had trapped so many visitors, and had at one time endangered his own people.

A bullfrog bellowed in the reeds by the water, its voice resonated throughout the countryside. When they came to the crest of the hill, the place near where Cassie had first entered the Realm, they sat in the grass and watched the reflections of the sinking sun glisten on the sea.

It must end tonight. She had already committed herself. Before the day lost its light completely, she reached into her pouch, pulled out her cell phone, and fingered the all too familiar numbers.

Martim sat up, his face grave. The hurt in his eyes pierced her heart.

"Cassie?" Dad's voice sounded so comforting.

"Dad?"

"Are you ready to come home?"

Cassie wiped her eyes and nodded.

"Cassie, do you want me to come and get you at the forest edge? Say, in half an hour?"

She nodded again.

"He can't hear you when you nod." Martim whispered.

"Cassie?"

"Dad, I love you." She looked at Martim, his eyes red. "I don't want to do this," she said to him.

"No. Go to your family. They need you."

"I don't want to leave you alone."

Martim smiled, but it was strained.

"I'm not alone. Look at all the fine people who live here. I'm strong. I have a kingdom to rule, which will keep me busy. You need to go home." He took her hand. "You'll come back."

She nodded. "Half an hour," she said to her father, and then she shut off her phone.

It hurt too much to lock eyes with him, so Cassie lay in the grass and watched the color of the sky fade to dark.

Martim rested his violin on his shoulder and gently passed the bow over the strings. The sound blended with the low whistle of the breeze and harmonized with the call of the birds. Even the bullfrog found his notes in the melody. It wasn't a sad song, though it rang sweet, like a lullaby, like the world was going to rest for a while, maybe for a long while.

The music welcomed the evening stars and echoed in the heavens, ending with a whisper.

When he finished, Martim set his violin on the grass. The silence was unbearable because it meant her days here were over.

"It's time, isn't it?" Cassie sat up.

He moved closer to her. "Do you mind?" he asked as he lifted her chin.

Cassie's heart raced and she tried to tell him no. She didn't mind, but already his breath warmed her cheeks as he drew near, his lips moist and gentle when they touched hers. They drew a breath together, pressing tenderly against each other. She closed her eyes, the melody of his song still ringing in her ears. She was in heaven. This moment can't end. It never will!

As gently as they had come together, they parted, the taste of his kiss sweet on her lips. Stunned for a moment, their eyes locked and then her embarrassed laugh matched his. She looked away.

"You're going to convince me to stay."

"I'm sorry."

"No. No, don't be sorry, please." She fought tears. "Don't be sorry." Cassie touched the camera option on her phone screen and then handed it to him. "You do it," she said.

Martim took the phone.

"And then you'll have my picture." She blinked at the tears from her lashes.

He smiled. "And your phone."

She nodded. "Dad will get me another one. Look, push this button."

Martim held the phone up. She tried really hard to smile.

A blue light flashed. Cassie blinked. When she reopened her eyes, Dad was there to hold her.

EPILOGUE

"Cassie, I can't take you to school today, dear. You'll have to ride the bus."

"I know Mom. I'm ready."

She gave her mom a kiss. Dad was on a business trip out of town, doing concept work for another film. Today was the last day of school, and the first day back since she had returned home from the Realm.

"Thank you for cleaning your room yesterday. It looks really nice." Abbi said as she gave Cassie a kiss on the cheek. "And you look lovely this morning."

"Thanks, Mom, so do you."

Abbi sighed and let her gaze remain on Cassie for the longest time.

"I'm so glad you're safe at home."

Maybe that was her cue to say she's glad to be home, but Cassie had mixed feelings, and wasn't ready to give them up. Not yet. She knew she would have to someday, but it would have to be later. Martim's kiss was still tingling through her body and when she thought of him her heart ached. She nodded, grabbed her lunch bag, and walked to the front door.

"Mom? Can you answer a question before I go?"

"Of course."

"I heard you and Dad talk this morning before he left and ... well... When Dad said to you he was concerned that I might have stayed in Alisubbo with Martim... what made him think that? Because I said nothing to him about how I felt about Martim. How did he know?"

There was an expression in her mother's eyes, and the tilt of her head that only moms and dads give their children when they understand something more than what their child is letting on. Cassie had seen it before, often on Mom's face, but sometimes Dad would look at her like that too. Only when he gave her that look, he'd always add a crooked smile... and a wink.

She couldn't put her finger on it, but she'd seen that same look recently and tried to remember where.

"I think your dad knows how you feel about Martim." Mom smiled. "Besides, kings don't give away expensive jewels to just anyone. Hurry now, the bus is coming."

The leaves on the poplar trees shimmered with light and stretched their branches to the turquoise skies. They danced freely in the summer breeze, a welcome song to the season that was coming. This, the last day of school, marked a pleasant finale to her adventures. She had two months of vacation with no proper plans but to day dream.

"Or, better still, maybe I'll volunteer at the local children's hospital this summer," Cassie whispered to herself, remembering the children in Medio.

She watched the yellow school bus pull away from Daemon's house and flash its lights as it slowed down to stop at her driveway.

Now she remembered where she had seen that look before. It was in the eyes of that Boreal when they were in the cave. He had looked right at her and had given her a crooked smile and a wink.

"Good morning, Cassie," the driver greeted.

"Hi," Cassie answered as she swung around the hand bar and sat down next to Daemon. She didn't mean to stare at him, but the silly kid-appearance was gone. He seemed older, even stronger. His lips curled when he glanced up from his book.

"Good morning, Cassandra," he said.

"Daemon?" Cassie gave him a curious look. He never addressed her as Cassandra.

"What?"

"Remember when you called my cell and told me to look behind me?"

Daemon's face turned red. He took his glasses off and wiped them with his shirt. "Vaguely."

"Where were you when you called me?"

He had a sheepish smile when he answered. "That's a silly question. I was on my phone."

Funny, she'd never seen his dimples in that light before.

"On your phone?" Cassie laughed. "That's funny, Daemon. And vague."

He shrugged and there it was again. The look and the wink. She didn't. mean to stare at him, but the silly kid-like appearance he was famous for was gone. He seemed older, even stronger. His lips curled when he glanced up from his book.

"Good morning, Cassandra," he said.

"Daemon?" Cassie gave him a curious look. He never addressed her as Cassandra.

"What?"

"Remember when you called my cell and told me to look behind me?"

Daemon's face turned red. He took his glasses off and wiped them with his shirt. "Vaguely."

"Where were you when you called me?"

He had a sheepish smile when he answered. "That's a silly question. I was on my phone."

Funny, she'd never seen his dimples in that light before. "On your phone?" Cassie laughed. "That's funny, Daemon. And very vague."

The End

Acknowledgements

Many thanks to all the people that have encouraged the telling of this tale. My grandsons, my husband, and the community of editors and small presses; and now as an independent publication and of course my Kickstarter backers who have been following the series!

Books in the Ian's Realm Saga
Ian's Realm Trilogy books 1 - 3
Layla book 4
Diary of a Conjurer book 5
Tale of the Four Wizards
Lost on Taikus
Cassandra's Castle book 6
Book 7 to be released in fall of 2023

You may also like The Sword of Cho Nisi Series

Find all D.L. Gardner's books in her eBook Boutique Bookshop
https://gardnerebooks.link
Subscribe to learn more
https://gardnersart.com

About the Author

D.L. Gardner is an award-winning artist, author and screenwriter. She writes primarily fantasy novels including all sub genres, with a love for historical fantasy.
A lover of the classics, both visual and literary, she believes a story should be good enough to hand down from one generation to the next.

Dianne was born in Ohio, raised in California, spent many years in Arizzona, and now lives in the beautiful Pacific Northwest where the oceans, mountains and woodlands are in inspiration to many of her stories.
Winner of Book Excellence Award for Cassandra's Castle and Ian's Realm Serles, Best Urban fantasy at Imaginarium Convention for Pouraka, and a host of screenings and trophies for her adaptions.